In the Shadows

J.A. Owenby

Download Your FREE Book

Trigger and Content Warnings

Please visit https://authorjaowenby.com/about/in-the-shadows-trigger-warnings-2/ for triggers, content warnings, and tropes.

Please do not proceed reading if these are potential triggers. Your mental health is too important.

xoxo,
J.A. Owenby

Playlist

"Sick Pretty Mind" by Upsahl
"Desire" by Violet Orlandi
"I Put Something in Your Drink" by Ramsey
"My Strange Addiction" by RAYNE
"Guilty" by Bobi Andonov
"Face in the Crowd" by Freya Ridings
"Silence" by Galli J
"Love Like This" by Zayn
"Holy Water" by Freya Riddings
"Unconditional" by Freya Riddings

Bend over and take it like a good girl. Just remember this ain't no fucking fairy tale, Princess. You have to take it all.

For my girls, Alida and Britny. You're true badasses, and I couldn't imagine my life without either of you in it. You keep me sane! Love you both. Dildos not Drama Forever!

Chapter 1

Death

"Liberty for wolves is death to the lambs" - Isaiah Berlin

I crept into Ella McCloud's bedroom. Through the parted curtains, the full moon cast a glow on her beautiful curves, and I settled into the grey chair nestled in the corner. Every luscious part of her body was exquisite, and I yearned to feel my knife run along the dips and valleys of her porcelain skin. The possibilities of how I could etch my marks into her flesh flooded my mind until my cock twitched, begging to be inside of her.

She sighed softly and rolled over, exposing her long, toned legs from beneath the blankets. Her neck was poised perfectly and allowed the access I craved. I willed myself not to run my tongue along the curve and taste her.

My dick begged for release while I fantasized that she woke up, terrified. I envisioned her eyes popping wide open as I slipped the knife into her stomach. The cut, as smooth as butter, would steal her breath as she realized what I'd done.

I clenched my jaw and berated myself for allowing my sinful thoughts to consume me. Not my Ella. That wasn't my plan for her. I bathed in my other victims' blood after slicing and dicing them, but not her. Ella was the flicker of light in my dark world, the color in my grayscale existence, and I yearned for her like the night yearns for stars.

The first moment I saw her and spotted her shoulder-length dark hair and piercing green eyes, I had to have her. The gentle touch of water on her face made her skin glisten, and as the droplets clung to her eyelashes, my world came to a standstill. Ella was breathtaking, and the only sound I could hear was my heart pounding in my ears. Her mere presence electrified my heightened senses, resonating deep within my soul and drawing me to her.

As I massaged the back of my neck, the heavenly but faint smell of her peach and vanilla bodywash lingered in the air, imprinting on my mind. Although I'd first seen Ella one year ago, this was the first time I'd entered her house. A thrill surged through me.

Captivated by her beauty, I pressed the flat edge of the blade against my lower lip and slid it back and forth. The cold steel sent shivers down my spine as I gazed at Ella's chest rising and falling, her tightly fitted tank top accentuating her full breasts. The sharp knife grazed my lower lip, drawing a drop of blood that I eagerly licked off with my tongue, savoring its metallic tang.

Life was so fragile—here one second and gone the next. It would be so easy to take away the life she'd built for herself—steal her soul and make it mine for all eternity.

My hand clenched the blade's hilt, the veins in my forearm branching out like a spider's web. I moved closer to her bed, my target oblivious to my proximity.

Her black hair cascaded like a midnight waterfall, deep and enigmatic, reflecting hints of blue or brown under the moonlight. Its richness and depth never failed to captivate me, embodying both the mystery of the night sky and the warmth of a shadowed ember. An overwhelming urge to touch her washed over me. I brushed pieces of hair from her forehead, the strands so delicate and pristine between my fingers.

I reached out my bloodstained fingertip and lightly stroked her cheek with just a whisper of a graze. My little lamb consumed my thoughts. With one glance in my direction, she had become my obsession, and soon I would be hers.

We were meant for each other—even if it meant killing people along the way. I had to have her for my own—no matter what it took because ...

Even Death deserved a Queen.

Chapter 2

Sebastian

"Hey, Bass, hook me up with two shots of your best tequila," Kip yelled at me over the loud, thumping music playing at Velvet Vortex, a popular, upscale nightclub.

Tossing the bar towel over my shoulder, I located his booze of choice. As I poured the liquor, my attention swept over the elbow-to-elbow crowd on the dance floor. The tables and booths were packed with people too. Since the remodeling with a kitchen and full menu along with a state-of-the-art sound system, top-notch DJs, and a custom floor that boasted the largest dance space in Portland, Oregon, the club had to hire additional bouncers to manage the long lines on the weekends.

I focused intently on the dark-haired girl who threw her head back, laughing as she danced rhythmically to the beat of "Sick Pretty Mind" by Upsahl. I noticed her. Noticed her in a way I hadn't any other woman in a long fucking time. There was something intoxicating about her.

It wasn't just how life-altering beautiful she was. I watched how her body moved, sinuous and free flowing; how her face lit up with

4

pure, unfiltered joy. She was guileless, provocative. Sinner and saint.

But once again her friends surrounded her, blocking my view, and I turned back to Kip.

"As always, it's on the house, mate." Kip was my best friend and coworker, and we knew even the rarest of details about each other.

My attention was once more drawn to the middle of the packed dancefloor, a slight smile tugging at the corner of my mouth.

"What's up, man?" Kip turned and followed my gaze back to her, and then he flashed a wide grin at me. "She's hot, Bass, but you know the gig. Don't get attached."

"I haven't dated in years. Only one-night stands, so I think I understand. But don't you ever think about settling down?"

Kip arched a brow and grunted at me.

"Shit, mate, I'm fucking forty. I want a family before I'm too old to run around and chase my kids." I placed the shot glasses on the bar top in front of him, the tequila sloshing over the rims. Grabbing my towel, I quickly wiped up the spill.

"Get laid and send them on their way. Works for me. Besides, she looks too young for you. I mean, wasn't your first pet a T-Rex?" Kip's laugh broke through a lull in the music.

"Fuck you. You're not that much younger than I am." I turned away from him and took the drink order from a chick who was practically leaning over the counter, her tits about to spill out of her too-small, bright pink top. She screamed desperation. Not my type. Her eyes briefly widened when she heard my Australian accent. If I were an asshole, that accent would let me take home a chick every night of the week, but I wasn't looking for that. I wanted something substantial. Real.

Keep dreaming, motherfucker.

"Aren't you yummy?" Pinky climbed onto the barstool, practically salivating over me as if I were the last drop of water in a desert.

"Thanks. It's the accent, isn't it?" I flashed her a wide grin and shoved my fingers through my brown hair, playing her game in hopes of a decent tip instead of a phone number. I would throw her digits in the trash the second she left the bar anyway.

"English?"

I hid my smirk and prayed some dumbass would catch her attention and give me a break from who I suspected was a stage five clinger. "Australian."

A beautiful laugh floated through the air, and I glanced up at the group of ladies heading to the bar. The dark-haired beauty I'd spotted a few minutes ago was with them, smiling and giggling. I smoothed my black T-shirt and hoped I hadn't sweated through my deodorant.

"I've got this round," she said to her group of friends.

I looked over at Pinky and said, "I'll give you a few moments to decide what drink you want."

I strolled to the far end of the bar, captivated by her striking green eyes and raven-black hair. Her sun-kissed face showcased a sprinkle of freckles across her delicately upturned nose.

"What can I get for you?"

Her brow slightly rose right before she offered me the most beautiful smile I'd ever seen.

"I need four different drinks, please. A mai tai, Long Island iced tea, an appletini, and a sex on the beach."

"Which one is for you?" I grabbed the glasses I needed as I waited for her to respond.

"Uh, the sex on the beach." She looked at the floor, and her cheeks slightly pinkened.

Was she as innocent as she came across, or was she just shy when she met someone new? She shoved her hand into her pocket and produced a blue hair tie. While I made the drinks, she gathered her hair into a messy bun, and I caught myself staring.

"Here ya go." I placed the glasses in front of her.

"Thanks." She slid her credit card to me.

"Yours is on the house."

"That's not necessary." She tucked a wisp of stray hair behind her ear, offering me a shy smile.

"I wasn't asking." I gave her a wink before I walked away and glanced at the name on the card. Ella McCloud. Once I rang up the order, I returned to her.

"Here you go, Ella."

She frowned. "How did you know my name?"

I waved her credit card before I slapped it on the bar along with the receipt, and she laughed.

"It's a beautiful name for a beautiful lady." I smiled.

Ella sank her teeth into her lower lip, stifling her giggle, those eyes of hers full of mischief and amusement. A delectable combination. She filled in a generous tip and scribbled her signature on the small piece of paper.

"Thanks again." She gathered two of the drinks and handed them to her friends behind her.

Inwardly, I sighed. Ella McCloud had politely declined my flirtatious gesture by not flirting back or staying to talk, but it was for the best. My life was too dangerous and complicated. Plus, she looked like she was in her late twenties, maybe thirty, and she probably wasn't into older men. My phone buzzed in the front pocket of my slacks, but I ignored it. If it was important, they could call back.

As Ella sauntered away, I appreciated the gentle sway of her hips and curves of her ass calling my name, and my cock strained against my jeans. It wasn't just her physical beauty that mesmerized me—there was something different about her—a pull that drew me in. At the bar, I encountered numerous women, but none of them intrigued me as much as her. As she disappeared into the crowd, I wondered what secrets she hid beneath her beautiful exterior. Because everyone had secrets.

My phone vibrated again in my pocket, and I swore under my breath. After fishing it out, I stared at the screen, my forehead creasing with concern. I hurried to the backroom where Riley, the other bartender on duty, was heads down taking inventory. "Riley, I have to take this call. Can you cover for me?"

She blew loose strands of her brown hair out of her eyes as she stood. "Sure. I need a break from counting anyway." She patted my biceps as she passed me.

I raised the phone to my ear as Riley left and closed the door.

"What?" I asked, not disguising the irritation in my tone.

"Sorry, boss, I know you're working, but I have information you need. This is a save-your-ass call," Dope said.

We were twelve when I first met Dope, a.k.a. Hal. When he'd invited me to his house after school one day, he'd snuck into his brother's stash, and he got stoned off his fucking ass. He had me laughing so hard I was doubled over. As we got to know each other, I realized he was a genius. Then, about six years ago, I bought him a bag of some seriously sick shit that was grown by the best dealer in the state. I slid the product to him along with an ironclad nondisclosure agreement that my attorney had drawn up. Like most of my collaborators, I needed to trust them, and a signed contract ensured that. Kip, along with a notary, were present to observe Dope signing the document.

Adjusting the phone, I sank onto the edge of the barstool. I pinched the bridge of my nose, ridding myself of the distracting thoughts that riddled my brain.

"What is it?" I asked.

He cleared his throat before he began speaking again. "I've gained access to the information of everyone currently in the club due to the bouncers scanning their driver's license. While this method is effective for preventing drug dealers and pimps from entering, it's not as successful at keeping other types of criminals out."

My gaze narrowed, waiting for him to clue me in. "It's why there has to be eyes everywhere all the damn time." Releasing a soft sigh, I rolled my shoulders in an attempt to alleviate some tension.

"Our vulture has arrived, and unfortunately, there's a hitch. His wife is with him, which might make your job a little more difficult."

"Son of a bitch. Why is she here? That fucks everything up. I'll have to reassess."

"Sorry to deliver the bad news, but I didn't want you to start chatting with him, then get knocked off your game when she joined him. One wrong word and the entire plan turns into a shit show."

"And my goddamn ass is on the line," I muttered, standing before pacing the small room.

"Exactly. My recommendation? Steer clear. Go get laid and blow off some steam. You're no use to anyone all fucking stressed out."

"That would be great, but I've got too much shit to do." I blew out a heavy breath. "On the bright side, at least it gives me more time to analyze the situation."

"Just be careful. This guy's a fucking shark. You've been putting in a lot of hours, and I know you're running on fumes."

My body stiffened. "Are you doubting me, Dope?"

"Never. But even the gods make mistakes. Just watch your back."

My irritable reaction had just proven Dope right. I was exhausted and not my best. "Always. Thanks for the heads-up. I'll catch you later." I ended the call and stared at my cell in the palm of my hand. Maybe my friend was right, and I should enjoy my evening. Too bad it wouldn't be with Ella's thighs around my head.

I stood and approached the door, wondering why in the hell this woman had grabbed my attention so damn quickly. No matter what I longed for, though, I had to get her out of my system. I had shit to do and no room in my life for fucking feelings.

Chapter 3

Ella

"Laters, babe. Thanks for going out tonight," my best friend Cami said as she pulled her car into my driveway.

"It was fun. I needed to blow off some steam." I reached for the door handle.

"And that sexy bartender who flirted with you. Ella, you should go back and chat him up."

My lips pressed into a thin line. "I don't have time for a relationship."

Cami shifted in her seat and looked at me. "You've used that excuse since before we were in college." Cami smirked as she tapped her fingernails against the steering wheel. "I'll just sign you up for speed dating." An ornery glint filled her eyes. "Or better yet, I'll find you a hottie on FarmersOnly." She threw her head back and laughed hysterically. "I'll even buy you your first pair of suspenders and cowboy boots." She snorted loudly, then broke into laughter again.

"Don't you dare." I glared a hole into her, hoping like hell she wouldn't go that far just because she thought I needed a man in my life.

Cami's laughter died down, and she patted my leg. "I want you to be happy. That's all. I know you've been dealing with a lot."

I stared out of the front window. Cami and I had been friends for twelve years, and she knew nearly everything about me. Almost.

"It's life. I make it work."

"Ella, I have to practically kidnap you to have any fun in life. Look at tonight, you went to the club, danced all night, and even got a drink on the house from the sexy bartender. Hell, you're still home before your bedtime." She snickered, clearly entertaining herself.

My mood plummeted faster than a roller coaster on its steepest dive. "You know why I don't go out."

A heavy silence filled the car, shattering the lighter mood.

Her expression softened and compassion filled her pretty features. "Babe, you have to stop hiding. Live your life."

"I'm working on it." I shook my head. I opened the door and started to climb out. Glancing at my bestie, my heart softened. "I love you for being an amazing friend. And I'll think about talking to the hot bartender again."

"Do. Or do not. There is no try," she replied in her best Yoda imitation. "And the hot bartender is absolutely delicious with those blue eyes and broad shoulders."

With a mix of frustration and weariness due to my situation, I reminded myself that Cami was on my side and only wanted the best for me. "Drive safe." I blew her a kiss before I closed the door.

Drawing a deep, steadying breath, I made my way to the front door of my house, my sanctuary. Among my friends, I was the only one who had managed to purchase my own home. It wasn't luck or chance; it was sheer willpower and meticulous planning. I had set a goal for myself to own a place by twenty-nine, and I'd made it a reality.

Slipping the key into the deadbolt, it clicked, and I opened the heavy front door. As a single female, I wanted to feel safe at night and had selected higher-quality doors for greater protection.

Once inside, I slipped off my heels. My feet killed me from

dancing all night. I secured the lock and tossed my keys into the brown wood bowl on the hall table. It was almost one in the morning, and I was exhausted, but I had to unwind and then take a hot shower before I tumbled into bed.

I scooped up the pieces of mail I'd tossed on the coffee table before leaving for the club. The television remote caught the soft light of the lamp, and I retrieved it from the grey sofa before I sat down. The sound from the news filled the otherwise quiet space.

"A serial killer is on the loose, and police are reminding residents of Portland to lock their doors, windows, and use an alarm system if available," the female announcer said.

"What?" I leaned forward, listening intently.

"With three murders occurring in the last two months, police have come forward, and a full investigation to catch the murderer is underway. No other details have been supplied at this time."

Shocked, I collected my phone from my back pocket and messaged Cami.

Me:

> Shit, we have a psycho on the loose. Have you heard about the serial killer in the area?

Cami:

> Girl, what the hell have I told you about watching the news? It just creates fear and anxiety. However, I guess the serial killer is kind of important.

Me:

> Maybe I should get an alarm system.

Cami:

I'm on the eighth floor of an apartment building, so I think I'm safe unless the killer is Spider-Man and wants to scale the building.

Me:

Lock your doors and don't bring home any strangers. I'm taking you shopping at Adam and Eve to curb your insatiable appetite soon.

Cami:

Sweet! Just tell me when, and I'm game. LOL

Me:

LOL. Love ya, bitch.

Cami:

Right back atcha.

I set my phone on the end table and listened to the weather forecast for the weekend. Sunny and eighty would be perfect. I could open the windows and allow some fresh air into the house. On second thought, maybe not if a killer was running around.

With the murderer information finally sinking into my thick head, a wave of terror crashed over me as the thought cemented itself in my gut. A murderer, lurking in *my* neighborhood. My heart pounded in my chest as I checked all the door and window locks, the sound of each latch clicking into place echoing with a sense of finality and protection. But could anything truly keep out a determined killer?

Returning to the couch, I shuffled through the junk mail, then spotted the dreaded envelope I'd been expecting. My stomach somersaulted as I opened the bill and stared at the amount due.

"Shit." I threw the letter on the side table and rubbed my face with my hands. My mind raced, a frantic whirlwind of calculations, sifting through my expenses for areas I could tighten. Every hard-earned penny mattered. My day job as a paralegal took care of most living expenses—barely. When I'd bought the house, my finances were in perfect order, but those relentless medical bills wouldn't let up. Yet, wallowing in despair over circumstances out of my control was pointless.

With a renewed determination to push forward through the overwhelm, I hopped off the sofa and swiped my cell off the end table. I walked past the kitchen and down the short hall.

My one-story home was tucked away at the end of the cul-de-sac, and the back of the house faced a green space. Within, it boasted two sunlit bedrooms, each decorated with soft shades of browns, personal mementos, and pictures of family vacations evoking warmth and comfort.

The en suite bathroom showcased a large jetted tub and separate shower while the other sported a sleek, modern shower and tub combo. The open-concept layout seamlessly melded the living, dining, and kitchen areas, letting conversations and scents flow freely between them.

Vaulted ceilings towered overhead, adorned with wooden beams that added depth to the space. Large windows sprinkled throughout allowed generous sunlight to spill in during the day, casting golden hues and dancing shadows upon the dark hardwood floors. But beyond its physical attributes, what filled me with immense pride was the fact that every corner, nook, and cranny of this cherished space was completely mine.

"Alexa, light on." My lamp blinked to life as I entered the bedroom.

A lavender duvet was draped over my queen-sized bed and

matching pillows were propped against the headboard. On the opposite side, a vintage wooden dresser stood, its surface neatly organized.

My favorite part of the space was the cozy reading nook nestled by the window, equipped with a comfortable grey chair, soft throw pillows, and a lavender blanket.

Against the other wall was my workstation that housed my MacBook. Opening my laptop, I turned it on and waited as the machine whirred to life. My fingernails clicked against the keys as I pulled up the website and logged in. Once I'd collected my mobile camera, I headed to the en suite bathroom. In seconds, I'd stripped and discarded my jeans and teal-colored top onto the tiled floor. Maybe I should feel shame or guilt about how I earned my additional income, but I didn't. It was my secret. No one knew. Not even Cami.

Suddenly, an overwhelming wave of loneliness washed over me. Instead of taking home hot bartenders at the end of the night, my interactions were limited to men on the other side of a screen, lacking any real personal connection. For me, the job was primarily a means to pay my bills, and usually, the absence of a meaningful relationship in my life hadn't bothered me, but for some reason it stung at the moment. Although I had a few relationships in the past, none were worth reminiscing about. Maybe the rush of emotion was because the bartender had flirted with me, or maybe it had been my conversation with Cami. I wasn't sure.

"It's not like you don't enjoy your work sometimes," I reminded myself while I opened the shower door and walked inside. Pushing up on my tiptoes, I placed the camera strategically on the top ledge and turned on the water. Realizing I'd set my phone near my computer, I hurried to grab it. I pulled up the app and tapped the red record button.

Steam billowed from under the hot spray and into the bathroom as I stepped beneath it and secured the door behind me. Glancing up, I made sure the webcam was at the right angle. With a few pumps of my vanilla and peach body wash, I slowly lathered up my breasts. I took my time and gave them extra attention for the video. Water streamed between my soapy tits and trickled down my stomach, and my fingertips followed the trail until I reached my thighs. Careful to not lose my balance, I propped one foot on the shower seat, allowing the camera full access to my pussy.

My fingers spread my sensitive flesh and massaged my clit for the camera. I leaned against the wall for balance as I moaned. The longer I continued to touch myself, the more money I would make. The key was to draw it out for as long as I could.

Closing my eyes, the handsome bartender flashed before me. His corded biceps and strong hands were the first thing I'd noticed about him as he waited on customers at the club. The name on his tag had read Sebastian. When he spoke, his Australian accent had made my entire body tingle. Imagining that he was on his knees in front of me, his tongue expertly teasing and prodding at my tender flesh as he slid his finger inside me made my core clench with longing. My back arched as he ravaged my body with his mouth, then spun me around and plunged his thick cock inside me from behind.

My legs trembled with the fantasy as a sweet sensation swirled in my lower belly. After another five minutes of recording, I allowed myself to cum, adding a bit of extra drama for the performance. I licked the water droplets off my mouth as I rinsed the suds off my tanned skin.

I turned off the water and opened the door, displaying my backside as I stepped out on the fluffy brown mat and reached for the plush matching towel on the rack. Seductively, I winked at the camera before I disappeared out of the bathroom and turned off the recording from my app. With a few clicks of the mouse, I loaded the video. I wrapped the towel around me and sat in the chair, waiting.

Ten minutes later, the video was edited, and I uploaded it to the adult website.

Hope you enjoy how wet I am for you, I typed before I submitted it for anyone who wanted to pay to watch.

A smile twitched at the corner of my mouth as a message popped up in the chat box.

Are you there? Shadow Whisperer asked.

Whoever was behind the username was one of my best customers over the last year, and I always tried to give him a little extra.

I typed out my response. *For you, always.*

Can we talk tonight?

My shoulders sagged with exhaustion. Sometimes conversations would last for hours. Maybe I should mention that I had a very short block of time.

Only for half an hour.

Apparently, it was long enough because the payment bell dinged. A figure cloaked in darkness filled the screen, and I smiled.

"Hi, there," I said, starting the conversation. "Did you miss me?"

A disguised voice streamed through my computer speakers.

"You know I can't stay away from my naughty girl for long."

I responded with a soft purr, then, "I'm always happy to spend some time with you." It wasn't an out-and-out lie. Whoever this guy was showed up for me nearly every evening that I worked. I had a list of fans, but he was by far the most dedicated and brought in a lot of money. As long as Shadow Whisperer paid well, I would give him a good time. Even though I hadn't ever admitted it to him, some nights I liked our twisted fantasy time together. I also wanted to know who was behind the screen, and why did he spend so much time with me? Did he not have a family?

He cleared his throat, interrupting my thoughts.

"I just watched your shower video." He paused and shifted in his chair. "Who were you thinking of when you had your hand between your thighs, stroking your hot cunt?"

I purposefully took a deep breath, my breasts rising and falling just for him. "You know it's always you, baby."

"Tell me more," he demanded as the shadow of his hand disappeared. The sound of his zipper lowering made me smile.

"You're demanding and dominating as you spin me around and bend me over. I need you to fuck me hard and make me forget that anything else exists other than your huge cock pumping into my wet

17

cunt. You slide your hand between my legs and pinch my clit so hard I scream."

He growled as he stroked his cock in front of me, the shadows hiding his face and most of his body.

"You pull out of me, and I turn around while you grab my hair and force me to my knees. Telling me to part my mouth, you rub the tip of your cock along my mouth. Eagerly, I part my lips and flick my tongue across your sensitive head, tasting precum. Sliding you into my mouth, I moan as I take the full length of you until you hit the back of my throat. I stroke and suck you until you pull out and spray cum all over my tits."

"That's it. You're the only one that makes me come this hard." His breathing hitched in his throat as he groaned and released.

Secretly, I gravitated to him as well, but he'd made it clear I was his naughty girl, and no one could ever replace me. Maybe it was bordering on a sick obsession, but I fed on it too.

His chuckle filtered through my computer speakers, and I waited for him to speak. "I think it's time that you give me your real name instead of your screen name, Angel Fluff," he said.

"You know the rules, baby. No personal details." I nibbled on my manicured nail and peeked through my long, black eyelashes.

"Fuck the rules. I have a friend with a sex club. We could meet there, and you can give me my own private show. I'll remain behind the glass and watch you. I'll pay you fifty thousand dollars."

"What?" I shrieked as I leaned back too far in my chair, my arms flailing around, causing my towel to drop to my waist as I struggled to regain my balance and dignity.

His chuckle rumbled through his broad chest. "You heard me."

Once I settled in again, I gathered the towel and attempted to cover my breasts.

"Leave it down," he ordered.

Slowly, I lowered it away from my body. Something about his tone had me obeying before I realized I was giving into him so quickly. "Fifty thousand dollars to watch me in person? I don't understand."

Maybe I did. I was part of his daily sexual fantasies. Why wouldn't he want more? And fifty grand could put a nice dent in the bills I was struggling to pay.

"There's nothing to understand. I want what I want."

A few beats of silence passed before I responded. "You'll be behind glass and won't touch me?"

"Yes. For *now*. But before you say yes, you should know that I have some very particular tastes." He shifted in his chair.

My eyes narrowed at the screen as I attempted to figure out what his game was.

"Like what? Threesomes, BDSM, what's your dirty addiction?"

"When the time comes, you'll find out." His tone held an edge of darkness, danger.

A chill slithered over my arms, and I swallowed down the fear, telling my inner voice to hush. It wasn't about what I was comfortable with. It was about being able to make quick money. Desperate people sometimes had to silence their instincts. Desperate people didn't get to worry about things like fear or being uneasy.

"When and where?"

"You'll fly on my private plane. I'll confirm the time for you shortly, but it will be in the afternoon. When you land in Seattle, a car will pick you up and drive you to the club."

Goosebumps prickled my skin, and a sense of foreboding trotted in hot on its heels. I shook my head, baffled at his invitation. No one had ever offered me anything like this before. *I've fucking lost my mind, but how can I pass up money like that?* I took a deep breath and reminded myself of all the good that would come from working for one afternoon.

Once the details were settled, we signed off. Never in a million years would I ever tell Cami what I'd just agreed to even if it meant keeping me safe. When I'd first started to work online, I promised myself that I would never let them touch me, just watch.

"Nothing's changed, Ella. Stop being a baby." A prickly sensation washed over me, and I rubbed my arms, warding off the haunted feeling. Then, my brain gave me a big fuck you. *Holy shit. If he wants me to meet him at a club, does that mean he knows that I live in Portland?* A thick lump formed in my throat. I had to back out.

A chime from my laptop pulled me out of my panic, and I hurried to see who was contacting me. I propped a hand on the desk and leaned down, reading the message.

Shadow Whisperer:

Your flight leaves tomorrow at 1:12 in the afternoon from PDX and arrives in Seattle an hour and ten minutes later.

My heart broke into a gallop. *Fuck! He knows where I live.* I had to cancel now or never. Once I gave my word, I kept it no matter the consequences. My hand shook as I debated my response.

Me:

See you soon.

"Remember why, Ella. When you're terrified as hell, remember what this is all for," I said softly.

With that, I signed off and closed my computer before I crawled my exhausted ass into bed. I set my alarm, ready to grab some sleep before I had to be at the airport. But my brain had other ideas, and thoughts galloped through my head along with a wake of fear. What in the hell had I just agreed to? *Remember the why.*

Chapter 4

Death

"Remember that God under the Law ordained a Lamb to be offered up to Him every Morning and Evening." ~ Thomas Ken

Darkness shielded my presence as I waited for the perfect opportunity to catch Andrew alone. It shouldn't be difficult since he practiced bad habits after nightfall. Some people thought they were safe from me because they lived in a wealthy neighborhood with high-tech cameras and security systems. How wrong they were.

A white Pathfinder approached the house, and I stilled, willing my breathing to become so faint that it was almost undetectable even to me. Little did he realize that I'd been following him for almost a month now. I had gone to great lengths to learn his schedule, identify the cheating assholes that he called his friends, and even noted the days and times he attended the gym to keep up his buff appearance.

He was pathetic. A fake. He appeared to the public as a successful, loving family man. What his wife hadn't figured out yet was that he was balls deep inside a different chick every other night. He also had a nasty gambling habit and treated people like shit behind closed doors. That was just the beginning of his lies. But I knew the truth. All the ugly, ink-black truth about him.

He climbed out of the car and stuck a red pair of panties into his three-thousand-dollar briefcase, chuckling as if he was getting away with his affair. He was dead wrong.

Humming softly, he approached the row of garbage and recycling canisters along the darkest side of his home. Clueless to my presence, he tossed an empty Burger King bag into the green container.

Without a sound, I stepped from my hiding place behind him. "Hello, Andrew. Welcome to hell." I slapped my gloved hand over his mouth and with my other hand, I stabbed the needle into the side of his neck.

THE FULL MOON CAST AN EERIE SHADOW ACROSS THE WATER AS a small ripple traveled over the otherwise smooth surface of the lake. I had searched for the perfect place to bring Andrew to. It was a hidden, quiet area with no homes in sight for miles. The tree cover was perfect for what I had in mind for the evening.

Smiling as if I didn't have a care in the world, I turned when I heard muffled noises.

"Rest well?" I asked while I kneeled near Andrew, who was lying on his side on the hard, unforgiving ground wiggling back and forth as if it would help. The earth wasn't the only one who wouldn't grant forgiveness.

His mouth widened in horror as his mind scrambled to understand where he was. He squirmed against the ropes tied snugly around his wrists and ankles.

I ripped the duct tape off his mouth and left the corner dangling from one cheek, laughing as his screams turned into pitiful cries.

His face drained of all color, making the fine lines of age more pronounced. His eyes wide and bulging, darted frantically from side to side, desperately searching for an escape. There was none.

"Don't hurt me. Please. I'll give you anything you want." Snot coated his upper lip, and his tongue swiped along his parched mouth.

Unmoved by his pathetic begging, I sneered at him. "Welcome to your worst nightmare, Andrew. Let me introduce myself." I leaned close to his left ear. "I'm Death."

"What the fuck, man. You dress up as the grim reaper and terrorize people?" Tears rolled down his cheeks as he pretended to be tough.

"I don't terrorize, motherfucker." I rose and walked away, leaving him hidden beneath the trees a hundred feet away. No one lived near the area, so even if he screamed at the top of his lungs, it wouldn't matter.

Every flash of movement from a squirrel or hoot of an owl caused him to flinch or gasp, and the sweat on his brow gleamed in the dim light. His dilated pupils gave him a wild appearance. "Why am I here?" Horror twisted his voice.

Now that he was conscious, I would let him think he had an opportunity to turn his situation around. The moment he realized he was fucked, I would know. Until then ... I would enjoy toying with my prey.

A jagged strike of lightning split the darkness. I lifted my chin and sniffed the approaching rain. Time was running out. I would have to move faster than anticipated. On the other hand, as long as I was gone by the time the downpour started, any evidence of Andrew and me would be long gone once the water washed it away. By the shift of the wind and the scent of the storm, I had less than an hour.

Slowly, I strolled back to the now quiet man. Ah, he just realized how fucked he really was. My favorite part of our time together.

The tendons in his neck stood out, taut as bowstrings, and his shoulders were hunched as he stared at his swollen stomach. The myriad of stitches haphazardly holding the tissue together like a stitched-up football. Blood oozed out in trickles and his bruised skin expanded, turning a multitude of colors as it went.

"What did you do to me, you sick son of a bitch?"

"Tsk, tsk. No need for name calling." I stood in front of him and plucked a new pair of black gloves from my coat pocket. His gaze narrowed as he watched me pull them on one at a time. "We all have a time." I flexed my fingers, allowing the leather to mold to my hands. "A time to cry, a time to laugh, a time to ... die."

His whine broke through his sobs as he asked, "What did you do to my stomach?"

I laughed as I stared at his distended abdomen. The stitches were pure perfection and would rival those of any surgeon. "One of my favorite quotes is 'stand through life firm as a rock in the sea, undisturbed and unmoved by its ever-rising waves' by Hazrat Inayat Khan. Granted, we're not near the sea, but in your case, a lake will have to do."

His breathing came in short, erratic bursts, as if the very act of drawing breath was a struggle.

"What did I do to you?" Spittle flew out of my mouth as a flood of emotions twisted his expression.

"I knocked you out, and while you were sleeping, I split you open and sewed a bag of rocks in your stomach. You'll either die from the half-assed surgery I performed, or you'll drown when I toss your pathetic ass into the lake and sink to the bottom. The rocks will ensure that you won't make it to the surface. Ever."

Andrew screamed and thrashed on the ground before he vomited. I assumed the pain would render him unconscious shortly. Regardless, the thunder was growing closer, which meant I had to wrap up our time together.

"Any last words?"

"W-w-why? Why me? What did I do to you?"

I pretended to think about his question, but I didn't give a fuck. He was a monster, and I was ridding the world of one more. It was a tough job, but someone had to do it.

"Nothing. You did nothing to *me*. It was what you did to everyone else." I leaned over, careful to avoid the vomit crusting to the side of Andrew's lips, and slapped the duct tape over his mouth again before I whispered my goodbyes.

Adrenaline pumped through my veins, eager to give the sorry bastard what he deserved. I dragged his body onto the black sheeting, ignoring the fact he'd just pissed himself. At least I wouldn't have to smell it for long. I made quick work of securing him in the thick plastic, then dragged him to the edge of the water where the speed boat waited for us. Breathing heavily, I dumped his body onto the floor and climbed in after him. It was a beautiful evening for a ride, if I did say so myself.

I wiped the sweat from my forehead as I started the engine and pulled away from the land. Most of the time, I enjoyed slicing and dicing my victims, but I had to stay ahead of the cops and FBI, so I changed my methods on a regular basis. Keeping the authorities guessing was almost as much fun as the actual killing.

Whistling "Pop Goes the Weasel" as the rain began to fall, I guided the boat toward the middle of the lake where Andrew would take his final breath.

Chapter 5

Ella

I gently lifted my airplane seat from its reclined position, feeling the warmth and smooth texture of the luxurious brown leather beneath my fingertips as we were about to land. The moment I stepped onboard, a flight attendant handed me a drink, and the promise of a movie awaited on the sleek flat-screen television ahead. It was the most lavish experience I'd ever had. A girl could get used to this kind of treatment and fast.

I braced myself as the plane's wheels skidded against the airstrip. Besides my nerves jumping around like a cat on a hot tin roof in August, the flight had been uneventful. At least I was familiar with the Seattle airport and didn't have to worry about getting lost.

As I was escorted off the plane, I instinctively adjusted the strap of my crossbody Kate Spade purse over my shoulder, my fingers fidgeting with its edges. I navigated the bustling terminal, occasionally pushing a stray lock of hair behind my ear. Since I was flying on a private plane, I could avoid the added stress of elbowing my way through the crowd at baggage claim.

I pushed through the airport exit door and strolled into the early autumn sunshine. Leaves scraped the sidewalk as the wind swept them in the opposite direction. Slipping my sunglasses on, I scanned the area for a limo. From five cars away, I spotted one and quickly headed toward it, wondering if it was for me. As I approached, the occupant climbed out, revealing a handsome middle-aged man in uniform who hurried around to greet me.

"Angel Fluff?" I nearly cringed at my website name being used in public.

"That's me." I offered him a kind smile as he opened the back passenger door. I gently raised the hem of my long, blue cami dress to prevent tripping and gracefully stepped inside.

"I've been hired for the day to escort you to the meeting place. Please enjoy a glass of wine. We'll reach your destination in half an hour. Traffic is brutal."

I could use a stiff drink to knock the edge off, but wine would do. Settling into the seat, I glanced around at the fully stocked bar and the small television mounted in the corner. A chilled bottle and opener were waiting for me on the center console. I removed the cork and filled my glass. I let out a heavy sigh. I didn't know whether the next half hour would feel like the longest or shortest of my life, but I was about to find out.

Finally, the limo pulled around to the back of a large, red brick building near downtown. Despite the glass of wine, I was wound tight, my nerves standing on end. I'd tried to talk myself into having fun today, but I was walking into unknown territory. What if I never left? I chided myself for allowing my anxiety to dictate my thoughts. Shadow Whisperer had never given me a reason to fear him ... until now. I reminded myself that fifty grand would make me feel a hell of a lot better. The only thing that kept me sane and partially settled was the fact that he wouldn't touch me. He would remain behind the glass, watching.

The back door opened, and the driver extended his hand to me. The afternoon clouds had muted the sun, and I tucked my sunglasses into my handbag. I climbed out of the car, and as my heel touched the pavement, a shock of terror shot through me. *I'm actually doing this!* Goosebumps pebbled my skin as I stood and straightened my dress, my palms growing clammy with each passing second. I could back out, run, and never talk to Shadow Whisperer again. It was what I should do. It's what a sane person would do. I swallowed over the lump in my throat, images dancing through my terrified thoughts ... *remember the why.* After I collected my courage, I tipped my chin in the air and squared my shoulders. I had never been a girl to back down from a challenge, and I sure as hell wouldn't now.

"Follow me." He strolled toward a back entrance and scanned a key card. The lock clicked, and he pulled on the door handle as his cell rang. He ushered me into the dark hall before he answered.

"Sir?" His jaw tensed. "I understand. I'll let her know."

Frowning, I waited for him to end the call.

He replaced his phone inside his jacket pocket and cleared his throat.

"I'm terribly sorry. Your companion for the afternoon has been called away on unexpected business. He said he'll reach out to reschedule, and he'll pay you half of the agreed upon amount for your trouble."

My hand flew to my chest, relief nearly causing my knees to buckle. "That's too bad. I was looking forward to it." *Liar! You're scared shitless.* As soon as the relief had dissipated, curiosity took its place. *Who is the man behind the screen?*

"He asked me to accompany you back to the jet and make sure you arrive safely back to Portland."

"Thank you. It's a beautiful plane. It beats the hell out of flying commercial." Shadow Whisperer seemed to at least care about my safety. Maybe he was a good person to have around after all.

"I agree."

A silly grin eased across my face. "Is it wrong that I'm more excited to fly on his jet again ..." I cleared my throat. "Uh, more than meeting Shadow Whisperer at the club?"

His deep chuckle rippled through the air before he extended his hand to me. "Call me Thomas since we might see each other again."

I stared at him before shaking his hand and searching my brain for a fake name. "Janie, but maybe you already knew my real name."

"I do now." His warm smile reached his kind eyes. "Are you ready?"

"Yeah." He had no idea how eager I was to return home. I doubted whether I would receive payment, but the limo and jet ride had given me a small adventure that invigorated me. For the first time in years, I felt alive. My whole body had been infused with immense fear, but I still went ahead and did it all anyway. It was empowering. That disheartened and weak part of me that let paranoia, suspicion, and panic consume my daily life shattered. And all it had taken was one plane ride. I felt invigorated ... Powerful, like I could do anything I put my mind to, as long as I drowned out the little voice in my head, warning me, restraining me. That long dormant part that once took chances and jumped before looking was waking up, and I was going to make sure it didn't go back to sleep again. It was time to make some changes in my life.

On the way back to the airport, I scrambled for clues about who the man behind the username Shadow Whisperer was. He was wealthy and chose to remain hidden, which made me think he was someone in the public eye who didn't want his sex life in the spotlight. But who was he, and why had he chosen me from all the other women who worked online?

A muffled ding sounded, and I rifled through my purse and retrieved my phone. I held back my squeal as twenty-five grand hit my Venmo account. A rush of disbelief slammed into my chest as I focused on the zeros.

Holy shit. This guy is for real. My heart soared with gratitude for the much-needed money. It would give me a bit of breathing room until the next round of bills found their way to my mailbox.

Without delay, I transferred it to my checking account. I was afraid if I waited, the payment would disappear.

I settled into the plush seat, smiling to myself. Cami was right. It was time to stop hiding and live my life. Fortunately, I knew precisely the place to do it. I typed out a quick text, and Cami almost immediately confirmed our plans for the evening. Since I would be at my place in a few hours, I would have time to nap before going out for a few drinks later.

AFTER I'D ARRIVED HOME FROM THE RIDE ON THE JET, I'D TAKEN a long shower, unable to stop thinking about Cami's encouragement to date and have some fun.

At the same time, my mind was preoccupied with Shadow Whisperer and questions about his real identity kept swirling around inside my head. Maybe he was a good guy, just discreet in his sex life. I understood. No one knew about my night job or my fear of being judged. I was pretty sure even Cami would have something to say about it, so it made sense not to put myself in that position unless I had no other choice. Pushing the questions aside, I yawned as I made my way to the bed for some shut-eye.

After a long nap, I dressed in jeans that hugged my ass and paired it with a blue silk blouse. For an added touch, I curled my hair as thoughts of the attractive bartender took up space in my mind. The idea of seeing him again sent my heart racing, mingled with an intense curiosity about who Sebastian really was. Maybe it was time to find out.

"Babe, you look amazing. Stop fussing over your clothes," Cami scolded me outside the Velvet Vortex entrance. Her long hair flowed past her shoulders with loose curls at the end. Cami always looked picture perfect, even when she had just woken up. She adjusted her orchid top and revealed a little more cleavage before we strolled in.

"I'm trying." I tugged at my lower lip with my teeth, a bundle of nervous and excitement forming in the pit of my stomach.

What if Sebastian was actually interested instead of the harmless flirting he'd shown me last night? My tummy fluttered with the idea until I reminded myself that I had little time to have fun and unwind. The last year had been stolen with doctor appointments and work. Then I remembered my promise to myself. Things had to change. I needed some balance, or I would lose my mind.

"Can I admit that I'm a bit surprised that you wanted to come back here so soon?"

I laughed as I opened the front door and entered the building, following a long, dimly lit hall. The dance floor wouldn't open until nine, which was a few hours away, but food and drinks started at five. It was run a bit differently from most clubs, but I didn't mind. Once we began to dance, it was hard to talk over the music anyway, so arriving early gave me time to catch up with Cami.

"I thought about what you said last night. It's been a helluva year, and I need to relax."

We entered the restaurant area, and every corner of the room echoed with laughter, conversations, and the soft undertones of background music. Waitstaff gracefully navigated the maze of tables, their trays heavy with steaming dishes, drinks, and an assortment of desserts.

"Relax with an Australian bartender, maybe?" She grinned at me, then glanced around. "They're already busy." Cami flipped her long blonde hair over her shoulder, her smile sparkling.

"Yeah, they are."

A pretty hostess led us to a table, and Cami cackled with glee as she slid into one side of the booth. "Thought you might want that side since Sebastian is working. The view is much better."

I tucked my hair behind my ear and realized that I had a direct path to the bar and eye candy.

"Yes, it is."

Cami rubbed her hands together like a devious child plotting a prank. "He's sinfully gorgeous."

I smoothed my top and wiped my damp palms on my jeans. My heart tap-danced against my chest as I allowed myself to drool over Sebastian. Every contour of his body seemed etched with precision. His broad shoulders and well-defined pectorals stretched the fabric of his black T-shirt, making it cling to him as if tailor-made for his physique. I imprinted the details on my brain as his coworker joined him. Black T-shirts must have been part of the uniform. My brows knitted together as the two men stood with their backs to me, appearing similar in height with broad shoulders and short brown hair. From this view, they could be twins. I wondered if they were related.

Sebastian threw his head back and laughed, the sound muffled by the chatter of the guests.

"You should go say hi."

A tall waiter in his thirties approached our table, cutting off my response. "Hello, ladies, what can I get for you?"

Cami worried her bottom lip with her teeth. "One Jack and Coke for Ella and one Long Island iced tea for me, plus let Sebastian know that Ella is here."

My nostrils flared, but I would have to wait to slap my best friend until we had no audience.

"Sure thing. I'll be right back." The waiter offered us a warm smile before he disappeared.

"Cami! What happened to allowing me to talk to him in my own timing?" I didn't need to chide her in a soft tone. It was loud, and no one would even notice me yelling at her.

"What? I just thought I'd help move your evening along. He was clearly flirting with you last night, so maybe he'll be happy you're back. You'll never know unless you get out there, babe."

I watched our waiter approach the bar and chat with Sebastian. He turned in my direction, then flashed me a full-on, panty-dropping smile that turned my hormones into a puddle. My thighs clenched, and I crossed my legs as I gave him a small wave.

"Shit. He saw me." My pulse kicked up with every step he took toward me.

"Oh, tall, dark, and handsome is on his way over. This is so exciting." Cami said, wiggling her brows at me.

Sebastian's grin never wavered as he approached the table with our drink order.

"Ella." He set the Jack and Coke in front of me before he gave Cami her Long Island.

"I'm surprised but happy to see you again." He folded his arms over his chest, his pectoral muscles flexing as he moved.

"Yeah, my evening plans got canceled, so we came for a few drinks," I explained.

"And him," Cami mouthed behind him.

"I need to get back to the bar, but why don't you come see me after you eat?"

"Okay." A flush crept across my face as he turned and walked away, my interest firmly planted on his jean-clad ass and thighs.

Cami fanned her cheeks. "My. God. That accent is orgasmic! I'm pretty sure I just flooded the basement."

"Cami!" I hid my face in my hands, giggling. I peered at her through my fingers. "Did I just agree to talk to him some more?"

Cami rolled her eyes at me. "Yes. And you will spend time at the bar chatting up the hot Australian, or you and I are breaking up."

Laughing, I stirred my cocktail with the straw before I raised my glass to my bestie and waited for her to do the same.

"To hot men and best friends," I said.

"Yeah, bitch!"

We clinked the rims of the glasses, and then I took several gulps. I needed some liquid courage. Talking to a guy behind a camera or computer screen was one thing, but chatting with one face-to-face was another ball game, and I hoped like hell I was up to the challenge.

Chapter 6

Sebastian

"Watch the spillage, man," Kip said as his brow rose. "You're off your game tonight. What gives?"

On occasion, my best friend filled in at the bar for me, and since I had a long night of inventory and ordering ahead, I'd asked if he could pick up an extra shift.

I jerked the bottle of Crown Royal back from the highball glass, added some Coke, and handed it to the guy patiently waiting for his drink.

"Nothing's up." I wiped up the whiskey from the bar and shot a sideways glance in Ella's direction. To my astonishment, she'd showed up for dinner with one of her friends from last night. It was as if the universe sensed the moment I let her slip from my thoughts, only to bring her right back into them.

Kip popped me on the shoulder with his bar towel and shook his head. "Man, it's that chick again."

I chuckled. "Her name is Ella, which makes her no longer a random chick."

"I see how it is. Someone's caught your attention." Kip snickered behind his hand as he rushed to help the next patron.

The bar buzzed with energy and a waiting line. The thought of finding time to chat with Ella seemed impossible. I gripped the back of my neck, my frustration growing. "Don't you have work to do?" I snapped.

Ignoring my clipped tone, Kip nodded to the people filing in through the front door. "Looks like we both do. It's about to get busier."

"Bloody hell," I grumbled, quickly pushing my irritation aside. I plastered on a smile and tended to a pretty girl at the bar. Thankfully, after I served her, she didn't linger or try to flirt. Ella was the only person I wanted to talk to, but she was across the room.

The next two hours passed in a whirl as Kip and I zigzagged from one end of the bar to the other, serving a continuous wave of customers. Sweat formed on my forehead, and I made a mental note to freshen up when I could.

Then, as I turned to serve another customer, I stopped dead in my tracks. There they were—Ella and her friend, comfortably seated at the bar.

"You're slammed tonight." Ella tucked her long, dark hair behind her ear and smiled. "Good money, I hope."

"It's flat out busy, but yeah, the money is nice. Sometimes it gets old, though."

"Hey, handsome." Another girl leaned on the counter and shared her ample cleavage with me. I'd learned long ago to keep my attention on the face, not the tits. It kept me out of hot water.

"I'll be right with you." No way was I walking away from Ella until I got her drinks.

Ella's friend waved at me. "I'm Cami, Ella's best friend. It's nice to meet you."

"Sorry, I should have introduced the both of you." The thin strap of Ella's scarlet bra fell down her upper arm, the red a stark contrast against her porcelain skin. Unable to look away, I wished I was her hand when she slid the strap back up her skin, out of sight once more.

My dick instantly hardened. I wasn't sure if it was her gorgeous smile, or the smoking body, but there was something about this girl I couldn't shake.

"Sebastian." I nodded and smiled at Cami. She was pretty, but there was no comparison between her and Ella.

"Can I get a mai tai?" Ella asked.

"One for me too, please," Cami added, fishing her debit card from her back jeans pocket.

"This round is on the house." I winked at Ella before disappearing to make their order and handle the flirt still waiting.

Kip eventually made his way over. "Take a break, man. Go talk to her."

"You sure? It's crazy."

"Remove your name tag and stand next to her. If I need you, I'll wave you back over. And you've been here since noon. Grab some food. We won't have time to eat before we ..." He shot me a knowing look.

The crushing burden of my secret weighed on my shoulders. The hidden truth screamed at me, reminding me that I had no right to even glance at Ella—or any other woman, for that matter. With a shake of my head, I pushed away the thoughts. I was done sidelining myself from life. Ella's presence offered a glimmer of hope, suggesting she might be open, at least, to conversation.

"Sure thing, *Mom*." I laughed as I ordered a burger and fries from the kitchen before I removed my name tag and hurried over to Ella and Cami on the other side of the bar.

"Kip is making me take a break. Hopefully, hanging with you ladies for a few minutes is okay?" I could have sworn Ella's expression clouded. Had I said something wrong?

"We would love to." Cami flashed a big smile at Ella. "Right?"

I tilted my head at Ella and chuckled, amused as a soft pink dusted her cheeks. She was a breath of fresh air compared to most women who came into the club.

"Right."

Damn, she's beautiful.

37

"So, Ella, are you a college student?"

Open mouth, insert foot. She was definitely too young for me, but she didn't need to know that. Unfortunately, I had just opened that can and couldn't slap the lid back on fast enough.

"Wow. I must look really young." She laughed. "I graduated eight years ago from the University of Oregon. I'm twenty-nine."

"Almost thirty," Cami added. She nibbled on her stir straw, watching our conversation occur.

Too bad I couldn't tell what Cami was thinking. I wasn't stupid. I knew how this shit would play out. The best friend held the power to make or break a relationship, which meant I had to impress Cami as much as Ella.

Not to mention, I was eleven years her senior. It was better than I first thought, though.

"What kind of work do you do?" I stared at Ella's full lips as she drank her mai tai.

"I'm a paralegal at Barnaby and Smooch." Her forehead creased. "I have no idea why attorneys have such strange last names. Anyway, they're criminal lawyers. The work is interesting. I mean, I have front row seats to their cases. If I am really honest, I'm fascinated with some criminals. Why do they do what they do, hurt, or kill people? Is it psychological? Sociological? Were they born that way?"

"And some of us can't help but love the bad boys," Cami said.

Ella shook her head. "Ignore her."

Fuck. Fuck. Fuck. Just my damn luck.

I shoved my fingers through my hair, then instantly regretted it. Hopefully, it wasn't sticking up at an awkward angle. "I bet it's fascinating to see what goes on behind the scenes of the legal system."

"Sometimes it's scary. Like when you know someone is guilty, but the attorneys are so damn good they get them off the charges. But it's not my job to judge." She gave me a half-shrug, and I wondered if she ever battled guilt about her work.

"Here ya go, Bass." Kip set my food at the end of the bar.

Ella pointed behind me. "Someone's trying to get your attention."

Kip and I turned around to see what she was talking about.

A playful grin slipped over Kip's face as he approached the woman at the other end of the bar. The brunette handed him a red jacket that I immediately recognized as his.

Kip tipped his chin at the lady before he walked away. "At least she didn't keep it. I get tired of replacing jackets. Be right back, I'm going to put it away." Kip laughed as he held it up, then disappeared through the door that led to the inventory and locker room.

I scooted the plate over. "I realize that you two just ate dinner, but the fries here are amazing. Help yourself, ladies, otherwise I'll feel like an asshole eating in front of you."

Ella's smile reached her eyes as she snatched one up and popped it into her mouth. "Mmm, you're right, those are really good."

"Since you ladies are drinking, I'll get some fries going for you. Be right back." Not only did I have a legal responsibility for someone leaving Velvet Vortex drunk, I wanted to make sure the ladies were safe to drive home when they were ready.

A shadow of guilt crossed Kip's expression as I neared the register to place the food order. "Sorry to cut your meal short," he said, "but I need help."

I released a weary breath. "It's all right, mate. I knew it wouldn't last long. Let me tell Ella I'm not skipping out on her."

Replacing my name tag on my shirt, I hurried over. "I gotta save Kip from drowning. I'll be back when I can with your fries." I picked up my plate and hurried to the kitchen to box it up.

When I returned to the bar, I barely had time to think about Ella other than to grab another drink for her and Cami with their snack. At least the tips were flowing well. I didn't need the money, but it was a matter of principle to me. If a customer got good service, they should tip—end of discussion. Even though the staff was paid well, a good chunk of what they made in a night was from tips. When those were dependent on another person's mood that shit blew.

As Cami moved away from the bar and headed toward the restroom, my focus immediately shifted to Ella. A brown-haired guy quickly claimed Cami's seat, and my protective instincts kicked into overdrive. I'd seen plenty of crazy shit go down in my life that I could spot trouble a fucking mile away. The guy looked shady as hell. My gaze flicked her way several times, assessing the situation and gauging her body language. He chatted with Ella as she defensively crossed her arms over her chest. She wasn't interested in whatever he had to say.

Good.

As soon as I took care of the people at the end of the bar, I planned to make my way toward her without looking like an over-bearing asshole. Suddenly, her expression morphed into annoyance as she slipped off the barstool, scanning the floor below. Had I not been watching her; I would have missed what the motherfucker did.

A guttural growl rumbled through me as I stormed toward him with laser-focused rage. In a swift motion, I knocked over Ella's drink, shattering it into the wall. I jumped over the bar, narrowly missing her as she gaped at me, and I grabbed the fucking guy by his shirt. I tossed him on the floor like a sack of rotten potatoes before I pinned him down and raised my fist, pounding him with one good shot straight in the nose.

"Get the fuck out, and don't you ever come back here again, you miserable piece of shit," I roared.

Shocked, the man stared at me as blood poured down his face. I hopped off him, my hands clenching and unclenching with my barely restrained temper. "Out. Now."

"I'll fucking sue you for assault," he yelled.

By then, everyone in the restaurant was watching the drama go down.

I climbed onto the bar top, cupped my hands around my mouth, and talked as loudly as possible. "Take a look at this man. He just tried to slip drugs into a woman's drink. If you see him here again, notify me or Kip immediately. And for the rest of the fuckers that might even think about drugging and raping a girl in my club, I'll come for you, too, but I won't be so damn nice. Consider yourself warned." I looked down the length of the bar at Kip as a wicked smile slipped into place. "I'll be back. I want to make sure Ella is all right." I hopped off the bar and headed over to a shocked and rattled woman. Her hands shook as she picked up the pieces of the glass on the floor.

"Shit." She jerked her hand back, blood pooling on the end of her finger and dripping onto the floor.

"Ella, are you okay? Let the staff take care of that." I gently took her arm as she trembled. "Let's get you cleaned up and make sure there's not any glass in your finger."

"Okay." Her voice wobbled as she focused on me.

"I need to let Cami know I'm with you. She'll freak out if I leave without telling her."

"Kip. Tell Cami that Ella is with me," I said as we passed by him.

He nodded, then I led her through the kitchen and to the door marked "employees only." I passed through the break room, collected a Band-Aid and antibacterial wipe, and took her outside.

My temper was still at full throttle, but I didn't want to scare Ella any more than she already was.

We stepped outside into the cool night air, and I closed the door behind us.

"Are you all right?" I gripped her shoulders. "Did you drink anything from the time he sat down next to you?"

Her eyes widened as she shook her head. "No. I ... he put something in my drink?" Anger brewed to life behind her gaze.

"Yeah. Thank god, I saw him before it was too late. Let me see your finger." I gently cleaned it and inspected the small slice before I placed the Band-Aid around the cut. "There you go."

To my surprise, Ella hugged me. "Thank you. I could tell he was an asshole as soon as he took Cami's seat. I told him she would be right back, but he didn't care."

Her entire body leaned against mine, tremors still racking her small frame. She buried her nose against my neck, and her breaths grazed my skin. Ella's full breasts pressed against me, and her warm, soft curves were short wiring my brain.

41

I wrapped her in my arms, comforting her. My heart skipped a beat as her body fit perfectly against mine. Reluctantly, I stepped back and allowed a little space between us before she could feel my dick straining against my jeans. It wasn't the time, but my cock didn't seem to care.

"I won't put up with that shit in my club."

Confusion skipped across her face. "Wait. Your club? You own Velvet Vortex?"

I rubbed my jaw, the stubble rough against my fingers. "Yeah. I have a few business partners. Kip is one of them, but I hold the majority share."

"I had no idea. I guess I thought you were just the—"

"Bartender?"

A deep blush darkened her cheeks. "Sorry, that was going to sound super shitty, and I didn't mean it like that."

"It's okay. No offense taken." I massaged the back of my neck as I realized that she had shown an interest in me before she knew I was part owner of a thriving business. I was sick and tired of meeting women who were after my money. The tension in my shoulders eased with the realization that this woman was different.

"Now that you know I have a temper, would that deter you from going out with me?"

A small smile crept across her face, making my heart skip a beat. It had been way too long since I'd taken someone out.

"What did you have in mind?" She shoved her hands into the front pockets of her jeans.

Her shyness was endearing.

"Not here, that's for damn sure." I chuckled. "A nice dinner at a restaurant. I want to talk and learn more about who Ella is, so not a bar and grill. What kind of food do you like?"

"Most food. Pizza, popcorn, Chinese."

My brows knitted together. "Steak? Lobster? Seafood?"

She nodded, excitement flickering through her gaze.

"Excellent. How about tomorrow evening? I'll pick you up at eight. Wear something nice."

"Oh, you're taking me somewhere fancy?"

I frowned for a brief second. "Hasn't a guy taken you to an expensive dinner before?"

She scrunched up her nose. "Most of the guys I know are paying off college loans, so that would be a no." She looked away and cleared her throat. "I realize that you're older than I am, but how old are you?" Her voice was thin, as if she really didn't want to hear the answer.

"I'm forty." My pulse spiked as I waited for her to respond. "I hope that's not too old for you."

Chapter 7

Ella

After beating the hell out of a guy for nearly drugging me, Sebastian held me, and then I didn't give a shit how old he was. Unless my instincts were wrong, he was safe and dependable, something I hadn't experienced in a long time. More than that, even before he went all hero on my behalf, I was definitely interested. For forty, he was so damn good looking and fit. His body toned and sculpted ... *oh god, if I didn't stop, I would be a total goner.*

"Eleven years doesn't bother me. Being an asshole does."

Sebastian gave me a devilishly sexy smile, making my knees go weak.

"Good. I was a little worried that you might not want to go out with me if you knew I was older."

I nibbled on my lower lip. Why did being around him send my belly dipping like I was on a wild ride at Disney World? Still, it felt nice to be excited about getting to know a guy. "Well, stop worrying."

"I better get back in there and help Kip. I'm guessing no other douchebag will try any more shit around me for the remainder of the evening."

"I hope not. And thank you again." With an appreciative gesture, I squeezed his biceps.

Sebastian gave me a little bow. "At your service, ma'am."

A giggle broke free as his words warmed me. "I'll probably find Cami and head out. If I'm completely honest, I only showed up tonight to see if you were working."

Sebastian's eyes darkened as he closed the distance between us.

He took my hand and raised it to his mouth, turning my palm up, and pressing his lips against my wrist. My pulse stuttered wildly under his touch, and our gazes locked. I fought the urge to shiver. Not once had a sweet gesture sparked such a reaction from me—a desire to be cherished. I was used to rude, crude, dominating men on the website and at work. But Sebastian seemed different, and I was looking forward to finding out. My heart fluttered against the walls of my chest, and I reined in the impulse to kiss him silly.

He gently lowered my arm but kept a light hold on it. Moving closer to me, he softly said, "Until tomorrow evening, be a good girl for me." With that, he released my hand and stepped toward the door.

I sucked in the air and realized that my panties were soaked.

Maybe it's time someone else gave me an orgasm. My hand and a vibrator were only appealing for so long. I wanted to be wined, dined, sixty-nined, and whisked away to another reality, even if for only a few hours.

Sebastian walked away, then opened the door for me.

"Before we part ways for the evening." He removed his phone from his back pocket and handed it to me. "Your number, please. I mean, you don't have to give it to me, but it will be difficult to pick you up at your place if I have no idea where I'm going." His deep chuckle infused the space between us.

I took his cell and added my digits. "I was wondering when you'd ask me for it." Once I finished, I held it out to him, and his warm fingers brushed against mine, sending a spark of delicious electricity through me. My phone buzzed and I grinned as Sebastian's text popped up on my screen. I quickly saved his number.

The kitchen's heat blasted against my cool skin as we walked through it and back to the bar where Cami was waiting for me, her forehead pinched with worry. When she saw me with Sebastian, her shoulders relaxed.

"I'll see you tomorrow," Sebastian said.

"Okay." I offered him a warm smile as he hurried to help Kip. Sebastian's magnetism hadn't escaped me the first time I saw him, and once again I noticed all the girls sitting along the bar. Several of them sighed when Sebastian joined his friend—both men tall, broad-shouldered, and completely drool-worthy.

Cami hurried over to me, wearing a bewildered expression. "What the fuck did I miss? I swear, I can't leave you for one minute without shit hitting the fan. I heard Sebastian beat the hell out of some dude for no reason."

I frowned. "He had every reason. Some sick bastard tried to drug my drink. I didn't see him, but Sebastian did. He flew over the bar and punched the guy in the nose. I bet that guy was so fucked up, he'll probably need a plastic surgeon to put his face back together."

Cami gasped. "Holy crap, and good for Sebastian! I wonder if he ended up in the emergency room. If I were working in the ER tonight, I would have someone make sure he was reported for trying to drug you. Even if there wasn't proof, he would be on the cops' radar. Plus ..." A silly smile eased into place as she shrugged. "I might be friends with a certain hot cop who visits my nurse's station and maybe he'll find out who the asshole is."

Appreciating my best friend for having my back, I was still a little unnerved by the shady incident. The situation could have turned into something so much worse if Sebastian hadn't caught the asshole. "Do you think your cop friend would try to find out? Maybe the guy already has a record." My brows pinched together. I loathed the idea of that man doing this to other women. He needed to be stopped for good.

"We'll see. He stops by almost every shift I work, but I think he's working nearby. I'll check the records during my next shift to see if anyone came into the emergency room. If I can get a name, I'll mention it to him."

"Thanks." I blew out a heavy sigh. "After all the excitement, I'm ready to call it a night. Are you ready to leave? If not, I can take an Uber to my place."

"Bitch, no. I'm ready too. I'm super tired after the last week at work. Arguing with management takes it out of me."

Cami rose from her seat, and I slipped my arm through hers. "Well, you wouldn't have to argue if they realized you were right, and they should just do as they're told."

Cami laughed as we made our way to the exit. I glanced over my shoulder at Sebastian, who gave me a small wave.

"Looks like someone is smitten. I hope he's good to you, or I'll have to beat the hell out of him." Cami pushed the door open, and the fresh evening air greeted us.

"I'm sure he would be absolutely terrified at the mere thought." Our laughter echoed off the brick building, and even though I was chatting with my bestie, all I could think about was my date tomorrow evening. It had been a long time since I'd had one, and the idea sent butterflies scattering in my stomach.

"Now that we're out of the club ..." I opened the Mustang's door and climbed into the passenger seat.

"Yeah?" Cami buckled up and started the engine, grinning as it roared to life.

"Sebastian asked me out for tomorrow night. I'm not sure where he's taking me, but I need to wear something nice."

Cami gaped at me, and then she snorted. "Do you know how long it's been since I've had a guy take me somewhere nice?"

"Same."

"Well, I've seen your clothes, and you don't have anything to wear. I mean, you have corporate suits and shit. Not something sexy. But don't worry, babe. I've got your back."

"You're not taking me home, are you?"

"Nope. We're going to make drinks and rummage through my closet. You can stay the night or Uber to your place later, but I plan to get shitfaced."

Cami was fucking hilarious when she got drunk, and I welcomed the entertainment. A few more drinks sounded nice, but I had to work later. For a fleeting moment, I wondered what Sebastian would think if he knew how I earned my money after ten in the evening.

IT WAS ALMOST TWO IN THE MORNING WHEN I FINALLY LEFT Cami's and took an Uber home. Work would have to wait until Monday evening, but I could afford to take a few nights off since I'd made twenty-five grand.

Once I brushed my teeth and changed into my pajamas, I strolled to the kitchen to grab a glass of water. Hydrating always helped me avoid a hangover, and I hadn't done well in the water department that night.

Gathering a glass from the cabinet, I pushed the rim against the water dispenser on my refrigerator. A reflection caught my attention in the window directly above the sink, and a shudder ran through my body as the hair rose on the back of my neck. Spinning around, I clutched the glass as water sloshed over the edge and landed on my bare feet.

My legs threatened to buckle and betray me. He stood tall and wore a black hood that shrouded his grim reaper mask, and I looked into cold, grey eyes peering at me through the shadows. His lips curved into a terrifying smile through the face covering, and a deafening scream erupted from my throat. I dropped the glass on the tile floor, the fragile pieces shattering in every direction. *Fuck!*

Rather than fleeing, he stared at me. Without looking away from him, I stepped backward, mentally scolding myself for not installing an alarm system already. If I had, the police would be on their way once I pushed a hidden button in the house. Instead, I was left glancing around for my phone, which was most likely on my damn nightstand.

An eerie calm washed over me as our eyes locked, the deafening roar in my ears the only sound.

He moved away from the window before he appeared at the door leading into my kitchen from the backyard. The top half was glass, and all he had to do was break it, reach in, and unlock it.

Goosebumps skated across my skin, and my teeth chattered, waiting for his next move. Rooted in place, I fisted my hand as my chest heaved, and I willed myself to fucking run.

He raised a black-gloved hand, placed his palm against the window, and paused before disappearing into the night.

My legs collapsed beneath me, and my knees smacked the unforgiving ground as I dragged myself around the treacherous shards of glass that littered my path. Closing and locking the door behind me, I pulled myself onto my queen-sized bed and snatched up my phone. In seconds, 9-1-1 was on the line.

I stumbled through answering the questions, barely remembering my address as the lady took my report.

"The police are on the way. Please stay on the line until they arrive."

I curled into a ball at the head of my bed, shaking so hard I was afraid I might puke, and my frantic heartbeat ticked away the time as I waited.

"Ma'am, they've reached your residence and will ring the doorbell. Please stay on the line until you confirm that Officer Bexley and Officer Huang are with you."

With a trembling voice, I replied, "Okay. Thank you." I hurried to the front door and peered out of the peephole, verifying two uniformed men were standing on my porch. Carefully, I left the chain in place and cracked it open.

"Ma'am, we're Officer Bexley and Huang. We received a call that you had an intruder."

I nodded and returned my attention to the operator listening to our conversation. "Thank you for staying on the phone with me. The cops are here."

"You're welcome. Have a good evening." The woman disconnected the call.

Once I removed the chain, I welcomed the police into my home.

"Do you mind if we have a look around?" Officer Bexley asked.

"No, of course not." I glanced over my shoulder and spotted a tall figure across the street. Before I had time to point him out to the cops, it disappeared into the darkness. I rubbed my bare arms, willing the nightmare to disappear along with the masked man. But somewhere inside, I knew it was the same person who had stared through my window and into my soul. I just wanted to know how long he'd waited for me.

My thoughts were in a dangerous whirlwind as I followed the police around the house with my heart in my throat.

Chapter 8

Ella

"Stop stressing. You look stunning." Cami thoughtfully tapped her chin and paced the width of her bedroom.

Since our college graduation, Cami had lived in the same building in the Pearl district. Before I bought my house, I'd shared the apartment with Cami. Even though it had an older interior, we'd revitalized its white walls with art and decorations. When we learned that we could add a removable accent wall, we nearly peed our pants with excitement. We chose a dark, shabby-chic theme, which added depth to the space. We adored the look so much that we gave the living room the same treatment.

"You're missing som—" Her eyes widened, and she snapped her fingers.

"Apparently you've figured it out." I smoothed the form-fitting, backless, black dress with a slit up the right thigh, my thoughts returning to the man at my door last night. *I'm safe here.*

I inhaled deeply, forcing myself to return my attention to the dress. It had taken Cami a good hour to talk me into wearing it for my evening with Sebastian. This dress was sexy—really sexy. It was one

51

thing to be provocative in the cam job, but this was real life, and I was terrified of going out with Sebastian. With his heart-stopping smile and accent, I could see him charming his way into my bed.

"Pff, of course I did." She waved me off before she hurried to the jewelry box and removed a strand of pearls. "This will be perfect."

I swept my hair off my neck before she fastened the necklace. "Thanks for your help. I need the distraction after last night."

"Don't forget that you're not going home until your alarm system is installed tomorrow, so after your hot date, have him drop you off here."

I chewed on my bottom lip and willed myself not to cry. After the cops had taken my statement and left, I'd called my bestie. She'd rushed over to be with me at my place. Cami packed some clothes and toiletries, insisting I stay at with her until it was safe to return to my place. A new back door without a window and an alarm system would be installed tomorrow. I was willing to pay a rush fee to have it done.

My thoughts and emotions were in turmoil as I tried to identify the man and wondered why he hadn't broken into my home.

Was he someone I knew? Could he be the serial killer? Without Cami's support while preparing for my date, I might have completely lost my grip on reality.

"Do not ruin my artwork, girl!" Cami blew in my face until I started laughing. "Seriously, you look mouthwatering yummy. I mean if I were into chicks and not dicks, I would take you home with me." She gave me an exaggerated wink and giggled.

"Well, I hate to break it to you, but you've already taken me to your place." I laughed and pulled her in for a hug. "Love ya. Thank you for making me laugh."

Cami clung to me. My bestie was strong. We both were, but it was moments like these where I caught a glimpse of how she was really feeling. Last night had scared the shit out of her as well.

"Love you too." She dropped her arms and stepped back, placing her hands on her slender hips. "My work is done here. It's up to you now. And you gave Sebastian my address to pick you up, right?"

I rolled my eyes at her. "For the tenth time, yes. You're worse than my mother."

Cami glanced at her Apple watch. "Well, the man better not be late. That doesn't make a good impression on me." She tilted her head, attitude rolling off her.

"Cami. I'm nervous enough. You're making it worse." I wiped my sweaty palms on the dress's bodice, and Cami groaned.

"Dammit, I'm going to have to get my dress dry cleaned now!"

I was about to wipe my hands off some more just to see her turn beet red with frustration, but the sound of the doorbell interrupted me. My heart galloped into overdrive, and I took several soothing breaths.

"I've got it!" She ran out of her bedroom before I could catch her.

I blew out a big breath and waited to make sure it was Sebastian. Pacing the room, I couldn't stop my smile as his deep voice soothed me. I squared my shoulders, grabbed my clutch with my phone, ID, and credit card tucked inside, and joined them in the living room. The second Sebastian saw me, his blue eyes widened, and he paused mid-sentence.

"Hi," I said softly. "You look amazing." My pulse jumped as I took in the sight of him: towering and imposing, his well-defined muscles evident even beneath the elegant navy suit. The pants accentuated his powerful thighs, while the jacket showcased his broad, muscular shoulders. His chiseled jaw, freshly shaven, beckoned to me, and I yearned to trace its sharp contours with my fingers. I swallowed over the dryness in my throat.

A lopsided smile eased across his face. "You look breathtaking."

His accent was thicker than usual and anticipation swept over me.

"It's all Cami." I folded my hands in front of me in order not to fidget.

"No offense, but Cami couldn't have done this. Natural beauty can't be—"

"You two are sucking all the oxygen from the room." Cami turned to me. "Have fun. Be home late." She gave me a quick hug before she turned to Sebastian. Her entire body stiffened. "Hurt my girl, and I will very slowly saw off your balls with a butter knife and feed them to you."

Sebastian glanced at me before he answered. "I would expect no less from a best friend. Message received."

"Excellent, then get out of my apartment. Both of you." She squeezed my arm as I walked by.

"Keep your doors locked," I whispered.

"Always, don't worry about me. Go have fun." She shooed me out and laughed as she closed the door behind us.

Sebastian extended his arm, and I slipped mine through his.

"Sorry about her."

He patted my hand. "Don't apologize. I know plenty of people that would give anything to have a friend like that."

We made small talk as we walked down the hall and to the elevator. Once we entered and the doors closed, I realized no one else was in the small space. Between his proximity and the light musk of the cologne he was wearing, my body went into overdrive.

"If I weren't a gentleman, I would pin you against the wall and kiss you until neither of us could breathe."

Tilting my chin up, I composed myself. "Sometimes being a gentleman is overrated."

His gaze darkened, and he cleared his throat as the lobby button lit up. "I might need a longer elevator ride for that."

I laughed as we entered the main floor of the building and headed to the exit. Sebastian cracked the door open and then paused. "I'll bring the car around."

Before I could argue with him, he darted outside and jogged toward the parking area.

My heart hammered against my ribs as a familiar, fleeting

shadow from the window danced behind me. With a startled gasp, I whipped around, my high heels betraying me as they wobbled. With trembling hands, I desperately grasped the wall and managed to steady myself, narrowly avoiding a collision with two departing men.

A furious blush danced across my cheeks. "I'm so sorry."

A man with sun-kissed blonde hair extended a reassuring hand to my arm. "It's okay. Are you all right?"

Taking a shaky breath, I replied, "Yes. I just ... for a moment, I mistook you for someone I met last night. It caught me off guard."

From the lobby entrance, Sebastian's commanding tone sliced through the murmured conversation around us. "Is everything okay here?"

Composing myself, I met his gaze. "I lost my footing. He was making sure that I was all right." With a chilling dread, I realized I couldn't let Sebastian discover that I'd confused this innocent stranger with the menacing figure from last night.

Sebastian's expression softened as he nodded appreciatively at the man. "Thanks for looking out for her." His large hand found its place on the small of my back, radiating a comforting warmth.

The man smiled. "Stay safe," he said and then he and his companion exited the lobby.

Sebastian's voice lowered as he ushered me away. "I was worried they were bothering you."

"No, it was the other way around, I'm afraid."

Sebastian led us outside to his car, idling at the curb.

He held the door for me, and I tried my best to land in the seat and tuck my legs beneath the dress, so the long slit didn't show my ass cheek. I'd opted for a seamless thong, but now I was rethinking my choice. My butt was freezing, and I'd almost mooned my date.

The sound of Sebastian's throat clearing pulled me from my thoughts, and I looked up at him. His eyes were dark, pupils dilated. He was staring at me like he wanted to fuck me on the spot, and from the impressive outline of his cock pressing against his navy slacks, I wasn't wrong. Heat flooded my body, and I crossed my legs at the ankle.

He leaned over and slid the seatbelt around my waist, his face a mere centimeter from mine. I sucked in a breath as the heat of his body consumed the small space between us. His attention flicked to my mouth and then to my eyes as a wicked grin curved his full lips. I mentally begged for him to drag his knuckles over my painfully hard nipples, but he took extra precautions not to make contact. The click of the seatbelt snapped into place, and he straightened slowly. I inwardly groaned, disappointed that he had only teased me.

Once Sebastian was in the driver's seat, and we were buckled up, he merged into the oncoming traffic.

He reached over with his free hand and took mine, and butterflies fluttered madly in my chest. My fingers traced over his swollen, red knuckles, a reminder of the moment he had punched my would-be rapist. My stomach twisted with guilt and gratitude; he had injured himself to protect me. But I also felt admiration for his fearlessness and willingness to do what was right.

Every feminist cell in my body melted into a puddle with memories of how he'd beaten that asshole's face in. It had left me shocked and intrigued. Something deliciously mysterious about this man intrigued me, and I wanted to uncover more.

Sebastian glanced at me, then continued to focus on the drive. "How was your day?"

Thank god he wasn't looking at me. I couldn't have hidden the surprise from my expression. I'd never had a date where I was asked how my day was.

"It was nice. I hung out with Cami until you picked me up. Yours? Did you work at the club?"

Sebastian looked at me, his jaw clenched visibly, muscles taut and straining beneath his skin. A storm of emotions briefly flashed in his eyes—anger, confusion, and maybe a hint of pain.

I folded my hands on my lap as I studied him, wondering what was behind his reaction. Had I said something wrong?

"No, I had some things to take care of and didn't want to get locked into working tonight. Kip was supposed to cover for me, but he called in sick. Riley is filling in. Not sure you've met her yet. Anyway, I rarely take time off, but I wasn't about to miss our evening together." Sebastian shifted in his seat, appearing uncomfortable for a second.

His words sent my pulse skittering. "You seem to like your job. At least bartending, anyway. Or you could like beating guys up more." An offhanded laugh escaped me.

"Only if they're trying to hurt others. That's a fucking trigger for me, and my temper can get the best of me in those circumstances." His accent thickened, revealing his growing frustration with each word.

Sebastian signaled left, then drove down toward the river. I remained silent, attempting to guess where he was taking me. A few minutes later, he pulled into a building's valet parking. Our car doors flew open, and one of the employees extended his hand and assisted me out of the car.

Their greeting was filled with warmth and familiarity. Sebastian clearly had a rapport with them. As I approached him near the entrance, he gently placed his comforting palm on my exposed back, guiding us into the restaurant. I was immediately enveloped in a cozy ambiance — the soft glow of candlelight, plum-colored seats, and matching fabrics on the walls. My heels sank into the plush carpet as the host gracefully led us up a set of stairs and through a glass door.

A semi-private dining area was perched on top of the building, and I gasped, taking it all in. The rooftop offered a panoramic view of the vast, tranquil river. Nightfall draped the world in a velvety darkness, and the moonlight danced across the gentle ripples of the water. Elegant string lights adorned the restaurant, casting a warm, golden glow that contrasted with the stars overhead.

Once seated, I set my clutch on the side of the table and offered Sebastian a shy smile. No one had ever taken me somewhere so nice. "This is beautiful."

Sebastian's gaze met mine. "Not as beautiful as you."

Out of nowhere, my nape prickled with unease. I discreetly tucked a strand of hair behind my ear, trying to suppress the rising panic. The memories of last night's unwelcome visitor flooded my mind. Desperate to dismiss the idea that I was being watched, I looked away and pretended to adjust my dress. I closed my eyes and took a deep breath. But the unnerving sensation persisted, and I was left with an inescapable feeling of being stalked.

Chapter 9

Sebastian

Although I suspected Ella tried to hide her reaction, something had rattled her.

"What's wrong?"

Her eyes widened, and her smile slipped into place. "I'm sorry. I thought I saw someone I knew, and it surprised me."

That was twice tonight.

I had years of experience reading people in numerous situations, and Ella was lying to me. Granted, this was our first date, and I had no right to get into her business, but the fear that flashed across her face bothered me. I hated seeing her upset. I reached for her hand, hoping to soothe her.

The waiter approached us with our waters and set them on the table. Once we ordered a couple of cocktails, we fell into a comfortable silence while we studied the menus.

"What do you recommend?" she asked, her voice soft. She sank her teeth into her lower lip. I stifled my groan, but my dick was all about getting to know her. All of her.

"The lobster is amazing. If you prefer beef, the filet mignon melts in your mouth."

"Oh, wow. They're both really expensive. I can get a salad." She closed the menu and set it on the table, folding her hands in her lap.

"Ella, it's not about the money. It's about giving you an experience that you'll never forget. Wined and dined. No strings attached. I don't expect to spend the night with you, and you don't owe me anything. Not a single damn thing. If I can get you to smile or laugh, then it's already been the best night of my life."

Ella stared at me as if I were an alien that had just landed on planet Earth.

She looked away, then returned her gaze to me. Our eyes locked as I tried to reassure her that I meant exactly what I said.

"Tell me the truth. What do you love to eat or have wanted to try but never allowed yourself to?" I stroked the back of her hand with the pad of my thumb.

Ella McCloud had a way of captivating me, and she was taking pieces of my heart without my consent. Yet, there was a depth to her that I couldn't quite understand. She carried herself with a sense of wisdom and life experience that I hadn't seen in someone her age before.

She licked her lips, and I focused on her full mouth. Incredibly uncomfortable, I shifted in the seat in a failed attempt to give my poor cock some relief.

"The lobster, but I can pay half."

I chuckled. "You don't quit, do you?"

"I don't want us to leave at the end of our night, and you're pissed because I didn't suck your dick or sleep with you. Most guys think if they pay for a nice dinner, that the girl or guy owes them."

Anger licked through me with the idea that any man would make Ella feel pressured into something she didn't want.

"Then it sounds like you've gone out with the wrong guys. That's changing. Now be a good girl and order the lobster. If you don't, I'll order it for you."

Ella gasped, her cheeks burning bright red as she sucked in an audible breath. Maybe I'd been too forward, but if she worked with attorneys, she should be used to it.

Before she could respond, the waiter appeared, and she ordered the lobster.

"So what part of Australia are you from?"

"The capital of Australia, Canberra. It's about a hundred and fifty miles southwest of Sydney. Have you ever visited?"

She shook her head. "No, but I'd love to visit. Have you been in the states long?"

"Since the sixth grade. I met Kip not long after."

Her eyes widened. "I didn't realize you guys were childhood friends. From what it sounds like, you and Kip are family like Cami and I are. Having a lifelong friend who will trudge through the trenches with you is priceless and difficult to come by."

"It's one reason I trust him as a business partner."

"That makes sense." She smiled at me. "Are your parents still in the states or did they move back to Australia when you were old enough?"

A lump lodged in my throat as my chest tightened. I suspected the conversation about them would pop up tonight, but I was still hoping it wouldn't. Shifting in my seat, I offered her a regretful smile. "They're no longer with me anymore. I lost them after we moved here."

The color drained from Ella's face, and I reached out for her hand. "Maybe I'll tell you more another time, but for tonight, I just want to enjoy our time together."

"Of course. I would never want to intrude."

"It's fine, really. But tell me about your job. You've seen me at mine. Why a paralegal for criminal defense attorneys?"

She took a drink of her mai tai, peeking at me over the rim.

"The legal system intrigues me. I'm not sure if I'll go to law school or not. Since it's so expensive, I decided to get some experience first and see if I like it. The attorneys I work for let me attend trials, so that's super helpful. I started working for them right out of college, and they've taught me everything I know. I have a lot of respect for both of them." Her head tilted slightly to the side. "Call me crazy, but as I said before, I'm fascinated with the criminal mind."

The more she talked, the more she reeled me in, which was a dangerous game. Even with Dope's warning, I wanted to spend more time with her. "Do you think the law is fair?"

I could see her mind working as she pondered my question.

"No. I think it's broken. There are instances where guilty individuals go free while innocent ones are incarcerated. The most effective method to assist those wrongfully convicted is to challenge the verdict and advocate for their release. However, the process is slow, costly, and lengthy."

I leaned back in my seat, studying her. She was smarter than I'd realized, which was a huge plus. Not only was she beautiful, but she was intelligent. I bet all the girls hated her, and all the men wanted her.

"How do you feel about people who don't find justice in the courts and decide to take matters into their own hands?"

One dark eyebrow slightly rose with my question. "You mean a vigilante?"

"Yeah, let's say Robin Hood." I grinned.

She stared at me, and a surge of intense energy coursed through my chest as she prepared to speak. I leaned into the table, mesmerized, as I didn't want to miss a single word that came from her mouth. My fingers gripped my water glass, waiting for her answer.

"I think they do best if they don't get caught. You can't quote me saying that, though."

"It's true. If they die or get thrown in prison, it's not much help to anyone."

"The biggest reason I've not moved forward and continued the path to becoming an attorney is that sometimes the world needs someone who is morally grey. For instance, the television show Dexter. He was a crime lab tech but tortured and killed serial killers, which made *him* a serial killer."

"Such a good show. Do you think things like that happen in real life?"

Ella leaned across the table, then whispered, "I fucking hope so."

Dammit, I want to kiss her so fucking bad right now.

"And where do you stand on that same issue?" she asked.

I cleared my throat and opened my mouth to respond as our dinner arrived.

"This looks delicious." Ella unrolled her napkin and set it on her lap.

Unable to take my attention from her, I replied, "It does." Before she realized I was referring to her and not the food, I busied myself with my utensils.

Ella paused and waited for me to select the tiny fork, and she did the same. I took the lead, pried a bite of the juicy white meat from the shell, and dipped it into butter before I popped it into my mouth. "Try it. See if you like it. If not, we'll order you something else to eat. It would not hurt my feelings to eat your lobster."

Ella choked, her eyes watering. It took me a moment to realize what I'd said and how she'd taken it. I threw my head back and laughed as she attempted to compose herself.

"I meant the food." I pointed to her plate.

"I know, but it was the way you said it ..." She looked away at the other guests, but no one was interested in us.

"Take a bite."

"Bossy much?"

"Oh, Ella, you have no idea." I smirked at her. I would have paid a million dollars to read her thoughts right then.

"I have a feeling you're full of surprises." She dug her fork into the lobster, dipped it in butter, and put it into her mouth. Her eyelids fluttered closed, and a seductive moan slipped from her. "Holy hell. That's the best thing I've ever tasted." She set the utensil down and wiped the corner of her lips with the blue linen napkin. "Sorry, Sebastian. You won't be getting my dinner." She gave me a playful smile.

She took another bite, chewing slowly and savoring the moment. "Next time, you should let me cook for you."

My fork paused in midair, and my gaze softened as her cheeks heated with embarrassment. I quirked a brow and forced myself not to smile. "We're going out again?"

Her face briefly fell. "I hope so." She pursed her lips. "I didn't mean to assume though, so let's just forget I said anything."

A fleeting look of disappointment slipped over her expression before she plastered on a smile.

Her attention drifted down to the tablecloth, her body language revealing her insecurities that she tried to mask with pleasant conversation. But I saw beyond her practiced smiles and small talk. All it took was someone who truly saw her to understand what lay beneath the surface. There was so much more to Ella McCloud, and I couldn't wait to uncover each layer, slowly.

"Ella. Eyes here." I waited until her attention was fixed on me, taking heed of the subtle command in my tone, making sure she could see the sincerity in my gaze. "We're definitely going to do this again. You and me."

"Are you sure? I really wasn't assuming. I just stuck my foot in my mouth." She glanced around before her attention landed on me again, almost as if she was concerned other people had overhead her. "To be honest, I don't go on many dates. Actually, this is the first one I've agreed to in a long time." Her gentle laugh danced across the table.

"I'm positive." Her unexpected vulnerability touched me, and an overwhelming urge to shield her from the world rippled through my chest.

Ella's shoulders sagged with relief as we agreed to see each other. I was aware that she was nervous about our evening, but I hadn't realized how much until now. I wanted her to feel relaxed and safe with me, to be herself, for as long as the night lasted.

We continued to learn more about each other during the remainder of our dinner. When the subject of my future came up, I shared my dreams of an early retirement and globe-trotting adventures. She leaned in, her eyes shining with genuine intrigue, and even chimed in with her travel plans.

A high-pitched *ping* rang out from Ella's empty glass, followed by another just as she turned her head toward the dark, threatening sky. Holding out her hand, palm up, in front of her, I watched transfixed while Ella blinked rapidly, as if trying to clear her vision. Her expression morphed into one of bewilderment, and she wiped a water droplet from her eyelash.

"Sebastian, look—it's starting to rain."

The plump drops fell faster, landing on the blue tablecloth. Ella sprang up, her laugh carefree and wild, as rain pelted her pale skin. It fell in rivulets, transforming her already impossibly dark hair into midnight velvet.

"We're lucky we finished eating!" she exclaimed with a giggle, using the leather menu as an impromptu umbrella.

The other guests scurried inside, leaving Ella and me behind, simply standing grinning at each other through the downpour. Our hair and clothes were already soaked through. She looked like a woodland sprite, glowing and mischievous, standing underneath the fairy lights. Her dress molded to every dip and curve of her body, droplets sneaking their way down into the valley of her cleavage, as the rain drenched us both.

The hum of the classical music that flowed through the outdoor speakers blended with the rhythmic sound of the raindrops and Ella's husky laughter.

In that moment, it felt like a memory that would stay with me forever.

I stood and held my hand out to her. "Dance with me."

Surprise flickered through her expression as she looked at me. Moments later, a smile graced her lips, and she accepted my hand. Drawing her close, we began to sway in a gentle dance.

"You're crazy." She laughed, tilting her face to the rain. I reached out and touched her cheek, using my thumb to brush away the water from her soft skin. She playfully licked her bottom lip, catching a few droplets on her wet, full mouth. "I like it," she said as she snuggled against me as we danced.

My palm gently trailed up her bare back, and she shivered against me. "I won't keep you out here long. I don't want you to get sick. If you do, I'll take care of you, though."

Her eyes softened. "I might let you." To my surprise, she stopped dancing and lifted her chin. "I've wanted to do this all evening." She tilted her mouth up, brushed her lips against mine, lingering for just a moment before she broke our embrace.

Every fiber in my body responded to her, but more than that, I loved that she'd made the first move.

I took her hand in mine. "Let's get inside. I'll pay the bill and we can dry off."

"That's probably a good idea." She shrieked as a sudden wind blew the rain sideways, pelting against our skin. She scooped up her clutch off the table and laughed.

I loved seeing her happy.

Careful, Romeo. Anxiety wrapped its fingers around my chest, reminding me that Ella and I were on borrowed time. She might never want to see me again if she ever uncovered the truth.

Chapter 10

Ella

I was freezing my ass off, but dancing with Sebastian in the rain was worth every tooth-chattering moment.

He hugged me from the side and rubbed my arms to help me get warm as we walked to the entrance of the restaurant.

"I'm sorry," he said. "I shouldn't have kept you outside."

"Don't apologize. It was fun. I haven't danced in the rain since I was little."

Memories flickered through my mind of my orange rubber boots Mom made me wear along with my green raincoat. Back then, I wanted to be unique and stand out in the sea of kids wearing the same boring yellow rain jackets. My wish to be different came true, just not in the way I'd hoped.

That memory was a painful reminder of what I'd worked so hard to hide. If I continued to date Sebastian, I would eventually have to reveal the truth to him. A shiver rocked my body, and I shelved the idea for now. I just wanted to enjoy his company.

Sebastian approached a female staff member who was offering towels to everyone caught in the downpour. He grabbed several and returned to me with a silly grin. I reached out to take one, but he pulled away. "I'll dry you off. After all, I was the one that got you all wet."

I hid my smile as he gently lifted my drenched hair and draped a towel over my shoulders. He took one arm at a time and, with great care, tenderly dried the water droplets from my skin. My belly flip-flopped at his attentiveness, and I wondered what he would be like in bed. From how he had treated me so far, he would take his time and take care of me first. I tingled with anticipation.

His gaze never left mine as he kneeled before me, drying the top of my feet and ankles. He slowly made his way up my calves but stopped.

I reached out to touch his hair, and my fingers sifted through the wet strands. Swallowing over the lump in my throat, I tried not to haul him off to the bathroom and let him fuck me senseless in a stall. If he continued touching me that way, I might combust right there. Apparently, foreplay was his nickname, and I wanted every second of being teased until I lost my mind.

He rose and leaned near my ear. "I'm glad we'll have more time together, Ella. I'm looking forward to it."

I sucked in a breath, searching his blue eyes for the promises that hadn't rolled off his tongue.

"Let me take those for you," a young lady said, breaking us out of our trance.

I handed my towels to her before she turned to walk away. "Excuse me. I need a few more for him." I pointed at my still-drenched date.

"Of course. I'll be right back."

"Thank you."

Sebastian placed a finger beneath my chin and forced me to look at him.

"Why, Ella McCloud, are you the type of woman that gets what she wants?"

His accent was thicker than usual, and I wondered what he would do if I said yes. He brushed his lips against mine, forcing my response to lodge in my throat.

"Sir. Here you are," the lady said and handed him some towels.

He nodded at her. "Ella, I'll be right back."

My attention was trained on him as he went to the men's restroom. Minutes later, he returned with the crumpled towel in one hand and his suit jacket in the other. His white shirt was glued to his skin, and I couldn't pull my gaze away from his muscled chest and abs.

"I have clothes, including a few spare shirts in the car. I'll change when we're there."

"You do?" Puzzled with why he had a change of clothes, I followed him out of the restaurant. We stood beneath the awning as the valet located his car.

"I always have a change of clothes in case I need to head straight to the bar from the gym."

"That makes sense. I'm getting the impression that you practically live there."

"It's definitely my second home."

Once we were settled in the car, Sebastian blasted the heat. He pulled around to the other side of the parking lot and stopped on the side of the restaurant. "I'm going to park here for a minute to change my shirt. My bag is behind your seat." He reached over and grabbed it. "Is it okay if I change in front of you?"

"You're soaking wet still. You don't need to ask my permission."

He removed a white folded shirt from the bag, then tossed it on the back seat. "Making you uncomfortable on our first date isn't on the agenda." He winked at me, and I was pretty sure I melted into a puddle.

"I've seen plenty of men without a shirt on. For instance, at the lake."

"You have a point, but those guys aren't on a first date with you."

He removed his shirt and tossed it over his shoulder. I sank my teeth into my bottom lip as his well-defined, broad shoulders narrowed down to a slender waist, the contours of his stomach muscles looking incredibly yummy. I wanted to lick my way straight down to the sculpted abs that led into his jeans, the thin strip of hair guiding the way. His arms flexed as they moved, pulling on the clean shirt. I shifted, thoroughly enjoying the front-row seat. My thighs clenched as I pretended not to ogle him, but dear god, I was. I definitely had a date with my vibrator once I got home.

"Sebastian," I said, my body consumed by a hunger overtaking any logical thoughts. He turned to me, and I leaned over the console and pressed my lips to his, my hands roaming over his chest, feeling the heat radiating through his clothes. He responded eagerly, his hand tangling in my hair as our tongues intertwined in a passionate dance. A guttural moan escaped his lips as he attempted to get closer.

"Damn console," he grumbled.

"I can solve that problem." I gave him a wicked little grin as I hiked up my dress to my thighs, then crawled over to his seat and straddled him.

His pupils darkened with need as his cock pushed against my core. Sebastian's hands gripped my waist possessively, pulling me closer as I moaned softly, the heat between us becoming more and more intense. I reached down, my fingers brushing against his rigid length through his slacks, and he shuddered at my touch.

"I want you," I whispered, leaning down to press my lips to his ear, my breath hot and heavy. "I need you."

He groaned, his eyelids fluttering shut as he thrust up into my hand, his hips bucking against me.

"Ella," he moaned as our bodies melded together. The hunger inside me intensified, and the wetness of my desire seeped through my thong.

I leaned forward, my nipples brushing against his chest through the material of the dress.

With a growl, he lifted me just enough for his hand to slide around my thigh and cup my ass.

He thrust upward, our bodies grinding against each other as his tongue swept over mine. Sebastian slid his fingers between my legs and massaged my clit through the thin fabric of my thong.

"You're so wet," he said, his voice low and husky.

"Oh, god that feels so good."

I moved against his hand, desperate to have more. As if reading my mind, he slid my thong out of the way, exposing my sensitive skin to his touch.

He slowly eased a finger inside me, matching the rhythm of my hips. The sensation was overwhelming, pushing me to the brink of ecstasy.

My breath hitched as his piercing gaze locked with mine.

I couldn't hold back my moans as he added another finger, stretching and building the tension within me. His lips trailed down my neck, leaving a trail of fiery kisses that left me gasping for air.

"Be a good girl for me, Ella," he whispered huskily. "Cum for me and mark me with your scent for the rest of the night." A shiver ran through my body at his command.

I grabbed his biceps and dug my fingernails into the corded muscles. "Sebastian." I leaned forward, and my lips grazed his ear as I exploded, trying not to scream his name.

"That's my girl." He removed his fingers from my drenched pussy, then slowly licked them clean.

I straightened with a silly smile as I reached for the button on his slacks.

My cell rang, pulling me out of my hormone-induced fog, and I gathered my clutch from the console. I located my cell and glanced at the screen and frowned. It was Cami. She knew I was out with Sebastian, which meant it was important.

"I'm sorry. I have to take this." I awkwardly climbed back into my seat, my attention still on Sebastian as he fixed his hard cock behind his slacks before he made sure I was buckled in.

"Do your thing." Sebastian shifted into drive and drove out of the parking lot.

"Hey, is everything okay?" I asked Cami.

"Babe, you didn't see your missed calls yet?" Cami sniffled, and her nose sounded stuffy.

Shit. She'd been crying. "What missed calls?"

"Your parents and me. Ella, your dad is in the ICU. Get there as fast as you can."

My stomach dropped to my toes, my vison tunneling, everything so far away. I could hear Cami's quiet sobs, tinny and distant in my ear, and Sebastian's worried questions, muffled and muted, but it seemed as if it was happening to someone else. My breath caught in my throat and cold, hard panic rose as the tingling started in my fingertips. *No. This can't be happening.* "Cami, is he ... is he?" I couldn't force the words out of my mouth.

"I don't know. Just ask Sebastian to bring you to St. Vincent."

"Okay. I'm on my way."

My heart galloped against my chest, threatening to break free.

"Ella, what's wrong?"

"My dad." Tears welled in my eyes, and I blinked them away, embarrassed at my show of emotion in front of Sebastian. "He's in intensive care at St. Vincent Hospital. Can you please take me there?"

"Of course." Sebastian signaled to change lanes and merge on the highway.

"I should tell you something." I focused on the wipers as they cleared the relentless drops from the windshield. If only it were that easy and could whisk away the pain.

Once he merged into traffic onto highway 26, he took my hand. "I'm listening, Ella, but take your time."

"He's sick. He has a rare cancer, and I'm covering his medical bills for a new trial. It's his only hope and ..." My shoulders shook as I broke down. "I'm so sorry. I didn't want our date to end like this. I wasn't going to tell you about him unless we continued to see each other. It's a lot to deal with. *I'm* a lot to deal with when we think we're losing him." I grabbed a tissue from my clutch and dabbed my cheeks, hoping like hell I didn't look like more of a hot fucking mess.

"Don't apologize, Ella. That's too much to carry alone for anyone."

"Cami knows, but she's family. I don't talk to anyone else about it."

"Hold on for a minute. We're about forty-five minutes away. Let me see if I can speed things up."

He pressed a button on the steering wheel, and a phone ringing filled the car speakers.

"Sup, Bass?"

"Hey, Zayne. I need a favor. Are you still working in Portland this weekend?"

"Yeah, Giselle and I are here for a few weeks. What can I do for you?"

"I need a police escort to St. Vincent's. Can you get me one?"

"Are you okay?" Zayne's voice was heavy with concern for Sebastian.

"I'm good. It's for ..." He paused and glanced at me. "A special friend of mine."

"Let me see what I can do. What car are you driving tonight?"

Sebastian rattled off the make and model of the vehicle along with the license plate.

"Got it. Hold the line."

Sebastian reached over and squeezed my hand as he focused on the road and waited. "Zayne has his own security company on the East Coast, but he works on this side of the world sometimes too. I met him and his wife at the bar one evening. We've been friends for the last few years. Damn good guy."

Zayne returned. "Officer Bexley is a half mile away. Get into the right lane. Once he sees you, he'll turn his lights on. Get behind him and he'll escort you in."

"I owe ya, man. Thanks."

Bexley ... where did I know that name?

Son of a bitch. It was one of the officers who had been at my home last night when I'd reported an intruder. Dammit, I hope he doesn't say anything in front of Sebastian. If Sebastian found out that I had a possible stalker, he'd run in the opposite direction. No one wanted a suitcase full of drama.

Chapter 11

Ella

My knee bounced as Sebastian drove like a bat out of hell. "Thank you for calling in a favor. I'm sorry I didn't tell you sooner about my dad. It's just not first date material."

"It's all right, Ella. We're still getting to know each other, but I'm here if you need anything."

"I just don't want to bother you with my drama."

His forehead pinched. "Don't think like that."

With the police's help, Sebastian pulled into the emergency parking lot in record time. I wasn't sure that he would truly understand how grateful I was to reach the hospital so quickly.

Sebastian eased up to the curb behind the cop car, and I held my breath as Officer Bexley approached at the driver's side window.

Please don't recognize me.

"Hi, Sebastian, I hope everything is ..." His words trailed off as he stared at me. I shook my head slightly, hoping he would understand not to say anything about my possible stalker. Until I had more information, I couldn't risk Sebastian thinking I was a total shit show, or worse, put him in danger.

Officer Bexley cleared his throat as I climbed out of the car before I poked my head back in. "Thank you both. As soon as I know how Dad is, I'll message you, Sebastian."

"Do you want me to come in with you?" Sebastian's tone was soft and concerned.

"No. They only allow families into the intensive care unit. Plus, I'm not sure how long we'll be waiting to hear something. I'll talk to you later." I closed the car door and hurried to the entrance. I slowed, then walked back to the car. Sebastian rolled his window down, and I leaned in and kissed him on the cheek. "Thank you for everything."

"I'm here if you need anything," he said before I gave him a small wave and left.

A few minutes later, I joined Cami. The intensive care waiting room was abuzz with tension. Fluorescent lights overhead gave a sterile glow, revealing off-white walls with informational posters about health and safety precautions. The seats were arranged in short rows, and Cami was pacing between them, nibbling on her thumbnail.

"Hey, how bad is it?"

"Thank god you're here." Cami hugged me, sniffling.

"They wouldn't tell me much because I'm not family, but since I work here, I was able to talk them into letting me wait until you or your mom arrived."

Realizing my mom wasn't around, I asked, "Where is Mom? They've talked to her, right?"

She must have seen the fear on my face because she started explaining. "Your mom's safe and sound, Ella. Take a breath. Since her job practically forced her to Seattle, she couldn't get a flight home fast enough." She placed her hands on her hips, pausing. "I stopped by the house to check on him, and when I arrived, he took a sudden turn and was having trouble breathing. His heart rate had dropped really low, so I called 9-1-1 while his nurse tried to help him. Once the ambulance arrived, I followed in my car and called your mom while I was driving."

"Fuck." I pressed the heel of my hand against my forehead. "I'll see what I can find out. Thank you for being there and calling Mom." I hugged Cami again before I hurried to the nurse's station with her behind me. I clenched my hands together, trying to ward off the rising panic. Every second felt like an eternity, and the suffocating fear that I couldn't do anything to ease my father's pain threatened to consume me.

"Hi, I'm Alexander McCloud's daughter. He was brought in by ambulance. I was wondering what condition he's in?" I took out Dad's additional insurance card I carried with me, no matter what purse I used. With Mom occasionally traveling for work, it was the best way to ensure the hospital received the information. At first, I was furious that Mom still traveled, but my parents risked losing their house if she didn't. Bills didn't stop just because someone was skating along the edge of death. It had taken both of us pitching in to hire a full-time nurse for him, but it allowed us a little peace of mind. Sometimes, anyway.

"He's in the ICU waiting for tests, hon. Do you want to see him? He's in 515."

"Thank you very much." I turned to my best friend. "I'll text you when I get more information, but at least I can talk to him if he's awake."

"I'll wait for your mom." She gave me a reassuring smile before I disappeared down the hall.

I reached his room and slowed, staring at the door number. Taking a few, deep, calming breaths, I wiped beneath my eyes and attempted to rid any evidence that I'd been crying. I wanted to be strong for Dad. Finally, I poked my head through the cracked door.

"Dad, I'm here."

"Ella?" Dad asked from the hospital bed as he pried his tired green eyes open. "Come on in." His voice sounded strained.

I closed the door behind me and hurried to his bedside. "When will the doctor come in?" I pulled up a chair, the legs scraping across the white tile floor. Taking his hand in mine, I sat next to him.

"He just ordered the tests. He's concerned the trial is weakening my heart."

I clenched and unclenched my hand. "No. Dammit, no. We can try something else. There has to be another trial we can get you into. Something better. If this one isn't working, we'll find one that will. We can't just—"

"I love you, baby girl. But we might have to stop fighting."

I pressed a kiss to the paper-thin skin of his knuckles. My jaw clenched with determination, and our gazes locked. "I will never stop fighting for you. Never. So do *not* ask me to."

An exhausted smile slipped into place. "Sometimes the heavens make that choice for us, honey."

I shook my head. "No. I refuse to accept that until the test results are back." I patted his skinny arm. Over the last fourteen months, Dad had lost so much weight that it was hard to picture him as the man who used to work out every morning. He was healthy for sixty-two. Then, almost overnight, he was sick ... dying. While Mom had taken a medical leave at work to care for him, we'd tried an aggressive chemo without any positive results. It had left his pale skin paper thin from the extensive sessions. Afterward, I'd scrambled to find a clinical trial for him. He'd finally been accepted into one. It was our last hope.

A looming shadow of dread lurked over me as memories of his decline grabbed me by the throat, sending my pulse racing with anxiety. The mere thought of being without him was like standing at the edge of an abyss, the ground beneath my feet threatening to crumble beneath me. He had always been my rock.

"Stop," he said.

"Stop what?"

"Thinking about what it will be like when I'm gone. You're strong. You'll be okay. I've prepared you for this, honey. You're smart, you have a good job, great friends, and your mom." He pulled in a long breath before he continued. "Do you have someone special in your life yet?"

I rolled my eyes. "What kind of question is that at a time like this?"

"Appease your old man and answer me."

I shifted on the hard plastic chair, my ass protesting loudly.

"Maybe. It's too early to tell." For a moment, my body relaxed, and a smile pulled at the corner of my lips. *But tonight was amazing.*

"From the look on your face, you really like this boy. Tell me more."

Dad always had a way of guiding conversation when there was a tense situation. He said it didn't make sense to waste time wondering about something out of your control. It helped pass the time with a more uplifting topic. I always appreciated his wisdom, especially now.

"His name is Sebastian. He's a few years older but has an established career. So far, he's attentive, kind, funny, and very handsome." I couldn't help but smile at the thought of the man quickly gaining my interest, whether we were together or not. I decided it was probably best that I leave out telling my dad that I wanted to lick and fondle every square inch of the man. My dad didn't need to know about Sebastian's defined abs and sculpted arms. How the rain had molded his pants to what looked to be a very impressive cock.

"What does he do for a living?"

I squirmed on the seat, wondering how Dad would take the fact that he owned a restaurant and club. Dad was a bit old-fashioned and was a firm believer in working for a corporation until you retired. Times had changed though, and companies laid off the highest paid people first. Security was a thing of the past. But even if he weren't crazy about the idea of Sebastian being self-employed, the thought that Sebastian had money and could take care of his daughter would soothe his concerns. Not that I needed anyone to take care of me, but my security was important to him.

"He owns a restaurant and club. He's wealthy, but you'd never know it because he bartends. He said it keeps things interesting."

"He sounds like a good guy. If you think there's something

between the two of you, I would like to meet him." Dad squeezed my hand, his eyelids fluttering closed.

I froze, waiting for the soft rise and fall of his chest that would indicate he hadn't died. A lump formed in my throat, and I struggled to swallow over the fear. Frantically, I searched the room to see what machines he was hooked up to. I heaved a sigh of relief when I saw the monitor tracking his heartbeat. It was the soft beep I was hearing.

Dad's eyes flew open, and he chuckled. "Sorry, honey. I guess I dozed off."

The door opened, and a nurse joined us. "We're ready to take him for his tests. You can stay here or in the waiting room." She offered a gentle smile to us.

I rose, then leaned over and kissed Dad on the forehead. "Hurry back. Mom should be here any time."

"Thank you for taking care of him," I said before I left the room.

"It will be about an hour or more. Try to get some food or coffee, hon." The nurse gave me a kind smile.

I nodded, then stepped into the hall, my heels echoing off the walls as I headed back to the waiting room.

"How is he?" Mom asked, rushing over to us. Her eyes, usually so full of life, were rimmed with red and shadowed with fatigue. They darted around restlessly, scanning Cami and me for any signs of hope, or perhaps bracing for the bad news.

"Sleeping." I threw my arms around her, hugging her tightly. "He went in for tests a few hours ago, and he's been sleeping since then. I've checked on him several times but wanted to be here when you arrived. Thanks for texting and letting me know when you landed."

"Of course." She turned and hugged Cami. "Thank you for being here."

"Always. I love you guys."

Mom's hand trembled as she smoothed her hair. She'd been dying it her original color since she was forty, and the beginnings of grey wisps peeked through the jet-black strands. I got my green eyes from Dad and my hair from Mom.

I was lucky. My parents were both loving, compassionate, and intelligent people.

"Let me take you to his room, Mom. He'll be happy to see you when he wakes up."

"That would be good. I want to be in the room waiting for the doctor when the results come back." Mom hugged Cami again. "I'll see you in a while."

Slipping my arm around Mom, I steered us toward Dad's room. When we arrived, the door was wide open, and the doctor stood beside his bed. He glanced up as we joined them.

"Hi, baby." Mom kissed Dad's cheek, and his face lit up.

"You must be Mrs. McCloud. I'm Dr. Coppinger. I was just about to give your husband his test results."

"We're just in time, then," I said from behind Mom.

Dr. Coppinger folded his hands in front of him, expression full of compassion.

Shit. This wasn't good. I gripped the back of the chair and attempted to steady myself for the blow.

"I understand that you're in a trial treatment for your cancer, Mr. McCloud."

"Yes. Please call me Alexander."

"Got it. Alexander." A kind smile eased across his face. "In these situations, there are always greater downsides than a tried-and-true treatment. I'm afraid that the trial will have to come to an end. If we continue, you risk heart damage. I know this is incredibly difficult to hear, and I'm so sorry."

I shook my head, refusing the doctor's words. My jaw clenched as I struggled to formulate my thoughts. "If he's not on it, his cancer will kill him."

"I understand, but there's nothing else we can do. If you have a nurse, then I can send your father home and keep him comfortable for as long as needed."

"You mean until he dies?" My pitch rose with my question while Mom's muffled cries filled the room.

"Spend time with him and try to make some lasting memories. It will help the difficult process. I can also offer a counselor to help process the grief."

My hands clenched and unclenched, anger roaring to life inside the pit of my belly. We'd worked so hard to get him in the trial. I'd talked to a multitude of doctors to get Dad the best care. How could our last hope be gone in a fleeting second?

"Shouldn't the decision be his choice? Have you even looked at other options, or are you just giving up on my dad?" I gritted my teeth, tears spilling down my cheeks as the grief twisted my me into knots.

"Honey, we can look into this some more. Find another way," Mom said, consoling the both of us.

"I reviewed his charts after the tests results came back. There aren't any additional trials he would qualify for. I understand your pain, but I've truly done everything I can. So have the other medical professionals who have worked with him. I'll be around tomorrow if you have questions."

He nodded and left the room, leaving me with the earth-shattering truth that my dad was on limited time.

My cell chimed in my clutch, and I retrieved it.

Sebastian:

> Is your father okay? Are you?

I squeezed my eyes closed against the pain. I wanted to see him. Despite my life being a complete disaster, I needed something new and good for just a few moments. Even though I didn't owe him anything, I should give Sebastian the news about Dad and the opportunity to bow out before things became more complicated.

Me:

> Can you meet me at the house tomorrow? I'm having an alarm system put in, so I'll be home all day. We can talk then.

Sebastian:

> What time?

Me:

> Would eleven work?

Sebastian:

> See you then, but message me if you need anything before then.

Me:

> I will and thank you. My address is 1072 Daisy Drive. See you soon.

Chapter 12

Sebastian

"Focus, Dude." Dope's expression twisted with worry. "This shit should be the most important thing on your mind."

I paced the small room overflowing with Dope's cameras, video equipment, and devices I didn't even know the names of. Other than his gaming chair, the only other piece of furniture was an ugly plaid loveseat pushed up against the wall. Every time I stepped foot into his secret dungeon, his intelligence and knowledge of all things tech overwhelmed me. Dope had taught me enough to make me dangerous, but nowhere near his skill level.

"Before we get down to business, there's something else we need to chat about." Dope laced his fingers behind his head.

"What's that?"

"Kip, man. He's missing work and acting weird as fuck."

I stood still, staring at Dope and chewing on what he was saying. I'd worked with Kip weekly, but his sudden disappearances for a few days at a time with zero communication with us was messed up. "Do you think he's using drugs again?"

"No. I think his eyes would be bloodshot, he'd be forgetting things, he'd be all twitchy and shit if he was using. I was there five years ago when he got clean and off heroin. I would recognize the signs. This is something else. Maybe you can talk to him and find out what's up."

"Yeah. I'll do that. I guess I get so busy I didn't realize how many times it had happened." I placed my hands on my hips.

"Something is definitely off."

I rubbed my forehead, trying to relieve the tension. "Why don't you talk to Kip and let me know what he says."

"Hopefully that problem will be resolved soon." Dope slapped his hands together, the noise indicating we were done discussing Kip.

"Moving on to other important business. I need you present and concentrating on what we're doing. As you're always telling Kip and me, we can't afford to fuck up. And I'm happy that you're into someone, but Ella is all up in your head, man."

I groaned, refusing to agree with him. "I'm worried about her. She's got a lot on her plate. If it were good news about her dad, she would have texted me already. And if he's dying, she might want to try to push me away and not see me again. I hope not, but it would be a normal reaction."

Dope rolled his office chair backward, glaring at me, his red hair flopping onto his forehead. "You gotta shake it off, man. You know how fucking dangerous it is to get involved with someone. No. Hell, no. Not you, Kip, or me. We made a commitment. If we get caught ..." Dope folded his arms across his chest, sucking air through his teeth. "Don't. Do. It. Break shit off with her *now*. Like the next time you see her. We can't afford for you to fall head over heels for her or anyone for that matter. And do you really even know who she is? Have you checked her out? No. You haven't because you would've asked me to dive into her business."

He raised a finger, halting me from telling him to fuck off.

"No worries. You know I'm already on it." Dope rolled up to his computer, and his fingers flew across the keys.

Feeling protective of her, I objected. "Piss off. You're not going to dig into her background." He ignored me, and I grabbed the back of the chair and jerked, causing Dope's arms to flail like a windsock in a hurricane.

Dope paused and stared a hole through me. "I'll make you a deal. Let me deep dive, and if she's as amazing as you hope she is, then I'll give you my blessing to date her."

I groaned as I placed my hands on my hips. "That's not cool, mate."

"I know. But hear me out. If you like her, then let's start vetting her. I mean, eventually she's going to find out what you're up to. You talk in your sleep, and one confession will fuck us all, and not in a good way." He arched a light red brow at me, waiting.

"Goddammit." I scrubbed my face with my hands, weighing out the pros and cons as quickly as possible. Dope wouldn't wait for me to think about it for a few days.

"I don't even know where Ella and I are headed. All I know is that I enjoy being around her. She's special." But he was right. I couldn't jeopardize her learning shit she had no business knowing. Not yet anyway.

I blew out a heavy sigh. "I can't believe I'm saying this but go ahead. It would be better to end things now with her if we found out anything concerning. She's a paralegal, though, and her bosses would run a background check, so I'm sure she's clean."

Dope grinned and cracked his knuckles. "Those fuckers have no idea what they're doing."

"Quit running your fucking pie hole and work your magic." I swiped the black pen from Dope's desk and clicked the end several times as he began his search.

"Name?"

"Ella McCloud."

"Middle name?" he asked.

"No idea."

"Address?"

I rattled off the information and the name of her place of employment.

I shifted from one foot to the other, watching the computer screen fill with information.

"Oh shit. Ohh shiiit. Damn, bro! You know how to pick 'em." Dope turned to look at me. "Yeah, she's something else all right."

"Fucking spit it out before I lose my temper," I growled.

Dope tossed his hands up in surrender. "It's nothing you gotta stop seeing her over, but you might want to after learning—"

Before he could say another word, I grabbed his arm and pulled him out of his chair. I sat down and began to read. Ella hadn't lied about her employment, college, best friend, dad's cancer trial, or where she lived. All of that checked out. I breathed a sigh of relief but then realized I was relieved too fucking soon.

"What the hell?" I leaned closer to the screen, not wanting to believe what I was reading. I glanced at Dope over my shoulder. "This information is on the dark web. That's how you found it, right?"

"Yup. It's the best way to find out shit about people. I just wasn't prepared for ... that." He pointed at a video. The screen flickered to life, revealing a still image with a triangle in the middle, taunting us to press play. And there was sweet, innocent, blushing Ella with her legs spread wide, pussy on display, fingers dancing over her clit as water cascaded over her naked form. My jaw clenched, and my hands balled into fists at my sides as a surge of conflicting emotions washed over me in waves. Anger and arousal battled for dominance inside me, fueling a fiery inferno that threatened to consume every inch of my being.

"Out. You're not watching this with me."

Dope's expression fell. "Dammit. I should've demanded to watch as payment. Besides, you know I have access to her now."

A surge of primal rage and fierce protectiveness coursed through my veins and ignited every nerve in my body. I launched myself from the chair in a blur of motion and sent it flying across the room. Before Dope could register what happened, I grabbed his shirt, slammed him against the wall, and snarled in his face. His features contorted with terror as he realized the mistake he made. "If you ever look at any of her adult videos, I will dismantle you myself. Got it?"

"Yeah, man. Of course. I was just giving you shit. I swear on my grandma's grave I won't ever check her out like that." The color in Dope's cheeks drained. "Bass, you know I'll always have your back, and I did all of this to prove a point. She's not good for you. For whatever reason, she's got you all hot under the collar. We've known each other since grade school. You trust me, but you just backed me into a wall over a chick you barely know. What gives?"

Flashes of painful memories ricocheted through my mind. "You know how I feel about disrespecting women, Dope. It's why we do what we do."

"I get it, man, but you gotta stop letting your past control you. That's all." The corner of his eye twitched, his telltale sign disclosing the level of stress he was under.

My heart banged against my ribs, and I realized Dope was right. Regret washed over me as I let him go and stepped away. Maybe I wasn't capable of handling a relationship with Ella.

But that fact wouldn't stop me from taking her out again, and I knew it.

"Please leave so I can see what's going on." I retrieved the chair as the door clicked behind Dope and sat down. Grabbing the mouse, I directed the arrow to one of several adult videos. The music played in the background as she showered, the suds running over her large tits. My cock sprang to life as I watched her. Good god, she was beautiful. I stopped that video and clicked on another and another. Video after video was of her naked and getting herself off for the camera. Jealousy stirred inside me, and I clicked out of the website. My damn dick hurt so bad, I considered using Dope's bathroom to rub one out, but the more I thought about thousands of other men looking at her, my cock deflated. I couldn't reconcile that this was the same woman who blushed and smiled shyly at me over dinner.

I forced myself to read the rest of the information Dope had pulled up. "Damn. It makes sense now," I mumbled. Ella was paying her father's medical bills, and they were astronomical. She could buy another house with the money she was spending.

Sinking back into the chair, I matched the dates between her father's diagnosis and her cam job. They lined up. My stomach twisted into knots. She was selling her body the safest way possible to save her dad. Fuck, that took guts, and instead of turning me away from her, it pulled me toward her. Even though I didn't like the idea of other men getting off watching her, I had mad respect for her determination. Before I got carried away with my rationalizations, I wanted to see if I was correct, but getting an answer would take time. I pulled up an additional tab and typed the hospital name where her father was being treated. Once I found what I was looking for, I removed my wallet from my back pocket and paid every penny of his medical bills. She would probably hate me if she ever found out, but it was a chance I was willing to take. All I wanted was to help and give her a choice whether to work the cam job or not.

"Dope! Come on in." I stood as he joined me again. "She's working a cam job for fuckers to watch her so she can pay her dad's medical bills. He has cancer that attacks the nervous system."

"Yeah, primary central nervous system lymphoma. Or CNS." Dope took his chair back, eyeing me. He was probably wondering if I was about to fly off the damn handle again.

"No offense, dude, but your temper is getting worse since you first saw her. Keep it focused in the right direction, man, and that ain't me." He leaned over, grabbed his weed off the desk, and rolled a fat one. "I highly recommend a smoke." Dope extended it to me.

"You know I'm not worth shit if I smoke, but thanks."

"Then we gotta schedule a time out for ya. Knock the edge off your sharp corners. The last time we were supposed to lie low, you nearly—"

"Say it," I snarled, my hands fisting tightly.

"You nearly cost us. We can't get caught. We'll fucking lose everything we've worked our asses off for."

"I didn't cost us shit, asshole."

"The son of a bitch saw you." Dope shook his head, perplexed.

"Not for long he didn't." I smirked.

"Bass, come on, man. You beat the shit out of him, and his life is hanging by a thread. That's not what *we* do."

A heavy beat of silence pulsed through the air.

"Maybe you should consider some underground fights again if you need to work off that adrenaline."

It wasn't a bad idea. I fed off the fights, the way my fists connected with the cartilage, the sound of the snap when bones broke. It was brutal and vicious, and it had consumed me for years until I found a new way to direct my pent-up energy. It was another reason I worked so much, to keep my fucking ass out of jail.

"The last time I stepped into the ring the cops had been tipped off." I clenched my jaw, reliving the crowd running wild and people being trampled and killed in the process. My opponent and I were the last to find out the police had shown up, and we almost didn't make it out in time. I refused to ever be someone's prison bitch, so I'd hung up my fighting days three years ago. But I'd be lying if I said I didn't miss it. Over that time, I'd worked hard to smooth out my rough edges, at least around other people, but Dope and Kip still saw that part of me that loved to live on the edge of danger.

I rubbed my forehead, exhausted from the long hours at the bar as well as our extra excursions. "Enough. This conversation is fucking over. I can't risk being covered in bruises, mate. It will cause too many questions." I didn't want to talk about my issues anymore.

Dope returned to the computer, the sound of the keys clacking beneath his fingertips the only sound in the room. He slid me a sideways glance, probably gauging my temper before he said anything else.

"Okay, Bass, listen. Let's just rip the Band-Aid off. The worst is the cam job. I didn't find anything else. My guess is that no dudes are rocking her boat since she's only on the screen for viewing, not tangled up with guys for the camera. That's a plus."

My fists clenched and unclenched as my anger punched me in

the chest. "You want to help me with my temper? I suggest you shut the fuck up."

I was done. I'd already been on fucking edge about seeing Ella tomorrow, and after what I'd just learned about her, my nerves were as taut as a high wire in the wind, on the verge of breaking.

"Fair enough. Didn't mean to get your panties in a twist." He grinned at me, and I had to laugh. The motherfucker never let up. Dope knew me better than anyone else, and I trusted him with my life, but some days he annoyed the shit out of me. But if I was going to date Ella, I had to make sure I could trust Dope with her life, too.

"You good now? We gotta figure some shit out, but you have to be right in the head." He tapped the side of his skull with his first two fingers. "As you tell us all the time, no mistakes are allowed. It's too dangerous out there."

I briefly closed my eyes, calming my mind and ridding it of any thoughts that would jeopardize us. Standing behind him and forcing myself to focus, I said, "Let's do this."

"That's what I wanted to hear."

Dope's fingers flew across the keyboard again, pulling up information on Sarah Thompson.

"Okay, she's got two kids, ages twelve and nine. A boy and a girl. They're rich as fuck, so that might make things more difficult. Cameras are located around the house and property, which won't be a problem when we make our move." Dope sucked air through his teeth, creating a soft whistle.

"Looks like the husband travels only a few times a year. However, he's on the board of directors of BioSync Tech, so we know he's not home at least a few nights a month." Dope continued to sift through the information. "Shit, this guy stays close to the family."

My eyes narrowed with the revelation. "Makes it more difficult for damn sure. We might have to schedule the plan on an evening he's working late."

Dope glanced over his shoulder in my direction. "Don't you find it odd that the meetings are at night? I smell something rank, Bass."

"See what you can dig up."

I paced the small room, my thoughts bouncing from Ella to Sarah Thompson. Once I'd seen the videos, I'd morphed into a jealous, possessive asshole and selfishly paid the medical bills without her permission. I did it for Ella, but my desire to keep her to myself was a factor.

"Sneaky bastard," Dope said.

"What?" I hurried over to him, peering at the screen. Once I read the details about the board meeting, I laughed. "Jackpot, motherfucker." I slapped Dope on the shoulder with the back of my hand. "Let's do it. Let's fuck up his world."

"Now you're talking."

Dope rubbed his hands together, giddy with the idea. "Let me check his schedule."

I shoved my hands into the pockets of my slacks.

"Oh, hell, it's our lucky day! It's in two days. Just enough time."

"Perfect. We'll be ready."

I pulled my phone from my back pocket to check the time, seeing Ella's message. I fired off a response, then focused on the next steps with Dope.

Chapter 13

Ella

Once I saw Cami in the waiting room, I told her they were removing Dad from the trial, and we both broke down sobbing.

"I'll do everything I can to help, babe. I'll vet hospice nurses if you want, check on him daily, and move in with your parents if I need to."

I sniffled through my tears. "I know you will. Me too." My shoulders slumped with the exhaustion I'd carried over the last year. The medical bills, the constant spikes of hope, and the nearly debilitating drops of defeat almost crippled me emotionally. It was a stab in the heart over and over as the new treatments failed. "Cami, I don't know how I would make it without you, especially this last year. I'm so fucking lucky to have you as my bestie."

I wiped away the moisture from my cheeks. "I think Dad is tired. When the doctor told us about the trial, he closed his eyes, and his entire body relaxed."

"How can he not be exhausted? Hell, we are, and we're not sick." Cami dabbed the teardrops from her face with her fingertips. "Let's go. You're going to sleep in your own bed tonight. I'll stay with you."

I slipped my arm through hers as we walked down the hall. "I love that idea, but the alarm system won't be installed until tomorrow."

She patted her purse and grinned. "Don't worry, babe. If the stalker shows up, I'll pop a cap right into the middle of his fucking head. I've got Old Faithful with me."

"I'm glad you have your permit. I do need to check on the house, and taking a long, hot shower sounds like heaven."

"I already have clothes at your place, so let's just go on over. Well, I'm starving, so let's grab some food on the way." Sadness flashed through her eyes. "I need to soothe my grief with unhealthy carbs."

I glanced at my watch. "The only places open after midnight are fast food, so you're in luck."

We reached the elevator and rode it down to the lobby. "Yup. Arby's or KFC, babe?"

"Arby's. A chocolate shake sounds really good."

It finally dawned on me that tomorrow was Monday, and I was in no shape to go to work. Checking the time, I pulled up my boss's cell number and left him a voice message, updating him about my dad and that I wouldn't be into work for the week, but would call him in a few days.

I was quiet as Cami drove to pick up food and then went to my place. I tried to sort through the information the doctor had provided, but I didn't want to accept what he'd said. A part of me refused to give up, but the logical side reminded me that there were no more trials for Dad to try. Even if there were, would he put himself through one again? He'd fought hard for a long time. When he'd lost the will to fight, I'd picked up the mantle for him.

My shoulders and neck stiffened the thought that it was time to accept the cold, hard truth. Dad was on borrowed time. Whether I liked it or not, I had to make the best of it with him.

Ten minutes later, we were inside my house, and I immediately locked the front door.

"I'll have a look around. Stay put." Cami withdrew her pistol and checked all the rooms, under the beds, and the locks on the windows and doors.

"Looks good."

"Thanks, babe. I'm so fucking tired, but with the hard news tonight and knowing a serial killer is in the area, I might not be able to sleep." My shoulders slumped in exhaustion.

"Girl, you're so wrung out. I will stay awake to make sure you're safe if that will help you sleep."

Cami and I walked to the kitchen, clutching Arby's bags of fries, cheese sticks, and chicken sandwiches. I took a long sip from my drink. A wave of rich, creamy chocolate goodness burst across my taste buds, causing me to moan. "This is almost orgas—" As I struggled to swallow the thick drink, my eyes widened as they locked onto something that wasn't there before. My breaths slowed, see-sawing in and out, keeping tempo with each step I took while approaching the granite counter. My senses stood on high alert as I set down my bag and milkshake, my heart pounding.

"I saw that someone sent you a present. Look at the pretty gold wrapping. If you don't want the red ribbon, I'll take it." Her gaze narrowed on me. "Wait a minute, you're holding out on me, girl. Who is sending you gifts?"

A tight knot of fear held my voice captive, causing me to hesitate to speak to her. I was riveted with the exquisite box in front of me. My rational thoughts were overridden by intense curiosity as I reached for it, ignoring the warning signs that screamed danger. Maybe I should have called the police. Maybe I shouldn't have opened it without them there. Despite a nagging sense of unease, I gently tugged at the large bow with unsteady fingers, unraveling it.

Cami's warm breath on my neck told me she was just as curious and apprehensive. As I peered into the box, my brows furrowed in surprise and shock. Frowning, I lifted out the sheer black lingerie, its design leaving little to the imagination.

"Damn, Sebastian is smitten big time if he's sending you sexy stuff already. Good job." She elbowed me in the arm, slurping on her soda.

A cold wave of dread washed over me, making me hastily drop the gift back into the box. An unsettling thought raced through my mind. How on earth had someone entered my home? My heart thudded as I recalled Cami's words moments ago—all the doors and windows were securely locked.

What if it was Shadow Whisperer? The serial killer? I couldn't shake my questions. If it was the killer, why me? Mentally, I combed through recent criminal cases, wondering if one of the accused had seen me in the courtroom and developed an obsession with me. The scenarios swirled chaotically, a tumultuous waltz of uncertainty and fear.

"I don't think it was Sebastian, Cami. He wouldn't have broken into my house to leave this." Anger pumped through my veins, and I tossed the gift into the trash. I placed my hands on my hips, furious that someone had the balls to break into my home without my permission and violate my space. *Violated me. Fuck that.*

"Maybe I missed something," she said, her gaze darting around the open floor plan before she stared at me. "What are you not telling me, Ella? Something is off."

"There's a good possibility it was the same man that was at my window the other night." I swallowed several times, trying to collect my words. "I think I have a stalker, Cami."

The color drained from Cami's cheeks as my confession registered. "W-why would you say that? Whoever it was only showed up once ... right?"

I hadn't told her about the second time, and I was too upset to tell her that night. It wouldn't make a difference any way. "Dammit, I can't eat. I've lost my appetite." I scooped the bag and drink off the counter and tossed it into the fridge. Next, I grabbed the bottle of vodka from the cabinet and poured two shots for myself. I added ice and a bit of water. This conversation called for a stiff drink. "Want one? You might need it."

Cami nodded and climbed on the barstool, munching on her fries and staring a hole through me. I made her a drink and set it next to her. After a few gulps of mine, I sucked in a sharp breath.

I had no intention of ever sharing with Cami about my cam job, but if Shadow Whisperer was stalking me, then she needed to know in case he went off the rails and hurt me. At least she would know the full story and be able to talk to the police.

"I need you to hear me out with an open mind."

"Of course I will." She picked up her drink and took a sip, wincing before she set it down. "The alcohol is smooth as hell, but I think I need a splash of something else. Do you have any cranberry juice?"

I located what I needed and topped off Cami's drink, my palms slickening with sweat as the seconds ticked by.

"Much better." She smacked her lips. "Sorry, it's already been a shit show of a night, and I have a feeling I'm going to need more than one."

"If you can still hit a target drunk, then I'll keep pouring for you." I leaned against the counter, my attention sweeping through my kitchen and living area.

Over the next several minutes, I confessed to Cami about working the cam job to help pay Dad's medical bills. She sat still, listening until I told her I'd flown to Seattle to meet with Shadow Whisperer and was paid twenty-five thousand dollars when he canceled.

"Are you fucking insane?" Her screech bounced off the walls, and I covered my ears.

"Yes, but you knew that, Cami. I'm drowning in debt. I barely have enough to cover my bills, and I was the only hope Dad had. I would do anything to save him. Anything. You know how close we are." I paced the room, angry at the shit show called my life. "The money was originally fifty thousand to watch, and Shadow Whisperer promised he wouldn't lay a hand on me." My throat tightened as a wave of blame crashed over me. If I hadn't agreed to meet him and allow the situation to become more personal, maybe it wouldn't have pushed him over the edge.

If it was even him.

Cami's shoulders rolled forward as she slumped in her seat. "I wish you'd told me. I could have moved in and split the bills. Hell, I would have picked up extra shifts to help pay for his medical trial, babe. You didn't have to go sell your gorgeous body to strange men."

"It wouldn't have been enough, and even though you're family, this wasn't your fight. I love you for wanting to help. And thank you for not judging me."

"You're hard-headed as hell, but I'll let it slide for now. We have to figure out who left the creepy present for you."

Unease ghosted over me and a thought just out of reach tugged at my mind. Although I was being ridiculous, I decided to text Sebastian.

I pulled my phone out of my clutch, realizing I was still in my dress and heels. My fingers flew over the keyboard as I messaged him.

Me:

> Crazy question, since we only had our first date tonight … but you didn't happen to leave a gift for me?

I set the cell on the counter. "I'm going to change into something more comfortable. I'll also pay to have your dress cleaned. We danced in the rain on the rooftop of the restaurant, and we were both soaked. It wasn't long after that when you called me." I offered her a sad smile.

"Jesus, that sounds romantic as hell. I hope it's not him breaking into your home, Ella. I really do."

"That makes two of us." I took my drink and phone, heading into my bedroom. A soothing hot shower would have to wait. I was too exhausted and mentally wrung out. "I'm going to call it a night."

"Sounds good. I know the way to the guest room." She smiled and gave me a little wave goodnight.

Once I changed into my comfy pajamas, my cell chimed with a message. Picking it up from my nightstand, I stared at Sebastian's text.

Sebastian:

> I wish I'd thought to send you something to make you feel better since your father is in the hospital, but I didn't.

Me:

> I appreciate the thought. I'll see you in the a.m.

It would have been super easy for Sebastian to lie to me about the lingerie, but something in my gut said it wasn't him. I chewed on my thumbnail, then hopped online to see if Shadow Whisperer had messaged me.

I wiggled the mouse, and my computer lit up. After I logged in to the website, my mouth dropped at the number of notifications. Two hundred and eight, and they were all from Shadow Whisperer. I clicked each one, reading the short messages.

Where are you?

Why aren't you working tonight?

It's your night to work. I want to talk.

Are you out spending my money?

Ella! Yeah, I know your real name. Are you out fucking other guys on me? That's the wrong thing to do.

You're such a slut, Ella. I paid you. You're supposed to be here with me. You owe me, bitch.

Where are you? Are you being a little cum whore with someone's cock in your cunt?

You're really pissing me off. Where the fuck are you?

With each message I read, he grew angrier, bordering on desperate.

I gripped the back of my neck, anxiety coursing through me. The messages confirmed what I was worried about. There was no doubt that Shadow Whisperer was my stalker. For a moment, I put myself in his position. We'd talked for over a year, and he'd watched every video I'd posted. It would be easy for him to build me up in his mind, shaping the idea of what he needed me to be, while reality painted a different picture.

With my job, I'd spent a lot of time around unhinged men, and I'd always been attracted to the bad boys. They didn't scare me. I massaged my forehead, a whirlwind of thoughts and emotions pumping through my mind. Maybe I could breathe a little easier since I knew it was him. Shadow Whisperer had a temper, but when it came down to it, I hoped like hell he wouldn't hurt me.

I groaned and slapped my hands over my face, wondering what the hell was wrong with me for not being terrified out of my mind. Most women would be, but with my job and the clients my bosses represented, I had spent time with some shady characters—murderers, thieves, drug deals, and worse. My arms dropped to my sides as I read the messages again, more irritated than scared.

"I'm so damn stupid. If I hadn't agreed to his money and to meet him, none of this would be happening. Now I have an obsessed stalker," I said aloud.

Standing, I closed my laptop before I sank onto the edge of my bed, numb from all of the emotional turmoil that was like a roller coaster with sharp turns and steep drops, unpredictable and intense.

Despite my exhaustion, I seriously doubted my brain would allow me to sleep. An idea stirred in my mind, and a renewed determination bubbled to life inside me. Shadow Whisperer was fucking with the wrong girl.

Chapter 14

Death

"Whoever becomes a lamb will find a wolf to eat him." ~ *Vilfredo Pareto*

I glanced around the dimly lit room, shadows dancing on the walls as the flickering candle in the center of the table cast an eerie glow. The air was heavy with the scent of roses in Ella's yard, mingling with the metallic tang of blood still lingering on my hands. I took a deep breath, savoring the quiet moment before the storm.

As I peered through the window, a twisted grin crept onto my face. There she was, Ella ... my Ella, unaware of my presence as she moved about her kitchen. Once she'd arrived home from the hospital, I crept through the darkness and identified my secret spot. I wanted to watch when she spotted the gift I'd sent her. But her reaction wasn't what I'd expected, and it took me an hour to rein in my fury when she'd tossed the box in the trash.

"Don't worry, little lamb. You can't get rid of me as easily as you did my present," I whispered into the darkness.

When Ella had disappeared into her bedroom, Cami had made

101

her way to the guest room and retired for the night. Not long after, Ella returned to the kitchen unable to sleep. Her movements were graceful, almost hypnotic, as she prepared something to eat. The soft light from above illuminated her delicate features, casting a halo around her dark hair.

With my grim reaper mask in place, I watched with hungry eyes as she carefully chopped vegetables, her brow furrowed in concentration. The knife in her hand gleamed, a deadly dance partner in her delicate hands.

A delicious thrill rippled through my body as I imagined the blade slicing through the flesh of my next kill, Ella by my side as the blood splattered, staining her porcelain skin. I would paint her naked body with crimson as I forced her to kneel and worship me.

I would savor every minute of our encounter. A perverse sense of pride rose as I thought of the intricate plan that had led me to this point. It wasn't just about the thrill of the hunt or the taste of the kill. It was about the artistry involved, the perfect execution that elevated it from mere violence to an exquisite dance with death.

Ella paused momentarily, a faint frown marring her features as if sensing something was wrong. I held my breath, willing myself to blend into the darkness outside. But then she returned to her food.

The time was near. A surge of anticipation coursed through my veins. Soon, Ella would be mine, to mold into my masterpiece. My heart raced as I imagined the terror in her eyes when she finally realized the danger lurking around the corner. Her year had been filled with the ups and downs of her father's illness, but my little lamb had no idea how much her life was really about to change. My hands tingled with excitement, the muscles in my fingers twitching.

Ella strolled to the cabinet, removed a Tupperware container, and loaded the vegetables in it before she sealed the lid and placed the dish in the refrigerator. She returned to the sink and washed the knife and cutting board. As she grabbed a paper towel and dried her hands, her shoulders slumped with exhaustion, and she rolled her neck, stretching. Ella adjusted to the darkness at that moment, and she gaped as her attention landed on me. Time froze as we stared at each other, locked in a silent battle of wills.

Terror flashed in her green-eyed gaze as she struggled to speak. "What do you want from me?" she yelled, her voice trembling.

A twisted, menacing smirk slid into place, "your soul," I mouthed before I disappeared into the night.

Chapter 15

Sebastian

After I left Dope's place last night, I thought I'd be able to sleep, but it had eluded me. Ella's video was on replay in my mind, but her text had taken me off guard. Was some other guy sending her gifts? It wasn't any of my fucking business, but I wanted to know if I had competition. Most importantly, I had to tuck away my ego and remember that she was going through hell with her father's medical issues. If anyone understood parental struggles, I did. Something about her soothed me, and I wanted to be there for her as well. We would see if she would let me help or let me off the hook.

The next day, Ella greeted me with a soft smile. Her hair was up into a high ponytail, and she wore a light pink tank with black running shorts. She looked good enough to eat, but I had to remember why I was here, and it wasn't to fuck her senseless on her kitchen counter, but it wouldn't stop me thinking about it.

The weight of fatigue was evident in every inch of her face. Her eyes were shadowed with dark circles, and her once-lively gaze seemed dull. Had she slept at all?

"Hi. Thanks for coming over."

"Of course." I reached over and gently moved a loose strand of hair off her cheek, then pressed my forehead against hers. She leaned into my embrace, and the tension in her body melted away as she relaxed against me.

She broke our hug and took a step back. "You just missed Cami. She stayed over last night." She tipped her head toward the window. "As you could see from the truck in my driveway, the guys are installing a security system. I figure with the serial killer running around, it would be a smart idea. I also took this week off, so I could spend time with Dad." Her voice lowered, and grief shadowed her expression.

"I certainly don't disagree with that. Have them install multiple emergency buttons in your house. There are several in the club. If you want, I can make sure they're doing a good job?"

Ella's brows raised. "Really? I don't know anything about installation or camera angles." She rubbed her bare arms as if she were warding off an evil spirit.

Something was off, but I couldn't put my finger on it ... yet. Maybe inspecting the men's work would allow me to piece some things together ... like what she was so scared about.

"Of course. I want to make sure you're as safe as possible in your home." I gently squeezed one of her biceps.

"Would you like any coffee? I can make some more."

"I'm good, thanks. Point me in their direction, and I'll take a look at the cameras."

She massaged her temples. "I think they're installing an emergency button in my bedroom. Down the hall, third door on the left."

The last thing I'd anticipated was double checking the alarm company's job, but I knew firsthand how sloppy some people's work was. I would make damn sure this wasn't going to be one of them.

An hour later, I joined Ella on the couch. She closed her laptop and set it on the coffee table in front of us. "How did it go?"

"They're doing a good job. I gave them some pointers with the angles and made sure that almost every inch of your yard and home are covered. There's a blind spot, but it's not too bad."

Ella placed her hand over mine. "Thank you. I really appreciate your input."

"Ella?" Jonas, one of the technicians asked. "We're all done. Your boyfriend was a big help, and we finished early."

Ella jumped off the sofa, not bothering to correct Jonas.

"Oh, good. Thank you."

I held back as he showed Ella how to use the monitor app on her phone, and where all the buttons were installed as well. Thirty minutes later, he and his coworkers loaded the van and left. I was finally alone with her, which might be a good or bad thing.

Ready to hear what she had to say, I asked, "Can we talk about your text from last night?"

She tucked a loose strand of her hair behind her ear, a wistful expression twisting her mouth. "I knew I'd see you today, so I figured an explanation would mean more face-to-face." She remained standing, pursing her lips.

I shifted in my seat, looking at her.

"When I got home from the hospital, there was a gift on the counter. At first, I thought someone had broken in, but Cami had checked all the locks and doors before we even came inside. Everything was fine."

"Then how did it get in your house?" I didn't like this situation at all, and I was glad she'd had an alarm system installed. Otherwise, I would have camped out on her couch, waiting for the fucker that thought it was funny to scare a single woman like that.

She gave me a small shrug and huffed out a little laugh. "I forgot my friend Alexa had a spare key. She dropped something off, forgot the card to say who it was from, and I just freaked out over nothing. It's been a stressful week." She propped her elbow on the back of the couch, assessing me.

Concern nudged me in the side. Although I wanted to believe her, something didn't feel right, and I suspected she was too scared to tell me the truth. Regardless, I would find out soon enough. "I'm glad you have good people in your life."

"Me too."

"How's your father?" I asked, redirecting the conversation away from Alexa.

Ella plopped onto the couch and tucked a leg beneath her. Tears welled in her eyes and slipped down her cheeks.

I leaned over and gently wiped them away with the pad of my thumb. "Talk to me, Ella. What can I do to help?"

"Nothing." She sniffled and looked away from me. "The doctor's said that he can't continue the trial. It will kill him before the cancer does. He should be released from the hospital in a day or two. Cami called a hospice nurse to monitor him, give him pain medication, and take care of him until he ..." Her shoulders shook as she sobbed into her hands.

"I'm so sorry." I wrapped her in my arms and pulled her in my lap, rocking her as if she were a little girl, and I was giving her a safe place to grieve.

Once her tears dried, she nestled her head on my shoulder. "I'm sorry that you have to see me like this. Everything in my life is so complicated right now."

Shit. Here it comes. I braced myself for her next words.

Her fingers trembled as they trailed up my biceps. "Am I allowed to sound like a clingy girl for a minute?"

My chuckle rumbled through my chest. "From what I've seen you're definitely not clingy. Strong, determined, but clingy isn't on the list."

"My world is shitty right now, but you give me a light in the darkness. I need that. I need something to look forward to while Dad is ... making his transition." She hid her face in my neck and snorted. "God, that sounded lame. I barely know you."

I threaded my fingers through hers, recalling my mother's words when I was eight and had caught her crying after Dad had left the house. Maybe they would help Ella too. "Even the strongest women need support sometimes." I wrestled with the idea of telling her that I had paid her father's medical bills, but I didn't think it was a smart idea. Letting her believe it was an anonymous gift would probably be best for now.

"Tell me about your family. Where did you grow up?" Instead of getting up, Ella remained snuggled against me.

I rubbed her back and wondered if she might fall asleep. If she did, I was okay with it. She was emotionally and physically drained.

"When I was in grade school, my family moved from Australia to the States. After that, I grew up in Minnesota. Mom was a school-teacher, and Dad was an underwater welder."

"Really? That's badass." Ella stifled a yawn. "I'm sorry. I'm exhausted, and you're so warm."

"It's all right. I won't take it personally if you doze off." I chuckled, happy that she felt safe next to me. "My dad was good at what he did and was in high demand. He took on private jobs as well and made damn good money. As I got older, I began to worry each time he left, wondering if I would ever hug him again. When he returned, I would hear Mom quietly sobbing from relief in her room. The strain it put on our family wasn't justified by the money. Mom was grateful when he quit that job. He was home a lot more after that."

A soft snore reached my ears, and I stifled my laughter. Carefully, I stood with her in my arms and carried her to her bedroom. Setting her down gently, I covered her with the blanket at the foot of her bed. At least she felt comfortable enough to fall asleep. It had also saved me from having to share the rest of my background. Eventually she would learn more, but it was too soon for her to swallow that fucking pill.

After a final sweep of her house, I ensured the windows and doors were locked.

My phone buzzed in my back pocket, and I retrieved it. Dope's name lit up my screen, and I declined the call. If Ella heard me talking, it might wake her, and she needed her sleep. To my surprise, it was almost two in the afternoon, and it was time to go to the club.

Quietly, I located a notepad and pen in her kitchen and left her a message that I would call her later. I let myself out and climbed into my car. Once I was buckled in, I started the engine and called Dope back.

"What's up?" I pulled away from the curb and headed downtown to Velvet Vortex.

"Guess who's going out of town tomorrow?" His voice was filled with excitement, and I imagined he was rubbing his hands together.

"Dammit, I don't want to play a guessing game. Just tell me."

"Sarah's husband."

As soon as the words left his mouth, I made a quick U-turn and drove the car in the opposite direction.

"Fuck yeah. I'm on my way."

Chapter 16

Death

"Lambs are sweet, but they're also a symbol of someone who is innocent and perhaps naive." ~ Unknown

Once Cami had left Ella's house early that morning, I waited for her to settle in for the night and then made my move when she was vulnerable.

My little lamb thought she'd taken all the steps necessary to secure her home but had overlooked one glaring detail—I could pick any lock, including state-of-the-art, high-tech security systems. Nothing could keep me out. I adjusted my grim reaper mask, allowing my eyes and mouth to line up with the holes as the fabric molded to my skin. My masks had been custom made to fit like a second skin, allowing me to breathe and see without any issues. I flexed my gloved fingers before I kneeled and examined the ancient tumbler lock. With a few delicate twists of my picks, I felt the last pin fall into place and heard the soft click of the mechanism. I stood and opened the kitchen door, walking into her house without a sound. Little did Ella know that I had connections everywhere, including one of the men who had installed the system. It had been easy to disarm her alarm. She was never safe from me.

As I entered her darkened bedroom, I licked my lips. I walked over to her bed, carefully gauging the rise and fall of her chest as she slept. I took a deep breath and turned to her laptop, which rested on the desk. Moving the mouse ever so softly, the light from the screen illuminated my figure in the darkness. A thrill of anticipation ran through me as I inserted the thumb drive and typed in a few quick commands that sent an insidious virus into her computer system. It would delete any evidence of our conversations from the webcam website we frequented. She'd assumed she could get away with taking advantage of me, but I'd caught her with that man from Velvet Vortex again. If my little lamb wanted to play this dangerous game, I would relish every moment. A smirk played at the corners of my mouth at the thought of teaching her a lesson. I wanted her to break down and plead with tears streaming down her cheeks, begging for forgiveness.

Once the virus had finished running its course, I slid the thumb drive into the pocket of my jeans and removed my knife from the sheath strapped to my calf.

My footsteps were silent as I crept toward her bed. She was fast asleep on her back, her breath soft and steady, and was completely clueless that I was looming over her. The sheet covering her body had slipped off, exposing her tanned legs. With a practiced hand, I sliced through the fabric of her shorts with my blade, the pieces falling to the sides. I focused on her bare cunt, but this was the first time I'd seen it in person. My dick pressed painfully against my jeans as I imagined how she tasted. *You'll have relief soon.*

I slid a finger between her slightly parted legs and stroked her sensitive nub. She sighed and shifted her hips closer to me as my massage intensified. Ella's juices slicked my fingers as her body quivered in pleasure.

"Sebastian?" Sleep coated her voice as she pried her eyelids open.

Terror flashed across her face, and I moved my hand from her pussy to cover her mouth. This was about to get good.

"Keep those pretty legs spread for me."

She slapped them together, ignoring my demand and narrowing her gaze.

"I love a woman with a fight in her. I'm surprised you have anything left after dealing with your dad this last year." I tsked as she realized what I'd said. "I know everything about you, Ella. With a few technology tricks, it was easy to eavesdrop. I also know that you love working for criminal attorneys, and I bet the idea of fucking a killer turns you on. Don't worry, little lamb, your darkest fantasy is about to come true."

She stared at me, digesting what I'd shared.

"You can part those thighs, or I can do it myself." I raised my knife, laughing when I realized there was still a spot of dried blood on the blade's edge. "Can you keep your mouth closed and not scream?"

She nodded frantically against my palm. Slowly, I removed my hand and crawled over her body.

"Are you going to kill me?" Her chin trembled with her question.

I sneered as I ran the tip of my knife down her tank top, the cut shirt sliding over her ribcage and exposing her stomach.

She visibly swallowed, and I fed off her fear.

I responded with silence. "You're even more stunning in real life." I moved the blade along her breast, a thin line of blood blooming from the surface wound. The sharp pointed tip traced around her nipple, causing it to harden in response to the cold metal.

Her whimper echoed through the space as the sting of the slice met with the cool night air.

Rage simmered inside of me, and I embraced it—welcomed the high that rode in on its coattails. "Did he touch you?"

"Who?" Her chin visibly quivered.

"Sebastian Fletcher. Did he touch your breast?"

"N-no."

My gaze never left hers as I leaned down and licked the blood from her tender skin, savoring every delicious drop. Taking my time, I ran my tongue over the other breast, relishing the taste of her flesh.

"Blood makes me crazy, Ella. I crave it, feed off it. After I'm finished killing my victims, I jerk off. These days my hand isn't enough. You're going to replace it just fine." My maniacal laughter echoed through the house.

I gripped the inside of her leg, her cry of pain making my cock hard with excitement. "I have so much planned for our time together." Flipping the knife around, I rubbed her wet slit with the handle, her juices glistening off the black leather. Raw power pumped through me as her body responded.

"Please," she whispered. "Please don't." She swallowed excessively, terror twisting her features.

I moved off her bed, adrenaline rushing through my veins as I stood in front of her nightstand, blocking her access from the panic button located beneath the drawer.

"I'm a fair man, Ella, so I'll make you a deal. If you can reach one of the alarm buttons in the other part of the house, I'll leave you alone. You'll be free of me. No more messages, no more stalking. I'll move on." Like that would ever happen, but giving her hope before I stripped it away was all part of the game. "And don't even consider the alarm I'm standing in front of. That would be way too easy."

She sat up and swung her legs off the bed. "Do I have your word? You'll leave me alone? I'll never hear from you again?" Little beads of sweat coated her forehead, her gaze darting toward the kitchen.

I fixated on Ella; her exposed and bleeding body sent shivers racing down my spine. My mind raced with a dangerous intensity, teetering on the brink of uncontrollable desire. The sight of her consumed me, and my senses heightened to levels only matched by the rush of torturing a victim. I was devoured by a primal craving, coursing through my veins like a drug I couldn't get enough of.

"Yes. But no more chit chat. Run, Ella. Run for your fucking life. I'll even give you a head start."

I sneered as she darted from her room, panic written all over her face. Even though I knew where each button was located, she didn't know that.

My long legs ate up the distance, and I quickly blocked her from reaching the first one beneath the kitchen counter just as she reached to push it.

Ella scrambled around the counter, her eyes wild with fear, desperate to reach the bathroom. Then, she had a moment of clarity and realized her mistake—she should have gone for the living room and the front door instead. She spun on her heels, zigzagging through the furniture in an attempt to escape, but I was quicker. As she lunged toward the gas fireplace mantle, I blocked her again before she could press the button that would have saved her. She scrambled to the front door, tripping and landing on the floor with a thud.

I stalked menacingly behind her as she frantically tried to make her escape.

I lunged forward, grabbed her ankle, and jerked her away from freedom. She screamed in terror, thrashing wildly in an attempt to break free, but I easily overpowered her. I pressed the blade of my knife against her throat, silencing her instantly.

"One more scream, and your blood will be all over the floor. Am I clear?"

"Yes," she whimpered.

I stepped back and hauled her off the ground by her arm, dragging her into her bedroom like a rag doll.

"No one defies me, little lamb. You just lost the fight."

She wiggled against my hold on her, somehow managing to slip away. In a desperate attempt for freedom, she sprinted toward the back door. Her hands frantically fumbled with the locks before flinging the door open and running outside.

One, two, three, four steps out on her patio. I had to allow her a little hope before I brought her to her knees.

I clamped my hand over her mouth as I quickly lifted her off the ground and dragged her back into the house. She howled and screamed beneath my palm, her limbs flailing in desperation. I kicked the door closed with a loud bang and threw her onto the floor. She landed on her back with a delightful thud, the air whooshing from her lungs. I towered over her, smiling at the fear danced across her features.

"Why me? You could have picked any girl who worked for the website." Her jaw clenched and a spark ignited in her expression—determination and a fight I had known was inside her. Every cell in my body burned to tame her, bend her to my will, and mold her.

I unbuttoned and unzipped my jeans, her attention trained on my every move as I freed my throbbing cock. She flinched at my size. She should. I would split her open with it soon.

Ignoring her question, I sneered at her. "Get on your knees and crawl to me. Beg for my cock, little slut."

Slowly, she did as I asked.

It took everything inside of me not to come at the sight of her. "I can't hear you, whore."

Her tongue darted over her lower lip. "Give me that big cock." Her voice cracked.

"Not good enough," I growled.

"What do you want me to call you? Daddy? Sir?"

I couldn't help but laugh. She didn't know who I was beneath the mask I used to hide my real identity. "I'm Death, Ella. Call me by my name."

She slammed her eyes closed and began crawling again. "Will you fuck me with that big, thick dick? I bet Death can fuck me better than anyone else."

When she was close enough, I fisted her hair and tipped her head back, forcing her into submission at my feet. She glowered up at me, her gaze filled with defiance and hatred.

"Suck my cock, my dirty bitch." I shoved my fingers into her mouth and pried it apart, spitting into her mouth. "Swallow."

She flinched but did as she was told.

"Now take my dick. If you bite me, I'll fuck you raw and carve your skin up like a Halloween pumpkin while I'm deep inside you."

Her jaw relaxed, and I thrust myself into her mouth until I hit the back of her throat and cut off her air supply. I pulled her hair, moving her mouth up and down my length.

Her fingernails dug into my thighs through my jeans, and I chuckled.

"My little lamb is getting off on this. You like being dominated. I bet your cunt is dripping wet for me."

She sucked me better than I could have imagined, and I allowed myself to ride the edge before pushing her away. As much as I wanted to fuck her, it wouldn't happen tonight.

"Get on your back."

Fear flickered in her face again. "Why me?"

She lay down on her back, her gaze searching for an answer.

I grabbed her by the throat so she wouldn't run as I shoved the handle of the knife inside her pussy. Shock twisted her facial features.

"Because you're different from the others. Ella McCloud is a good girl with a dark side. I'm your sickness, and I'll infect you with a fever."

Ella's eyes closed, and her breath came in short, ragged gasps that turned into a shuddering moan as I thrust deeper and deeper.

"My dirty girl likes me fucking her with the same weapon I use to kill. We're more alike than I thought." I picked up the pace, my cock begging to cum as she moaned, and her entire body trembled with her release.

With a primal growl, I crawled over, then forced my throbbing shaft into her mouth, thrusting with savage abandon as she gagged and choked on me. The sound of her muffled moans only fueled my desire as I reached the edge and exploded, filling her throat with hot, pulsating spurts of my seed.

I pulled out and ran my thumb through the last few drops of cum and painted her lips, then smeared her tears and my semen over her flushed cheeks.

"I've never seen a more beautiful piece of art."

Goddammit. I never left DNA behind, but she'd gotten under my skin, making me lose my mind as soon as I touched her.

"Sleep well, my little lamb."

I gave her a feral smile. "Soon enough, you'll beg for me to visit."

Slipping through the darkness, a newfound energy pumped through my veins. It was time to select my next victim to kill.

Chapter 17

Ella

The sun beamed through the window, casting a spotlight on the beige tiles. I lay motionless, numb, and lost as I stared at the cabinets. The minutes felt like hours as I tried to process what had happened.

Peeling myself off the floor, I shook from head to toe as the mixture of adrenaline, fear, and the forced orgasm had left me weak. I struggled to stand, my knees cracking with the effort. I glanced down at my naked body. My shins were covered in light brown bruises, and a thin line of dried blood marked each breast.

I stumbled to the en suite bathroom. Emotionally and physically drained, I turned on the shower and fisted my hands against the glass. I should call the cops, but something inside ... some twisted, sick, dark part of me didn't want to. Because for one depraved moment I was entirely lost to sensation. My brain switched off, my body handing itself over to Death to do with me as he pleased. I didn't have to think about my dad dying, saying goodbye, paying medical bills, keeping my head above water. I was free to drown. The sting of the blade marking my skin had made me feel ... made me *feel*. Death's words bounced around in my mind. *I'm your sickness, and I'll infect you with a fever.* Maybe he was right.

I stood under the scalding hot water, the cuts stinging as the water glided over them. My brain pounded with a confusing array of emotions. I tried desperately to reconcile the two versions of Death that I had encountered—the one online and the one in person. It wasn't like Death was a total stranger. I'd met a version of him on the website but experienced a completely different side to him last night. He was brutal and terrifying.

My thoughts raced with the conversations we'd had over the last year. His voice had always been disguised by the computer he used, so it was impossible to know if he had the same Pacific Northwest accent Death had. Plus, the man I knew as Shadow Whisper had shared things about his life that made him look like a saint. If what he'd said was true, he donated to charities and mentioned mentoring kids living in bad areas. But the man I knew as Death had marked me, stained my soul, and no amount of scrubbing could wash me clean. I'd been stupid to think I knew him without spending time with him in person first. It was easy to hide behind a screen and pretend to be someone else.

"Stop making excuses for him. He's a fucking criminal. He broke into your house and raped you," I muttered.

My jaw clenched and unclenched. I should turn him in. From the clues he'd given me, I strongly suspected that he was the Portland serial killer destroying lives, and now he was my stalker. I barked out a laugh. *How the hell did I end up here?*

I tried to fit the puzzle pieces together, forcing myself to think logically. Who was this man? Was he a client at the law firm? Maybe we'd worked together on a case, and he developed an obsession with me. Fear coiled like a snake in the pit of my stomach. I inhaled deeply, the steam filling my lungs.

Was it possible that one of the men from the alarm company was behind the mask? I certainly couldn't rule it out, but this fucked-up situation with Death was deeper and more personal than someone simply lurking in the shadows.

Once I'd finished scrubbing my body and conditioning my hair, I turned off the shower and grabbed the towel. Minutes later, I had rechecked the locks, ensured the alarm was set, and dressed in clean pajamas. Glancing at the clock, I climbed onto the comfortable mattress. I realized that Death had access to my house but only visited when it was dark, and I couldn't see him. Apparently, I was safer in the daylight. My eyelids fluttered closed as I nestled into my pillow.

I ROLLED OUT OF BED, THE DIGITAL CLOCK READING EIGHT P.M. I had been sleeping all day, but my mind was bogged down, and my stomach twisted in knots. Cami had gone to work, so I was alone with my tangled thoughts about Dad's illness and Death's threats. My skin crawled, and I needed to leave the house before I burst apart.

An hour later, I strolled into Velvet Vortex, the smell of hamburgers and fries heavy in the air. Since it was Tuesday evening, the dance floor wasn't packed, but the restaurant was. I made my way to the bar, searching for Sebastian, but I didn't see his broad shoulders and the black T-shirt he usually wore. It was someone else.

I climbed onto a barstool and set my handbag on the counter.

"Hey, you're Ella, right?" the bartender asked.

I frowned, anxiety shooting through me. I wasn't keen on anyone knowing who I was after Death had broken into my home and hurt me. "Who's asking?"

"I'm Kip, one of Bass's best friends and part club owner. I've heard a lot about you. I've seen you as well, but I figured I should introduce myself."

I hid my sigh of relief. "It's nice to meet you. Is Sebastian here?"

"Yeah, he's in the office. Go on back."

I slid off the seat, waiting for him to point me in the right direction.

"Walk past the kitchen and enter the 'Employees Only' area. In the hallway, his door is the third one on the right."

"Thanks." I gave him a small wave as I followed his instructions. Once in the hall, I spotted Sebastian's office. The door was closed, but I could hear his voice.

Ready to knock, my hand froze in midair. I glanced behind me to make sure no one else was around before I pressed my ear to the door.

"Are you sure he won't be home? If we need to scout the house ..."

What the hell is he into?

"Yeah, Britny will be there at the designated time, and I'll hide the goods from there. You do your thing, hack the security system and loop the feed, so we cover our asses. I don't plan on being anyone's prison bitch."

Fuck! Prison? Hacking a security system?

A whirlwind of thoughts cluttered my mind, and I wondered if Sebastian might be the masked man. Is that why he had asked my opinion on the law and justice system over dinner? Whatever switch inside me had flipped, I was bound and determined to learn what was going on. I refused to wait at home, hoping to find my answers.

Reality punched me in the chest as I realized I had to do something to calm my curiosity, the drive to learn the truth leading to my decision.

I spun on my heel and ran back down the hall as I decided the best thing to do was follow him and find out what he was up to.

Shit. Shit. Shit. If he was dirty, no wonder he was so interested in my work. He was determining if I posed a threat to him if we became close.

Apprehension gripped me as I stepped into the restaurant again, my heart beating erratically. I glanced at the bar where Kip stood chatting up a brunette, oblivious to my presence. I reminded myself to act normal and not appear suspicious, so he didn't spot me and call me over.

Once I managed to escape to the safety of my car, a wave of relief washed over me, but it was short-lived. Steering the Toyota to the side of the building, where I suspected the employees parked, my eyes darted around until they locked onto Sebastian's black BMW. Trying to manage the adrenaline rush, I drove a little farther up the street and parked, my breath shallow as I waited for Sebastian to emerge.

The minutes ticked by, and right before nine-thirty p.m., Sebastian exited, hurried down the stairs, and climbed into his car. My pulse kicked up, and I wiped my damp palms on my jeans. Even though I hadn't ever tailed anyone before, I knew to stay back far enough not to raise suspicion.

Sebastian drove for ten minutes as I hung back, keeping him in my sight. He drove to a nearly deserted parking lot, parked his BMW next to a white van, and hopped in. The van exited through the back part of the lot onto a side street, which made sneaking up on them more difficult. I counted to ten and watched the red taillights blink in the darkness as it turned right.

Finally, they stopped in a back alley of a wealthy neighborhood. *Holy shit! Is he casing a house?* Disappointment overwhelmed me. I really liked Sebastian. I thought he was different from the other men I'd been interested in.

It was nearly ten o'clock when Sebastian jumped out of the van, but this time he wore a black baseball hat low over his forehead. He also had a mustache and beard. *He's wearing a disguise.* I hid my purse beneath the back seat as he jogged down the alley, and I hopped out of my car, closing the door softly to not alert anyone. With my phone ready to record, I hurried in the opposite direction. A row of hedges bordered the property, which meant I had cover. I crouched down and slipped between the greenery. Branches scraped across my bare arms, and I quietly swore. When I'd dressed earlier in my jeans and sleeveless navy blouse, I hadn't planned on hiding in a thicket to bust a burglary, yet here I was.

As Sebastian appeared at the home's entrance, I frowned as he rang the doorbell. *Is he just making sure the house is empty?*

I hit the record button, holding my breath. To my surprise, the front door swung open, and a tall, blonde-haired woman answered. She peered around before she ushered him in. What the hell was happening? An unexpected tinge of jealousy tightened my chest. He must have someone helping on the inside. The home was fucking huge, and if he was stealing all the valuables, it would take time.

Several minutes later, the terrified women emerged with two children clutching backpacks and pillows followed by Sebastian ... with a gun in his hand. *What the fuck? Kidnapping? Had he pulled a pistol on them as soon as he was in the house?* The sound of their tennis shoes against the sidewalk echoed through the yard. I assumed the woman was their mother, but what was her connection to Sebastian, and why had I overheard him discussing scouting the place?

Questioning my sanity with all the shit, I stood as I continued to video.

I snuck out of my hiding spot and paused the recording as Sebastian and the others disappeared.

Leaves crunched behind me, and I spun around, spotting an angry man stomping toward me.

"Hey! What the hell are you doing on my property?"

Dammit! I was so focused on Sebastian that I didn't see a car pull into the driveway. I squared my shoulders, noting the make of the black Cadillac. I assumed he owned the home.

"I'm sorry! My dog ran through the bushes, and I was searching for her. Have you seen her? She's a mutt, part lab and part collie." I flashed him a grin, praying he bought my lie.

"You have no right to be here. Get the fuck off my property and look for your dog somewhere else."

I raised my hands in the air, showing my compliance. "Again, I'm sorry. I wasn't trying to step on any toes."

I made my way through the bushes and ran to the alley, where I found Sebastian blindfolding the kids and a woman seated on the floor in the back of the van.

Oh, god. This is bad. Really bad. I had to help that poor women and kids. There was a lot of criminal activity I could overlook, but not hurting children.

I quickly restarted the video, catching all of it for the cops. Sebastian closed the doors, then hurried to the passenger's side.

"Stop!" I yelled.

Sebastian turned, glaring in my direction.

"I've got this recorded. Let them go, or I'll go straight to the cops and have you arrested."

Sebastian's eyes narrowed and his shoulders tensed before he darted to me and snatched my phone out of my hand.

"You don't know what the hell you're doing," he hissed. "When Kip mentioned you stopped by the bar and sent you to my office, I suspected we might have a problem since you never showed up." He forcefully grabbed my wrist and spun away from me, jerking me behind him.

Footsteps sounded from behind me, and I peered over my shoulder.

"You didn't lose your dog, you bitch! You're trying to rob my house." The man's fists clenched and unclenched.

"Goddammit." Sebastian hauled ass to the van, and I quickly weighed the pros and cons of going with him or staying behind and dealing with the raving lunatic behind me. If I went willingly, I would have a better chance of helping the kids. *Go!*

Flinging the door open, Sebastian forced me into the back with the others before he climbed into the passenger seat.

"Go! Go! Go!" He barked at the driver, his tone thick with anger that I suspected was teetering on the edge of outrage.

I settled in behind Sebastian's seat, a mixture of fear and fury bubbling inside me. I hadn't ever seen him so pissed before. Guess I was getting a first-row seat to this shitty side of him.

"I thought you were better than this, Sebastian. You're kidnapping people?" The van took a sharp turn, sending me toppling to the other side and into the woman.

"Sorry." I reached for her blindfold.

"Ella, do *not* do that. You'll be sorry if you do," he barked.

Chapter 18

Ella

My hand froze, shaking in response to Sebastian's threatening words. I'd never imagined him capable of such horrendous acts, and the idea of abducting women and children was unforgivable. Provoking him further was the last thing I needed. I had to stay calm and rational.

Reminders of Death invading my home last night sent a shiver through my body, and goosebumps trailed across my skin. Sebastian was a fucking picnic compared to Death. I could do this.

"Ella, you don't know what the hell you're doing. I'll explain it later, but for now, hold on. That motherfucker is following us." He looked at the driver. "Goddammit Dope, you gotta shake him. *Now.* If I have to deal with him, it won't be pretty."

"I'm in a fucking van, dude. It's not like I can hit ninety miles an hour and take sharp corners."

I leaned forward to see the driver, Dope. He shoved his long fingers through his short red hair and then replaced both hands on the wheels. Dope gripped it so hard his knuckles turned white. From where he sat, he appeared a little taller than Sebastian but had a slim build.

"God, if you're real, please save us," the woman said softly.

I grabbed her hand. "I don't know how, but I swear I'll get you out of this and help you and the kids."

She shook her head. "You don't understand. Sebastian is helping us."

My brows shot up. "*Helping* you?"

"Yeah, my children and I are here willingly. In order to keep everyone safe, we can't see where we're going. Sebastian is a wonderful man. He'll have to explain to you if ..." She swallowed. "If we get away from whoever saw you."

"It's a tall, blonde guy. He caught me on his property ... your property."

"Shit. That sounds like my husband. Did he have a small birthmark on his forehead?"

"I don't know. It was dark. He was super pissed, though."

"Mom?" the little girl asked.

"Yeah, baby?"

"Is he ... is Father going to get us?"

The tremble in her little voice ripped my heart out of my chest and stomped all over it.

The van whipped in another direction and sped down a street before it came to a stop.

"Keep an eye out, but I think we lost him," the driver said.

A heavy silence filled the small space, our breathing the only sound.

"Hopefully we're good." The vehicle slowly eased forward. "I hope you know what the fuck you're doing, Bass. That shit back there ain't cool at all. You've been doing this a long time, and you should have realized she was following you."

"I'm right here," I said, defiance thick in my tone. He was talking about me like I wasn't right behind them. "And I'm good at tailing people." I snorted. They didn't need to know that I'd never followed anyone in my life. Sebastian's head was probably somewhere else.

Sebastian glanced over his shoulder. "Get comfortable, Ella. It's going to be a long ride, and I don't have time to blindfold you. Hell, you've seen too much already, it wouldn't matter anyway."

I folded my arms over my chest, pissed that I was trapped here without answers. At least the woman next to me had stuck up for Sebastian. I just needed to know what the hell he was doing with two kids and a married woman blindfolded in the back of a vehicle with no windows. It looked really bad.

The soft hum of the engine and the children talking in muffled voices caught my attention.

"What's your name?" I asked the lady.

"I can't tell you, but it's not because I don't want to. It's safer if you don't ask me any questions."

Well, shit. I would have to wait on Sebastian after all.

IT WAS AFTER MIDNIGHT WHEN THE VEHICLE SLOWED AND THEN rolled to a stop.

"You can take your blindfolds off now," Sebastian said before he hopped out of the vehicle. His shoulders seemed more relaxed, and his tone wasn't so sharp with anger. The back doors clicked and then flew open, and I gulped deep breaths of fresh air. From the looks of it, we were miles away from civilization, with only rolling hills spreading out like an unending sea before us. We were in the middle of fucking nowhere.

A dark-colored car with its headlights on was waiting ahead of us. I stumbled out of the van, desperately needing to stretch my legs. One of the doors closed, the sound startling me. I was jumpy as hell.

Sebastian kneeled in front of the kids. "I know this is scary, but you both are so brave. I'm really proud of you. When you get scared, the most important thing to remember is that you're safe. He can't hurt you anymore." His blue eyes softened as the children threw their arms around him, almost knocking him to the ground. My throat tightened with a rush of emotion at his tenderness, and my heart broke at their courage.

A thin, pretty blonde approached us. "We need to move out."

Sebastian stood, the littles still sticking close to him.

"Sarah," he said to the mom. "This is Britny. She's one of my travelers and helps move families out of the state. She's going to drive you and the kids across the country. She has new identities, social security numbers, and a driver's license set up. You'll also have a job and temporary housing for as long as you need it. Britny will be your contact person with any questions."

Britny gave the family a sweet smile. "I know this is hard, but I promise that I'll help every step of the way. You can rebuild your life and never worry again."

I was still puzzled, but from the conversation, Sarah had been honest with me. Sebastian and Britny were helping.

"Thank you, Sebastian. I'm terrified and questioned myself a hundred times, but we had to leave. I wouldn't have been able to without your help. I'll never be able to repay you."

Sebastian placed his hands on his hips. "Repay me by helping you and the kids heal. Rebuild your life, then help someone else when they need it."

Sarah gave him an exhausted smile. "Deal." She hugged him briefly, then turned to her son and daughter. "Let's head out."

Sebastian stilled as the family climbed into Britny's car, and she waved at him. "I'll keep you updated, boss." A big grin lit up her features as she hopped into the driver's seat and drove away.

My heart worked its way to my throat as Sebastian blew out a huge sigh.

"Ella, you nearly cost them their lives. What the fuck were you thinking?" His tone was laced with steel as he took calculated steps toward me. I backed up until I hit the closed door of the van.

"I-I ... At first, I thought you were taking them to sell or something. They're just babies."

His palms landed on either side of my head, caging me in. My stomach dipped at his proximity.

"You what?" he barked.

My pulse spiked as I tried to back up, but it was no use. "I stopped by the club to see you and overheard a conversation. It sounded like you were breaking into a home. I followed so I could find out who you really are."

A rumble of laughter traveled through Sebastian's chest.

"I don't need to steal from anyone. What you heard was me making sure that Sarah's husband, Stephen, didn't show up when we were getting them out of the house."

"The man who was following us?"

"One and the same. Do you know what would have happened if Stephen had gotten his hands on Sarah and the kids?" His voice lowered.

"No, but he was pissed, so I can guess."

"Stephen beat the hell out of his wife on a regular basis. She's been to the ER for broken ribs, a collapsed lung, a broken arm, and more. But that's the nice part." Sebastian dipped his head, his breath grazing my ear. "He turned on the kids, but the little girl got the worst of it. He hurt her. Touched her in a way no man should ever touch a twelve-year-old girl."

"What?" Bile rose in my throat, at the thought of that sweet girl being abused, never mind by her own goddamn father. "The sick bastard deserves to die," I spat, meaning every word.

"One of many. This is what I do. My team and I help relocate abused women and children. We give them a safe place to start over, new identities, and set them up to succeed. It's dangerous and illegal, and I can't have people blowing our cover."

The weight of suspicion and doubt slipped away with his confession, and my heart swelled with overwhelming gratitude. A twinge of guilt rode on its heels. I had automatically suspected the worst of Sebastian.

"At dinner, you asked where I stood with someone breaking the law to help others." I looked into his eyes, losing myself in them for a moment. "You were asking about yourself."

"Yeah. I can't get involved with anyone that could jeopardize my work, Ella. Lives are depending on our discretion. If Stephen had caught up with us, he would have either been killed, or he would have taken his family back. Neither scenario was optimal. He'll figure shit out, but he didn't see my face. He saw *yours*." He cleared his throat. "You might be in danger because you were in the wrong place at the wrong time."

I glanced away, frustrated and pissed. *Fucking hell.* I might have two psychos after me now. How did I keep putting myself in these situations?

"I'm so sorry, Sebastian. I thought you were a bad guy."

"And now?" His heated gaze focused on my mouth, and I shifted from one foot to the other, the shitty evening dissipating as he leaned in closer.

"I love that you're helping women and children. I might think it's amazing that you're brave enough to get them to safety while breaking laws." I chewed on my lower lip and weighed my following words. "Let me help."

"Hell, no. Don't even think about it. It's dangerous. Stephen isn't the first problem we've ever encountered. This is the only time you get to be involved. Stay out of it."

Irritation bubbled up inside me, and I huffed. "And if I don't? I tailed you once, I can do it again."

Sebastian's jaw tightened. "Then you'll be putting people in jeopardy. Can you live with that?"

Defeat pulsed through my veins. "No," I whispered.

"Not to mention I'd be worried sick about you all of the time. Don't be the problem here, love, or we won't see each other again."

A part of me loved how protective he was of the families he saved, but he had put me in the same box. Sebastian was willing to let me go to protect me.

My chest rose and fell, brushing against his. "I don't think that will work for me."

"I was hoping you'd say that."

My heart pounded uncontrollably against my ribcage as his body pressed mine against the van. After Death's viciousness, I craved something softer. My mind skipped a beat and returned to the hot and heavy make-out session Sebastian and I had found ourselves in on our first date. Seconds later, my thoughts caved in on themselves as I struggled to reconcile my need for the darkness as much as the light.

His demanding mouth devoured mine, igniting a fire inside me that begged to burn brighter and hotter. He kept his hands planted firmly on the vehicle, as if steadying himself with them.

I moaned, our tongues tangling in the heated moment. And for just a few seconds, I allowed myself to get lost in Sebastian's touch and forget all about Death and his cruelty—stupid, stupid me.

Chapter 19

Sebastian

As much as I wanted to stand there and kiss Ella all fucking night, we had to leave.

"We need to go. Get in. I'll ride in the back." I climbed in and closed the door as Ella hopped into the front seat.

"Ella, this is Dope. Dope, meet Ella. Be mates. Talk. Get to know each other. Dope, I'll have her sign an NDA when we're back at the club, so answer whatever questions she has. Go ahead and tell her. I'm going to get some rest." I nearly laughed at the expression on Ella's face. I almost felt bad for her, but not quite. She'd shoved her nose where it didn't belong, and it landed her in trouble. Although I could easily forgive her for jumping to conclusions, she was smart enough to learn and not pull that shit again.

I pretended to sleep as Ella tried to strike up a conversation with Dope. He answered her questions about our work with short, clipped responses. It would take longer than a few hours stuck in a damn van for him to thaw, but I knew that. Dope was super protective of me and the families we helped.

I leaned up between the seats. "Dope, Ella's car is still in the alley behind Sarah's house. I would prefer that she not return there. I'm

133

sure Stephen is on a rampage by now. It would be better if you handled it; me running into him wouldn't work in anyone's favor."

Dope's brow rose as his lips pursed into a thin line before his gaze cut to Ella. "I'll need your key and address. I'll drop it off to you before you have to drive to work in the morning."

"I don't work tomorrow. I took the week off because ..." She smashed her lips together. "Because we just found out my dad is dying, and I need time to process and grieve. I'm planning on spending the day with him, so if you could have my car by eleven, that would be great."

Dope's expression fell with her words. "That fucking sucks. I'm sorry."

"Thanks." She stared out of the window, silent.

I leaned back against the side of the van and closed my eyes. After sharing her news, I doubted Ella would want to try to talk to Dope or anyone else for that matter. I didn't blame her.

I SCRUBBED MY FACE WITH MY HANDS, WILLING MYSELF TO PERK up, but my ass was tired after the excitement with Sarah and Ella. We had stopped by Velvet Vortex and Ella signed the nondisclosure agreement before we dropped her off.

I stretched my legs out and crossed them at the ankles, the keystrokes of Dope's keyboard filling the room. We'd returned to Portland, where I'd crash on his shitty loveseat, but I'd slept in worse places.

"Cheers for taking care of Ella's car, Dope. Why the fuck did she decide it was a good idea to trail us anyway? Son of a bitch, I had no clue she was even following me. *Fuck*."

Dope swiveled in his office chair, glaring at me. "She's in your head. We've been helping families for three years, and not once have you screwed up this bad. Are you sure I don't need to make some calls and schedule some fights for you? It might clear your mind."

My lips pursed. "I don't need to go down that rabbit hole, so quit fucking bringing it up, mate. For whatever reason, I trust her, or I wouldn't have told her what we do. She wanted to join us, and I said hell no. I'm not putting her in danger."

Dope scoffed. "You already have. The moment you banged her, you were a goner."

My head whipped around, my jaw clenching while my gaze narrowed on Dope. "I told you not to fucking talk about her like that."

Dope held his hands up in mock surrender, his eyes wide in confusion and apology, before he dropped his arms and returned to his computer. "Does she know you gotta dip for a while?"

"No. I'll tell her when I see her again. Probably tonight or tomorrow." I yawned. "I need some sleep first. Kip is covering the club tonight, so I'll call her later. She needs some time to chew on what went down with Sarah anyway."

"She seemed fine with it when we talked on the drive home, but I don't know her that well." Dope moved closer to his curved monitor.

"I just want to make sure."

Dope leaned back in his chair. "Well, I recommend you do it tonight. The team is ready to move the family out tomorrow evening. But they have two more families while we're there. I'd plan on being gone for at least a few weeks."

"Damn. That's longer than we thought." I stood and stretched, my fingertips brushing the low ceiling of Dope's dungeon. "I'll call Ella on the way to my place. I won't be worth shit to anyone if I don't catch some sleep and eat." I slapped Dope on his shoulder. "I'm out."

"Later, man."

"Later." I climbed the stairs to the main floor of Dope's house and let myself out. The bright sunlight caused me to cringe as I shaded my eyes with my hand. Climbing into my car, I wondered how long I would continue running the relocation program. For the first time in years, I had started wondering what a different life might look like.

I drove away from Dope's place and pressed the call button on my steering wheel. Ella's name and number lit up the display screen.

"Hey," her soft voice filled my car.

"Hi. How are you after last night?"

"Tired, but okay. Every time I try to sleep, my mind returns to Sarah and the kids. How are they doing?"

"Good. Britny will stay in touch as the family adjusts, so just know that they're in safe hands, but they have new identities now, and I can't discuss any more with you." I massaged the back of my neck.

"I understand."

"I have to leave town for a few weeks. I was hoping to see you tonight before I go?"

"A few weeks?" Disappointment clung to her words.

"Yeah. It's for ... work."

"Come over now if you want."

I smiled. "I would love that. I need to shower and change clothes, though."

"Use my shower. I'll make a late lunch while you're cleaning up."

My dick jumped to attention, wondering if she would offer the same shower she used to film for the adult website. No matter how badly I wanted to pin her beneath me and ravish her, it would have to wait.

I glanced at the clock. "I'll see you in ten."

"I'll be waiting."

It had only taken me nine minutes to reach her house, and I spotted her car in the driveway. Before I could ring the doorbell, Ella opened the door.

Her soft smile lit up her face as she took my hand and led me inside. My dick refused to give up as my gaze trailed up her body. Her hair hung past her shoulders, and her tank top molded to her breasts while her running shorts barely covered the curve of her ass cheeks. I resisted the urge to pull her shorts down and taste her right then and there.

"I'm glad you're here." She turned to me.

"Me too. Two weeks is a long damn time." I tucked her hair behind her ear before I pressed my lips to hers. "Even though I would prefer to kiss you all day, I really need to clean up. If you'll point me in the right direction."

"Use my bathroom. There's a clean towel and washcloth for you on the counter. Are you okay with a salad and turkey sandwich?"

"Sounds perfect." I kissed her again before I headed to her bedroom. Passing her desk, I spotted the medical bills and wondered if she'd noticed the balance had been paid off. My instincts said no since she hadn't mentioned it. She'd never know it was me since I instructed the hospital and clinic to tell her it was an anonymous person.

I continued toward her bathroom and reminded myself to chill the fuck out and to enjoy our time together. Maybe I could even move the schedule up for relocating the families. But only if it didn't cost them their safety.

Chapter 20

Ella

Over the next week, Sebastian wouldn't tell me where he was, but he sent a few texts and called every other day from an untraceable burner phone. I questioned the unfamiliar number, but he explained he used it to protect the families he was helping.

It was strange how much I missed him and found myself bonding over text messages and deep conversations about his work with the families, what he loved about working with the bar, and even about his underground fighting days. I probably should have been shocked, but this man was breaking laws and had most likely found himself in situations he had to use his fists to get out of if he wanted to live. Worst of all, my heart broke when he told me both of his parents had died when he was twelve. Even over the phone, I could tell it was a closed conversation, so I didn't ask many questions.

I loved the moments we chatted about travel dreams and where each of us wanted to visit and maybe even move. Sharing these thoughts with each other made me happy.

Sinking my teeth into my lower lip, I recalled dancing in the rain with Sebastian. He'd felt so strong—safe. I hadn't experienced that with anyone before, and it drew me to him. Surprised, I realized I missed him.

My mind returned to the moment, and I blew out a heavy sigh. After spending the day with Dad, I was emotionally and physically drained. The irony of meeting Sebastian and beginning something new while Dad's life was ending hadn't escaped me. There would come a time when I traded one hero for another, and the mere idea fucking gutted me.

After a hectic but good week at work, I was glad it was Friday and I could relax. After I parked my car in the driveway, I grabbed the trash canister and rolled it to the side of the house. I was ready to get into my pajamas and curl up with a good book before getting some sleep. Reaching the back door, I fished for my key in my purse, then slid it into the lock.

Cold metal pressed against my temple as a strong hand slipped over my mouth. The hair on the back of my neck stood on end as the person's breath grazed my ear.

"Not a word, Ella, or I'll put a bullet in your head right now. Thanks to your license plate, it was very easy to find you, you conniving bitch. Now, open the door and walk inside."

My blood chilled as recognition dawned on me. The voice didn't belong to Death, but to Stephen—Sarah's abusive husband. At least Sarah and the kids were safe thanks to Sebastian and his team ... but I wasn't.

His maniacal laugh reached my ears as I walked inside, Stephen right behind me.

My mind scrambled for a way out of the situation, but the sick bastard had a gun trained on me. Sebastian's words echoed in the back of my head, reminding me of Stephen's sins. I had to keep my mouth shut. I had a suspicion that he would end me if he realized that I knew what he'd done to his daughter and family.

"Turn around and look at me."

I obeyed, the glint of light on the barrel of his weapon catching my attention. "Don't do this, Stephen," I pleaded, my voice quivering. "I'm not worth it."

"Where's the cunt?"

"I'm sorry. I have no idea what you're talking about."

"Sarah! Where is she? Where are my kids?"

I gritted my teeth. "I don't know."

"Liar!" His intense gaze narrowed, his chest rising and falling with his rage. "Get on your knees."

My legs trembled, entirely at his mercy. He was too far away for me to tackle, and I had to give him a reason to move closer. Vomit traveled up my throat, and I swallowed the bitter bile down.

Stephen paced in front of me. "Where are they, Ella? You helped them escape, pretending you lost your little dog. Well, guess what? You don't have one. There are zero signs in your house that you have any animals at all. As a single female, it's a stupid move."

"Thanks for the advice," I muttered, immediately scolding myself for what I'd just said to the man holding me at gunpoint. Fear showed itself in crazy ways under duress.

Stephen stomped toward me, his black boots thundering against my hardwood floors and my heart along with them.

He aimed the gun at me. "Get on your knees." He pressed the weapon against my temple and moved his finger to the trigger.

He threw his head back and laughed. "I want you to take a moment to think about this. Are you willing to die for that cunt? She's my problem, not yours, and she sure as fuck isn't worth dying for. But you have a big backyard, and I have no qualms about burying you there."

Thoughts of Sarah and the kids broke through the fear, followed by Sebastian's kindness as he kneeled in front of the children, encouraging them. I could be strong for them. I had to.

I stilled, clearing my mind the best I could. That little girl was worth saving. She was worth dying for. The fucking bastard would never hurt her again. My fear twisted into a dark, nearly blinding hatred, and my determination to protect Sarah and her family returned full force. Slowly, I looked from the weapon in his hand to his hardened gaze, full of rage.

The corners of my lips kicked up as I planned my next move. I would rather die rebelling and protecting innocent children than submitting.

"You stupid bitch!"

Time seemed to grind to a halt as I plowed forward, and head butted him right in the junk. He yelled as his arms lowered, and the weapon clambered to the floor.

The momentum of my hit sent me tumbling toward the gun, and my fingers closed around it before he could react. In one smooth motion, I spun around and pointed it at him. He froze, his expression wide with terror as I cocked the hammer back, ready to pull the trigger if he came at me. But it was too late.

"Hello, Ella. Nice of you to give me a new body to bury," Death said from behind Stephen.

I stilled as the glint of his blade against Stephen's neck caught my attention.

Death's grey eyes peered at me through his mask as a swell of gratitude bloomed inside my chest. "Did he hurt you?" His tone was void of emotion, cold and calculating.

"No," I managed to choke out as the realization sunk in that Stephen had almost killed me, and Death had snuck into my house and *saved* me.

"Who is this man to you?" Death asked.

"He's looking for his family who escaped him a few nights ago. He abused his wife and son but even worse ... he molested his daughter. He's a horrible excuse for a human being." I stood, the gun still in my hand as I righted myself.

"That's a lie!" Stephen yelled, his voice quivering with fear.

"Make another sound, and I will slice you open from throat to groin. You will drown in your own blood, and I will cherish the sight of your last breath leaving your body." Death dug the sharp edge of the weapon into Stephen's neck, causing a trickle of crimson liquid to stream down his shirt.

"Little lamb, go to your bedroom right now and lock the door. Don't come out until I give you permission. Do *not* call the cops. Do you understand?"

Fear surged through my veins like icy water as I ran toward my room. My hands trembled as I threw the door shut and pressed my ear against it, desperately trying to make out what was happening on the other side.

Death's voice was a mumble, but Stephen's pleading was clear as a bell. Every fiber of my being rooted for Death to end the fucked-up bastard for hurting his family. My heart thundered in my ears as I continued to listen.

I chewed on my thumbnail as the conversation's volume dropped, and seconds later the sound of a lamp crashing to the floor split the silence. Cringing, I grasped the gun again, unsure if Stephen would barge through my bedroom door and hurt me. If he did, I was prepared to shoot ... and kill.

Another crash echoed through the house, and I held my breath and waited for his reply. Instead, I heard only the sound of glass shattering against the walls of my home. Gripping the pistol tightly, I tensed, ready to defend myself. My pulse skipped several beats as another deafening crash rang out.

Then there was nothing.

Minutes seemed like hours as I strained to hear any additional noises, but there was only an eerie silence. I braced myself as I slowly turned the doorknob and cracked the door. I tiptoed into the kitchen, wondering when Stephen would grab me, but I didn't see him. My gaze swept the area, and before I could scream, a large hand slapped over my mouth.

Blood. So much blood coated the kitchen floor. Stephen laid on his back, his unseeing eyes staring at the ceiling. His throat gaped where it had been slashed, still gushing crimson.

Bile rushed from my stomach, and I smacked Death's hand away as I puked. The sound of it splattering over my feet made me retch again, and I grabbed my belly as my nostrils flared from the stench. I'd seen horrendous crime scene pictures at work but witnessing it firsthand was more than I could deal with.

"Are you kidding me?" I forced myself to look at the man standing next to me. It was the first time my brain registered the black grim reaper mask over his face. Even if Stephen had made it out alive, he would have never been able to identify Death.

"You killed him in my house? How am I going to get the stains out of my floor?" My voice shook as disbelief and the aftermath of adrenaline spiked my heart rate. Straightening, I wanted him to kill Stephen, of course ... just not in my home. What a fucking mess.

I stumbled to the sink. Distraught and angry, I turned on the water and hopped onto the counter, placing my feet in the stainless-steel basin. I washed the chunks of vomit and splatters of blood away, watching as the remnants circled down the drain. Impatiently waiting for Death to answer me, I glowered at him. My glare slipped into a frown. It was then that I realized he was bleeding. "You're hurt." I nodded at the gash in his long-sleeved black shirt that was covered with Stephen's blood. Strangely, a flicker of knowing crept into my thoughts. He'd gotten hurt because of me. For me.

"It's only a flesh wound." He placed his hand over the gash on his left arm, red liquid seeping between his fingers.

I strained to identify his low and husky growl along with his Pacific Northwest accent, but it was useless. There was a good possibility that my brain was too scrambled to figure out who was behind the mask.

"You deserve worse for killing the bastard in my house, Death." I blanched, fear bubbling inside of me for speaking to him so boldly, but apparently, I was in shock and my mouth had a mind of its own.

Through the haze of my shock, it dawned on me. He'd just saved my life. He'd protected me when I needed him the most. A tug of war between logic and my emotions kicked into overdrive, and I shuddered with the twists and turns my thoughts were taking. Tonight, he'd shown me a different side. He was a murderer, dark and cold, but ... I snorted before a crazy laugh bubbled up as I washed my feet. I was fucked in the head. Every fiber in my being should hate him. I should have called the cops when he stepped foot in my home uninvited, but I couldn't. Something inside pulled me to him. "You saved my life."

Death responded with a grunt.

"And his family's too."

Frowning, I grabbed the dish towel beside the sink and dried my feet. My shoulders slumped as I stared at the body. *Fuck! I have a dead person on my floor.*

"So you're one of those serial killers who saves people?"

That time, I didn't even get a grunt. He just remained silent.

I hopped off the counter, careful to avoid the vomit puddle on the floor. I had a long night ahead of me, scrubbing and bleaching my floors.

I pointed at his arm. "Let me see." I approached him and examined his wound through the cut on his black shirt. His grey eyes flickered with amusement as I gently moved the fabric away.

My chin jutted up, and I squared my shoulders as my gaze found his. "You're going to help me clean up this mess and get the body out of my house. I can't have you bleeding all over the place as you do. Follow me." Maybe I was stupid turning my back on the man who had raped me. Then again, he'd also just killed for me.

I led him to my bathroom and turned on the light. He stood at the edge of the room, watching every move I made. Maybe he thought I had a weapon under my sink. I should have. It was something to consider, for damn sure.

Locating the first-aid kit in the cabinet, I placed it on the counter and pulled open the top. "Sit." I tilted my head toward the toilet seat.

To my surprise he didn't argue with me.

"Thank you," I said softly. "For taking care of Stephen." I didn't expect an answer. "Take your arm out of your shirt and give it to me." I busied myself as I cleaned the wound. "How did he cut you?"

144

"I thought you'd left the bedroom against my orders, and I lost my advantage."

My eyes cut to his grey ones. "So it's my fault?"

"Yes."

The sound of my phone buzzing against my nightstand startled me. In the shock of the moment, I had forgotten anything or anyone else existed.

"Great. I guess it's my fault that you killed a man in my house too." I snorted. "Let me make sure I'm understanding correctly. You'll save me from the boogeyman, but there's no one to save me from you."

"I'm glad you have that figured out."

I shook my head while I secured a few butterfly bandages over his arm. "There. At least I won't have anyone else's blood on my floor." I turned to wash my hands. "You're helping me clean up. Don't even think about ditching me."

Death shot off the toilet seat, whirled me around, and forcefully slammed me against the wall, the air whooshing from my lungs.

"Don't forget your place, little lamb. You serve me, not the other way around." He dragged his knuckles down my cheek.

I swallowed my fear and clenched my jaw. Adrenaline snaked through my body, and my core clenched with the memories of him marking me with the hilt of his knife. *Dammit, my body continues to betray me.* "Then I'll ask thee, my lord, to please assist your servant." I licked my lips, my body responding to him pressing against me.

He stepped back and allowed enough space between us to lower his head and bite my nipple through my sleep tank.

A cry escaped me as he cupped my breast hard and inflicted more pain. He laughed as he straightened, his nose grazing my cheek. "You'll learn to watch that smart mouth of yours around me, Ella."

My chest rose and fell, my breath coming in short bursts as my panties dampened.

"I smell your desire for me. There's no pretending, little lamb. You want me to do dirty, unthinkable things to your body. Don't worry. You're not getting rid of me." His hand trailed down my side and to the leg opening of my shorts. He slipped a finger beneath them, brushing the fabric of my underwear.

"That's my dirty bitch, so wet for me." He massaged my sensitive nub, and I stifled a moan.

My body betrayed me, but I refused to give him the satisfaction of knowing how much I craved him. "You terrify me. That's the only reason I'm wet. It's a natural fear response."

"Tell yourself whatever lie you need to. You're the only one believing it." His hand eased inside my panties, and his knuckle brushed over my slit.

I gasped as he expertly played with me. My eyes fluttered closed as he shoved a finger inside me, fucking me roughly.

"For the last year, I watched you get yourself off for the camera, but tonight ... tonight, Ella, you're mine. Don't deny it. Have you been touching yourself while I'm gone?"

Heat swirled deep in my belly, the delicious tingling coursing through my body as he brought me closer to the edge.

I gritted my teeth, refusing to give him the satisfaction of my orgasm. "You raped me. Why would I want to think about that again?" I wanted to apologize before my mouth landed me in hot water, but the stress of Stephen nearly killing me plus his dead body on my kitchen floor had my mouth running in overdrive.

A dark chuckle escaped Death as he withdrew his hand. "Little lamb, I can't take what already belongs to me."

Terror and eagerness warred inside my chest. A part of me wanted him. I wanted this twisted, sick, psychotic man to fuck me senseless and pull me into a world I hadn't ever experienced.

"Take off your clothes."

Realizing there was no room for discussion, I discarded my pajamas and tossed them onto the floor. Death grabbed my wrist and dragged me behind him to the kitchen. He picked me up and set me on top of the granite counter, the cold stone chilling my ass cheeks. I focused on the dead man on the floor. Pockets of red had started to congeal.

"Don't deny that your soul is as dark as mine." Death backed away, admiring me.

My stomach clenched with nerves as he kneeled next to Stephen. He removed his knife from the sheath on his leg and plunged it into Stephen's chest. Too terrified to watch, I slammed my eyes closed as I waited for him to finish. A few minutes later, I sensed his presence next to me, and I peeked at him as he sheathed his weapon into his leg holster. Slapping a hand over my mouth, I stifled my scream as Death set Stephen's heart in my sink. He dragged his fingertips over the organ and through the dripping blood.

Death palmed the organ before he faced me. "You won't ever disappoint me, will you, little lamb?"

"N-no." I wasn't stupid. I understood that the same could happen to me if I ever turned on him. As I stared at the lifeless heart, mine raced at Mach speed.

He flashed me a maniacal smile as he painted my breasts and abdomen with Stephen's red, sticky substance. I couldn't pull my attention away as he continued streaking his fingertips through Stephen's crimson life force. My chest heaved with horror at the gruesome sight in front of me.

"I would give you his dark heart as a trophy, but I can't leave evidence behind."

Disgusted, I looked away from the nightmare that was unfolding.

"Open your eyes, little lamb. Your shepherd has brought you to the slaughter."

I forced them open, hating the feel of his slick fingers on my skin.

"In my world, you celebrate the kill with the person that means the most to you."

I blinked several times, trying to follow what he'd said. *I* was the most important person to him.

"Lean back."

Dazed, I did as he asked. He dug his fingers into my thighs and roughly pulled them apart, then positioned himself between them, his tongue darting through the mouth opening of his mask before he bit the tender inside of my leg. My cry filled the room as tears blurred my vision.

"Pain before pleasure, Ella." He licked the bite mark before he flattened his tongue and slowly ran it along my slit.

A guttural growl worked up his throat. "You taste better than I ever imagined."

He sucked on my clit, pulling on it with his teeth. I gasped as he soothed my sensitive skin. I should kick him away, make him stop. But his tongue was as wicked as his soul. My head dropped back, my mouth slack as he feasted on me. Heat swirled in the pit of my stomach, and my pussy clenched as he continued. Teetering on the edge of ecstasy, I rocked against his face in a desperate frenzy.

Seconds before I shattered, he stood and yanked me onto my feet. He bent me over and pinned my cheek against the counter as the sound of his zipper filled the room. Before I could protest, he rubbed the tip of his rock-hard cock up and down my pussy and then thrust inside me with so much force I cried out.

"Such a tight cunt, and now it's mine."

He seized my head and forced me to look at the morbid scene before me. Stephen's lifeless body. Blood spattered across the kitchen floor like a gruesome painting. Death's hand crept up my body, fingers coiling tightly around my neck like a collar while his other hand viciously pinched my nipple. As he plunged into me with an insatiable hunger, he taunted me with his words.

"You are mine. And I will bathe you in the blood of my victim."

My body convulsed in pleasure at his twisted confession, reality fading away as every nerve sparked to life. I embraced the dark desires consuming me.

"My little lamb loves that idea." He chuckled darkly as his tongue traced the pulsing vein on my neck.

With a firm grip on my hair, he pulled out of me and led me to Stephen's lifeless form.

"Lie down," he commanded.

I sank to the floor, torn between screaming out against this depraved act and begging for Death to ravage me once more. In this dark, twisted ritual, I realized we would be bound together forever.

Stephen's blood coated my back and ass as I complied with Death, feeling like a puppet on strings without any control over my actions.

With a cruel smile, Death positioned himself between my legs and penetrated me with his large shaft, stretching me to accommodate him. He thrust forcefully, his body quivering with pleasure as he groaned in satisfaction.

I wrapped my legs around him, leaving smears of crimson on his jeans and skin as he continued to pound into me. My breasts rubbed against his shirt, creating an intense sensation that sent delicious chills through my entire body. Every nerve was on fire, and I craved more.

As if sensing my desires, Death rolled over, and I straddled him, taking control of the rhythm now.

"You wanted this all along, Ella," he growled, and a tantalizing chill ran down my back. "I've just awakened your deepest, darkest fantasy. You hide from the world, but I see you."

He lifted his hips and grabbed hold of my breasts, squeezing them tightly. Placing my hands on his chest for support, I rode him eagerly, craving the unique combination of sensations that only he could provide—pain and pleasure intertwined together in perfect harmony.

The stench of blood and sex hung heavy in the air as Death's rough hands gripped my hips, pulling me onto his cock. My body quivered with desire and fear as he whispered degrading words in my ear, his breath hot against my skin. Stephen's lifeless body in front of me reminded me of the depravity we were engaging in.

"Your cunt is dripping wet. You love my cock inside you, don't you, my naughty whore? You're enjoying being fucked in Stephen's blood." Death chuckled, and my body tightened around his shaft.

I writhed under Death's touch, my slick walls clenching and releasing around him as he continued to thrust into me relentlessly. His fingers slipped between my legs, expertly stroking my clit as he plunged deeper into me. The pleasure was overwhelming, driving me closer and closer to the edge.

"Look at him," Death commanded, his voice low and menacing. I turned my head to gaze at Stephen's corpse, a mix of horror and arousal washing over me.

"Cum for me while you stare at his dead body," Death growled, pushing me harder toward climax. And with one final thrust, I shattered into a million pieces, screaming out in both pleasure and revulsion.

Death's breathing quickened and a guttural growl escaped him.

"I'm not on birth control!" I cried.

"I know." With one final slam, his body jerked as his seed spilled into me.

He stilled, then he pulled out and stood. Death grabbed my arm and jerked me to my feet. He led me to the counter, picked me up and placed me on top of the cold granite. He spread my legs, focusing on my pussy.

"You look so beautiful with my cum dripping from your cunt." He swirled his fingertips through it, then pushed his seed back inside me. The corners of his mouth twitched as an evil grin curved into place, mixing our juices.

He seized my jaw and thrust his fingers between my lips. "Suck." His semen exploded on my tongue and coated my throat, every second enthralling yet terrifying me at the same time.

Once I'd cleaned off all traces of him, he backed away. "Don't move."

My fingers clenched and unclenched as he began to collect cleaning supplies. I could feel the color drain from my cheeks as reality seeped through the cracks of my addled and thoroughly fucked brain. Death knew exactly where everything was in my kitchen.

Chapter 21

Ella

I shifted on my living room couch, staring at the ceiling. My heart was heavy, and my mind swirled in a whirlwind of emotions from the events. I stared at the spot where Death had overpowered Stephen and slit his throat, then fucked me into delirium. I questioned my sanity as I recalled the mind-blowing sex next to Stephen's corpse. But I wanted it. I wanted Death. Something inside me had shifted toward him instead of away.

I shuddered at the memory of me standing in front of my mirror, naked and covered in blood. It had taken me an hour to scrub off every drop of crimson sin from my skin and hair. Once I'd finished, Death hauled Stephen's now naked body to the bathtub and dumped him in. He handed me a full-faced gas mask, and I gawked at him in disbelief.

My stomach clenched. "You're not going to do what I think you are."

"Put it on." He waited as he slipped his into place.

"Where did you get all of this?" I pointed to the jugs lined up on the floor near my tub.

He ignored my question, focusing on the body.

151

Horrified and repulsed, I gasped as Death poured multiple bottles of chemicals over Stephen's body. As hard as I tried, I couldn't turn away as Stephen's body dissolved within minutes and disappeared down my drain.

"I'll clean your tub and leave the fans on. Don't come back in here for at least eight hours. Use your other bathroom."

Even after I'd opened myself to Death and my darkest desires, I couldn't deny that a monster had saved me from a monster. I had no fucking clue how to reconcile that. I should tell my therapist, but I couldn't confide in someone about Death, they were legally bound to report a killer to the authorities. And how the hell would I ever explain that I was ravished in his victim's blood and not be arrested right along with him?

My feelings flip-flopped again, and a rush of fear and anger consumed me as I recalled how he'd forced me to stay still and allow his seed to remain in my body. The moment he'd left, I rushed to my bedroom and opened my nightstand drawer, frantically searching for my morning-after pill, but it was gone.

A quick phone call to the pharmacy had taken care of that, and I took the first dose as soon as I picked it up. I refused to carry a serial killer's baby.

Three texts from Sebastian had come through in the last twelve hours, and I hadn't responded to any. Scrolling through Spotify, I found my "pissed off" playlist and "Desire" by Violet Orlandi blasted through my Alexa speaker.

I stumbled through a strange combination of fear, excitement, and longing as I thought of Death's touch and mouth on my body. I shouldn't want him. Sebastian was the kind of man that I should be pursuing. He was strong, solid in his beliefs in wanting to help women and children. He was a *good* man. My pulse raced as I thought about him, wishing he were here with me. Sebastian's presence was safe and comforting and a part of me wanted to get lost in him—escape the insanity I was living in.

I shook my head in an attempt to clear the dark clouds muddying my brain, but I could not deny the way my heart raced when I thought of both men—the angel and the devil. I was ashamed for daring to have such conflicting emotions, yet powerless to resist the pull between them. I buried my face in my hands, feeling foolish but unable to stop the thrill that came from pushing boundaries.

But Death saved my life. It's proof that he isn't completely consumed by the urge to kill. I suspected that in Death's mind, his killings had a rhyme and reason. I just wasn't sure what that was yet.

"I Put Something in Your Drink" by Ramsey pulsed through the house, and a plan began to form. I had no idea who Death, a.k.a. Shadow Whisperer, was. I knew two different personas, the one on camera and the other in my home, but I'd never seen him unless it was dark, or he had a grim reaper mask over his head. I wanted to learn more. I *needed* to know more. My curiosity had always gotten me in trouble, and this situation was no different.

With a solid plan in place, I attempted to relax and finally read Sebastian's messages.

Sebastian:

> I miss you. I can't wait to see you.

A few hours later:

> I know you're busy, but text me when you can.

I groaned. I sure as hell couldn't mention that I'd been busy getting fucked senseless while a dead body was on my kitchen floor.

153

.   .   .

THE LAST MESSAGE:

> I hope you're okay. You usually respond sooner. I'm just worried because of Stephen. If I don't hear from you by noon tomorrow, I'll send someone to check on you.

I CLOSED MY EYES AND HELD THE PHONE TO MY CHEST, HIS words warming my heart. How could I want to be with him but be drawn to Death, as well? Blowing out a breath, I texted Sebastian.

ME:

> Sorry! I'm fine, I promise. I was with Dad, then came home and crashed. It's been a long, exhausting day. Miss you too. Stay safe.

GUILT GNAWED AT ME FOR LYING TO HIM, BUT IT WASN'T LIKE I could tell him the truth ... that a serial killer was stalking me and had killed Stephen in my kitchen.

Turning my thoughts from the gruesome situation, I focused on the fact that Sebastian was helping women and kids escape abusive situations.

My phone rang with Cami's special ringtone, and I answered.

"Bitch! I know your Dad isn't doing well, but I haven't heard from you in two days. What the hell is happening? You're scaring the crap out of me."

I cringed as Cami continued to let me have it.

"I'm sorry. I never meant to scare you. It's just ..." How the hell could I explain to Cami about Sebastian and his work, especially since I'd signed a nondisclosure form after Sarah's drop-off? "I wish I could talk to you about it, Cami, but I signed an NDA."

"What?" Her voice dropped, curiosity lacing her words. "Why?"

"I can't tell you. It would risk a lot of lives."

"So it's a work thing? Like about a criminal case?"

Bingo! I'll run with that. "Yeah. It's pretty big, and it has me stressed out, but there's something else, too. I just can't talk here."

"Then what are you waiting for? Get your cute ass over here."

"See ya soon." I ended the call, relieved to be getting out of the house.

Once I had dressed and brushed my hair, I headed out to gather what I needed for Death's next visit.

I KNOCKED ON CAMI'S DOOR, ANXIOUSLY TAPPING MY FOOT ON the floor. The choice to share certain details about Stephen had me nearly crawling up the walls with anxiety, but I couldn't process it all on my own. Dad had always told me it took more strength to ask for help than to shoulder it on my own. My throat tightened as tears welled in my eyes. Soon, he wouldn't be around to drop those tidbits of wisdom, and I wasn't sure how I would manage without him.

The door swung open, sucking me out of the devastating reality threatening to gobble me up.

Cami took my wrist and tugged me inside her apartment before tightly hugging me. She broke away and grabbed my shoulders. "Don't you ever scare me like that again, or I'll beat your ass and brag to your dad how easy it was."

We stared at each other in silence, then burst into giggles. I hugged her again. "I'm sorry. You'll understand when I tell you what I can. Plus, I need your help."

Cami closed the door behind us, flipped the deadbolt, and secured the chain.

"Drink? I can make some mimosas, or if this is some really big shit, we can just pass the bottle of Jack around."

I glanced at my watch. "It's not even noon yet."

"Your point?" She dug a hair tie from the front pocket of her boyfriend jeans and pulled her hair up. "I have a feeling this is about your stalker. If I'm right, we'll cut to the chase, and I'll get two straws and the bottle of whiskey."

I pointed at her. "Probably that, but I need some food, or I'll get sick from drinking."

"Like I don't know that after our college days." She motioned for me to follow her into the kitchen. I grinned as finger sandwiches, crackers, meat, and cheese were on plates, ready for us to munch on.

"Start talking, I don't have all day. Where the hell have you been? I still want to know more about this mysterious NDA, but if it's for work, I understand that you can't." She pushed up on her tiptoes and located two glass tumblers.

I climbed onto the black leather barstool and grabbed a few crackers and squares of meat and cheese.

Cami poured a shot into my glass and slid it to me. She leaned against the opposite side of the counter and propped her elbows up, staring a hole through me. "Talk."

I squared my shoulders, prepared to tell her about last night.

Are you sure? If she were in my shoes, I would be worried about her and call the cops if she told me she was raped by her stalker and liked it. It wasn't healthy, especially when I had an amazing guy wanting to spend time with me. He was a hero, not a murderer.

"There's a case, and I can't give you the details, but the man involved came after me last night."

Cami's mouth dropped. "What the hell? Hon, are you okay?"

"Traumatized, but he didn't hurt me. He tried, but um ..." I

156

snatched up my whiskey and downed it, needing some liquid courage before I told her the rest.

"Holy shit, this must be some intense stuff if you just slammed that back like it was water." She grabbed my glass and poured another shot for me.

"I had just gotten home when the guy showed up." I shivered, the memory of the pure hatred in Stephen's eyes twisting my nerves into a pretzel. *He's gone. He can't hurt you again.* "He held a gun to my head and forced his way into the house."

Cami's gaze narrowed while she stood. "What the actual fuck? Where is the son of a bitch now? We're going after him."

"No need," I whispered. "He threatened me, but I calmed him down, and he finally left."

Cami stared at me like I'd lost my mind. I had. "I'm sorry, what? That seems odd, Ella. You're not telling me everything."

I nodded. "I know. I can't. He did leave, though, and I'm safe. Those are the important highlights."

She blinked at me rapidly before she responded. "Ella, if you're in trouble, then I'm in trouble with you. We have each other's back. I understand that this is a case, but what happened to you is terrifying." Her shoulders slumped and she placed her palms on the counter, leaning on it.

Gratitude flowed through me. "Thank you. I love you for that, which is why I've debated telling you or not. You were worried about me, though, and I would need some kind of answer if the situation had been reversed."

"Girl, I hear some crazy ass shit in the ER. I can take it, but not as much when it's about my bestie." She pounded on her chest, grinning. "I feel like I should do something to help, but I don't know what. Did you call the cops?"

I grimaced. "No. I handled it and will tell my boss." *Death handled it.* A flood of emotions knotted in my stomach. My stalker and serial killer saved my life, and I was seeing him differently. That was fucked up. *I* was fucked up.

Cami rubbed her temples. "Of course, you got scared and went toward the danger instead of crawling out of a window and calling the fucking police. I can talk to my cop friend, if you want me to."

I rubbed my palms on my jeaned thighs. "No, I promise you that I'm all right. I don't think the client will be a problem anymore. If he is, I'll ask you to talk to your friend." Worry needled my skin as I wondered if Cami's relationship with the cop would cause issues down the road for Sebastian ... and Death. *Shit! Like I don't have enough on my plate as it is.*

Cami looked at me skeptically, but she remained quiet.

She folded her arms over her chest and glared a hole through me. "Are you going to say anything to Sebastian?"

I squirmed in my seat, not liking her line of questioning.

"I don't think so, but I'm not sure yet. The last thing I need is to have Sebastian worry and hover over me." I ran my fingertips along the rim of my glass, wondering how the hell my life had gotten so complicated.

"Sebastian is out of town for another week, so it should give me some space to figure things out. I really like him, and I don't want to scare him off with my drama."

"I get that. I'm glad that Sebastian is gone for a while, too. It will give you time to clear your head."

Over the next hour, Cami and I caught up on her life. As hard as I tried to focus on what she was saying, my mind continued to drift back to Death. I had to find out his real identity. The wheels in my brain began to churn as I mentally weighed the pros and cons of my plan.

Little did I know that Death had one of his own.

Chapter 22

Death

"In a world filled with wolves, the lamb must learn to be brave." ~
Unknown

Killing Stephen had whetted my appetite instead of dampening it. When he'd pointed a gun at Ella, rage coursed through me like an untamed animal. In any other situation, I would have enjoyed drawing out the suffering of my targets before ending their pathetic lives, but this had been different. For Ella, I was willing to do anything and unleash a fury that every man should fear.

Earlier, I had taken my second victim of the day, Morris. Normally, I spaced my kills out a few weeks apart, but the rage inside had consumed me, and I'd crossed another name off my list. Just like Stephen, Morris was a piece of shit. He beat his wife and son, but instead of molesting his kid, he sold him for sex. I'd been watching him for months, planning his torture and demise.

Unfortunately, Ella had taken up residence in my head, and I got sloppy. Instead of disposing of the body to stall the cops from finding him, I strung the motherfucker on a meat hook in his warehouse. It

159

was too late for me to go back, plus I would risk leaving evidence behind.

I always made a painstaking effort to make sure that I left no trace of who I was on or around my victims. If I got caught, my good work would have all been for nothing. Cleaning up the scum was a dirty job, but I was more than thrilled to do it.

As I arrived at Ella's home for the second night in a row, flashes of her on her kitchen counter with my cum seeping out of her cunt flashed through my mind, my cock responding to the delicious images. If I hadn't fucked her, I wouldn't have messed up with Morris, but I couldn't get hung up on him. I had to see her again. Ella was my obsession, and if I weren't careful, she would also become my weakness.

I crept into her backyard, cloaked by the cloudy night sky, and adjusted my grim reaper mask. Not even the moon was out, which made seeing my girl much easier. Out of habit, I jiggled the doorknob on her kitchen door, but instead of finding it locked, it gave way. *Odd.* Cautious, I eased it open and slipped into her home. Silence consumed the house, threatening to swallow it. My ears perked up as I heard the sound of the shower coming from her en suite bathroom. It had been a while since I'd seen a video of Ella in there. I entered her room, grinning as I noticed the door was wide open. Ella's curvy silhouette grabbed my attention. My cock twitched, wondering if my little lamb was carrying my baby yet. I suspected that she ran to the pharmacy and bought more pills to force her body to expel my attempts. That was a mistake, but it didn't matter. I would win in the end.

The shower turned off, and she stepped out, grabbing a towel from the toilet seat and patting herself dry. When she finished, she finally looked up. Stumbling backward, she screamed and covered herself.

"I thought you were welcoming me in, little lamb. Your back door was unlocked, and you were putting on quite a show for me. I wish I'd arrived sooner, but I had ... plans."

160

"You scared the shit out of me. I wasn't sure if you were going to drop by or not, but you could have said something, let me know you were here."

I threw my head back and laughed. "Why would I do that when seeing the terror on your face is so much more entertaining?"

"Asshole," she mumbled as she hung up the towel over the shower door.

"Careful," I growled dangerously.

My eyes feasted on her large tits and curve of her hips. She was built to carry my spawn.

Ella grabbed her black robe with pink flowers across the chest and secured the tie around her waist. "What are you doing here? I gave you what you wanted." She strode past me as if she hadn't a care in the world. My molars ground together. I was about to give her one.

My attention landed on her full, curvy ass as she walked to the kitchen with her shoulders squared. My little lamb was feeling confident around me.

"I assume you're staying for a while. Can I offer you something to drink? Whiskey? Water?" She looked up at the ceiling and placed a contemplative finger on her chin. "Bleach?" She offered me a sweet smile, her gaze flashing with defiance.

I tugged on my black gloves and flashed her a sinister grin. She was giving me attitude. Let her because she wouldn't like mine when I gave it back to her. "A shot of whiskey."

With her back turned to me, I folded my arms across my chest and focused on her every move. My cock throbbed with the idea of her cunt wrapped around my shaft. *Soon.*

Ella poured our drinks, then offered mine to me. "Cheers."

"And what are we toasting to?" Now that she was looking at me, I realized her eyes were swollen and red. My little lamb was hiding behind a facade.

I set the glass down on the counter, noticing a slight twitch at the corner of her lips. "Why have you been crying?"

She sipped her drink, staring at the floor before her gaze returned to mine. "Why do you want to know? It's not like you care."

"Try me."

"I spent the day with my father. The treatment isn't working," she said, the grief in her tone heavy with the confession.

"There aren't any other options?"

"No. This was the last hope. I was paying for his trial by working for the website. It was good money, but I suspect you were at least half of that income."

I offered her a sinister grin as I approached. Dragging my knuckles down her soft cheek, I leaned near her ear and whispered, "I was your *only* income."

Her body stiffened, and she attempted to pull away, but I was faster. I wrapped my gloved hand around her pretty little neck, choking her. "My cock is so damn hard right now as your cheeks redden, and you attempt to beg me for air." Chuckling, I released her and stepped back.

"What do you mean you were my only income?" She rubbed her neck, her eyes flashing with hatred.

"Your first few videos were very popular, so I paid someone to reroute the future ones you posted. I was the only one watching you, little lamb. After your first four, any money you made came from my pockets, no one else's. Once we started chatting, you were mine. You just didn't know it yet."

Her expression twisted with shock and anger. "How much of my life has been dictated by you behind the scenes?"

I took her drink from her and set it on the opposite counter, away from mine. Removing one of my gloves, I tucked it in my back pocket before I pinned her against the refrigerator. My hand slipped beneath the hem of her robe, and I grabbed her pussy hard enough to make her yelp.

"I know about your father and the failed trial. I know your bosses and what cases you're working on. I know when you go to sleep, shower, wake in the middle of the night and check your phone, terrified that your father has already died." I moved the hem of her robe out of my way and gently spread her pussy lips apart. "My little lamb is nice and wet for me already." I shoved a finger into her cunt, and she gasped. "I know your darkest secrets, what drives you to dance on the edge. I'm here to stoke that fire. When I finish destroying you and piecing you back together ... my little lamb will burn for me."

Her tongue darted over her full lower lip, her gaze heavy with need. "I don't have any secrets. I'm an open book."

"How quickly a lie falls from that pretty mouth of yours." I shoved another finger inside her, manipulating her body just as I'd manipulated her life over the last twelve months. It had been fun, but it was time to take things to the next level.

Her chest rose and fell as she neared an orgasm. I pulled away before I gripped the back of her neck, forcing her to look at me. "I know you spiked my drink, little lamb."

Ella's eyes widened as she attempted to shake her head. "I don't understand what you're talking about."

"Another lie. While you were holding your dad's hand, I was here waiting for you. You didn't hide the sleeping pills very well. I'm curious, what exactly were you hoping to accomplish by drugging me?"

She gulped, terror flashing through her gaze. "Ripping your mask off to see who you are would've been a lame attempt. Before my hand even reached your neck, you would have overpowered me. I want your fingerprints. I want to know who you are."

An intelligent, cunning woman deserving of a crown. "I've already told you. I'm Death."

"Who are you beneath the mask? Behind the screen?" She asked, her hand trembling at her side.

Rage and admiration for her failed attempt to blindside me raced through my veins. I guided her to her knees, then stood and walked across the room. I grabbed a chair from her dining table and sat on it, adjusting my cock through my black pants. "I'll tell you who I am, but you have to earn it, my little cum slut." Even with fear evident in her face, she melted with my words. Ella McCloud loved to be degraded.

It turned her on. Grinning, I removed my other glove and tossed it on the table. "Do you want to know who I really am?"

"Yes." She rubbed her arms, eagerness flickering to life in her expression.

I spread my legs, the outline of my dick evident through my slacks. I indicated for her to come closer. Like a good whore, she crawled to me with her head down, bowing. She was a fast learner. Ella kneeled in front of me, and I flipped open my pants button. My zipper slowly lowering was the only sound in the room. Wrapping my fingers around my thick shaft, I reached down and tilted her chin up. "I'll tell you who I am, little lamb. I'm the only man allowed to break you. I am your god, and you will bow and worship me."

A little whimper escaped her, and it stirred my dark soul. "Who do you serve?"

"You." Ella's nipples pressed against the satin fabric of her robe.

I fisted her hair as I continued to stroke my dick. Standing, I repositioned her and pushed her head back on the seat of the chair before I straddled her face. "Open."

My little lamb parted her mouth, and I rubbed the tip of my cock along her lower lip. She licked the precum off and looked up, her green eyes flashing with hunger. Hunger for me. Hunger for the darkest fantasy she was too terrified to indulge in. I eased past her teeth and groaned as her tongue pressed against the underside of my shaft.

"Worship me, Ella. If you do well, I'll forgive you for your lack of judgment. I might even reward you."

Her hands flew up and jerked my pants down to my thighs. Her fingernails dug into my flesh, drawing blood as she worked my cock with desperation and need. She moaned around my dick, sending heat up and down my spine. Saliva coated me as she wrapped her hand around my shaft, stroking and sucking in a rhythm that threatened to send me over the edge. Feral desire consumed me, and I pulled out of her mouth. My growl filled the room as I forced her to her feet. I sat on the chair and pulled her down, shoving my cock into her wet hole so hard she cried out. I roughly grabbed her hips, forcing her to take all of me. When I took her the other night, I hadn't given her every inch. If she wanted to earn something, she had to serve her master, which meant she would bend to my will.

With one hand, I ripped her robe open, her full breasts bouncing as desire consumed her, and she rode me hard. Heat shot up my back as my attention landed on the still healing cuts on her breasts—*my* marks on her skin. I leaned over and plucked her taut nipple with my teeth, pulling until I knew it hurt her. Taking her into my mouth, I sucked and lapped up her pain.

Ella's moan reached my ears, and I looked at her. Her lips parted as she bounced up and down.

"That's it. I knew my dirty little lamb could take all of me. Now I'm going to cum inside you."

I dug my fingers into her ass cheeks and bucked my hips, hitting the innermost parts of her. My balls tightened as I shot my seed deep inside her. The world around me disappeared. The only thing that existed was this stunning woman and the feel of her drenched pussy wrapped around my shaft. Before she had a chance to try to turn on me while I was vulnerable, I placed my hands beneath her and stood.

"What are you doing?" She yelped as she threw her arms around my neck for balance as I walked toward her room.

I kicked the partially closed door open, then laid her on her bed and grabbed her wrists with one hand. Opening her nightstand drawer, I snatched up the pair of handcuffs and made quick work of securing her to the bed frame.

She tugged on them, fire burning in her eyes. "What are you doing?"

I tenderly brushed her hair off her forehead. "Getting you pregnant."

Chapter 23

Ella

Furious for allowing myself to get into this position in the first place, I tugged at the stupid cuffs for the tenth time, just in case they loosened. Of course, they didn't. The sound of my shower running pissed me off even more. The son of a bitch handcuffed me, then strolled to my closet like he owned the damn house and removed a duffle bag full of clothes and toiletries. He'd planned it all.

My cell phone buzzed, and I searched the room, finally spotting it on my desk. He must have put it there, too far away for me to grab.

Fear pulsed through me. Was he going to keep me captive in my own home so I couldn't take the Plan B pill? Even then, I could terminate the pregnancy. I forced myself to think through the scenario and make a plan. The only thought that gave me a thread of peace was if I disappeared, my parents and Cami would come looking for me. Sebastian would also check in since he was worried about Stephen hurting me.

The bathroom door swung open, and a billow of steam swirled around Death as he stepped out in jeans, shirtless. He wore his grim reaper mask.

166

"How's my Queen feeling?"

Quickly, I scanned his chest for any marks that might help me identify who he was, but I didn't see any scars or tattoos. Maybe he'd kept his skin free of any marks that could give him away. He smirked as he leaned against the door frame.

"Peachy. You?" I muttered.

He responded with a low chuckle. He strolled over to the bed, spread my legs, and stared at my center.

A lump of anxiety formed in my throat before I spoke. "I'll never have your baby. You're wasting your time." My voice trembled as I attempted to hold my ground.

"Don't be so sure." He lowered his head and flicked his tongue over my clit. "If you don't fight me, I'll make you cum over and over until you're screaming my name."

I blew out a shaky sigh, doing my best to ignore his touch and the heat building between my thighs. "Why me? I mean what was it about me that you just couldn't pass up?"

"Other than your beauty? Your brain? Your good heart?" He sank his teeth into my inner thigh, causing me to scream and writhe on the bed. "It was none of that. It's the darkness you hide so well from others. But I saw it, Ella. All you need is some training, and you'll stand by my side."

"I'll never hurt anyone. I'm not a killer like you are."

He sucked my clit, then stroked it with his tongue.

"Oh, god." My hips had a mind of their own, and I shamelessly ground against his mouth as he slayed me, shaping me to his will.

"I'm not dark like you. I have a soul," I squeaked out. "No matter how many times you fuck me, I won't carry your baby." As accurate as that was, I was totally down for him fucking me.

He lifted his head, and something I hadn't seen before flashed in his eyes. His fingers pushed against my entrance before he slid them to my asshole.

"Don't make promises you can't keep." He eased a finger into each hole.

I fisted my hands, my fingernails digging into my palms, and mentally begged for him to let me cum.

He removed his hand, leaving me desperate once again. I pursed my lips together in order not to groan. He walked back to the bathroom and returned, pulling on a grey T-shirt before he disappeared again. A few minutes later, he was back with what I assumed was a fresh drink. He set mine on the nightstand.

"How am I going to take a drink?"

"If you want one, I'll give it to you." He sat in my office chair and faced me.

"How long are you keeping me handcuffed to my bed?"

"As long as I want to, but it depends on you. I have somewhere to be in a few hours. I'll either take the cuffs off or not. We'll see how it goes."

I gritted my teeth to not get snarky with him. Why in the hell my mouth had a mind of its own when I was scared was beyond me. "If we're going to spend quality time together, will you tell me something about yourself?" Maybe talking would soothe my soul, but I doubted it.

He chuckled. "You'll use it against me."

My focus shifted as I stared at him, seeing a man who hadn't completely given himself to the darkness. Working with criminal attorneys allowed me to study the men and women who walked through our office doors. Maybe I could still reach him and save lives. When he'd mentioned I also had darkness inside, he was partially right, but we weren't the same. Although I'd been pulled toward a darker existence for a long time, my desire to help others trumped it. If I played my cards right, maybe there was hope for him too. Or maybe I was just crazy as hell.

"I'm an accomplice to murder, or did you forget about Stephen?"

"Of course not. I track all of my kills."

"I heard serial killers keep a memento from each event. Is that true?"

He crossed his legs and smoothed his hand down his thigh.

"Most do. I don't, nor do I revisit where I took their life—your house is the exception. For the most part, I'm not your textbook criminal, little lamb. Don't put me in the same box as others."

The more he talked, the more questions I had. Since I'd sat in on many cases where my bosses questioned the criminals they represented in court, it was only a matter of time before Death gave me a tidbit I could sink my teeth into and find out who he was. *And when you do, what then?* "Are you different in other ways?"

"I was trained to kill and walk away without attachment."

Holy shit. Trained?

My forehead creased. "You had a mentor?"

Death threw his head back and laughed. Hard. Goosebumps peppered my skin with the deep, rich sound. After that, I would recognize his laugh in a crowded football stadium filled with chatter and cheers. He was leaving me crumbs, and I would take them. Grateful for something else to think about other than the fact that I was naked and handcuffed with a serial killer's sperm inside me, I quieted my mind. He might want me to have his baby, but our time together was a big mistake for him.

He flexed his fingers, and I studied every movement of his muscled and toned body and broad chest. Apparently, he wasn't going to answer me about a mentor.

"You killed Stephen because he was a threat to me, but I'd also mentioned the fact that he'd hurt his family ... he deserved to die. Do you pick your victims randomly, or?"

He leaned forward and placed an elbow on his knee, remaining silent.

My brows rose with his offer. "Are you so confident that when you uncuff me I won't run out of here and straight to the cops?"

"Yes. Because you just said you wouldn't since you're an accomplice to murder."

I shrugged. "Isn't that a good enough reason to trust me and explain how you choose your victims?"

He leaned back in his chair. "No. And the more I say, the more dangerous you are. If you ever talked to the cops, you would tell them everything."

"I would put both of us in jeopardy."

"Not really. You work for powerful men who could clear your name within a few days. Stephen held a gun to your head; it would be considered self-defense. And when proof of what he was doing to his daughter landed in the judge's hands, the case would miraculously disappear. Stephen's death sentence would be justified."

I stared at him, his words sinking in. "Who are you that you can sway a judge?"

The muscles in his broad chest flexed as he lifted his glass and took a drink. "A more powerful man. Always know your opponent before you strike, little lamb."

I racked my brain for anyone that I knew with that kind of influence. My bosses were well respected, and I suspected a bit shady, but not like Death.

"I hand pick my victims. Men who are pedophiles, deal in sex trafficking, beat their wives, or rape their children. I wash the earth in their blood."

My heart thundered, pounding against my ribs with his confession. "You're an unhinged savior." A flicker of knowing flew through my mind faster than I could grasp it and form a full thought. My gut was trying to tell me something, but I wasn't sure what yet.

"Call it whatever you want." He walked over to the bed and sat on the side, the mattress dipping beneath his weight. He smoothed my hair, and for a second, I lost myself in his touch.

"You're not a monster," I whispered.

"Don't fool yourself, little lamb. I am most definitely a monster."

Fear bubbled up inside me, but I pushed it down. I was about to do something potentially stupid.

"Come here." My voice was soft and filled with yearning.

Our gazes locked and my throat tightened with fear, but what I was about to do was worth the risk. I shut my eyes and pressed my mouth to his. He jerked away as if I'd burned him, but before I could

170

say anything, his lips crashed down on mine again. His touch was like a thousand needles piercing my skin, commanding and consuming me in one swift motion. As I opened up entirely to him, I felt the power shift as he took control with a ruthless determination. I arched my back and moaned, eager for him to dominate me. This monster was turning me inside out, and all I could do was beg for more.

He broke the kiss and ran the tip of his nose across my jawline to my ear. "If I'm not careful, you'll be the death of me."

Unable to help myself, I smiled.

"You've earned something tonight, little lamb. I have the power to make your deepest desires come true."

A wave of sadness warred with longing. I was afraid that no one could do that, no matter how powerful they were. I forced my thoughts away from the direction they inevitably headed and back to his kiss. "An orgasm?"

"No. Something that will last you a lifetime."

His mouth brushed my neck, and chills coasted over my skin. As the words fell from his lips, my world stopped, tilting on its axis as the air whooshed from my lungs. Sucking in a sharp breath, I clung to his promise.

Chapter 24

Ella

I climbed into my car and drove toward my parent's house from the law office. My heart pounded in my chest as I remembered the shock that coursed through me when, four days ago, Death shared that he could save my father. The more I learned about him and saw the glimmering humanity beneath his exterior, the more a twisted attraction continued to grow and deepen within me—an alluring fascination with his dark side. Knowing he lived on the edge, as both judge and executioner of his victims, I should have been shrinking away from Death instead of gravitating closer to him.

Twenty minutes later, I pressed the doorbell to my parents' home and then gently pushed open the door. The comforting aroma of freshly baked pumpkin bread enveloped the air, bringing an instant smile to my face. I placed my purse on the familiar coat rack and slipped my phone into the back pocket of my jeans. Locking the bolt behind me, a wave of nostalgia and security washed over me.

Over the years, my parents had renovated each room. The dark, polished hardwood floors gleamed beneath my feet, perfectly set against the warm tan walls. They were adorned with family photos, each frame capturing a moment, a memory, a shared adventure of our family's journey together.

I followed the sounds from the kitchen, my tummy growling in anticipation of Mom's baked goodies.

"Hey," I said, entering the room and smiling at the woman covered in flour.

Mom wiped her hands on her once-black apron decorated with tiny apples, then warmly embraced me.

"Hi, honey. I'm stress baking." She stirred the mixture in the stainless-steel bowl and glanced at me.

"Is it helping?" I leaned against the tan granite counter, staying out of her way as she continued to whip up a batch.

Mom turned to me and wiped her forehead with the back of her hand. "Nothing helps, but you know that." Her voice broke with the weight of the situation. "I'm losing the love of my life, and you're losing your father." Tears welled in her eyes, and her shoulders sagged.

"Mom, it's why I wanted to see both of you today. Is he awake?"

Confusion clouded her expression as she walked over to the kitchen table and peered at the camera that she'd set up to watch Dad when she wasn't in the same room as him.

"I think so, but maybe tell me what's going on first?"

"Sure, but it's nothing bad, so don't worry. It might actually be an answer we've been searching for." I offered her a sincere smile. "A few days ago, a friend told me that he has access to a new clinical trial that's in its testing phase. It's not even available yet, but the success is astronomical. There are also some political and financial issues going on behind the scenes, slowing the process of the treatment, but it's doing really well with minimal side effects."

Mom stilled, staring at me. "Are you saying that your friend can get your father in?"

"Yeah. He gave me the doctor's name, and I reached out to him on Monday, but it took him a few days to get back to me. We had a nice chat. I told him all about Dad and what he'd been through. Dr.

Magna said if we can get him to California, then he can work with him. He thinks Dad has a good chance of beating the cancer, Mom."

To my surprise, she burst into tears, her thin body shaking with her sobs.

"This is wonderful news. Why are you crying?" I strode across the kitchen and wrapped her in my arms.

"I'm scared to hope. We've tried so many things, pumpkin."

"I know. It's been a messed up emotional roller coaster. We see some hope, then the rug is jerked out from beneath us again. I have a good feeling about it this time. We just need to get him on board."

She broke our embrace and wiped the moisture from her face. "If you think this will give him a chance to live, then if I have to, I'll knock him out and throw him in the car."

Unable to suppress my laughter, I hugged her again. "I would love to be involved with a kidnapping." If she only knew I was an accomplice to so much more.

"Are you at a place to take a break from baking so we can talk to Dad together?"

She glanced at the ingredients that were scattered across the kitchen island. "Yeah, now is good, then I'll finish this batch of banana bread. I promised Cami that I would make some pumpkin muffins for her too. She's been such a sweetheart, stopping by several times a week. I'll give your dad a pot brownie while we have fresh muffins and milk." She cracked a grin at me. "Never in my lifetime did I think I would be happy about getting your father high, but here we are."

"If things go well, it won't be for much longer. Let's stay as positive as possible for him. You and I can talk in private and say anything that we need to."

Mom took a deep breath. "Can you tell your friend that we want to accept his offer?"

"Of course. I'll let you know when I talk to him, and we can plan for you to take time off work and stay in Mount Shasta, California. We'll figure out the money." My stomach churned at the idea of having to work online again, but then Death's words tapped me on the head. No one else was viewing them. He had put a stop to that.

Shit! I would have to think of another way to cover the medical costs. Inwardly I shuddered. I was still paying off Dad's other bills. It was time to see if I had enough equity in my home. If so, maybe it would be enough to cover the trial. I would do anything to save his life.

EXHAUSTED, I LET MYSELF INTO MY HOUSE AND SET THE ALARM. I wasn't sure why I bothered anymore—nothing would keep Death out when he wanted to see me.

After tossing my handbag on the couch, I walked to the kitchen and poured myself a whiskey and Coke. The rest of the afternoon had gone well, and Dad seemed hopeful about the trial. Since he had nothing to lose, it was worth one final shot. As soon as I saw Death, I would make the arrangements.

I sank into the sofa and rubbed my temples as I attempted to sort through my feelings.

"I'm so fucked up," I muttered. "I'm falling for a serial killer, and I have no clue who he is." Or did I? When I was cuffed to my bed and Death talked, something about his mannerisms piqued my interest. Unfortunately, as soon as the thought popped into my head, it was gone again.

My phone chimed in my purse, and I rummaged around until I retrieved it from the bottom. The screen announced a call from "unknown," but I had a sneaking suspicion I knew who it was.

"Hello?"

"Hey, it's Sebastian. Is this a bad time?"

My chest warmed at his voice.

"No. I just got back from my parents and settled in on the couch with a drink. How are you? When are you coming home?"

His sigh traveled over the line. "Tired. More so than normal, but this particular job was more difficult than expected. It's taken a lot out of me, and we have another one before I can come back to Portland."

"Why was it harder?" I chewed on my bottom lip, knowing better than to ask. "I'm sorry. I understand you can't give any details, but can I help in any way?" I sipped my drink, the bubbles from the soda tickling my nose.

"Simply hearing your voice is helping." His tone held such warmth and vulnerability that a wave of longing washed over me.

Everything inside me responded, and I was overwhelmed by the need to be with him. How could I be torn between two men?

"Sebastian," I began gently, "We're still getting to know each other, but I can't help but feel there's something else on your mind. I can't imagine how hard your work is. Seeing what you see can mentally wear you down. I just want you to know that I'm here if you need to talk."

The seconds ticked by as a heavy silence fell between us.

"I'm starting to think that this life isn't for me anymore, Ella. I'm gone all the time, and it's dangerous. I don't mind because I'm helping women and kids, but ... I'm considering handing things off to Dope and a few others. I can still fund the projects but work more in the background versus in the field."

My brows arched with his confession, and I wondered what was driving the change. "Have you been thinking about this for a while?"

"Off and on, but I won't lie. I miss you, Ella. I feel like I'm missing out on spending time with you, and I'm not liking it very much. I've not felt that way about anyone before. Not like this."

Belonging engulfed me like a blanket, its warmth threatening to swallow me whole as I grappled with the realization that I cared deeply about both Death and Sebastian. I doubted my feelings for Sebastian would disappear just because I found myself seamlessly drawn to both, caught in their magnetic pull of good and evil.

"Really?" I chewed on my bottom lip, loving the sound of seeing him more often.

"Yeah. It's different for me. I'm forty, I've dated, but I haven't ever felt like there was a possibility of settling down with anyone until recently. I'm not saying let's run off and get married or anything crazy, just that I would like to spend my time differently ... and with you."

Closing my eyes, I allowed my thoughts to soar with the idea of dinners, long walks, movie marathons while wrapped in Sebastian's strong arms, and lazy afternoons. I missed him, and I couldn't wait for him to come home.

"Sebastian, I would love to see you more, but I can't be the reason that you step down from the work you're doing. The world needs you."

"And *I* need time with you. I can still do a lot of good work behind the scenes."

Responding to his blunt honesty, I fought the urge to tell him I needed him too. Losing myself in the moment, I sucked in a deep breath as my pulse pounded against my wrist.

"Since I've met you, Ella, I look forward to seeing you when you visit the bar. You've given me a new perspective, and I'm interested in seeing what could happen between us."

My heart and mind played tug of war as I weighed out my developing feelings for Sebastian and Death—two completely different men. One fed my darkness. The other fed the light. Inwardly, I groaned. I was in bigger trouble than I realized.

"I'd like that too. And I've missed you more than I thought was possible. At least you were able to call."

"Good, I'm glad you're wanting the same thing. I'll call as soon as I can. As far as I'm concerned, burner phones are a gift from the heavens. I'll use one to call you, then stomp on it and throw it away. I know you can't reach me, Ella, but if you need anything, go see Kip at the bar. He stayed behind this time. Besides, I don't trust that Stephen won't show up. It's making me uncomfortable."

I didn't miss the edge in his tone, but I wasn't sure if it had something to do with Kip or Stephen since he didn't elaborate.

"I've not seen Stephen, but I'll keep it in mind. Thank you."

Liar!

"I have to go. Be a good girl for me."

My shoulders slouched. I'd been anything but his good girl. I'd fucked a serial killer, among a laundry list of other things. "Please be safe."

"I will. Later."

I tapped the red button on the screen and ended the call. My heart melted into a puddle on the floor in response to Sebastian's concern for me. He had every right, but he wasn't overbearing or crowding me. He seemed like the type of man that would be protective, but at the same time gave me space.

Anger stirred to life inside me. How had I gotten so sucked into Death's grip? There was no way I wanted to drag Sebastian into the middle of my mess. At the same time, I couldn't walk away from him. He was a good guy with a side of bad boy, and that was sexy as hell. We had potential together, and I wanted to go out with him again. My relationship with Death was toxic at its best. He'd sucked me into his sick, fucked-up world without a second thought. There was no remorse for his actions, and I wasn't a real person to him. I was just a doll he could manipulate in his world. Yeah, I liked parts of it ... a lot. The sex was out of this world, and there was a part of me that loved being degraded. But we would always be on the run. I wanted more in life than to constantly look over my shoulder.

Sebastian could offer everything I'd dreamed of—a deep connection, lazy afternoons in each other's arms, traveling, and so much more. I couldn't wait for him to get home, so we could spend more time together.

Reality snapped me out of my brain fog, and my body stiffened. I set my drink on the glass coffee table and jumped off the couch. It was time to do some digging and find out who was beneath the mask and rid him from my life once and for all.

Chapter 25

Death

"Wolves know when to be silent, lambs do not, and in that silence, the wilderness listens." ~ Anonymous

The last several days had been hell without seeing my little lamb, but I had work to do. My next victim was in Washington state, close to the Canadian border. The son of a bitch had struck close to home, and my revenge was personal. My mission should have coated me with the rich velvet of satisfaction, but all I could think about was the unbearable loneliness that awaited me afterward.

I stood near the property's tree line, my black clothes and grim reaper mask blending effortlessly into the darkness. John Bordeaux sat in his living room, the light of the television casting an ominous glow over him. His tumbler full of his favorite bourbon was within reach as he relaxed in his tan leather recliner, wearing only his boxers and white tank. The disgusting bastard was utterly oblivious to the fact that I was watching.

Movement on his TV caught my attention, and I moved through the trees for a closer look. A girl appeared on the screen, then another, and another. Each was young, and their heads hung down. They all wore the same thin, drab dresses that reached from their neck to their bare feet. He paused the video, his expression twisting into one of pleasure as his hand disappeared inside his boxers. I hoped he enjoyed his orgasm because it would be his last.

Without a sound, I slipped into his house and left the back door cracked just in case I hadn't anticipated the unexpected and needed to haul ass out of there.

Luckily for me, but not so much for John, he had traveled extensively searching for the next girl he wanted to buy, which made it easy for me to spend time inside the house and install some fun gadgets.

I shoved a hand in my jacket pocket and pressed a button on the small remote control. The long, navy curtains began to close.

"What the hell?" He shot out of the chair, staring as the heavy drapes completely concealed the floor-to-ceiling windows.

He had gotten cocky, thinking no one could see his activities since thick woodlands surrounded his house. What he hadn't counted on was me having had eyes on him for over a year. This particular kill would be worth the wait, but I had so much more in store for him than my other victims.

I pushed another button on the remote, and the television turned off and on multiple times.

Over the next several minutes, I continued to fuck with his head, playing with his recliner and lights as he grew more and more frantic.

Terror registered on John's face as he stilled.

"Hello? I know someone is here. Show yourself."

Maybe he wasn't as stupid as he looked, since he realized I was inside his home, but I doubted it. The son of a bitch was shopping for little girls in the middle of his living room with the curtains open. That shit got you ... killed.

With a click of a button, I turned off all the gadgets' illuminating lights, and pitch-black darkness replaced them.

"Who are you?" He asked, his voice hoarse and barely hovering above a whisper.

Silent as a ghost, I stalked toward him, the sound of my pulse thundering in my ears. Adrenaline surged through my veins like a drug as I imagined his lifeless body splayed out on a table, blood spilling from his wounds and pooling on the floor beneath him.

The familiar itch under my skin returned tenfold as I drew closer behind him, and a burning sensation of power licked through me. I flexed my gloved fingers before I wrapped my hand around his throat, cutting off his air supply. I wanted the bastard to beg for his life.

"Welcome to your worst nightmare, John. Let me introduce myself." I leaned close to his right ear. "I'm Death."

He clawed at my arm in a futile attempt, but it was useless. Over the years, I had built extraordinary strength in my fingers. His pulse throbbed against my thumb as I reached into my jacket pocket with my free hand and located the needle. I pulled off the cap with my teeth and jabbed it into the side of his neck. Within seconds, he dropped to the floor with a hard thud, completely unconscious.

I scowled in hatred as I drove my booted foot into his side, feeling the sickening crunch of his ribs breaking. With a smirk, I grabbed his right leg and wrenched it sideways, hearing it snap at its joints. Then I brought down my boot with force onto his knee, crushing bone and cartilage with an audible crack. If I hadn't just shattered it, I would soon. If the motherfucker woke up, he had zero chance of running now.

Clenching my jaw shut in a victorious sneer, I double checked that he was truly out cold before I moved through the house.

I grasped my trusty mini flashlight in one hand as I used the other to methodically rip out the overhead lights and tiny cameras that I'd planted in each room to track John with minimal effort. All the while, I stayed alert for any sudden movements from him.

A soft scuffling pulled my attention away from the current task, and I stilled, listening intently. *What the fuck?*

I hurried toward the noise and to his bedroom. As I approached his closet, the sound grew louder.

"Son of a fucking bitch. Either he has giant rats, or ..." I pushed the hanging clothes to the side and used my flashlight to search the wall.

I clenched the light between my teeth and pulled my knife out of the sheath attached to my calf. My gaze narrowed on the thin crack in the white plaster, barely noticeable to the untrained eye. It was still wide enough to fit my blade, and I pried the makeshift door open with a creak. That son of a bitch had gone to great lengths to keep it hidden.

Slowly, I moved the section of the wall and shined my light through the darkness, my knife ready to slice and dice anything that might jump out. My teeth gritted as I focused on the nightmare before me.

"Don't hurt us." A dirty, skinny young girl crawled in front of another one, shielding her.

A seething anger boiled up within me, threatening to consume my entire body. My fists clenched as I thought of that despicable man enslaving girls in his home. I would take pleasure in tearing him apart piece by piece.

I removed the flashlight from my mouth so I could speak. "I won't hurt you. Come out." My voice startled them, but they would be okay. I stepped to the side while they obeyed and crawled out of the hole and into the closet.

"How did you get here?" I asked.

They hurried to their feet, and the older one grabbed the younger one's hand. "I don't know. One minute, I was hanging out at a park with my friends. I went to the bathroom and don't remember anything after that."

The youngest nodded, her stringy hair falling into her face. "I was walking home from school when a car pulled up and took me."

I didn't have to ask if he'd hurt them. They were too skinny, dirty, and terrified for me to assume differently.

"Get on the bed."

Tears flowed down the older one's cheeks. "Please, don't hurt us."

"I won't. I don't like young girls." But I did love torturing sick motherfuckers, and this one was going to pay not only for what he'd done to these girls but ...

They moved on wobbly legs, their dresses barely long enough to cover their butts.

"Get under the covers and warm up." I opened John's nightstand and found the television remote control. Turning it on, I located a kid's movie on some channel. It had just started, which would buy me an hour and a half.

"When this show is over, use that phone and call 9-1-1. Understand? Not before. Do not leave this room until the police arrive."

The younger girl snuggled up to her friend. "You're letting us go?"

"Yeah, but you must follow the rules to stay safe." And me too. If they reached out for help too soon, I would be fucked.

"We will. And mister?"

"What?"

"Thank you."

I grunted at them before I hurried out of the room. My time frame had just been cut in half, and I still had to move the bastard to my car parked up the road. At least the piece of shit wasn't a fat fuck, and I could throw him over my shoulder and carry him for a while.

After I ensured that I hadn't left any traces in the house, I stood near John and took a deep breath, allowing the darkness inside to completely consume every part of my twisted being.

Chapter 26

Ella

Realizing I hadn't checked the mail in several days, I grabbed the stack from the box and tossed them on the hallway table. The logo for the medical company peeked out from the rest, and I groaned. I didn't want to deal with bills today. It wasn't due for a few more weeks anyway, it could wait. I was too exhausted after mulling over a difficult case at work and spending the evening with my parents. I had promised to help Mom prepare to leave for California.

Plus, a part of me was on edge, anticipating Death's arrival at my house at any moment. Eight nights had passed since he'd last appeared, and though I wanted to believe that maybe he had lost interest in me, deep down, I knew better. He would be back soon enough.

"My Strange Addiction" by RAYNE played while I drove to the club to meet my best friend. I started laughing at the irony that my strange addiction was twisted and warped. I supposed I should be grateful I hadn't totally fallen off the edge of sanity and had some normal feelings toward a great guy and not just a serial killer.

Minutes later, I parked behind the Velvet Vortex and messaged

Cami that I would meet her inside and grab a table. Climbing out, I closed the door and locked it. As I hurried toward the entrance, the soles of my black ankle boots scraped across the asphalt.

My heart sank as I realized that Sebastian wouldn't be there, but a part of me hoped he would show up and surprise me. It was funny how much I'd changed since my date with Sebastian. I wasn't the same shy, awkward woman unsure of how to flirt and constantly second guessing myself. I wasn't sure when the shift had occurred, but I was stronger, more resilient, and self-assured.

The warmth of Sebastian's kiss before he left still lingered on my skin, but his words echoed around me like a whispering ghost. I wanted to be his good girl, but I was petrified of what would happen if he learned the truth. Fear knotted my stomach whenever I thought about the possibility, and it made me question my decisions.

The sound of laughter snapped me out of my reverie, and I followed a group of people inside. As I wove through the chattering crowd and scanned the room, I looked for Kip. I could at least say hello.

"Guilty" by Bobi Andonov played through the speakers as I climbed up on a barstool. I searched the bar but only spotted a female.

"Hey, what can I get you?"

I glanced at her name tag and realized this was the Riley Sebastian had mentioned. "I'm not sure. It's been a long day, so I'm trying to decide what sounds good." Although I'd seen Riley behind the bar the first evening I met Sebastian, I hadn't had a chance to say hello.

She flashed me a wide smile. "I've seen you here before with your female friend, right?"

"Yeah, Cami. She's meeting me in a few minutes."

She grabbed a glass and made a drink, then set it in front of the guy four chairs down. "Aren't you friends with Bass too?"

Her tone was warm and friendly, and I tried to still my bouncing knee, wondering if she would like me. I hoped so. If she worked here, I suspected she was important to Sebastian. "I'm Ella."

"Ah, he talks about you a lot." Her smile widened.

Happily surprised that he'd at least mentioned me in passing, I nodded.

"It's nice to officially meet you."

I leaned on the counter. "You too."

She tossed a white towel over her shoulder and drew closer to me. "In the years I've known Bass, I've never seen him strung out over a girl before. A lot of women have tried, but no luck. It's nice to see that he's finally interested in someone." She flashed me a grin.

I willed my cheeks not to flush, but they just gave me a big fuck you.

Riley laughed. "Drinks are on the house, by the way. Bass made it clear you don't pay for anything here."

My forehead scrunched. "No, that's okay. I can take care of myself."

"Sorry. If Bass finds out, he'll have my head on a platter, and that's not a good look for me."

"Fine, then I'll tip you really well." I placed my hands on the counter and pondered what I wanted, but my usual was all that sounded appealing.

"Deal."

"Jack and Coke," a voice said beside me.

I turned to Cami as she claimed the seat next to me. "That's her drink of choice." She pointed to me. "I'll have a Long Island iced tea."

"Coming right up." Riley went to work as I turned to my bestie.

"Hey, glad you could make it." I gave her a quick hug. Cami was stunning in her dark wash jeans that hugged every curve of her body, and the slender straps of her plum-colored top revealed her graceful shoulders. As I pulled away, she flipped her long hair back and smiled, her posture relaxing.

"Me too. Being with sick people at the hospital drained me." She folded her hands on her lap and gave me her undivided attention. "You look hot as hell in that form-fitting black dress with your legs for days. I've never seen you wear it before. Shit, you even curled your hair." Her gaze narrowed on me. "If Sebastian were in town, I would think you were getting laid. You have a ..." Her hand fluttered in front of me. "Glow."

Dammit. "It's been in my closet. I just haven't worn it yet. With everything going on, I haven't been myself lately, and I wanted to look nice."

Cami leaned closer. "Do not wear that at work with a bunch of criminals in and out of that office, Ella. Don't tempt the devil."

I grinned at her, appreciating that she was so protective of me, but I'd already tempted the devil.

"I won't. This isn't professional attire, anyway. It's pencil skirts paired with blouses up to my neck or suits."

Riley set our drinks in front of us before she hurried to the opposite end of the bar to take care of another customer.

"Yeah, stuffy clothes. You're definitely not stuffy. You've always enjoyed dancing on the edge of trouble. It's only been after college graduation that you reeled it in."

"I had to. It's not like I could do a good job and start a serious career while drinking, fucking all the bad boys, and sleeping all day." A touch of a smile graced my lips before I took a drink of my Jack and Coke.

Her brow arched. "You miss it, don't you? I can tell. Not the drinking and sleeping all day, but the assholes who treated you like shit."

"Why would you say something like that? I mean, Sebastian is a great guy."

She gave me a half-shrug and chewed on her straw before she stirred her drink. "Just a gut feeling." Cami grinned at me. "But maybe Sebastian will tame the beast inside you."

The corner of my mouth twitched. Cami's words struck home harder than she realized, but I couldn't tell her about Death and my pull to him. He was my twisted, dark secret ... Maybe forever.

Ready to change the topic, I asked, "How's your hot cop? Has he visited you at work lately?"

She scrunched her nose and grinned. "His name is Ryan, and he asked me out today."

"What? Why didn't you lead with that?" I playfully smacked her on the shoulder. "Now who's holding out?"

Cami laughed. "I've only been here for ten minutes."

"Well, are you going out with him?" Acid churned in my stomach as I realized she might date a cop. What if he suspected something about Sebastian and me, or I let something slip about Death?

"Yeah. Tomorrow night after we're both off work. I'll hurry home, shower, and get ready, then he'll pick me up. He's going to take me out for dinner."

"I hope he takes you somewhere nice. You deserve to be pampered."

"Actually, I don't know where he's taking me, but I'm looking forward to spending time with him outside of the hospital."

"If nothing else, dine and ride." I winked at her.

"Oh, I plan to ride just to test his stick shift out. It's been *way* too long."

I can't say the same. "Me too." My pulse kicked up a notch. I hated lying to my best friend. If I was going to continue to live a double life, though, it was a fact that I would have to adjust to.

Cami groaned before she fished out her phone and looked at the screen. "Dammit. I just got a text from work. They called me back to the hospital."

"What? Do you have to go?" I asked, disappointment clear in my tone. "You just got here."

She slid off her seat and pushed her Long Island iced tea at me. "Either drink it or toss it. Just don't drive drunk." Cami leaned over and kissed my cheek. "Love ya, bitch."

"You too. Be safe."

Cami waved goodbye as she made her way to the front of the club, and I blew out a heavy sigh. My thoughts raced as I secretly hoped that Cami found someone else other than a police officer. The idea of spending time with her and a cop boyfriend sounded like an absolute nightmare. Sebastian and I would be walking on eggshells, watching every word that came out of our mouth. I reined my thoughts back in. If her relationship progressed, I would deal with the complications then.

"Did she leave?" Riley asked, nodding at Cami's drink.

"Yeah. She's a nurse and she got called back to the ER."

"Do you want her drink?"

"No. I'm good, thanks for asking."

Riley picked up the glass and tossed the contents into the sink before she loaded it onto a rack to be washed.

"Is Kip working tonight?"

Riley nodded. "He'll be in soon. We both close since it's Friday."

"Well, tell him I said hi." I ordered some fries to go and finished my Jack and Coke while they cooked. I tapped my fingers on the counter, realizing I had time alone. When my order was ready, I told Riley good night and hurried to the parking lot. I needed to head to the office.

The bosses worked from home most weekends, so I would have some privacy. Since I had a key, I could do a little research and dig into some client files. Not only did I want to know who Death was behind the mask, but there was also something about him that tickled my brain, and I couldn't figure it out for the life of me.

As I drove, I munched on a few fries and sifted through potential men who had been to the firm in the last twelve months. Three stuck out in my mind, and one in particular. I needed to see his file again since it had been a year.

Ten minutes later, I steered the car down the dark alley next to the office and parked behind the building. The moon was full, lighting my path as I hopped out, locked the doors, and hurried to the steps leading to the building. Although it was a nice neighborhood, I didn't like to make a habit of running around at night alone.

Once I unlocked and locked the front door, I walked to my desk. I flipped on the light and then settled in. Spotting a sticky note on the bottom of my monitor, I swore under my breath. I'd almost forgotten to pay my dad's medical bill.

Powering on the computer, it whirred to life, breaking the silence in the room. I opened a browser, logged into the website, and clicked the pay my bill option.

"Huh? A zero balance? That can't be right. Their system must be down."

I searched around, but all the other online options seemed fine. Suspicion tiptoed through my mind, leaving chills in its wake. Death had arranged Dad's trial for me. He'd also admitted that he was my only income on the adult website. Had he paid the bill?

I heaved a sigh, my mind racing as I tried to piece together who the hell he was. I shot up, sending my chair rolling to the side of the small room as I grabbed my cell and hurried to the locked filing cabinets in the library. Since our clients were criminals, my bosses left nothing to chance, including any of them snooping around where they shouldn't. Everything was locked down and hidden.

After my first year working for Barnaby and Smooch, I was trusted with the knowledge of where the safe was located and how to access it. I placed my phone on top of the cabinet, then located a key that was nestled in a combination safe behind a scenic picture of the ocean. I opened the first drawer and thumbed through the folders.

"Gotcha."

Next, I pulled files on two other men, gathered them along with my cell, and returned to my desk.

Carefully, I cracked open the first one, my heart racing as I read over Barnaby and Smooch's notes. It seemed that my notorious criminal attorney bosses were on retainer for some of the city's most wealthy and powerful individuals, all accused or involved in shady money laundering and fraud schemes. Sweat beaded on my forehead as I focused on the name on the third file. Fear wrapped its icy fingers around my throat as I slowly opened the last one and flipped through the pages.

I gawked in disbelief. Every damn piece of paper was blank. A corner of something caught my curiosity, and I located where it had stuck to another sheet. I peeled the photo away from the page, and my mouth hung open as I stared at it in dismay, confirming the name that I saw was accurate. "Son of a fucking bitch." I double checked the information, not believing my eyes. "How in the hell does this all fit together?"

Chapter 27

Death

"A wise lamb knows when to bleat and when to silently walk, just as a wise wolf knows when to hunt and when to watch." ~ *Anonymous*

The light inside Barnaby and Smooch's office was barely visible as I crept up to the side of the building and peered into the window. There she was, my beautiful little lamb with her nose where it didn't belong. If she dug too deep, she would connect me with people she already knew, and that couldn't happen. Not to mention, whoever thought of hiding a key behind a picture should be—killed.

After a long day of relocating John to an abandoned warehouse in the middle of fucking nowhere, I hammered railroad spikes into his feet, anchoring him to the floor. The sound of his agonizing screams bounced off the walls, and my dick got so hard I thought I was going to cum. I needed to ravage my little lamb until she screamed and drained my dick dry with her tight cunt. I eagerly made the eight-hour drive to see her.

To my disappointment, Ella wasn't where she should've been … at home waiting for me. Not only had I placed a tracker on her car, but I'd also bugged her phone and camera. I heard what she said—saw what she saw.

When I realized she was at the office digging through files in a futile attempt to discover my identity, rage churned in my stomach like a violent storm at sea. She had crossed a line, and she would be punished. I gripped the handle of my knife, my knuckles turning white as the blinding anger boiled in the pit of my stomach, giving birth to the dark thoughts that swirled in my mind. Ella would regret the moment she decided to dig deeper. I submitted to the all-consuming need to destroy and teetered on the brink of madness as every cell in my being burned to make her bleed.

"Oh, little lamb, you should be afraid," I whispered.

The front door opened, and Ella walked down the stairs and side-walk, looking completely fuckable in her tight dress and black heels. I counted her steps as she rounded the corner of the building where her Camry was parked. One, two, three ... as soon as her back was to me, I slipped up from behind and slapped my gloved hand over her mouth. She froze, her breathing quickening as I held her against my body. The curve of her ass pressed against my hard shaft, and I growled.

"I see you've been busy while I've been gone."

Her shoulders slumped when she recognized my voice—another mistake.

"Little lamb, you should know better than to relax in the presence of a wolf." I forced her to walk to her car. "Hand me your car key, and then drop your purse and files on the ground."

She handed me the key fob, and I unlocked the doors before shoving it into my front pocket. The clatter of her items hitting the asphalt rang through the parking lot as she trembled, her fear so thick in the air I could fucking taste it.

I ran the sharp tip of the blade between her breasts and down her stomach, splitting the fabric of her dress in two. With quick movements, I slipped the material off each shoulder and laughed as it fell to the ground. Ella trembled as she stood in her bra and panties.

"Are you scared, little lamb?" I ran my tongue along her jaw and pressed the knife against her neck. "At some point, you forgot who you bow to. Now ..." A dark chuckle rumbled through my chest. "Take off your heels."

She slid them off, her bare feet touching the asphalt of the parking lot.

"Listen closely, Ella. I'll only say this once." My voice was clipped, cold—deadly. "You should have never gone snooping around in those files. I thought I could trust you, but now it's time to experience the consequences. This time, it's not Stephen being led to the slaughter."

Her body shook violently as she sniffled, and I realized she was crying.

"See the woods? You're going to run into them, and if I catch you ..." I laughed, allowing her imagination to take over with what I had planned for her. "I'll give you a head start, but if you scream, I'll make sure that you'll never be able to speak again. I'll carve your tongue out just like I carved out Stephen's heart." I ran the side of the blade down her throat. "Run as fast as you can, little lamb. This wolf is about to hunt you down and devour you," I whispered against her ear.

I lowered the knife, pushed her, and sneered as she stumbled forward.

Ella glanced over her shoulder as I ran my tongue along my blade. "Run," I growled, stalking toward her. The fear in her eyes ignited a raging fire of lust inside me, one that demanded I possess her until she completely submitted to my will.

"One, two, I'm coming for you," I chanted. "Three, four, kneel on the floor. Five, six, I'm up to my old tricks. Seven, eight, lay in wait. Nine, ten, never to be seen again."

Ella knew she could never outrun me, so she would have to resort to the only thing she had left—hiding behind the trees and trying to avoid her impending fate as I hunted her. But Ella was no fool. Deep down, she understood that no matter where she tried to hide, there was no escape from me.

Slipping my blade into the sheath attached to my calf, I narrowed my eyes as I watched her arms furiously pump at her sides while her bare feet flew across the parking lot pavement and into the adjacent woods. I tracked her with a primal hunger, mesmerized by the grace of her movements. It had been a while since I'd chased my prey. When I caught Ella, I would destroy her. I wanted to mold her into a queen who would rule by my side, but only if she surrendered fully to my will.

I jogged into the darkness, allowing her time to suffer the thick underbrush that tore at her feet. I savored the thrill of the chase, listening eagerly for the slightest hint of where she was hiding. A twisted grin crossed my face as I slowed and entered the trees, practically tasting my victory.

Ella's fear was so thick that it hung in the air like mist. "I smell your desperation, Ella. It's so strong I can taste it." I fed off the scent of her terror, and when I got her beneath me, begging and pleading for me not to hurt her, I would strip her courage and need to learn the truth about who I really was. She would beg me to spare her life as I watched the light in them flicker away.

A cry reached my ears, and I quickly pinpointed her location. The crunch of leaves under her feet led me toward her.

"You're making this too easy, Ella. I thought you would be more of a challenge." I stumbled over a decaying trunk and took a sharp left, catching the briefest glimpse of her in the faint moonlight. I wanted to speed up my search, but at the same time, I didn't want the fun to end too quickly. Adrenaline raced through me as I held back my wild laughter. I had her in my sight, crouching behind a large tree.

Her eyes widened as soon as she saw me, and terror fueled her feet in the opposite direction. Primal instinct urged me forward, and despite her best efforts, I was relentless and managed to snag her arm. Yanking her off balance and flinging her to the ground, I laughed as she landed with a thud and the air left her lungs in an agonizing gasp.

Jerking her up on her feet, I shoved her against an oak tree. Terror

"I'm sorry. Forgive me," she said, choking on her tears. "I won't try to find out who you are anymore."

"That's my good little bitch." The bitter taste of forgiveness lingered on my tongue like a forgotten poison, burning through my senses and memories. Its sourness clung to me, leaving its mark as an ever-present reminder of what she'd done.

"You pretend to be a good girl, but I know the truth. You're nothing but a hungry slut for my cock and the dark fantasies that only I can deliver."

She whimpered her response.

My balls tightened as I slammed into her. I reached for her neck and wrapped my fingers around her throat, squeezing as I exploded deep inside.

She scratched at my gloved hands, fighting for air.

I leaned forward, my cock driving deeper inside her one more time before I pulled out and stood.

I secured myself in my pants before I scooped her up in my arms and carried her out of the woods. Carefully, I opened the car door and set her limp body in the backseat. I collected her belongings off the ground and set them on the floorboard before I covered her with the blanket that I'd located in her trunk.

Chapter 28

Death

"The lamb must learn to live with the wolf, but never trust him." ~
Anonymous

My little lamb remained quiet on the drive home, and I trusted she'd learned her lesson. Once we'd arrived, I carried her to the bathroom, where I turned on the water in her bathtub. She stood before me, scratched and bloody from running through the woods in the dark. I gently removed the sticks and leaves from her hair, then brushed it through. I wondered if she knew how close I'd come to killing her. But something had held me back, and as hard as I tried, my feelings for her had overrun my dark thirst to hurt her.

Tracing my fingers down her neck, I removed the blanket from her shoulders. She stood obediently, allowing me to touch her.

"Little lamb, if you'll embrace your destiny by my side, I can give you things you've never dreamed of. Stop fighting me. In due time, I'll reveal myself to you, but not yet." I placed a gentle kiss on her shoulder.

"Why won't you tell me who you are?" Her voice cracked, heavy with exhaustion as she spoke.

I tested the temperature of her bath. Satisfied with the result, I turned off the water.

"Get in."

Ella took my extended hand. She dipped a toe into the bath, wincing from the sting of her lacerations before she got in. Once she was as comfortable as possible, I knelt beside the tub.

"Get your hair wet."

She stared at me, probably wondering if I was going to drown her. Ella tipped her chin up, held her nose, then submerged her head. She popped back up and wiped the water from her tired face.

Pouring some of her peach and vanilla shampoo into my palm, I lathered her long strands. My fingers worked into her scalp, massaging away the pain I'd inflicted only an hour ago.

She moaned, and her eyes fluttered closed as I continued.

"I will destroy you, then piece you back together to match me, little lamb."

Her gaze landed on mine, her breasts moving with each breath.

"Rinse off," I ordered.

Once the soap was gone, I applied the conditioner.

Over the next several minutes, I lathered her body, massaging her shoulders and caring for my queen. She had learned a hard lesson but earned her reward when she promised to stop digging into my identity.

After she was clean and her hair was rinsed, I pulled the stopper and drained the water. I collected the large, plush brown bath towel that was hanging on the towel rack and carefully wrapped her in it. I picked her up and carried her to bed. Sitting down on the edge, I pulled her into my arms.

She grabbed the front of my shirt and then slowly peered into my eyes. At times I hated the damn mask, but it was a necessity. It was a barrier between us, and just like her will, it would soon be stripped away.

199

"Why does a part of me like everything that you do?"

I forcefully gripped her chin, narrowing my gaze at her. "You know why you feel like this? Because a part of you knows that you and I are the same. We have both danced in the darkness, and now we are forever intertwined."

Her mouth opened to refute me, but I cut her off. "No more lies. I killed for you in your own home, yet you never contacted the police or turned me in. What does that say?"

My lips curved in a hungry smirk as I pressed my forehead against hers. "Let me remind you: You've already had this conversation with me before, and now you want to deny it all. Not anymore. Tell me, Ella—what did they do to make you like this?"

Fear flashed across her features before she could hide it behind a stoic expression. Her jaw clenched as she fought the tears that rolled down her cheeks. "How do you know?"

Bringing my mouth close to hers, I felt the warmth of her breath on my skin as I whispered, "You have no secrets from me, Ella. It's time for you to embrace who you really are. Confess your shame out loud and accept it."

Still shaking her head frantically, she managed to choke out three words between sobs. "I-I can't."

My grin widened into a predatory smile as I moved closer until our mouths almost touched. "Say it, Ella. Give me your darkest secret. I can give you whatever you desire. All that stands between us is voicing the truth and embracing it completely. What did they do to you, little lamb?"

Instead of turning away, she buried her face in my neck, her tears marking my skin with her pain. I rubbed her bare back.

"Who were they?"

A deafening silence filled the room while I waited for her to speak.

"A family friend."

Shivers racked her body, and I moved her wet hair from her shoulder.

"How did it start?" I wrapped my arms around her, protecting her from the monsters lurking in her memories.

"He bought a new camera and told my parents that since I was so photogenic, I would be a great study. They'd known him for years and never questioned his intentions. I didn't have a lot of friends since we were new to Portland, so I hung out with him most of the time when my parents were still at work. To them, he was a great babysitter, trustworthy." Her tongue darted over her lower lip before she continued. "When I was alone with him, he dressed me up in frilly outfits and told me how pretty I was."

I rubbed the back of her neck, absorbing her fear and tension in the warmth of my palm.

"It continued for a few months before he ..." She sniffled and swiped at her nose. "He talked me into taking off my shirt. I was eight, so I wasn't developing much yet, but he didn't care. He made me promise that I wouldn't tell anyone, or he would murder my mom and make me watch. By the time I was old enough to understand that he was a pedophile, I was so brainwashed and terrified, I didn't know what to do."

"You're safe now, little lamb." I stroked her hair as if she were still a child but secure with me instead of that sick motherfucker.

"When I was twelve, he started touching me. But I wasn't the only one. He had some other kids a few years younger than me by that time too. He made them watch as he forced me to pose for the camera, how to spread my legs for a better angle." Her voice trailed off. "His threats to kill my mom extended to my dad and our dog. I was terrified that I would do the wrong thing all the time. Finally, something in me snapped when he brought over a little girl who was only seven. I realized that I had to make him stop." She snorted. "If only."

I watched as she struggled to take an even breath.

"One day, he left us unattended for a few minutes while he took a phone call upstairs in his house. I stole one of the VCR tapes that he'd used. All of the kids were on it. I slipped it into my backpack before I replaced it with a different one in the recorder. I wasn't sure how often he checked them, but I only needed a few hours to do what I had planned. After we were finished that day, I walked the little girl home, scared to go to my house in case he found out what I'd done. It was getting dark early, so I took a back way to the police station a few blocks away. When I was close, I scribbled a message on a scrap of paper and told them to watch the video and catch the bad man that was hurting the kids. I never signed my name, just stuck the tape and note into my brown bag I'd used for lunch. It took me forever to work up the nerve to slip into the building undetected and leave the evidence on the receptionist's desk when she'd stepped away."

As she continued to tell me about the horror she lived through, my feral anger festered like an abscess inside my dark soul.

As a sob escaped Ella and more tears rolled down her cheeks, my heart and mind waged a silent war. My little lamb needed peace from her tormented past, and I could grant that. First, though, she had to tell me the rest.

"Was he caught?"

"No." Her nose sounded stuffy from her cries. "He must have seen the cops at his house and ran because no one saw him again."

"What's his name?" My tone was soft. The darkness she'd been battling was too heavy to fight alone any longer.

She bolted upright, her eyes wide with a mix of fear and morbid curiosity. "Are you going to track him down?"

"Give me his name."

She swallowed excessively, the wheels in her head turning as she processed what I was asking.

"I assume that I wasn't the only one, Death. When he left, he most likely found new children to hurt. I've never searched, but I'm sure the videos are all over the dark web."

I stood and placed her on her feet. She grabbed the towel, held it in place, and stared up at me.

"Give me his name," I growled.

In the Shadows

Her chin shook as a rush of emotions flashed across her face. "Are you going to murder him if I do?"

"I will torture him, then kill him slowly as he pleads for forgiveness before I rip his foul soul from his body. Just thinking about what I'll do to him makes me want to cum." It fueled the violent storm that existed inside of me, driving me to rid the world of yet another disgusting monster.

Ella dropped her towel on the floor. My attention traveled from her full breasts, over her stomach, and to her creamy thighs. She reached out and cupped my hard cock through my slacks, massaging me.

As I roughly grabbed her wrist and moved her hand away, shock and rejection pinched her features.

"Name," I demanded, seething.

She opened her mouth, but nothing came out. Seconds ticked by before she finally spoke. "Promise me that you'll make him suffer before you kill him." She closed her eyes as if it could change her past and future if she refused to face it.

"You have my word, little lamb." I would take the weight of the world for Ella. Take her pain and carry it on my shoulders straight to the pits of hell as I sought revenge on those who hurt her.

Her steely gaze found mine. Then his name tumbled off her pretty lips.

Chapter 29

Ella

So many emotions swirled inside me that I couldn't make heads or tails of what I was feeling. After I confessed to Death the name of the person who had hurt me, I wrestled with the fact that I was potentially responsible for a man's murder. At first, I struggled with remorse and guilt, but I quickly got over it. A few hours later, I wasn't suffering with one fucking drop of regret that I gave him up. It was freeing.

The thought of that sick bastard answering for what he'd done to me and the other kids had sent my emotions into overdrive. Yet when Death had sworn revenge, my hormones kicked into high gear, leaving my body wanting him again. I was ready to fuck Death's brains out for taking care of me, but he'd deflected my advances and tucked me into bed. Once I was snuggled beneath the covers, he also crawled in and held me until I fell asleep. Not once did I wake up fearful of who would hurt me next. For the first time since I was young, I felt safe and hopeful that I could shed the shame I'd carried for so many years.

I tossed and turned, my damp sheets sticking to my clammy skin.

Apparently, Death had left sometime in the middle of the night, and my mind started to race with possibilities—where was he now? Was he tracking down the monster? A chill ran through me as I realized that I should have been disturbed by the fact that I was enjoying the thought of Death killing my molester, but instead, I felt a strange connection to Death. Even if I wasn't the one to end someone's life, I was helping direct him toward justice. It should have made me uncomfortable, but my heart beat faster in anticipation.

I placed my bare feet on the area rug, digging my toes into the soft, beige fabric. I stood and stretched, groaning from the previous evening's chase and capture. My body ached and the cuts on the bottom of my feet were tender. My pulse spiked, reliving the chase in my mind. I blew out a heavy sigh as my body trembled with fear all over again. I hadn't ever seen Death so furious. Somewhere in my mind, I suspected I was always safe with him. I was so wrong. In his rage, I'd been terrified Death would snap and kill me, but thank god he wasn't ready to let go of me yet.

I attempted to steady my frayed nerves and focused on the good part—the rough sex had been mind-blowing. He intuitively knew some of my darkest fantasies, playing them out as it served him.

Glancing at my phone on the nightstand, I stared at it, frowning as I saw two missed texts and a call from last night. I tapped the screen, Sebastian's name lighting up.

Sebastian:

> I'll be home in a few days. I can't wait to see you.

SEBASTIAN:

> I'd hoped to talk. Sorry we missed each other.

Not wanting him to panic that Stephen had come after me, I messaged him immediately.

Me:

I'm sorry. I fell asleep early last night. I can't wait to see you too.

I groaned, once again torn in two different directions about the men in my life. A part of me craved Sebastian's gentleness as much as I craved Death's abuse. He could offer me a life, a family, security. I could offer him the same. There was no possible way that I could build a future with Death. I didn't even know what the fucker looked like or who he really was, but more than that, he was unhinged and fucking crazy.

Before making coffee, I threw on a pair of black yoga pants and a grey hoodie. My parents would be stopping by on their way to the airport for their trip to California, and I needed to hide the cuts and bruises on my body. It terrified me to think it might be the last time I saw Dad, but I reminded myself that this trial had done well for the cancer patients who had gone through the treatment already.

My doorbell rang, and I set my coffee mug down and hurried to answer. I opened the door, greeting my mom.

"Hey, thanks for stopping by." I hugged her, wishing I could go with them, but she insisted I stay and keep an eye on their house, water their plants, and leave lights on. She also promised that she would update me every day.

"Of course. I wouldn't leave without you and Dad having a few minutes together first. It will be strange not seeing you all the time. It's been a nice perk since I haven't been traveling." She patted my cheek and offered me a warm smile.

My thoughts drifted to my confession to Death, my heart breaking at the idea of Mom and Dad learning the truth about me. About their friend. To my parents, I could do no wrong, and I think with their love and support, I couldn't stand to disappoint them by falling for a pedophile's lies. As an adult, I understood it wasn't my fault, but it didn't make the feeling go away. It would crush them that one of their closest friends was an evil, twisted man. I'd chosen to carry the burden myself until I'd shared it with Death last night.

Pushing the thoughts aside, I slipped my arm through Mom's as we walked to the car, where Dad was settled into the front seat.

"There's my girl." He offered me a weak smile.

I opened the passenger door and sat on the edge, hugging him. "Hi. Are you ready for your trip? I have faith that this trial is the one, and when it's done, I'll be right here waiting for you." With my head on his chest, I listened to the steady rhythm of his heartbeat, burning this moment into my memory for the rest of my days. Tears pricked my eyes, but I forced them back. I could cry later. I didn't want to waste the few minutes I had with him by sobbing.

"I get to fly in a medical helicopter, Ella. You know I've always wanted to fly in one. Granted not for medical reasons, but hey. Now's my chance." His soft chuckle was music to my ears. "I would have taken another ride in an ambulance but refused since they wouldn't stop by to let me see my girl. Hell, I hate those damn things, anyway. No windows."

"You should have gone in the ambulance, Dad. I could have met you somewhere to say goodbye. They need to monitor your heart constantly and make sure you have the medical attention you need when you're not home. It's why you're flying to California, remember?"

"You know your father. He's determined to do things his way even when it's a stupid idea," Mom said from behind me.

"At least Mom doesn't have to drive and can join you in California in a few hours. Maybe she can rest on her flight."

Dad's brows knitted together. "You think they'd let her on the helicopter with me."

"They don't have enough room, and family typically isn't allowed on flights like that."

He mumbled in agreement.

Raising up, I kissed him on the cheek. "No matter what happens, just know that you're my hero. Thank you for believing in me, Dad."

"It was the easiest thing I ever did." A sparkle glinted in his eyes. "And pumpkin?"

"Yeah?"

He placed a bony finger beneath my chin, lifting it. "I'll see you soon." He pressed a tender kiss to my forehead before we said goodbye.

After I hugged Mom, she climbed into their SUV and drove away. I rubbed my arms against the loneliness that crept in as I watched the car disappear down the street.

My slip-on Uggs scuffed the sidewalk as I entered my house with my stomach in my throat.

I locked the door, but before I set the alarm, black boots caught my attention. Ones I was beginning to know all too well.

"You're here in the daytime," I said to Death.

"I wanted to see your father off. He will come home a new man, Ella. I promise."

I strolled past him and to my kitchen, where I located my coffee again. Hopping onto the counter, I blew on the hot liquid before I took a sip.

"Thank you for doing this. For helping Dad."

Death approached me, then took my cup from my hands and set it down. He forced my legs apart and tugged me to the edge. I waited for him to speak, but instead his mouth crashed down on mine. A bolt of heat punched through me, and I wrapped my arms around his neck and pulled him closer.

His kiss was so intense I lost the ability to form a coherent thought. With quick movements, Death pushed me backward, yanked my yoga pants off, and tossed them on the floor. He dropped to his knees and placed his mouth on my center before I could comprehend what was happening.

Sparks skittered down my spine as his tongue darted over my clit. My eyes rolled back into my head as I surrendered to the pleasure. Every nerve in my body screamed and trembled at his touch, a blissful heat radiating from where he licked my sensitive skin. I moaned deep in my throat, my back arching as I melted beneath him.

He explored my body with the reverence of a worshipper, uncovering hidden pleasures and sending shocks of desire through me with each caress. Death pushed two fingers inside me, and I sighed.

I panted as his hands gripped my thighs hard enough to leave bruises.

His mouth left my pussy as he stood and quickly undid his jeans. My juices glistened on his lips as he lined himself up at my center. Instead of slamming into me, he slowly pushed past my entrance. I gasped as I took every inch of him.

"That's it, little lamb. Take all of my cock." He trailed kisses along my jaw, and I tilted my head, giving him access.

I quivered as a wave of pure pleasure washed over me. His feral growl echoed through the room, sending shocks of electricity ricocheting throughout my body. His need was palpable, radiating from his body like wildfire, igniting my desire. A moan escaped me as he found a rhythm. His thrusts grew faster and deeper as I moved against him, demanding more. Every ruthless snap of his hips sent me spiraling into an oblivion that I hadn't ever experienced before.

I was so wet that my juices slicked my thighs, and I couldn't get enough of the man I was terrified of.

Death slipped his hand between us, massaging my clit with the right amount of pressure. "Oh shit."

Gazing at me with a combination of hunger and danger in his eyes, he pumped into me until my pussy spasmed around his shaft. I ground my hips against him as he threw his head back and came while I drained every delicious drop from his cock, my body soaking it up.

Then, he released a possessive growl like I hadn't ever heard before—one filled with pleasure and defeat.

I blinked several times, clearing the haze from my vision as I focused on him. What had just happened between us?

Chapter 30

Ella

The man I'd just had sex with wasn't the same one I ran from the previous evening. I couldn't deny it. There was a shift between us—a tenderness, however slight, that had awoken something in me. Even though I knew he was complicated and dangerous, I couldn't ignore the small gesture of his gentle kiss. My monster had a side to him he hadn't allowed me to see until after he brought me home and bathed me last night.

His cock began to soften, and he pulled out. A sudden emptiness consumed me, and I struggled against it.

The sound of my phone buzzing interrupted the moment. Death left me on the counter and disappeared into my bedroom. Seconds later, he leaned against my door frame, wearing a menacing glare.

Without a word, he slipped out the back door and left. A chill gripped my bones—something was off, but I had no idea what.

Sighing, I struggled with the idea of being alone and curling up with a good book or seeing if Cami could hang out for a few hours before her night shift. I wanted the scoop on her and this cop. If I was going to be sneaking around with a serial killer and protecting Sebastian, I had to know exactly where and who our enemies were.

CAMI WAS AT MY PLACE AN HOUR LATER WITH A PIZZA LOADED with cheese and pepperoni. I hadn't realized how hungry I was until the heavenly smell consumed my house.

She sat it on the counter while I collected some plates from the kitchen cabinet.

"I said bye to Dad this morning. It was really hard." I flipped open the box lid and grabbed a piece, plopping it onto my plate.

Once Cami did the same, she hopped onto her favorite stool and focused on me.

"I'm sure that was hard. Hell, I bawled my eyes out when I saw him yesterday." She took a bite of her pizza, the cheese leaving a string from her mouth to the crust. She swiped a finger through it and licked it off.

I couldn't help but laugh. "I'm sure Mom will call me later when she and Dad are settled in. Until then, it's not going to do me any good worrying. Besides, I need an update. Are you ready for your big date tomorrow?"

She shook her head, her lips pursed. "No, I'm scared to death, Ella. I really like this guy."

"Yeah? What's so special about him?"

"He's not from Portland, for starters. He's from Connecticut." She grinned at me around the food in her mouth. "Plus." She leaned toward me. "Can you keep a secret?"

If she only knew the dark secrets I was already keeping.

"Of course." I waved her off as if it were the silliest thing she'd ever asked me. It was.

"Not a soul, Ella. But Ryan is working on the Portland serial killer case."

My phone clattered to the floor, and ice flowed through my veins, rendering me momentarily immobile.

"Are you okay? What did I say wrong?"

Fear bubbled up inside my chest. "Did you tell Ryan about my stalker, Cami?"

She shook her head slowly. "No, you've not mentioned it again, so I figured it wasn't as concerning as we first thought."

I mentally sighed with relief, but the concerns weren't over. "It wasn't. I only saw him once, and honestly, I think he was just passing through the neighborhood and decided to scare me on the way out." My pulse spiked with my lie. How would I protect Death if Cami's boyfriend was sniffing around? My heart skipped a beat as I realized that I actually would protect him. He'd saved my life and there was no doubt in my mind that he would kill for me again.

"With everything happening, I forgot all about it. I should have told you sooner that he hadn't been back around."

"Yeah, it was weird, but I'm glad he's not been around anymore. Honestly, I don't think the man who scared you and the serial killer are the same guy, anyway. I'm sure there would be some seriously weird behavior going down with you if it were."

She had no idea how much she'd hit the nail on the head. "No shit." I massaged the back of my neck, trying to see how to play this. "Has Ryan given you any details about the case at all? I mean, I realize we hear things on the news, but it's only what we're allowed to know."

Cami chewed, then swallowed her bite of pizza. "You can't tell anyone. You swear on your life?"

"Who am I going to tell, babe? You're my best friend and you're giving me the tea, so that pretty much cuts down who I'm going to blab to." I laughed.

She pondered for a moment. "Yeah, you have a point." She rubbed her hands together as if she had a super juicy secret. Hell, she might, and I needed to know what it was.

"It's a male, for sure. They've not found any evidence as to who, though. It's like the killer is a clean freak or something because he hasn't left anything behind except once. There was a partial boot print at a murder scene. From that clue, they can guesstimate he's about six foot three and approximately two hundred pounds."

I nearly choked on my panic but instead played into Cami's fascination with what the man might look like. Hell, I was also curious about who Death was beneath the mask. "Hm, maybe broad shoulders and a solid wall of muscle. I mean, you've got to be strong to kill someone, right?" I pulled at the cheese hanging off my slice of pizza and popped it into my mouth.

"The way he's doing it, yeah." Cami flipped her long hair behind her shoulder.

Frowning, I took another bite and said, "What do you mean? The news hasn't said anything about his methods." Neither had Death. Other than Stephen, I had no idea how or who he was murdering. I stared at my feet, realizing that Cami was sitting only feet away from where Stephen died. Images of his lifeless, bloody form played through my head, and my feelings about the sorry bastard bounced around inside me like a kangaroo on crack. All in all, I was glad the fucker was dead.

"Girl, Ryan said they found a body in the lake near Bend. Rocks were sewn into his stomach to keep him from floating to the top of the water."

I scrunched up my nose. "Gross, but efficient."

"The guy wasn't small either, so whoever did it is strong enough to snatch and carry his victims." She tapped her chin for a moment, pretending to be deep in thought. "I wonder if Ryan is strong enough to carry me?"

I snorted, Death had carried me a few times, but not in the way most women wanted. "Maybe you'll find out."

Cami grinned at me.

"Did Ryan say anything else?" I asked, bringing the conversation to the front and center again.

"No. That was it. At this point, they've not closed in on a suspect at all, so the killer is still on the loose." She grabbed another slice and set it on her plate. "Other than your dad, what's going on with you?"

I licked the cheese off my fingers, loudly smacking them to annoy my best friend.

"Well, I'm not working for the adult website anymore."

Cami's eyes widened. "Really? That's fantastic!"

"Well, maybe. I still have to figure out a way to pay for his new trial, but ..." I flattened my palms against the kitchen counter, staring at my friend. "The bills are paid for now, at least."

"Wow! You must be popular on the website because those trials are thousands of dollars."

I tilted my head, waiting to see her expression when I told her. "It wasn't me."

A crease dented the smooth skin in between her eyebrows. "What do you mean?"

"I mean someone else settled the bill."

Cami's mouth opened and closed like a fish out of water. "Wait. Maybe I didn't understand you correctly. An anonymous person paid your dad's medical bills?"

"Yup." I popped the *p* for extra emphasis.

"Do you think it was Sebastian?" She practically whispered her question as if we were in a crowded room full of nosy people.

"I have no idea. He's been out of town, so I've been unable to ask him. Honestly, if they took care of it anonymously, I'm guessing they don't want their identity known."

"Well, shit that's great, but *I* want to know."

I grinned at her. "Me too. If I find out, you'll be the first person I tell."

"Hmm, I still think it might be Sebastian, but that's a lot of money for a bartender to cough up."

I pondered if I should tell her that he actually owned Velvet Vortex. It was most likely common knowledge so it wouldn't be a big deal. Apparently, I was getting used to keeping secrets and weighing everything before the words left my mouth. I just wanted to protect Sebastian and his work outside the club.

"He's not just a bartender. He owns Velvet Vortex along with another partner, Kip, who has also worked at the bar when we've been there."

"Damn, so the guy is loaded. Velvet Vortex is always hoppin.' Well, good for them." She grabbed a napkin from the pile on the counter and wiped her mouth. "And here I thought you were dating a broke-ass older man with no hopes of retirement."

I released an exaggerated, dramatic groan, grinning. "Nope, it's not the case."

"Kip is pretty hot too. Maybe if it doesn't work out with Ryan, I can learn more about Kip." She laughed. "A girl has to keep her options open."

"If you were interested in Kip, it might be fun to double date on occasion. The guys are close, and so are we, so we'd all get along. I think I like that idea." It was hella better than her dating a cop and learning about my double life.

"Yeah, I could see that. For now, I'm excited about Ryan. I do worry about his safety working on the serial killer case, but I guess it's something I'll learn to deal with."

"That would be hard." I understood. I was concerned about Death and Sebastian's safety all the time.

Hopefully, Death would show up tonight so I could tell him to watch his tracks since the police were hot on his heels. They would connect me to him if they learned his identity. That shit couldn't happen.

Chapter 31

Death

"Even in a flock of lambs, there can be a wolf at heart, and among wolves, there can be one with the gentleness of a lamb." ~ *Unknown*

T houghts of my little lamb swirled in my head as I entered the abandoned warehouse where I was keeping John. I'd left some food and water next to him to keep him alive for a while. I hadn't told Ella that I had the man who'd hurt her in captivity. Once she'd spoken his name, I nearly told her I'd kidnapped him already. And she was right, I'd stumbled across John's activity with her and other children on the dark web before I ever appeared in her home.

I whistled "London Bridge is Falling Down" as I walked to the back of the building where John was held. The song was almost as dark as I was, but not quite. One theory suggested it referenced Viking attacks in the eleventh century. Another explained it was about entombing live children in the foundations of bridges to ensure they wouldn't collapse. Buried alive—what a shit way to die. As I continued, the lyrics stirred my imagination of how to possibly kill the bastard, but I hadn't decided yet.

The rusty door creaked as I opened it and then walked into the dank and dark room. I flipped on the light switch and waited for my eyes to adjust.

"Have you missed me?" I asked John as he huddled in the corner, still wearing his undershirt and boxers. I'd considered giving him warmer clothes, but I didn't want to waste them on someone who would die soon.

"Have you gotten any muscle cramps?" I laughed, enjoying my warped sense of humor. It wasn't as if he could walk around and stretch since I'd nailed his feet to the floor when I'd arrived. This particular room had been used as an office and had wood floors. It was perfect for nailing the son of a bitch down.

John grunted at me with his eyelids half closed. His pain must be overwhelming, and his knee would never recover—not that he would ever need it again.

"I met one of your *friends*." I kneeled and adjusted my mask, staring straight into his corrupted soul.

"Yeah?" He laid his hand on his broken leg and winced. He'd propped himself up on the wall, weak and exhausted. His boxers were stained from pissing himself, but I'd smelled worse.

I sucked air between my teeth before I responded. "Ella McCloud."

He chuckled as a twisted smile slipped into place. "She was a pretty little thing. How'd she turn out?"

My hand shot out and wrapped around his throat. "Beautiful and strong, but you touched what is *mine*."

His round cheeks reddened as I tightened my hold, ready to kill this motherfucker for what he said about her, but I couldn't—not yet.

"Who else worked with you and found the kids for your disgusting pictures and videos?" My hand fell away as he sputtered and coughed.

"Like I'd tell you. Just know that killing me won't stop it. Someone will take my place and continue with our art."

A blinding rage gripped me and ignited an inferno of inescapable wrath.

"Art? You call sexually abusing kids art? You're more screwed up in the head than I thought you were." I drew closer, a mere inch from his ugly mug. "If I wasn't a fucked-up individual as well, I would snap your neck right now and put you out of your misery, but I have other things planned for you."

I rose and stomped on his other knee. His screams of pain and swearing bouncing off the walls of the small room gave me almost as much pleasure as being inside Ella's cunt.

Strolling out as if I'd just won the lottery, I secured the door behind me and left.

Chapter 32

Ella

I paced my living room, chewing on my thumbnail like a bunny munching on a carrot. It had been four days since Death had visited, and I was terrified that he'd slipped up and the cops had arrested him. I slapped my hands over my face and groaned at the fact that I'd gone from not wanting him here to developing feelings for a maniac. It was as if he'd breathed new life into my boring existence. The irony of that tidbit hadn't escaped me. My heart betrayed me again, flip-flopping to wanting the safe and comfortable with Sebastian returning. It had been almost three weeks since he'd left, and I longed to see him, kiss him. Dread seeped inside me as I reminded myself how tricky managing Death and Sebastian at the same time would be. Not only tricky, but dangerous.

"You're lying to everyone you love," I muttered to myself.

"Don't worry, little lamb. You'll get used to it."

I whirled on my heels and ran to the masked man in my kitchen. Throwing my arms around his neck, I wrapped my legs around his waist and buried my cheek against his chest. "You're okay?"

His body stiffened but after a few seconds he pulled me against him. "Always." He held me tightly.

"I was worried the police had arrested you." I released him and slid down his muscular body until I could set my feet on the ground.

He wound strands of my hair around his fingers and jerked my head back, his eyes narrowing. "What's going on?"

"We need to talk." He released me and I led him to the couch, then quickly closed my curtains to prevent any nosy neighbors from looking inside.

Sitting next to him, I tucked one of my legs beneath me and turned to him with a serious expression. "Cami, my best friend is going out with a cop. He's on your case, and they found a partial boot print. You have to be more careful."

He clenched his right hand into a tight fist. It was the only visible indication that he was worried. "What else?"

I grabbed one of his bulging biceps and gave it a soft squeeze. "They found a murder victim with rocks in his stomach near the Idaho border." Panic seized my chest. "Was it you?"

Death responded with a wicked grin.

"I trust you had a good reason to open up that man's stomach and sew rocks into his body before you tossed him in the lake."

Death shifted in his seat but neither confirmed nor denied it. "The less you know the better."

"Except that if you get caught, they're going to trace Stephen's murder right to my fucking doorstep! Surely someone has reported him missing by now. I stopped watching the news, so I don't know."

"I'll take care of it, little lamb. There's no need to lose your mind over the cops."

I shot off the couch, steaming at the entire fucked-up situation. "Not lose my mind? I don't need this right now. I'm hiding the truth from my best friend, and I'm lying to everyone that I know. I was a good person until you dragged me into your cold, twisted world." I moved closer to him. "Let me go. If you really care about me, and I'm not just an obsession that you can replace ... Let. Me. Go."

Death stood so quickly I nearly toppled backward. He reached out and grabbed my upper arm, sending pain ricocheting through my entire body. I tried to pull away, but his grip was too firm.

"The quicker you understand the situation, the easier it will go for you, Ella. You belong to me, and there's no turning back." He pressed his body against mine, his eyes a steely grey that cut right through me. "You will protect me as I do you, or ..." His sneer appeared through his mask. "You. Will. Die. Are we clear?"

His hard-on pressed against my waist, and my body trembled against him. "How am I going to protect you if I don't know who you are? When are you going to trust me with all of your secrets?" I asked, my voice shaking almost as much as I was.

"When you earn them." Death didn't move. He simply stared right through me, and my stomach knotted with his threat.

"All I want to know is who I'm falling in love with."

I would have moved heaven and earth to have seen Death's expression when I'd confessed my feelings to him.

His arm protectively slipped around me. "You already know who I am, Ella."

A spark of boldness shot through me. "The man who will break me and put me together again? A killer with a thirst for vengeance? A man of great wealth and power? Yeah, you've said it all before, but you know I want more—need more."

A possessive growl rumbled in his throat. "I'll give you more soon, little lamb. You have my word." As quietly as he slipped into my house, he left again.

I spent the next hour frustrated as hell with Death's elusiveness. After heaving a sigh, I heard my phone buzz, pulling me away from my pity party. Maybe it was Mom.

Searching for my cell, I finally found it in the kitchen beside the sink. My brow shot up as I stared at the number.

"Hey," I said, grinning. "How are you?"

"Home. You're my first call," Sebastian said.

I tapped my fingers against the granite counter, grinning as if I'd lost my fucking mind. I hadn't realized how much I'd missed him until I heard his soothing voice and accent. It smoothed out my jagged edges and cauterized my frayed nerves, piecing me back together again.

"When can I see you?"

"Now?" His warm chuckle filled the line, and my entire body tingled with warmth.

"I would love that."

Chapter 33

Sebastian

I hadn't expected to see Ella so soon, but I was thrilled she'd wanted to meet at my place in an hour. I was excited to see and kiss her as well as find out how she was. The hole in my damn chest had grown bigger during the weeks we were apart.

After I had texted her my address, I turned on some music, and "Face in the Crowd" by Freya Ridings played softly in the background.

A few minutes before eight, I stepped out of the shower and dried off before I pulled on a pair of jeans and a black polo shirt. The doorman had alerted me that Ella was on her way up, and a few minutes later the doorbell rang. I strolled to the door, eager to see her.

"Hi," she said, beaming at me, her eyes flashing with excitement.

"Hi, yourself." I pulled her against me, nuzzling her hair and soaking up her intoxicating scent of peach and vanilla. Everything inside of me wanted her to stay by my side for the rest of the night.

"I've missed you." I rubbed her back as I spoke.

"I guess what they say about distance making the heart grow fonder is true. Plus, I was worried. When you called last week, you didn't sound so good."

I broke our embrace and squeezed her shoulders. "As I mentioned on the phone, this trip was a lot harder for multiple reasons." It was tough to let my guard down, but I was ready to make a change. I just needed to know if she was too.

She took my hand, concern in her gaze. "Are you able to tell me about it?"

"Some, but first, would you like something to drink? I have your favorite, Jack and Coke." I offered her a warm smile.

"That sounds great, thanks."

I extended my hand to her. "Come on, I'll show you around."

She slipped hers in mine. "You didn't mention that you lived in a penthouse. The building is stunning."

I led her to the living room, where I'd turned on the gas fireplace earlier. "It's a nice place. Plus, when I'm gone, no one really notices. It's not like my mail stacks up or the grass grows too high. One of the reasons I wanted to live here was the low maintenance since I travel so much."

"That makes sense."

She looked around the living area, eyeing the pictures I had on the wall of Dope, Riley, Kip, and me. Something similar to sadness flashed in her expression as she stood before the images. She touched Kip's red jacket, then jerked her hand away. "Sorry, I didn't mean to fingerprint the glass."

I wasn't sure what was going on in that beautiful mind of hers, but I didn't want to pry.

"We've all been friends for years. Riley is newer to the bar and group, but she's also a part of the Safe Horizon Society."

"Oh, I didn't realize she was a part of it too. I mean not that it was any of my business, but I swear I won't breathe a word to anyone, Sebastian."

"I trust you."

She looked at me quizzically. "How? How do you know that I'm not some horrible person who does terrible things? You have a double life that only a handful of people are aware of. What makes you think I'm any different?"

I gently turned her toward me and placed my finger under her chin. "Gut instincts. I'm rarely wrong about someone, Ella. When you were tailing me the night we were moving Sarah, I didn't miss the look in your eyes, the longing to help even if it meant risking your life. The rest of the details are just fun things I'll learn about you on the way."

Her gaze softened as she nodded and before I could talk myself out of it, I leaned down and pressed my lips to hers. Warmth flooded my body as my cock lengthened. She parted her lips, and I slipped my tongue into her mouth, tasting her. She kissed me with such tenderness it caught me off guard. I wasn't expecting her response to say so much without uttering a word.

I threaded my fingers through her long hair. A soft moan escaped her as she slipped her arms around my waist. Feeling her body against mine was heaven after missing her over the last few weeks.

Finally, I pulled away and placed a light kiss on her forehead. "I'll show you the rest of the house, then get you a drink."

She gave me a sweet smile. "That sounds nice."

Her mouth parted in awe as she walked through the penthouse with large windows that overlooked the city and sported a breath-taking view of Mount Hood. I showed her the guest bathroom, additional bedroom, and kitchen.

"There's a loft?" she asked, glancing up.

"My office. Come on." I started up the stairs, holding her hand as we climbed. "I like the view here too." I pointed out the window at a different angle of the mountain.

"It has snow on it already. I wonder if it will be a good ski season."

I turned to her. "Do you ski?"

"No, but I've always wanted to."

"I'll have to take you to the ski lodge for a long weekend." I was testing the waters to see if she would want to spend that time alone with me. In bed and naked, preferably, but I wouldn't admit it to her yet.

She placed her small palm against my chest. "I would love that." Her expression flickered with a hint of something I couldn't pinpoint, and once again I wondered what was going on with her. Maybe she would tell me soon.

Guiding her to the kitchen, I made her a drink and grabbed myself a cold one before I led her back to the living room, where we settled on the brown leather sofa. "There's a coaster for you." I pointed to the coffee table in front of us.

"Tell me what you can about your trip." She took a sip of her drink and laughed. "Sebastian Fletcher, are you trying to get me drunk so I can't drive?"

"Should I add more Coke?"

"No, it's fine. I was just teasing you." She grew serious. "Why was this business trip so difficult? Did something happen?"

I cleared my throat and set my untouched beer down. "A lot can go wrong when we're out there. Neighbors could be watching the house. The spouse could come home, like when Stephen caught you when we were moving Sarah and the kids."

Her body stiffened, but she didn't say a word. Had he been around, and she hadn't said anything? *Fuck. I should have been there to make sure she was safe.*

"Ella, tell me the truth," I ordered. "You've seen Stephen, haven't you?"

Her face froze, panic-stricken. "It's fine. There's nothing you need to worry about anymore."

"What exactly does that mean?" I leaned closer. "Ella, if he's threatening you, I can take care of it. You have my word that he won't ever bother you again."

She shook her head. "I've not seen him in weeks. He did stop by my house, but I told him if he didn't leave me alone that I would call the cops."

"That's not enough to scare off a man like him. Let me hire a bodyguard for you."

She clenched her jaw. "No need. Plus, if some of our clients sniff out a bodyguard, it could cause issues. I swear to you that I'm safe, and he hasn't been back around." She took my hand in hers. "Thank you for worrying about me. It means a lot."

"I care about you, Ella. If anything happened to you because of me, I would never forgive myself."

She leaned up and pressed her lips to mine. "As you can see, I'm in front of you and perfectly fine." Ella sat back and rested against the arm of the couch. "It's your turn, mister. What's going on?"

A powerful urge exploded in my chest, and it took everything inside me not to pick her up and hide her away from all the bad in our fucked-up world. That wasn't reality, though. Not to mention, Ella was strong and would refuse to let anyone coddle her.

I took a deep breath, my thoughts returning to the first family we'd relocated. Since Ella had experienced what I did firsthand, I knew I could trust her with what happened.

"The boyfriend had recently been released from prison, and even though the woman had broken things off with him a year ago, he was determined not to let her go. The same day he was a free man, he showed up at her house and beat the shit out of her right in front of their six-year-old son. The kid was the one who called 9-1-1 for his mom."

Ella's hands flew over her mouth as tears welled in her eyes. "Oh god. That poor baby. Even for an adult that's a lot to try to process."

"I hate fuckers who take out their anger on a woman and kids." My pulse thundered in my ears, and I reminded myself the family was safe.

Anger simmered in her gaze. "Me too. I wish you'd caught that guy in the act and pummeled his face in."

I cracked a grin. "If I'd tied him down, would you have beat the hell out of him?"

She laughed. "That's a strange question, but yeah. I'd take you up on that offer. I wouldn't kill him, just give him the same level of pain that he'd inflicted on his ex." She shot me an impish grin. "I'm an equal opportunist." Ella took a drink and propped her arm up on the back of the couch, peering at me over the rim of her glass.

Unable to help myself, I stared at her. "You're so beautiful."

Her cheeks flushed with my compliment. I hadn't meant to embarrass her, but she would eventually get used to the praise.

"Thank you. But back to the story." She giggled behind her hand.

"Yeah, that." I rubbed my jaw. "We were able to reach her while she was in the hospital and arrange a safe place for her and the kid. Once she was discharged, Dope and I wheeled her out and to the pickup lane, but that sorry bastard was waiting for her. We had our disguises on, but he spotted her. We had to turn around and run through the building, hoping we could lose him while Dope called the police. The cops searched for a few hours, but they never found him. After we reached the van, Dope drove like a bat out of hell to get the son who was staying with a friend. She was terrified that her ex had gone after the kiddo while we were trying to get out of the hospital. Apparently, he'd used their son to manipulate her before, including holding a knife to the boy's neck."

Ella's mouth dropped open. "That's horrible. What the fuck is wrong with people?"

Dammit, I like this girl. We were on the same page in so many ways, but this—her protective nature with the ability to inflict some damage, when necessary, had both my heart and dick begging for her.

"We got the son, but as we were pulling away from the home, he showed up. Once he realized we had his kid, he came after us. He was hard to shake the second time, but Dope can drive that van like no one's business. He's got skills for damn sure."

Curiosity flashed in her gaze. "Why not a smaller car then?"

"We have one, but it depends on the size of the job. In this case, we were able to gather some of her and her son's belongings like clothes, toiletries, and some of her boy's favorite toys before we picked her up at the hospital. She'd given us a list of items and told us where the spare house key was when she called the hotline for help. She was attached to a few books, pictures, etcetera. We couldn't fit everything in a car. At one time, we wouldn't allow any personal belongings to be taken, but the grieving process when the women lost everything was intense. It helped to have a few things with them."

"I get that. I know they're only things, but it's also a part of who that person is. Are they safe now?" She shifted in her seat, stretching her legs in front of her.

I slipped off her shoes and placed her feet on my lap, then rubbed her calves and knee through her jeans.

"Oh. My. God. That feels so good." She groaned and my cock lengthened until it was painful. Could I give her an orgasm from rubbing her legs? I was willing to try. My chuckle rippled through the room as she moaned some more.

"I'm putty in your hands, Sebastian. Keep talking to me, though." Her eyes fluttered closed, and then she pried them open again.

"If he'd caught us, it would have ended badly. Plus, I'm trying to stay off the cop's radar so I can continue helping families. This time, my mind was elsewhere. I don't fucking make mistakes like that. I should have known he would be waiting for her at the hospital." It had been a big turning point for me. "Each night, I thought of you, Ella. All I wanted was to be here." I ran my thumb up the arch of her foot.

Her eyelids drooped. "You should stop before I fall asleep."

Ignoring her, I worked my way up her calf, massaging her tense muscles. "Be a good girl and just relax for me. I know it's been difficult with your dad. How's that going?"

She looked at me and licked her lower lip, nearly driving me over the edge. I wanted to taste her and have her beneath me, thrusting into her as she screamed my name. But it was too soon, and she was worth taking it slow. I wanted more than her gorgeous body. I wanted her heart.

Chapter 34

Sebastian

"Dad is hanging in there. He and Mom are in California for a new cancer trial."

My brows rose as a huge smile eased across my face. "That's good news, right?"

"I'm afraid to hope, but apparently this drug has had excellent results. Maybe Dad will come home a new man."

"He will. From what you've told me, he's a fighter, and I suspect it's where you get it from." I wanted to try to reassure her even though I had no way of knowing the outcome for him.

Silence hung in the air as I continued to rub her feet.

"Sebastian?" My name rolled off her tongue, her voice heavy with need.

My willpower disintegrated the moment my eyes met hers. An animalistic craving to consume her blazed through me.

She pulled her foot out of my grasp and moved it to my crotch. She sunk her teeth into her lower lip as toes rubbed along the clear outline of my thickening cock, her gaze hungry and blazing. Ella applied more pressure to my shaft, driving me wild.

"What do you want, Ella?" I growled.

Her long lashes fluttered, revealing intense longing behind them. Our eyes locked and we both stood without a second thought, drawn to each other by an irresistible force. I cradled the back of her head in my palm, pulling her closer as her fingers tangled in my hair. Every touch ignited sparks, fueling the desire until it consumed us completely. Our kisses were fervent and urgent, our teeth clashing together. With each move, our bodies tangled with each other while we stumbled toward my bedroom. As we collapsed onto the bed, Ella's laughter filled the room before our eyes met once again.

I crawled onto the king-size mattress next to her.

"Are you sure, Ella?"

She nodded, then lifted her head off the mattress and kissed me. "I've missed you. Somehow, you've worked your way into my heart, and I want more." Her fingertips traced my jawline, the emotions in her eyes speaking loudly.

Placing my palm on her hip, I held her gaze as my hand slipped beneath the hem of her blue shirt. I slowly moved my hand upward until I reached her right breast.

"Take your shirt off for me."

She sat up, peeled her top off, and tossed it on the floor.

The swell of her full breasts peeked out of her pink lace bra, and I couldn't wait to trail kisses over her soft skin. With a flick of her hand, she opened the front clasp before lying down on the bed again.

I moved the cup out of the way, watching her nipple harden against the cool air.

I lowered my head and kissed the swell of her breast. Then I grazed her flesh with my fingertips, sending electric shocks through my veins as desire pooled in my gut. I captured her mouth in a deep kiss, pressing myself against her and feeling the heat radiating off her body.

"Does that feel better?"

"Almost. More please." A smile played at the corners of her lips.

My hands explored every inch of her as I kissed my way down to her neck, loving the way she moaned softly as my tongue slid along her collarbone. I teased her nipples until she was writhing beneath me, begging for more.

"Your body is made for me, Ella. Let me worship you the way you deserve."

I nipped and licked between her breasts, taking my time to play with each tantalizing bud, before caressing and biting her pure perfection. Trailing kisses down her stomach, I hovered above her waistband.

"Keep going, Sebastian."

That was all I needed to hear. My heart raced as I unfastened her jeans and tugged them down. She lifted her hips, and I pulled them down to her ankles.

I hesitated, taking in the sight of her naked before me on my bed.

"Are you my good girl, Ella?"

"Yes."

Her thighs parted and allowed me a full view, and I focused on the damp spot in the center of her matching pink thong. Gently pushing her legs closed, I peeled them down her toned legs and tossed them on the floor.

I frowned at the marks and cuts on her shins. Worried, I reached over to pull off her sock, but she moved her leg.

"My feet are cold." She smiled, softly.

"What happened?"

She rubbed her forehead with the palm of her hand. "I was working on the garden and didn't realize how long I'd been sitting on my legs. I didn't feel the rocks beneath my shins until it was too late."

"It looks painful." I kissed the inside of her thigh, working my way up to her pussy.

"It was, but it's better now." She sucked in a deep breath as I eased her pussy lips apart. Our eyes locked as I circled her clit with my thumb in slow, lazy circles.

"That's it. You're so wet, Ella. I can't wait to taste you."

She dug her fingers into the black bedspread, and her mouth parted slightly.

I lowered my head and pressed soft kisses to the creamy flesh of her thighs, her scent intoxicating as I worked my way up to her pussy. Slowly, I ran my tongue up her slit. Ella jerked from the sensation, and her juices coated my chin as I buried my tongue deep inside her.

Her fingers tangled in my hair as waves of pleasure coursed through us both. She gasped as I continued and dug her nails into my shoulders.

I eased two fingers into her core while I worshipped her sensitive skin, her cries escaping her with every push and pull. I curled my fingers, and Ella bucked wildly as I coaxed an orgasm from her. Her slick walls tightened around me, and I sucked and nipped her clit until she was grinding beneath me in a frenzy.

"Sebastian ... Jesus Christ. What are you doing to me?"

Her upper body arched, her full breasts bouncing with her movements as she came undone, and her release coated my mouth and hand. I licked her juices off her sweet pussy as she quivered.

Her cheeks flushed, and her lazy smile made my heart jump.

"That was amazing."

"I'm glad you enjoyed yourself." I moved up the bed, kissed the tip of her nose, and moved onto my side.

"How am I naked, but you're fully dressed?" Warmth spread through my chest with her soft giggle.

I rolled over, pinning her upper body beneath mine, and captured her mouth. Her fingers trailed up the back of my neck, and I pressed my hips into her.

"Why aren't you inside of me right now?" Her gaze searched mine, and I pressed my forehead against hers as my thumb stroked her soft cheek.

"Because when I'm inside you, I'll claim you. There's no going back, Ella. I have to make sure that your heart and not just your body is ready and willing."

With a sigh of contentment, she kissed me and confirmed I'd made the right call.

I flashed her a wicked little grin. "Until then, how many orgasms have you had in one evening?"

Her brows shot up. "Two," she whispered.

Surprised, I arched a brow at her. "Any man who wouldn't make you come all night long isn't worthy of you."

I lowered my mouth to hers, then nipped along her jaw and to her ear. "Let me take care of you tonight."

"But what about you, Sebastian?" Her hand moved down my side and rested on my lower back.

"Next time, baby. Next time."

Chapter 35

Ella

At six the following morning, I returned home and flopped down in the middle of my bed with a silly smile on my face. I squealed like a little girl, then burst into giggles. Shit, it felt nice to laugh. It had been too long since I'd been genuinely happy. With Dad's illness and Death's obsession, life had lost its allure. Sebastian was a reminder that good people and things still existed.

When Sebastian had invited me over, I hadn't planned on spending the night, but when the first hints of the sunrise appeared, I realized it was already morning. The edges of the sky were tinged with the faintest whispers of golden light. Streaks of pink and orange bled into the fabric of the new day as I lay tangled in Sebastian's embrace. Nothing had ever felt so right. Moments later, wariness and fear slithered into my thoughts. What would Death do if he learned I'd spent the night with Sebastian? I shook my head. I had managed to keep Sebastian a secret from Death and vice versa. I could do this.

While stretching, I relished in the afterthoughts of Sebastian's attention, ignoring the fact that I had to get ready for work. I had been thoroughly ravished and worshipped. No man had ever taken care of me the way he had. After I was sure that I couldn't have any more orgasms, he wrapped me in his arms, and we dozed off. It was heaven—sheer bliss. Unlike the fucked-up situation I'd landed myself in with Death, I could talk to Cami about Sebastian. Would I ever find our relationship boring in comparison? I seriously doubted it since he had a secret life he couldn't share with many people. That alone was sexy as hell.

Maybe I was a hormonal mush puddle, but I was definitely falling for Sebastian. Hard. He was the extreme opposite of Death. Even I realized that my dance in the darkness with Death could only last so long. The cops were hot on Death's heels, and I couldn't watch him fall. Once he did, though, my heart might break. At the same time, I would be free of him.

My cell buzzed with an incoming message, and I patted my hand on the bed until I located it. Sebastian's name lit up the screen, and my stomach somersaulted with excitement.

Sebastian:

> I can still taste you in my mouth. I miss you already. Stop by the club tonight?

I decided to make the best of my evenings and spend them with Sebastian. If I wasn't home, Death couldn't invite himself over. I wasn't ready to see him yet.

ME:

> What time?

SEBASTIAN:

> I'll try to take a break around eight if that works for you.

Me:

> I'll see you then.

I SENT HIM MULTIPLE KISS EMOJIS, MY THIGHS CLENCHING WITH the reminder of his skilled mouth between my legs. My entire body tingled with anticipation of his touch. Even though I offered to get him off, he'd refused. A part of me wondered if he was a glutton for punishment. Being turned on but denying himself must have been difficult.

Rolling over on my stomach, I texted Cami.

ME:

> I spent the night with Sebastian. I just got home.

CAMI SENT ME A MULTITUDE OF MIND-BLOWN EMOJIS, ALONG with water, peaches, and eggplant. I snickered.

ME:

> How was your date?

. . .

CAMI:

> Delicious. LOL. It was good. I'll see him
> again tonight. I can say that he definitely
> knows how to use his nightstick.

ME:

> What? You test-drove it?

CAMI:

> Girl, yes. And it was fucking amazing. Pun
> intended.

ME:

> I'm happy for you. Sebastian and I didn't
> have sex, but he took very good care of me.

I added the lick emoji.
Cami:

> And? You can't leave me hanging.

I snorted as my fingers flew across the keyboard.

. . .

ME:

> A ten+. The man knows his stuff.

CAMI:

> Good. It's about time for both of us. Babe, I gotta go work a day shift, and then Ryan is picking me up. Catch ya tomorrow?

I PAUSED, REALIZING THAT CAMI WAS REALLY INTO HIM. WHAT did they say? *Keep your friends close, but your enemies closer.* Shit, I wasn't sure if this was a smart idea, but if I could spend some time with Ryan, I might be able to keep Sebastian and the Safe Horizon Society safe. *And Death.* My desire to protect both men wasn't healthy, but I couldn't seem to stop myself. Besides, it would raise suspicions if we didn't all hang out. I would rather control the situation than let it sneak up on me.

ME:

> No. After you two get naked and of course dressed again, I was hoping you could stop by and see me at Velvet Vortex so the guys can meet each other. Plus, I could use the time to unwind after work. My ass will be dragging, but I'm counting on that adrenaline to kick in. LOL.

CAMI:

> I like the way you think. Priorities. Naked first, friends second. LMAO. Love you, babe.

ME:

> LOL Love you, too. Sebastian will take his break around 8 p.m., so any time before or after.

Thank god, I had time to take a nap after work and before I met Cami.

CAMI:

> Perfect. See ya later.

ONCE I'D MADE PLANS WITH CAMI AND RYAN, I TEXTED MOM to check on Dad. She responded with a thumbs-up and said she'd update me soon since the doctor had just walked in.

My thoughts wandered to the medical bills and how I would pay them without Death's assistance from the webcam job.

Honestly, I was surprised he hadn't been waiting for me when I got home this morning. I was so wrapped up in Sebastian that it hadn't crossed my mind until now. Maybe Death was on another hunt.

I STROLLED INTO VELVET VORTEX AND SMOOTHED MY SWEATY palms on my dark wash jeans, my attention traveling straight to the bar. "Silence" by Galli J reverberated through the speakers, pumping up the energy in the club. I hadn't visited Sebastian on a Wednesday evening before, so I had no idea how many people typically hung out. It seemed relatively low-key tonight, but maybe Sebastian wouldn't be so busy, either.

My stomach dipped when I spotted him chatting with Kip. There were only a few people at the bar, men from what I could tell. I grabbed the strap of my leather purse and squeezed it, my nerves dancing around like popcorn kernels in a hot pan.

Approaching Sebastian, I squared my shoulders and willed my palms to stop sweating. The moment he spotted me, heat pulsed through my body. *Damn, he looks good.* A gorgeous smile eased across his face, and I nearly melted on the spot. I climbed onto the barstool and set my purse next to me.

"Hey, beautiful." Sebastian leaned over the bar and kissed me. He winked at me, then said, "That's for any stupid fuckers that think they have a chance with you."

His comment should have irritated me, but it had the opposite effect. It was sexy as hell.

"Thank you. Are you going on break soon?"

Kip meandered over to us, grinning. "Hey, Ella. It's good to see you again."

Our eyes met and a small jolt of electricity zipped through me. For the first time, I was close enough to notice the outer edge of Kip's contacts.

"I didn't know you wore contacts."

"Yeah, they're actually brown contacts. I have ocular albinism, which reduces the pigmentation in the iris and retina. It tends to scare people off. This seems to have fixed the problem. I actually get laid now." He arched a brow at me and smirked.

Images of Death flashed through my head, and I sized Kip up, my brain nudging me with possibilities I didn't want to believe. Sweat slickened my palms as I reminded myself to breathe.

Holy crap. How had I not seen this before? The similarities were right in front of me—the size of the hands, the broad shoulders, the shape of the mouth. Oh god, no. No! No! No! It can't be. If Kip is Death, that means I've been sleeping with Sebastian's best friend. I had to be wrong.

My stomach churned, and my world screeched to a standstill as my breath hitched in my chest. Kip and Death couldn't be one and the same, but the similarities were overwhelming. *Goddammit. My relationship with Sebastian depends on me making a mistake about Kip's identity.*

I folded my hands on the counter, willing my feelings not to register on my face. If I was correct, then how was he so calm and offhanded about our interaction? "You too. How have you been?"

He popped Sebastian with the white bar towel. "Busy. This dude's got me runnin' hard."

Sebastian's gaze cut to the side. "Yeah, we're *so* busy tonight."

"Go take a break with your girl, so I can get the hell out of here when you're back. I've got a girl of my own waiting for me."

"Yeah? Is her name Dolly?" Sebastian asked.

I barked out a laugh, then raised my hand in surrender, my brain forming a mental image of a blow-up doll. "I don't need to know any details, guys. Save it for Dolly." I smirked at Kip before we all broke into laughter. Until I knew for sure who Kip really was, I had to pretend that I didn't suspect a thing.

I laughed as Sebastian and Kip gave each other shit in a good-natured way. It was clear they were good friends, which meant I was making a mistake ... or Sebastian didn't know what Kip was hiding.

Determination bloomed to life inside me, and I squared my shoulders. Come hell or high water, I was going to find out who Death was.

Chapter 36

Death

"The lamb may not recognize the wolf, but it feels the danger in its presence." ~ Unknown

The alleyway behind Velvet Vortex was peaceful at one in the morning while the rest of the city was pulsing with nightlife. I had found myself a nice hidden spot. I tapped my fingers against the steering wheel, my rage bubbling to the surface once again. My little lamb had thought I was gone for a while and had snuck out to play. I'd made it clear that she was mine, so the fact that she had tested those shark-infested waters was disappointing. She would pay. They both would.

My excitement to see Ella turned a one-eighty when I had pulled up the history of her phone location last night. It was one thing to suspect and another to have confirmation shoved in my face that she was with another man. Not just having coffee or dinner but spending the entire night with him.

My nostrils flared as I gripped the steering wheel so tight my knuckles turned white. The motherfucker had come home, and Ella risked seeing him. Now, he would die a slow, torturous death.

Thinking about all the ways I planned on inflicting pain on him, I settled on skinning him alive one slice at a time. He would pass out from the sheer agony, and I would laugh as I injected him with adrenaline, forcing him to stay conscious. A wicked smile tugged at the corners of my mouth. Two could play at Ella's game.

A few minutes later, Sebastian's black BMW drove out of the employee parking lot and turned right.

Taillights winked in the darkness as he slowed and turned left. My eyes narrowed, wondering where he was going. It wasn't toward his place.

"He's going to Ella's house," I growled, consumed with a sudden need to end Sebastian quickly instead of carving him up. I had other victims to torture, but Sebastian was on the top of my list, and I had an opportunity to take the son of a bitch out right then. Time management 101—work smarter, not harder.

Waiting to see if he would turn down Elm Street toward Ella's, I bided my time. There was a slight chance I was wrong about where he was headed, but I doubted it. What baffled me was the fact that Ella had been bold enough to invite him to her place.

My brain throbbed with possibilities, my anger simmering beneath my skin like a million little bugs eating me from the inside out. I gritted my teeth, focusing on the vehicle ahead of me.

I pressed the accelerator, sending it lurching forward. The sound of the impact split my head open. I blinked several times in an attempt to focus on the task at hand.

I put the car in reverse and hit the gas, slamming into it again. The car flipped a few times before the scrape of the fiberglass wrapping around the tree in the middle of someone's yard sent a satisfying shiver down my back. "Goodbye, Sebastian Fletcher."

Chapter 37

Ella

My phone rang and jarred me out of a peaceful sleep. Rubbing my bleary eyes, I glanced at the digital clock on my nightstand. Who the hell would be calling me at seven-fifty in the morning?

Dad!

I snatched the cell up, fumbling in the process and sending it sliding across my floor. Somehow, the sheets had wrapped around my legs, and I kicked furiously in an attempt to answer before I missed the call. Finally, I landed with a thud on the hardwood and crawled to my phone. Breathless and terrified, I answered.

"Hello?"

"Babe? It's Cami."

My spine tightened, and despite the fear pumping through my heart valves, I managed to remain calm. Cami would only call me at this hour if it were an emergency. "What's wrong? Are you okay? Is it Dad? Did you hear something before I did?"

"Your dad is fine as far as I know, but you need to get to the hospital as soon as possible."

"What? Why?" Still half-asleep, I pulled myself up and staggered to the bathroom.

"It's Sebastian. He was in a really bad car accident a few hours ago. They just brought him in."

Ice chilled my veins as the reality of her words bitch slapped me. I couldn't fucking breathe, let alone move or think coherently.

"I don't have any other details yet, but Ryan and his partner found the car. I'll see if he knows anything. Grab some coffee and get your ass over here. It looked really bad, babe."

I pinched the bridge of my nose, refusing to cry. Until I had more information, jumping to conclusions wouldn't do any good. "I'm on my way, Cami. Call me if there are any updates."

"See you in a bit. Drive safe, please."

I disconnected the call, my hand trembling as I set the phone on the bathroom counter and washed my face. After I peed and dressed in jeans and a hoodie, I made a large cup of coffee to go and called my boss on the way to the hospital. After I explained more in-depth about my dad's cancer and now the accident with my *uncle*, he told me to take the time I needed, but to call and check in. Collecting my purse, I hurried out the door and prayed that Sebastian wasn't going to die.

I PACED THE WHITE TILE HALLWAY FLOORS, CHEWING ON MY nails until one started bleeding. My nerves were fucking shot. Sebastian had sustained a head injury and a punctured lung, which was all that we were aware of so far.

After Cami finished her shift that afternoon, she joined me in the emergency waiting room. Tears streamed down my cheeks as I paced beside Cami, her hand wrapped tightly in mine. My heart felt like it was being torn out of my chest as I silently prayed for the miracle that

Sebastian needed to be able to survive the operation. All around us, the hospital bustled with activity, but all I could feel was the ever-growing weight of terror and despair pressing on me.

The world outside seemed miles away from where I stood, a place unable to help or intervene. I clung desperately to hope, as if I could save him by sheer will alone.

I slowed and stared out the hallway windows that overlooked the busy Portland streets.

"Ryan will be here soon. We might have some off-the-record answers about the car accident. I know it's not an update on Sebastian, but I'll keep bugging the nurses for any new information." Cami slipped her arm around me and squeezed my shoulder. "Deep breaths. When we're this stressed, we forget that our brains need oxygen."

I covered my face with my hands, my neck stiff with tension. "Cami, Sebastian and I had just told each other we wanted to see where our relationship might lead. I could imagine myself with him long term."

Cami blanched. "Really? You don't think it's too soon?"

I shook my head. "No. Sometimes you just know. Besides, we're taking our time, dating, hanging out, getting to know each other. It's not like we got engaged."

"That makes more sense." Cami rubbed my back, attempting to soothe me.

Tears streamed down my cheeks, and I angrily swiped them away. If I found out that Death had anything to do with Sebastian's accident, Death would be the one who would have to run from *me*. Maybe Cami had some more information.

"Do you have any idea if another car was involved, or if anyone else was hurt?" I'd told Cami that my stalker wasn't around anymore, and it was just a freak thing that he'd looked at me through my kitchen window that night, so I doubted that my question would raise any suspicions.

Cami's forehead pinched. "I have no clue. We can ask Ryan.

Normally I would see the people involved as they all come into the emergency room at once, but I hurried to help with Sebastian, so I don't know."

"Thank you, Cami. Thank you for helping Sebastian and calling me." I hiccuped through my tears while I soothed my battered soul with ways to capture and torture Death if he was responsible. Everything inside me screamed that it was him. What surprised me most was that a car accident wasn't his method of operating. He liked to play with his prey before he killed them. My insides twisted as I recalled that he'd killed Stephen quickly in my kitchen. He hadn't followed his normal pattern then, either. He had been saving my life, though. An idea formed in my mind, and a possible puzzle piece fell into place. Heavy footsteps slapped the tile floor behind us, and I peeked over my shoulder into the waiting area. A tall, muscular, dark-haired cop approached.

"Cami," he said, his voice deep. "I'm here."

Cami spun around and embraced him. "Hi, thank you for stopping by."

He kissed the top of her head. "Sorry it took so long, but an accident like that takes a while to report and take down the details."

"I understand." Cami turned to me, still attached to Ryan. "This is my best friend, Ella McCloud."

Ryan extended his hand. "Nice to see you again. I'm guessing you've not had any more stalkers dropping by your house."

Oh. Shit. Cami is dating Officer Bexley! I glanced at my bestie.

"You two know each other?" Cami asked, puzzled.

"He was the officer who showed up to check my house when I called 911 when that man was lurking around my property." I looked at Ryan. "I had no idea you were the same person. I feel like I already know you since Cami talks about you all the time."

He flashed me a kind smile. "I'm sorry about your boyfriend."

Sebastian wasn't officially my boyfriend, but I wasn't about to correct him.

"Thanks. He's in surgery now. Hopefully we will hear something soon."

"He's lucky he's alive. There were skid marks on the road, so he was trying to brake, and it sent the vehicle into a tailspin. It flipped a few times before the tree stopped him. The car wrapped around it, and we had to use the jaws of life to get him out."

My hand flew to my mouth, and my heart ceased beating. Panic rose, and I thought I might be sick.

"Was there another car involved?" My voice shook with my question, terrified to hear the truth, but one that I had to learn.

"I can't say anything else until the investigation is over. It's routine, but I'll let you know as soon as I can."

Dammit! What if Death had forced him off the road? There would have been evidence, right? *Not necessarily.* Death was an expert at covering up his tracks. Maybe he'd stood in the middle of the street at night and scared the shit out of Sebastian. If he'd done something like that, he would have had to track Sebastian's car. A jumble of emotions tumbled inside me—fear, fury, and confusion. So many thoughts—followed by even more questions—zipped through my head.

"So this was just a fluke accident?"

Cami suspiciously eyed me. She knew me well enough to understand that I was getting at something. I was, but I couldn't talk to her about Death. A heavy blanket shrouded me in loneliness. This mess was just another reason that Death and I could never work. I would live in a completely different world than my family and best friend, chained to silence to protect Death from ever being caught and constantly scared to piss him off.

"We're still waiting for the full report, but I'll let Cami know as soon as we find out anything else." Ryan nodded, then returned his attention to Cami, doting on her before he had to leave.

I was happy for her, but if she was serious about a cop, then it would definitely change our conversations. She could never learn about Sebastian breaking the law and helping women and children escape dangerous situations. Even though Cami might support what he was doing, if she ever slipped up with Ryan, Sebastian would be arrested along with everyone else who was involved.

Where are Dope and Kip, anyway? I searched the area, but I didn't see him anywhere. That was odd. Dope and Kip were Sebastian's closest friends, so it didn't make sense that they weren't there. Suspicions needled my skin as I wondered where they were, especially Kip.

A few minutes later, a pair of doors leading down a hallway whooshed open and Dope and Kip appeared.

"Sebastian's friends are here. I'm going to see what they know." I hurried over to Dope and tugged on his arm. "Hi."

Dope turned and flashed me a sad smile. "Hey. I'm glad you made it."

I gave a slight wave to Kip, and he nodded, acknowledging my presence.

"I didn't realize you guys were here." I folded my arms across my chest and hoped they had some information I didn't.

"Kip and I have been in an intensive care unit waiting room, and we just came out to grab some coffee and see if you were here. We actually arrived not long after they brought Sebastian in. When I talked to the doctor, I told him that I was Sebastian's brother, so he could discuss his medical needs with me."

My insides quivered as I worked up my courage. "Do you have an update? Is Sebastian going to live?" I asked over the thundering of my heart.

Chapter 38

Ella

"**H**e's alive, Ella. I just got a text message that he's still in surgery, but almost finished. They've been decent about sending me updates during the operation."

I blew out a sigh, tears spilling down my cheeks. "He can't die, Dope. He fucking can't."

Dope surprised me with a warm hug, then pulled away. "He's a badass dude. He's going to be fine. Wait and see."

Dope's words didn't match the fear in his voice, but I loved that he was attempting to stay positive.

"One of the cops that was on the scene is here. I just talked to him, but they're still investigating the accident. I'm trying to make sense of how this happened in the first place."

Kip cleared his throat. "He'd had a long night at the bar. Bass is a hard head and needs to take some time off to sleep and enjoy life, but he's always burning the candle at both ends. I suspect he fell asleep at the wheel."

I rubbed my arms, warding off an eerie chill. Images of the files at the law office flickered through my mind's eye, and I quickly masked my thoughts. For now, I would have to stay alert and attempt to figure out what my subconscious was telling me.

"My best friend Cami is with me. Why don't you join us while we all wait?"

"Sounds good," Kip said.

Dope stuffed his hand in his jeans pocket before he agreed.

I led them over to Cami and introduced them. Over the next several hours, Dope and Kip reminisced about old times with Sebastian, and I learned a bit more about how these guys met in middle school and grew up together. Dope wasn't shy about sharing hilarious stories about the shenanigans they got into, including hot-wiring his mom's car one night to drag race.

I laughed between my tears as they explained that his mom's car was a Pinto with zero horsepower, and they got their asses kicked. Apparently, Dope and Sebastian were the two in trouble all the time. Kip joined them but often cleaned up their messes.

I discreetly glanced at Kip, the wheels turning in my mind as I tried to piece my suspicions together. I wasn't sure who he really was or how he was connected to Death, but there were hidden secrets I had to uncover. For Sebastian's sake. The possibility that I had slept with Sebastian's best friend still rattled my soul, but at the moment, I didn't have any proof to back it up, only a bad feeling.

"I'm glad you're both here. It's comforting to hear about all the good times you've had with Sebastian. I have to trust there will be more." What I said was true, but there was another important factor I was searching for, and they made it easier to sift through since they were together. However, I wasn't ready to deal with that yet, and I shoved it out of my mind for the time being.

Dope set his arms on his legs and stared at the floor, the air changing from good memories to heartbreak.

I shifted in my seat and leaned my head on Cami's shoulder right before a tall man in green scrubs entered the room. "Hal Whitney?"

Dope shot out of his chair, raising his hand. Kip and I followed in case we could also learn about Sebastian.

The doctor took one look at us and turned to Dope. "I'm Dr. Roggins, one of Sebastian's surgeons." He peered at Kip and me and rubbed his stubbled jawline. "Only family, I'm sorry."

"We're all brothers and sisters," Dope explained.

"Half," I chimed in. "That's why we don't look alike. We all grew up in the same house, though." I hoped like hell my added lie would help.

"Ah, okay. Well, Sebastian made it through surgery. He had a punctured lung, head trauma, and internal bleeding. We stopped the bleeding of the liver. As for the head trauma, we won't know how serious it is until he wakes up."

"What does that mean, exactly? Will he have amnesia or be in a coma the rest of his life?" Kip asked, unable to disguise his frantic tone.

"We haven't seen signs of permanent damage, but again, we have to wait until he regains consciousness to assess the situation fully. I'm sorry I can't tell you more yet. But he's alive. Let's try to focus on the positive. Now it's just a matter of time to see what happens."

I pinched the bridge of my nose, soaking in what Doctor Roggins had just said. Sebastian was alive. "When can we see him?"

"He was just moved into a private room. You all can come back. Give him a bit of time to wake up and don't overwhelm him with questions, though. Let him acclimate."

"We promise," I said.

Dope and Kip agreed as well. I glanced over at Cami, who was standing by the chairs, her hands clasped together.

I gave her a thumbs-up, and her shoulders slumped.

"I'll text you," I mouthed.

Following the doctor, Kip, Dope, and I disappeared behind the locked doors. The overwhelming stench of antiseptic and death greeted me, and I recoiled inward. I thought I would be used to it after all the hospital visits with Dad, but I had the same reaction every time.

We walked to the end of the hall in silence before Doctor

255

Roggins slowed at room 502. He pushed the door open and motioned for us to go in.

"The nurse will be here shortly to check on him. Grab yourself a seat and let him sleep."

"Okay," I whispered. "Thank you for taking care of him."

"Of course," Doctor Roggins said before he left.

I hung back in the doorway, staring at Sebastian's sleeping form. Brown and black bruises dotted the right side of his swollen face. The soft beep of the machine monitoring his heart rate filled the area. An IV pole with two bags suspended from hooks stood beside his bed, administering pain meds and keeping him hydrated.

A blinding rage rooted itself inside me. If my suspicions about Death were true, he would pay for this. My attention landed on Dope and Kip as they pulled up chairs next to their best friend. I scoured every inch of both of them, searching for clues as panic clutched my chest. I forced myself to breathe as I approached Sebastian.

Gently, I brushed a lock of hair off his forehead and kissed his cheek.

"I'm here, baby," I whispered. Dope brought me a chair, and I settled in on the opposite side of the guys.

I took Sebastian's hand in mine and traced small circles on the back of it with my fingertips. His skin was warm to the touch, and I wondered if he realized I was there. We were all there for him, hoping and praying that he would wake up without any permanent brain injuries.

Dope, Kip, and I kept the conversation positive and in hushed tones. It took everything inside me not to try to wake Sebastian, but he'd just been through surgery, and his body needed rest.

Over the next few hours, I updated Cami and Mom and learned that Dad was doing well at the beginning of the trial. My heart soared with the news, and then I reminded myself how many times we thought he was going to recover before it all went to hell again.

I leaned back in the uncomfortable hospital chair, my ass screaming at me for sitting so long. There was no way I would leave

Sebastian, though. Pretending to close my eyes and sleep, I racked my brain for hints of what my subconsciousness was trying to tell me.

"You almost got caught," Dope snapped.

His deep voice was distinguishable enough to differentiate who spoke even as they whispered.

"Don't pin this on me," Kip said, his tone clipped and irritated.

"I'm fucking pissed that this happened. It could have been avoided if we'd ..." Dope blew out a big breath. "It's gotta stop."

"I've tried, but it's no use. I need help managing it."

Play it cool, Ella, and let them talk. I mentally urged the guys to continue.

"And what about Ella?" Kip asked. "I'm surprised she hasn't figured it out."

"Me too, but shit's gonna hit the fan soon. I warned you both this would happen, but nobody fucking listened to me."

Silence enveloped the room, leaving me hanging on their every word. Anxiety boiled in my veins as icy suspicion of what they meant by me not finding out pierced my chest. A flurry of possibilities raced through my mind, and a single revelation congealed in my gut like poison.

Chapter 39

Sebastian

I struggled to peel my eyelids open, but they felt as if they'd been glued shut. Once I won the battle, I was met with sharp shards of blinding white light. I attempted to pull my arms up to shield my sight, but it was as if they were glued in place.

"Sebastian. Can you hear me? It's Ella." Her sweet voice floated in the air around me, and I finally managed to make out her gorgeous features through the haze of pain that pierced through my skull.

"Do you want an ice chip?"

I nodded, unable to speak yet.

"Here. Open your mouth."

I groaned as I pried my lips apart, the skin of my upper lip tearing across my lower one.

What the fuck is going on? Frantically, I searched the room for anything familiar, but it was all so hazy.

A cold sensation coated my tongue, and I swallowed, allowing the moisture to dampen the fire in my throat. "More," I managed to say.

"Hey, man, it's Dope. Kip is here too. You had a car wreck, and you're in the hospital."

My eyes closed, the memories rushing back of a blinding light in the middle of the road. I didn't remember anything after that.

"You had surgery. Your lung was fucked up, and you had some internal bleeding, but the doctors got it stopped. Plus, you hit your head pretty hard. Do you recall any of that?" Dope asked, staring at me with an expression twisted with worry.

"Bloody hell, not a bit of it. But I know who you motherfuckers are." I attempted a grin, but it took all my effort. My curiosity swept the area as I identified the sterile room and small hospital bed that I was in.

"We told the doctor that we are all half siblings so we could stay with you." Ella's gentle smile made my heart sing.

"That's my good girl," I croaked.

The guys shot Ella a look and chuckled. I hadn't meant to call her my good girl in front of them, but the drugs had me loopy as shit.

"How long have I been here?"

"Since about four this morning. It's five in the evening now, so a full day," Kip explained. He placed his hand on the railing of my bed, and I could have sworn that I saw Ella flinch. Apparently, my hit to the head had me imagining things. Why in the hell would Ella react to Kip like that? I would have to ask her when no one else was around.

Ella continued feeding me ice chips until my voice sounded more like my own. The guys continued to talk, quizzing me about what I remembered. Hell, I wondered how much they would recall while fucked up on drugs.

A shadow flashed through my mind, and I winced. "I think someone else was there right before I had the accident."

Ella was the only one who didn't appear shocked by the possibility. She settled into her chair, refusing to let go of my hand. I was okay with that. When I first woke up, it was disconcerting until I saw her beside my bedside. Her presence instantly soothed me.

"What do you mean?" Kip asked.

I inhaled slowly, mindful of my injuries. Even with the pain meds, they hurt like a son of a bitch. "Maybe it's nothing, but I thought I saw a car behind me."

Dope's expression grew grim.

"I spoke with one of the cops on the scene, and they're still investigating," Ella said softly.

"Maybe I hit my head harder than I realized." I reached up and shoved my fingers through messy strands, realizing I had some dried blood and hair plastered to my forehead. Something wasn't settling right inside my gut. I was sure that another person was involved in my accident. I slowly turned toward Ella and smiled. "I'm glad you're here. You, too, motherfuckers, but especially Ella."

"Where else would I be?" She raised my hand to her lips and kissed my knuckles.

"Would you and Kip find the nurse or see if you can track me down some Jell-O and 7Up? Maybe they'll let me eat something."

For a second, I thought her shoulders tensed, but my head must have been messing with me. "Sure." She stood and squeezed my hand before she walked to the door.

"Dope, do you need anything?" Kip asked as he joined her.

"I'm good, thanks."

I waited for Ella and Kip to leave before I turned my attention to Dope.

"What the fuck happened, and don't give me any bullshit."

The color drained from Dope's face. "We're trying to figure it out, but you've got to stay quiet. If you need to talk, you gotta keep it between us, man. Don't drag Ella into this. It could put her in danger."

I pursed my lips together, frustrated that I didn't have answers. "Am I fucking crazy to think it was Kip who ran me off the road? We've talked about how he's disappearing and shit."

Dope winced as he rubbed the back of his neck. "No fucking way, man. Kip would never pull shit like that, even if he were pissed at you. But if you said there was another car involved, I believe you."

His words hit me in the chest, cracking me wide open. I shook my head, my hair rubbing against the pillow, making a rustling noise. "You're right. I'm all fucked up about him. I'm worried. We've been friends since middle school. I trust both of you with my life. These pain meds are making me jumpy." My voice trailed off as I realized what I said. "Why would someone have followed me and tried to kill me?"

"Not sure, Bass. I'm sorry, man. I'm looking into it because you have no fucking idea how badly I want to figure all of this out. But god knows we've made enemies while working at Safe Horizon. I know we try to keep our identities concealed, but someone might have learned the truth. Maybe a wife broke protocol and her husband tracked you down or something."

I closed my eyes against his words, not wanting to believe that someone hated me enough to be responsible for my accident. "What do you need from me to get to the bottom of this?"

"To get better. I think it would be a good idea if Ella stayed with you tonight. I'll ask Kip to take care of the bar. That will give me some time to chat up some connections and try to learn what the hell is going on. I need to follow up on a few more ideas."

I raised my hand, and Dope grabbed it. "We've got this. We'll figure out if anyone is responsible for your accident. Hang tight. I hope to have answers soon."

"Thanks, man. Lie low. If someone really wanted me out of the way, they might want the same for you. Especially if it's concerning our work."

"I'll watch my back."

Exhaustion tugged at me as my hand dropped to the bed. "Dope?" My head lolled to one side, still pounding.

"Yeah?" Concern laced his tone.

"Keep Ella safe ..." I licked my lips. "At all costs." My eyelids fluttered closed as I drifted off into a dreamless sleep.

Chapter 40

Ella

After five long days, Sebastian was released to go home. Dope had bought Sebastian a wheelchair, so getting him in and out of his penthouse would be easier. When Sebastian asked me to stay with him at his place while he healed, my heart screamed a thousand yeses. I phoned into work and requested some extra time off, updating them on Dad's progress. They agreed to a few more weeks but said I should start working part time from home as soon as I could. I was okay with that since Sebastian needed company more than my help. With him still healing, he would most likely nap a lot, allowing me to dive back into some cases.

I opened the front door of Sebastian's penthouse and set my suitcase down while Dope wheeled him in. Cami had been a lifesaver and packed a bag for me, so I didn't have to worry about it. It was evident that Sebastian was feeling better because he grumbled all the way, insisting that he could get into the elevator and stand on his own two feet. Maybe so, but he was still weak, and I refused to let him try. If he fell when I was the only one with him, I wasn't strong enough to pick him up.

"Here we are," Dope said, grinning at his best friend.

I glanced around the stunning place with its open floor plan for the living and dining area, eager to spend time with Sebastian privately instead of at the hospital with the nurses and doctors constantly running in and out. During those long days, I'd learned a lot about his friendship with Kip and Dope and how the club and the Safe Horizon Society had started. These men risked everything to save innocent people, and I quickly understood how much they had truly given up of their own lives. Sebastian was selfless, and I could see why he wanted to step down. Dope and Kip were more than capable of being in the field, while Sebastian stayed back and worked behind the scenes.

"You ready, man?" Dope secured the brakes on the wheelchair, backed away, and gave Sebastian some space.

Sebastian planted both his palms on the arms and stood. "Told you I was fine."

Dope shot me a "whatever" look, then clapped his hands together. "Never doubted you for a minute."

Dope folded the wheelchair and placed it near the front door while Sebastian gingerly walked over to me.

"Mmm, this is so much better." He wrapped his arms around me and pulled me to him.

I gripped his muscular biceps in case he got dizzy from the meds, but he seemed solid on his feet.

"Almost." I grinned at him before pushing up on my tiptoes and kissing him.

Dope cleared his throat. "Remember the doctor's orders, you two." He snickered. "I'll be back in a few hours with groceries and lunch."

"Thank you, Dope. For everything," Sebastian said.

"Keep my man out of trouble, will ya? Maybe now that you're around, shit will settle down."

I nearly choked on my spit. I highly doubted anything would calm down. They had no idea I had been deep diving to learn Death's identity. If Sebastian suspected someone else was involved in the car accident, I believed him. It had crossed my mind that it could be a vengeful husband of someone in the Safe Horizon, but as hard as I tried to talk myself out of it, I knew in my gut it was Death. I also understood that Death wouldn't storm into a hospital to hurt Sebastian. We were safe here as well. The security for the building was tight, and I had no intention of allowing grocery or fast-food deliveries either, minimizing Death's access to Sebastian.

"Are you tired?" I asked once Dope was gone.

"Yeah. It's crazy how the trip home drained me. I hate it. I feel weak and helpless."

"Stop. You're not either of those things. It's as simple as this. Rest and take care of yourself, and you'll be back to normal in no time."

Sebastian pressed his forehead against mine, and my heart stuttered. "Thank you for staying with me."

"I'm happy to be here."

He lowered his head, kissing me. "It would make me feel better if you wore a little nurse uniform for me while you're here."

His chuckle sent delicious shivers through me. As much as I wanted to tear his clothes off and feel him inside of me, it couldn't happen. Not yet. Maybe it was for the best, allowing us to spend time together before we ravished each other.

"I'll see what I can do. Let's get you tucked into bed." I playfully swatted his ass cheek.

"Come with me."

I arched my brow, giggling at his choice of words. "I'll join you until you fall asleep."

He flashed me an ornery grin as he led the way.

AFTER SEBASTIAN PASSED OUT, I SLIPPED AWAY AND CLOSED his bedroom door. I stretched, staring at the high ceilings filled with the bright light from the early afternoon sun. My stomach growled, and I strolled down the hall, my bare feet not making any noise as I headed to the kitchen. I had only been there once before, so I had yet to learn where anything was. I opened the stainless-steel refrigerator, searching for food that wasn't spoiled, but his fridge was practically empty, with only a half-gallon of expired milk. After I emptied the carton into the sink, I then located the trash at the end of the island. I searched the cabinets, still not finding anything worthy of consumption. My fingernails tapped against the black marble counters, and I realized that I was at Dope's mercy until he brought groceries by. I checked my watch, hoping it would be soon.

Soaking up the minutes of silence, I tried to relax, but my brain kicked into gear. I sifted through the conversation I'd overheard between Dope and Kip had at the hospital. What had they been talking about, and what hadn't I figured out?

The doorbell chimed, startling me out of my thoughts. I hurried to the door and peered through the peephole, nearly crying with joy. I flung it open and smiled at Dope. "Please tell me you have some food."

I moved out of the way and let him in. Both arms were loaded with reusable grocery bags. "I figured he had absolutely nothing in his house. The man lives at the club."

"Makes sense." I took a bag from each arm, and we walked to the kitchen. "He's still sleeping. He's been out for a few hours."

"Good. He needs it. He's a grumpy bastard when he's running on fumes." Dope started to unload and put the groceries where they belonged. "The brown bag has Chinese food. Help yourself. There's more than enough for all of us."

I rubbed my hands together. "You're my hero."

"Well, I wouldn't go that far, but thanks."

Once everything was put away, Dope grabbed us plates and silverware. We sat at the table, and I scooped some sweet and sour chicken onto my plate. We were quiet as we dove into our food. My stomach dipped as I realized that I needed to have a conversation with Dope, and I hoped that he would keep it between us.

"Can I ask you something?"

"Sure. What is it?" he asked around a bite of Mongolian beef.

"I overheard you and Kip talking about me. You said you were surprised I hadn't figured it out. What did you mean?"

Dope's fork hovered in the air, a chow mien noodle slithering off and landing on his plate.

I leaned forward and pinned Dope with an intense gaze. "I think Kip is into some bad shit, and you're covering for him."

Dope put his fork down and rubbed his jeaned thigh with his hand. "You don't understand, Ella. I really thought you were figuring it out, but guess I was wrong."

"Figuring out what?" I waited for him to respond, but he stayed silent. "Dope, tell me before Sebastian wakes up. If you don't, I'll tell him that Kip is behind the car accident and possibly more ..." My stomach catapulted to my toes as the rest of the words lodged in my throat. I couldn't deal with the rest of that mess at the moment. It would have to wait until I knew Sebastian was safe.

Dope's jaw clenched. "You can't do that, Ella. You've got it all wrong. Yeah, Kip was following Bass the night of the car accident, but it's not what you think. He was trying to protect him."

"Then start talking. *Now.*"

"Not here. Let me call Kip to come over and hang out with Bass. Tell Bass that you need to grab some things from your house, and I'll meet you there."

My nostrils flared as I protested. "Until I get answers, Kip can't be alone with Sebastian. I don't trust him."

"Once I explain, it will all make sense. For now, you have to trust *me.*"

Chapter 41

Ella

Two hours later, I met Dope at my place.

"On second thought, I don't want to talk here. It's too risky," Dope said as he stood outside my front door. "Grab your stuff, and let's take a drive."

"You're acting super strange, Dope. Before I go anywhere with you, I have to know that Sebastian is safe. I'm worried sick while he's with Kip."

"He's fine. Bass is my best friend, and I would never allow anything bad to happen to him. Trust me. Please." Dope's brown eyes pleaded with me, tugging at my heart.

Giving in, I collected my purse and phone before I locked my door behind me. "Where are we going?"

"Somewhere it's safe to talk."

He climbed into his dark green Honda Civic, and I did the same. Once I buckled up, he started the engine and pulled away from the curb.

"I guess I never thought about what kind of car you drove. I've only seen you in the van. For some dumb reason, I assumed it was your everyday vehicle too."

That got an arched brow in my direction.

"Ella, I gotta say that I think you're perfect for Bass, but the shit that comes out of your mouth sometimes is ... well." He grimaced.

"Dumb?" I finished for him. "I know. I blurt shit out at times without thinking it through. And, of course, the van isn't your everyday car. It's probably hidden in a garage somewhere, and you change out the license plate every trip you make in it, so if you're reported, it will be more difficult to find a white work van."

Dope grinned at me. "There she is."

I grinned. "I'm new to the criminal world. I mean I'm usually reading files and helping prepare to defend criminals in court, not living the life."

"You're a criminal, too, Ella. You tracked Sebastian, then helped us kidnap people and transport them over a state line."

"You can't kidnap the willing, Dope. Don't be so dramatic." I rolled my eyes. What he said still punched me in the stomach. I *was* a criminal. I had assisted Death in covering up a murder in my home, and that made me an accomplice.

My knee bounced, and I attempted to think about other questions to ask Dope. It would help me not choke him for withholding the truth as soon as we got into his car. Maybe he was anticipating me losing my shit, so he didn't want to be driving. Smart guy.

Twenty minutes later, Dope pulled into the parking lot of a park. Only a few people were walking their dogs or jogging along the path that disappeared into the woods. Portland had a plethora of public parks connected to protected forests. Suddenly, I wondered how many bodies were buried there.

"Let's go." Dope hopped out and waited for me to do the same before he locked the doors.

I threw the strap of my crossbody purse over my shoulder in order to be hands free in case anyone got a bright idea and tried to mug me.

I was a paranoid bitch, but I didn't care. Not after what I heard Kip and Dope say at the hospital. That's why I didn't hesitate when

Dope offered to answer my questions. But I had a few things to say too.

We slowed, and Dope jumped on top of a picnic table, reached inside the front pocket of his jeans, and produced a joint and lighter.

The wind kicked up, cold and biting, and I burrowed further into my coat. The leaves stirred and danced as they were scooped off the sidewalk and into the air.

"It got a little bent." He frowned as he straightened it out as much as he could. "Want a hit?"

"No. I'm just here for answers." I sat next to him, growing impatient with his stalling. "Listen, I understand that you didn't want to talk while driving, but please tell me what you wanted to tell me about. I want to get back to Sebastian as soon as possible."

Dope took a pull of the joint and blew it out several seconds later. "I should start at the beginning, but Ella." He looked at me, sadness in his gaze. "You have to swear to me this doesn't get repeated. If you want to talk to me about it, fine. Even Kip, but not outside our safe circle. What I'm about to tell you falls under the NDA, but I'm asking you again for my peace of mind."

"I promise. I keep secrets every day at work. You can trust me." Not to mention that I had Stephen's blood on my hands. Well, it was on my body, but still.

"For some reason, I trust you, probably because Bass does. Don't prove me wrong." He took another hit, the stench of the pot assaulting my nose.

"I won't." I shifted on my seat, giving him my undivided attention.

"I'll start when we were in middle school because it's the only place I know where to begin. I'm about to share some fucked-up shit."

A cold shudder coursed through me as I tried to brace myself for what he was about to tell me.

"Kip, Bass, and I go way back, but I'd met Bass first when he'd moved to the neighborhood from Australia. We lived a few houses apart from each other in a middle-class neighborhood. It was safe. We rode our bikes in the middle of the street, played football, and we never thought anything about it. Bass and I were just normal kids in sixth grade. Then, everything changed on a fucking dime." He looked out over the park as he spoke. Dope snuffed out his joint and set it on the concrete picnic table beside him before he continued.

"I didn't know anything until after the fact, so my information is all secondhand, and I suspect not the entire story. But." He wiped his palms along his thighs, clearly something he did when he was stressed. "One fall afternoon, Bass and I agreed to meet up after dinner to play Dungeons and Dragons. He never showed." He visibly swallowed, and I realized how difficult this was for him.

"Take your time, Dope." I wanted to slap myself for saying that. My heart was beating so hard I thought it would burst through my chest. I needed him to spill the details before he had to call 911 because my blood pressure was through the roof.

"I tried to call his house but there was no answer. I just figured he had to go somewhere with his parents, and he'd catch up with me later. No big deal. Shit happened. But he didn't meet me for school the next day, either, and I knew something was wrong. I could feel it in my gut, but I dismissed it as being stupid." He rubbed his jaw, his gaze connecting with mine.

"I do that, too, then I regret not listening to that voice."

He nodded. "Instead of going to classes, I hurried to his place and rang the doorbell repeatedly. No one answered. I knew where they kept the key, so I jumped over the back fence and located it under the shriveled-up tomato plant in the garden. Seconds later, I let myself into their garage and then into the house. It was eerily silent and dark. Not a single light was on. I didn't call out to Bass because I thought no one was home. What bothered me was why he'd take off and not tell me. We shared everything, ya know?"

"Cami and I are like that," I said, encouraging him to continue. Cami and I used to be like that before I had dark secrets that I couldn't share with anyone.

"I walked down the hall and spotted the locked front door before I turned to go to the kitchen ..." Dope's voice was so low I had to strain to hear him. He stared at the ground while his hands fisted, his entire body stiffening. "I've never seen anything like it."

Chapter 42

Sebastian

S hards of pain ripped through me as I stirred, trying to open my eyes as I acclimated myself to my surroundings. A thick fog lingered in my head from the accident, but I remembered that Ella had stayed with me until I'd gone to sleep. Eager to see her, I sat up slowly, making sure the room wouldn't spin. Every inch of my body hurt like a son of a bitch, but that's what a car accident would do. The fact that I'd survived was a miracle, and I planned to make the best of my life. Hopefully Ella would continue to be a part of it.

"Alexa, light on." My voice sounded foreign to my ears, and I blinked as I adjusted to the brightness. Glancing at the clock, I realized it was almost nine in the evening. I'd slept for hours without any interruption. The hospital had driven me fucking nuts with the nurses and doctors running in every fifteen minutes.

I stood, testing the strength in my legs, and straightened slowly. My stitches were still healing, but they would come out in a few more days. It took me a minute, but I finally made it to my en suite bathroom and took a piss. God, it felt good to be home. The loud growl of my stomach agreed.

Once I'd relieved myself and washed my hands and face, I left my room and made my way to the kitchen. To my surprise, I didn't find Ella. Kip was there instead.

"Where's Ella?"

"She had to run to her place to grab a few things. You're stuck with me." He flashed me a cocky grin. "Sit. I'll heat up some Chinese food that Dope picked up."

I grunted, holding onto the side of the table as I sank into the chair. "I'm starved for some real food." I massaged my forehead. "Is there any Advil around? I can't seem to shake this headache. You would think the pain meds would take care of it, but I guess it's Advil for the win."

Kip briefly hesitated before locating which cabinet I kept the meds in. "You hit your head pretty hard in the accident." He reached for the bottle and shook it. "It's all out, man. I'll ask Ella to pick some up for you on the way over."

"That's strange. I don't recall taking the last of it." The room blurred for a moment, and my stomach rolled. "I hate the fucking pain meds. They mess with me, and I can't remember anything. They're supposed to help, but they make me feel like shit."

Kip scooped some rice, broccoli, and beef onto a plate before he popped it into the microwave. "Maybe some food will help. If not, try some crackers and 7Up. Dope bought some for you, just in case."

"I hate this. I feel helpless."

"You're not. If someone broke into your home, you'd still put a hell of a beating on him." Kip chuckled. "I know you don't like being down and out, but you're healing fast. You'll be back at the club soon."

He set the piping hot food and a fork in front of me. "I don't recall the accident at all." I eyed him, a creepy sensation ghosting over me.

"As I said, you hit your head hard. The doctor wasn't sure if you had brain damage. It was a fucking relief when you recognized us. It could have been so much worse."

Silence settled over us like a wet blanket, heavy and suffocating.

Kip sat in the chair across the table from me as I played with my food. "I'm glad you made it out alive, man. We thought we'd lost you for a while. It sucked ass."

His words meant a lot to me, and I looked up at him. "Like you and Dope could get rid of me that easily." I cracked a grin at him. "It's weird as hell not remembering anything, though. It's like ... like I know someone else was there, but it's just a shadow in my memory."

"Probably the EMT. Maybe you had moments of consciousness while they were cutting you out of the car."

Hearing him say that, I leaned back in my chair, exasperated. "I don't have a fucking car now, do I?"

Kip's brows dipped with concern. "You've still got your other one. Since you drove the BMW more, your Mercedes is still in its parking space."

"Oh." I glanced at the food growing cold on my plate. "How did I not know that?"

"Don't think too much of it. Your body has been through hell. Just try to relax and let your friends and girlfriend take care of you for a week or so. If there are any more memory issues, we'll call the doctor, but stressing over it won't help any."

Finally, I shoved a forkful of rice into my mouth. "You're right. I remember a ton of other stuff."

"Do you know Ella stayed next to your bedside at the hospital?"

My heart skipped a beat, recalling the moment I saw her. "Yeah."

"Man, she never left you, Bass. Ella slept there, showered there, and ate there. You don't do that unless you really care about someone."

I swallowed my food and stared at him, finally feeling something good again. "Why do you think that?"

"Well, the way she looks at you for starters, like you're the only person on the planet. Chicks don't hang out at hospitals like that, either. There's definitely something there. Hell, she even got feisty with a nurse for wanting to wake you up again." Kip chuckled. "You did a good job when you found her. I think she's a great fit for our group."

"Her father has cancer. Unfortunately, she's had a lot of time in hospitals." I ate another bite, my stomach feeling better as it had some food. "And thanks. She's pretty special."

"I think she'll be good for you."

I set the fork on the side of my plate and looked at my friend. "Would you think I was crazy if I told you I think I'm in love with her?"

"You're already crazy, dude."

Our laughter was a nice change. "Everything inside me wants to move her into the penthouse with me, but it's too soon. I can't rush things between us."

Kip massaged the back of his neck. "Wow. I've never heard you talk about anyone like that before."

"I know. I just worry I'll do something to fuck it up."

He shook his head. "I don't think you can scare her off. Just don't cheat on her."

"You know me better than that. I'm a one girl kind of guy."

Kip cleared his throat, appearing uncomfortable. "Is she seeing anyone else?"

Something in his tone hit me the wrong way, and the idea of sharing a future with Ella suddenly came to a screeching halt.

Chapter 43

Ella

I reached over and took his hand. "What was it, Dope? It's okay, you can talk to me." I was afraid to hear what he was about to say, and I remained quiet until Dope was ready to tell me what he saw at Sebastian's childhood home.

He took a long, slow drag of his joint and held it for what seemed like an eternity. Finally, he exhaled and the wind swept away the acrid smell of the marijuana. His hands shook and his eyes held a faraway look as if he were living that day over again. "His parents ... butchered."

I gasped as my hand flew over my mouth, and my entire body stiffened with horror. *Oh god, I'm so stressed I'm hearing shit that isn't true.*

"There was so much blood. So. Much. Fucking. Blood, Ella. The stench was almost as bad. Even though I was fucking panicked, I forced myself to walk to the edge of the kitchen. I knew better than to go in. My mom watched a ton of crime shows, and all I could think of was not contaminating any evidence. Anyway, I stopped at the threshold and peered in. What I saw fucking snapped me in two.

Huddled in the corner was Bass, holding a bloody knife in his hand and shaking violently."

"Jesus fucking Christ," I hissed as I shot up from my seat. My emotions churned and burned inside me. Poor Sebastian. Poor Dope. Oh my god. He'd said his parents had died, but he hadn't wanted to talk about it. I thought they'd been in a car accident, but this ... holy fucking shit ... this. Could the situation get any worse? "Tell me he didn't kill his parents, Dope. Please," I begged, strangling on my own words.

"He didn't. Not really."

"I need a minute." I stomped away, a storm brewing inside me. My mind spun with a merry-go-round of questions. I whirled back around and placed my hands on my hips, my shock and pity morphing into anger. "What do you mean not really? You need to stop dragging your feet and tell me everything, Dope. You're fucking with my head and feelings for a man that I've fallen for. Just rip the damn Band-Aid off."

"I'm sorry, Ella. Reliving this all is gutting me. I understand where you're at, but you need to remember that Bass, Kip, and I are like brothers. Keep that in the back of your mind as I tell you the rest."

"So you're telling me that you're all insane or that this isn't what it seems like?" I tapped my foot impatiently while a sheen of sweat broke out across my forehead.

"Both." He shoved his fingers in his red hair, leaving it disheveled.

"Then get to talking."

"Yeah. I've got this." He nodded as if to reassure himself that he could go through with the conversation. "I ran out of the house and back to mine where I phoned Mom at work. I was nearly hysterical as I tried to explain to her what I'd seen. She called Dad and the cops and told me to stay put. It was then that I realized Bass was holding the damn knife. If the police showed up and he was still gripping it, they would arrest him and charge him as an adult. I snuck away and ran my ass off back to his place. That time I went through back yards so no one would see me. I barged into his home and ran to the kitchen. After I skirted the walls of the kitchen and reached Bass, I talked to him like I always did. I told him about the new Dungeons and Dragons story I was thinking about. I tried to be so careful walking into the crime scene as I spoke to him. He just rocked back and forth with a blank look on his face. My goal wasn't to get him out of there, just get the knife. If they didn't have a weapon, they wouldn't suspect Bass had anything to do with the murders."

The fear rising in my chest felt like an avalanche of ice-cold water. Terror rippled through me, and I could almost feel the sharp talons as they scraped along my skin. I gritted my teeth nervously, every inch of me shaking, desperate to ask a question but terrified at what the answer may be. "Did he?"

Dope's gaze softened, a deep sorrow in them. "I don't know," he replied, his voice full of sympathy. "Bass and I never talked about everything that happened, only bits and pieces. Even if we did, I'm not sure he'd remember what he saw. The memories are buried so deep inside him that I don't think he can tap into them. Sebastian blocked it out hard. Whatever went down, I doubt we'll ever get the full story."

I curled my hands into fists, fighting the rush of tears, ready to break free, but somehow, I managed to rein them in.

"How does Kip fit in all of this?"

"Let me get there. After the cops showed up, social services took Bass. He wasn't at school for weeks, and I couldn't get in touch with him. Mom was able to reach the social worker, but Bass was at a boy's home where they were keeping him until they found a family willing to take a traumatized preteen in. Mom and Dad were all over that, and it wasn't long after Bass moved in with us."

"Shit. Were you scared he'd hurt your parents too?"

"Fucking terrified. I didn't sleep for the first month he was there. But over time, I saw glimmers of my best friend. Mom was a huge fan of therapy, and the state paid for his sessions. Mom never told me what she'd learned, but whatever it was, she was even kinder to Bass. She went out of her way to make him feel like family. Damn, he's always been family, but his parents were brutally murdered in front of him. That shit scars someone for life, man. You don't ever unsee something that horrible. I sure as hell didn't, and I didn't see it all go down, just the aftermath." He took a steadying breath.

"Life returned to normal for the most part. Kip moved into the neighborhood, and we all hit it off pretty quick. There were days that Bass was super quiet, and I knew he was struggling with the loss of his parents. It wasn't until later that I learned how bad it really was."

Dope shuddered before he picked up his joint. I snatched it out of his grip as he was about to light it. "You'll get this back when you're finished telling me the rest."

Dope scowled at me. "Don't be a brat, Ella, give me my weed." He held his hand out, but I stood my ground.

When Dope realized I wasn't fucking around, he started to talk again. The heavy ball in my stomach churned, and I needed him to get to the damn point.

"Kip was staying over for a D&D weekend. We were excited about the expansion that had just come out. Dad actually picked it up for us. Mom bought snacks and drinks and checked on us a few times. Other than that, we were holed up in my room for those two days. Man, that time was so fun. It was like Bass hadn't lived through hell, and I had my best friend back. He seemed like he'd healed enough to move on. It was good to see him happy. Kip didn't really know any difference since he'd only been around for a year, but I did. I really thought Bass had turned a corner. I was so fucking wrong."

I froze, waiting for Dope to ease my fears.

"At first it was kind of subtle. Bass would imitate a character to entertain us. His voice would change and the expressions on his face were cool as hell. It was like he could become someone else. Kip told him he had found his calling and could make good money as a voice actor for Batman or some other superhero cartoon. By the time the weekend was nearly over, we were tired as hell for staying awake for almost forty-eight hours ... that's when shit hit the fan."

The pressure in my head grew more and more intense as fear consumed me.

"All the sudden, Bass shuddered like he was cold, then his entire face changed. His eyes looked different, and his accent was gone. He gave us the evilest smile I'd ever seen, and I almost pissed my pants when he started talking." Dope glanced at me, our gazes locking.

A dark and heavy dread licked up and down my body, and my palms grew clammy. *This can't be happening. He can't be saying what I think he's saying.*

"He said he'd gotten home from school and walked into his house like any other day. That time, there was a strange man there. Bass heard fighting and crept closer to listen. His father argued with the man, and his mother screamed. Bass got so scared he hid beneath the stairs. There was a little door there for storage, and he crawled in. He listened to his mom die a horrible death, Ella."

A groan of frustration and relief escaped me. "He didn't kill his parents?! Dope, how could you not tell me that first?" I fisted my hand and bit my knuckles, trying not to punch him in the damn jaw for not telling me that information to begin with.

"Because if I'd started with that, you wouldn't have listened to the rest. You would have made up your mind before I told you everything."

Finally, after learning that Sebastian was innocent of murder, I collapsed back into my seat, still shaking from the intensity of my emotions. "The important thing is that Sebastian didn't murder his family."

A heartbeat of silence hung in the air.

"I never said that. I said I didn't have the entire story."

Chapter 44

Sebastian

A sickly combination of fear and anger snaked through my body. I hadn't talked to Ella about seeing other people, so I had no idea if she was or wasn't.

"You're making me cranky, mate. Do you know something or are you just asking me if Ella is dating around?"

He raised his hands in surrender. "All I'm saying is, has there been a conversation and a commitment, or is there a possibility she might be seeing someone else?"

A low, guttural growl slipped from my throat and echoed through the kitchen. "She mentioned that she wasn't, but that was a few weeks ago, and I didn't pry at the time. I trust her. You should, too, unless you've seen her with someone."

"Nope. I'm just watching out for my brother. I think she's great, and I'd love to see the two of you together long term, but it's never safe to assume she's not dating anyone until there's been a conversation. Besides, she's young. Your rules aren't her rules."

As much as I hated to admit it, Kip was right. There was an eleven-year age difference. I was old school as far as relationships went. I'd planned on speaking to her after I got home from moving women and children to a safe environment, but then the car accident fucked up my plans.

"Just talk to her, man. Ditch any preconceived ideas and have that conversation, then you'll clear any doubt there might be on either side."

Picking up my fork again, I continued to eat. The thought of Ella being touched by another man had nearly sent me into a toxic rage, and I had to rein in my temper fucking fast. It was definitely time to change the topic. "This is good." I jabbed the fork at my food. "Maybe Dope will bring us some more."

Kip grinned at me. "It's nice to see your appetite is returning."

"What about you? What were you up to when I was laid up in a hospital bed?"

"Nothing new. I took care of the bar when I wasn't with you."

"Have you met anyone new lately?"

He laced his fingers behind his head. "Nah. Same ol shit, another day. Chicks throwing themselves at us, but nothing serious. I was interested in Ella's friend, Cami, but she showed up at Velvet Vortex with a cop as her date."

My entire body went ramrod straight. "And you didn't think to mention that to me?"

"I just did."

"Sooner?"

"Bass, dude, you were laid up in a hospital bed barely hanging on by a thread. Cut me some slack, for fuck's sake. I was waiting for the right time to tell you about it. At this point, it doesn't seem like it's serious between them. If it is, then we've got plenty of practice keeping the Safe Horizon Society under wraps. It's all good. I think your pain meds are making you irritable. Maybe see if you can dial it back before you hurt someone."

"We don't hang out with cops. End of discussion." I blew out a sigh. "I didn't mean to give you shit. It just surprised me. If Ella's best friend is dating someone on the police force, it could be problematic.

Hopefully Ella realizes that and won't ask us to go out with them much."

"If she does, we'll deal with it. Just be sure to direct the conversation and watch your body language. This is normal for us, though. I didn't tell you about Cami to stress you out, just to be cautious." He gave me a slight shrug. "Hopefully, their relationship will be short-lived."

Kip seemed confident about the situation, and I decided it wasn't worth wasting my energy over unless it became an issue. I would definitely be careful around them in the meantime.

"Thanks for having my back. You're a good bloke. You keep me on a good path."

I ate slowly, brooding about Ella. Kip and I had grown up together, and he carefully chose his conversations. At times he walked on eggshells around me. Hell, Dope did too. Usually I was pretty chill, but my temper occasionally got away from me.

Guilt drowned me like a tidal wave, and it finally hit me that I'd almost died. I had to stop being an asshole and make some changes. Kip and Dope were innocent bystanders of my rage, but I was really only angry at myself. When my parents had passed away, the world had ended, and my anger had seeped into every corner of my life. I could control it most of the time, but that wasn't good enough. It wasn't good enough for Ella. I had to find another way to release my pent-up aggression without returning to underground fighting.

Whether I liked it or not, Kip had a point, and I relaxed a little, realizing his intentions were in the right place. There was one quick way to get to the bottom of Kip's, and now my, concerns with Ella. Once she was home for the evening, we needed to talk and get on the same page. I wasn't interested in having my heart ripped out of my chest.

Chapter 45

Ella

M y hope folded in on itself with Dope's correction. "Keep going," I whispered.

"Bass kept talking about how the man found him hiding and jerked him out from beneath the stairs. Bass assumed he'd be killed next, but clearly, he lived. Anyway, Bass continued in that fucked-up character he was pretending to be and said the man dragged him to the kitchen where he saw his mom—dead. His father was tied up on the floor next to her, still alive. The stranger had duct taped his dad's mouth so he couldn't yell for help. The guy forced the knife into Bass's hand and ordered him to kill his father."

My world tilted on its side, and I gripped the edge of the table. The cold, rough cement bit into my palm. Choking out a cry, I focused on the ground and tried not to scream in agony.

"The man took his time and instructed Bass how to kill someone slowly, to make him suffer for his sins. He guided Bass's hand with each stab to his dad's body. As twisted and fucked-up as that was, Bass wasn't finished. He detailed the last blow to his father's chest that he alone delivered. He was covered in his father's blood and at some point, he lost his way from what the murderer made him do. The police report said there were twenty-three puncture wounds."

My heart stopped beating, and I stared at him in shock. Acid churned in my gut as I tried to reconcile that Sebastian had been forced to kill his flesh and blood, but somewhere inside him, he'd flipped when he delivered all twenty-three blows that ended his father. I rushed a few feet away before I bent over and emptied the contents of my dinner on the grass. Swiping at the string of spit, I wondered why I could witness Death murder someone in my house, but the thought of Sebastian doing the same sent me into a wicked tailspin. I slowly straightened and turned to Dope.

"Did they ever find the killer? Did he know the family? How did that even fucking happen in the first place?" I wiped my mouth with the back of my hand, the acidic taste of vomit still lingering in my mouth.

"No, they never found him. I have no idea how he knew or if he knew Sebastian's family. It's all still a mystery."

Overwhelmed, I shook my head, attempting to clear my thoughts. My forehead pinched as another piece of the puzzle clicked into place.

"Goddammit ... Dope ... you and Kip have protected him all these years?"

"Yeah. It's not been easy when he changes. He's the extreme opposite of Sebastian."

A boulder hit the pit of my stomach with my suspicions, but I had to listen to what Dope had to say.

"I need to hear the rest because right now my brain is full speed ahead, and I'm hoping like hell it's running in the wrong direction," I croaked as I wiped my runny nose.

"I get it. That weekend scared Kip and me shitless. Dammit, I lived with Bass, and as much as I wanted to believe that he was just messing with us, I knew in my gut that he wasn't. Over the next year, I couldn't ignore it anymore. I was terrified for a long time, but then I got to know his other persona. His name is—"

"Death," I whispered, tears clogging my throat.

"Yeah."

I shook uncontrollably, realizing that I'd fallen for two opposing sides of the same man. That twisted me into a fucking pretzel. Seconds later, a wave of short-lived relief consumed me as I realized I hadn't slept with Kip. *He* wasn't Death. Moments later, that relief turned to horror, quickly followed by love for both men. I was fucked up and unable to wrap my head around the situation. How? How was my sweet, safe Sebastian also Death, a cruel serial killer? I shoved my fingers through my hair and pulled until my scalp stung. I couldn't scream in the middle of the park, or I'd draw attention, but I was overloaded, and my emotions needed a temporary outlet until I had time alone to process.

"Does he understand that he's also Death?"

Dope pursed his lips together. "No. At least not that I know of. We have very different conversations with each personality, careful not to slip up badly enough that he catches on. I'm sure you're wondering why we didn't get him help."

"Yeah, that was my next question."

"I read somewhere that if the personalities are aware of each other, it could drive someone insane. I'm not sure if that's true or not, but I was afraid to risk it until recently. And if Kip or I ever turned him in, the courts would lock him away for the rest of his life. He'd already lost everything. His home, his mom and dad, his mind. Kip and I couldn't take his freedom too. About a year ago, he got onto the dark web, looking for porn. That's when he found you, and he was immediately obsessed."

I leaned over and pressed my stomach against my legs, slamming my eyes closed. Death had stalked me, forced himself into my life, and was a coldblooded killer. My fists clenched and I dug my nails into my skin as I attempted to marry the two different men together.

Dope stretched his legs out in front of him. "It's what Kip and I were talking about in the hospital. We were completely baffled as to why you hadn't figured out who Death was."

"Easy, he only visited at night for a while so I couldn't see him. When I could see him, he wore a grim reaper mask. His eyes are grey, but Sebastian's are blue, and Death doesn't have an accent. Do you have any idea how many men are tall with large hands, and broad shoulders? How in the hell was I supposed to know it was Sebastian?" I rubbed my arms, warding off the chill of our conversation.

"His masks are fucking badass, so I get that. Did you know that eye color can change when someone is in a manic state or a different personality emerges?"

"No. I had no idea, but I've never dealt with this situation before." A combination of relief and grief punched me in the chest as silence hung in the air. "Dope?"

"Yeah?"

"Why did you and Kip stick around when you learned about Sebastian's ... condition. And who else knows?"

Dope laced his fingers behind his head. "As fucked up as it is, he's family to both of us. And I'm sorry that Kip and I didn't come to you sooner, but we had to make sure that we could trust you." He winced. "I don't know how else to say it."

"You're fine. But why did you decide to tell me now?"

"Because we saw how much you love Sebastian. Maybe you've not said it out loud, but it's clear to us. Sebastian is in love with you, too. We figured if you were staying with him at the hospital, it was time to tell you the truth. Anyway, as for why Kip and I stuck around? He had no one else other than us. We thought at the time that if we could learn to identify what triggered him, we could manage the situation. It wasn't until we attended college in Washington state that I noticed Sebastian sneaking out of our shared dorm room a few nights a month. I hadn't talked to Death in a while, so I assumed shit had settled down enough not to trigger Bass. We tried to manage his stress level, but we're only human. We finally realized that when he got pushed to the limit, or it was the anniversary of his parent's murders, Death showed up. As we got older and become adults and owned a business, more stressful situations were added to the equation. He works long hours and lives off very little sleep, which doesn't help at all." He sighed. "Then rumors of a serial killer started floating around. I told Kip we had a problem, and we either needed to turn Bass in or cover his tracks."

My eyes nearly popped out of my head. "What?"

"Yeah. Well, we obviously didn't turn him in."

"Why? He's a killer."

"Yeah, Kip and I talked about it at length, and we chose to take care of him. Not only was he our brother, but he wasn't killing innocent people. The first time Kip and I tailed him, he killed a guy trying to rape a woman in an alley. The next, a dad beating the hell out of his kid. Finally, Death stayed out long enough to talk to Kip and me again. He told us how he stalked his victims, making sure that they were truly hurting others before he, as he says it, 'washed the earth with their blood.'"

"He's said that to me before too." I stared at the couple walking by, holding hands.

"Things took an interesting turn when Bass talked about wanting to build Safe Horizon Society for women and children. We worked on that project for three years and just helped local families at first. Bass has a heart of fucking gold even with his rough edges, Ella."

"But how does he pay for it all? It's not cheap."

"Nope, it's millions of dollars every year, but he doesn't care. He works at the bar as a cover, so no one suspects what he's doing behind the scenes. When we were still in college, his uncle in Australia passed away and left Bass his money. His uncle was a rich motherfucker. Then, Bass turned twenty-five, and he received the trust his parents left him. He bought the penthouse with it. The equity in that place after fourteen years—shit, he could sell it for ten times what he paid."

"Equity is a good thing." I chewed on my thumbnail, trying to process the information. "So, you guys built the Safe Horizon Society to help the families. How did that play into his other persona?"

"It gave Death targets and we were able to move him around so bodies didn't pile up all in one place. Some of the significant others we were helping these women escape from were straight-up evil. They were into the skin trade, drugs, and illegal weapons. You name it. Sebastian, Kip, and I help the women and kids, and Death kills some of the men. In our opinion, he was saving people, no matter what. Not once has he targeted an innocent. Now when Kip and I research to see what families need help, we make sure that the guys are fucking sickos too."

I did a double take, digesting what Dope had just said. "Shit, that's kind of genius." I bit my lip. "I'm not a killer, but one less sick bastard around isn't a bad thing."

"Exactly. Now we take on a few really big relocations because I hack into bank records and take money out of the target's accounts. We pocket the funds for the Safe Horizon Society, but what the investigators see is that he moved the money to an offshore account or paid off gambling debts. It's all different shit, but we've been able to fund the organization from them instead of Bass's pockets. He's still sitting on a pretty penny, though."

My brain sifted through the abundance of questions, choosing one to start with. "What about the accident?"

"Kip was following him. He probably got too close, and Bass caught sight of him right before the accident. Kip knew Bass was starting to change, and we were worried it would happen while he was driving. It did." Dope paused, appearing to collect his thoughts. "But Bass does hallucinate sometimes. Lately it's when Death is trying to overtake Sebastian. Bass gets a horrible headache before he changes. He said it's like knives being shoved into his skull. My guess is that he was Death, then he flickered between personalities. Death thought he was pursuing Sebastian, then right before he hit the tree Sebastian fully appeared. And as for Kip? He's been running around like crazy cleaning up behind Death in order to keep the cops off his scent. Kip would die for Bass. We both would. Both personalities have saved our asses so many fucking times. We will always watch out for our man." He chuckled. "Bass kept us busy as hell the last three weeks we were moving women and children. When we were in Montana, he kept disappearing, and I would have to tail him. Each time it happened, he went straight back to you as Death."

"That was one of the pieces that had me messed up. How could Death be with me when Sebastian was in another state with you?" I shook my head, mulling over everything I'd heard.

"His plane made it easy. I can track his flights and car." Dope folded his hands in his lap. "Ella, what are you going to do now that you know the truth?"

Chapter 46

Ella

I stared ahead, unfocused on anything or anyone except what Dope had just shared with me. Would I stay with Sebastian? I wasn't sure, but at least I finally understood that the push and pull inside me was for the same man. Could I handle Death now that I knew the truth? One thing I was certain of was that he would never hurt me. Not after he had killed Stephen for me and how he had taken care of me after he chased me through the woods. As hard as I tried to shut off my feelings for Death and give myself to Sebastian, I couldn't. I couldn't ignore the connection between us that went beyond how he'd protected me and his gentleness at times.

A sharp knife stabbed me in the chest and pierced my heart, leaving me crying tears of blood. As I sorted through the details like a massive pile of dirty laundry, more questions flooded my mind.

"If Sebastian and Death are the same man, can you explain how I was getting text messages from Sebastian when I was with Death? It happened multiple times."

Dope popped his knuckles before he responded. "Easy. It was me covering his ass."

"What? How?"

"I'm a hacker, Ella. It's what I do for the Safe Horizon Society. Bass pays me really well to get into websites, phones, and camera systems. Given enough time, there's nothing I can't hack into."

Cocky much? "Government files and information?"

"Yup. Done it. I'm just careful when and how I do it."

"Shit. Where were you when I needed to shut down ..." My brows raised. "Oh shit. He was Shadow Whisperer on the ... uh ..."

"I know about the work on the website, don't worry. Bass wouldn't let me watch the videos. He took care of you in that way."

Warmth seeped into my chilled body at Sebastian's protectiveness, then my brows furrowed together. "Do ... do you know about Stephen?" I swallowed the lump in my throat.

"Yup. Thank god we didn't have to clean up that mess in your house since Death dissolved the son of a bitch."

I placed my palms on the sides of my head, holding it together in fear it might explode. How was I going to digest this?

"I suspect Sebastian paid my outstanding balance when he learned about the web cam job, but the hospital just said it was paid by an anonymous donor. Death made the new medical trial happen. That part of Sebastian has shown me some kindness. Possessive, dominating, and at times feral, but I got used to it." I pursed my lips, refusing to share our personal moments. They were mine. Death was mine, and I was his. A part of me had wanted what Sebastian offered, but it felt as if I was smothering the other side of me. I forced myself to take a deep breath.

"I have to go back to the penthouse and pretend that I don't know anything. How the hell am I going to do that?"

"It's not easy, but if you love him ... if you love both Sebastian and Death, you'll make it work. Kip and I will help you. However, if you can't stay with him, you need to break things off with him now."

I barked out a laugh. "Death will come after me, Dope. I can't tell him I no longer want to be with him. I was afraid that he was behind the car accident, and in a way, he was. What would happen if I tried to break things off with him?" A twisted little thrill rippled through me while I reveled in the idea of Death's dark hold over me, but I had one over him too. His dark, obsessive need for me made my body tingle all over. I had grown to love him and all of his fucked-up ways.

"You might be the only person that could talk to him, Ella. I'm afraid the cops are starting to figure shit out, and he's in trouble. He has to stop killing people for now. Kip and I are hoping that you might be able to make a difference for him—calm the beast inside."

Unable to hold back the floodgates any longer, my body shook as I sobbed, reality slamming into me like an eighteen-wheeler on steroids. Sniffling, I gave Dope a sad smile. "When my mom used to read books to me as a child, I always wanted the bad guy. I was convinced that the big bad wolf just needed to be loved in order to change. I've been drawn to a darkness that I didn't understand, so when Death showed up, it was scary as hell, but then I realized there was a magnetic pull to him I couldn't control. He saw straight inside my soul and recognized things inside me I'd always been afraid to admit to myself. I hated him for seeing my vulnerability, playing on it to manipulate me. Then there's Sebastian. He's such a gentleman—caring, strong, and everything I could have ever hoped for." I looked at Dope, my shoulders shaking with my cries. "What am I going to do? How am I going to reconcile the idea that this amazing man in front of me is also a brutal killer? Everything I've experienced with him as Sebastian is ..." A frustrated groan slipped from my throat as I stared at the cloudy sky. "I don't want to hurt him. I'll never be free from Death, and I'm not sure I want to be. If I tell Sebastian that I can't see him anymore, then I would have to run and hide from Death. He would hunt me, and I would be constantly moving."

"He'll find you. He's almost as good a hacker as I am." The corner of his lips kicked up. "Almost. He had a damn good teacher."

"That wasn't the advice I was hoping for," I muttered.

"Truth trumps advice right now, Ella. You're going to have to decide just like Kip and I had to. Do you love him enough to keep his secret? Even cover up the murders of evil men?"

I picked at the hangnail on my finger, unable to answer him yet. I cared deeply for both men, but a true commitment scared the shit out of me. If Death went down, we all went down.

You're already covering up murders and lies for him. I told the voice in my head to shut the hell up. I was well aware of my actions. That was not the real issue, though.

"Listen, Sebastian doesn't know that I'm with you. He thinks you went to your house to grab some things you needed for work. Make up a bullshit story that you're sick and have the stomach flu and won't be back for a few days. Take a beat to process. Hell, Kip and I had to do the same thing. Kip almost ditched us the first time he met Sebastian's other personality. It's a lot to chew on. If for some reason you decide you can't stick around, Kip and I will help you relocate. Just please don't give Sebastian up."

I swallowed over the anguish. "I haven't given Death up to the police, and I won't now. You have my word."

"Okay, and what about Sebastian? You could nail him for breaking the law too."

"I won't. He's doing too much good, plus I signed an NDA." I stood and brushed off the back of my jeans in case there was dirt on my ass, but it was the least of my worries.

"Thank you, Ella. For the record, Kip and I are hoping you won't go anywhere. I think you're exactly what Bass needs. I know that's a lot of pressure, but I don't mean it like that. Just being you makes Bass happy, and he deserves a fucking break."

I turned to Dope as he stood and gave him a big hug. "He's lucky to have you, and Kip, as well."

As we walked to the car, Dope slung his arm over my shoulder as if he were an older brother. "Before I drop you off, I'll make sure you have my phone number if you need anything. I probably don't have to tell you not to say or text too much on the line, though."

"Yeah, it's the same with my bosses when we're talking about a case. We keep the majority of the conversation in person."

"Excellent. When do you go back to work?"

We reached Dope's car and hopped in.

"In a week. Guess that gives me some time to think some things through."

Dope started the engine, and before he shifted into drive, he asked for my phone and added his number. "It's under Hal Whitney instead of my nickname."

"Thanks. I appreciate the support. You're a good guy, Dope."

He pulled out of the parking lot and headed toward my house. "I wasn't sure about you at first, and when you followed Bass when we were trying to get Sarah and the kids out safely, I was fucking pissed. You were my least favorite person."

I cracked a grin. "When did that change?"

"When you didn't turn Death in for saving your life with Stephen, then for sure at the hospital. You refused to leave his side."

"In all fairness, I was afraid Death would slip into his room and finish him off." I stared out the passenger's side window.

His gaze cut over to me. "Even before you knew the truth, you were protecting Sebastian. Tell me why."

A few heartbeats of silence hung in the air.

Dope's brow arched, but he didn't say anything else. I heard his unspoken words loud and clear. I was falling in love with Sebastian.

ONCE I WAS INSIDE MY HOUSE AND THE ALARM WAS ON, I poured myself a hell of a stiff drink. Throwing myself onto the sofa by the window, I propped my feet up on the edge of the coffee table. First, I messaged Sebastian and told him I was puking and wouldn't be back until I was better. I couldn't risk him getting sick and ripping open his stitches. From his texts, I could tell he was disappointed, but he was sweet and understanding.

I tossed my phone on the cushion beside me, my body tense and waiting for Death to slip into my house. When I realized he wouldn't be back until Sebastian healed from the car accident, I breathed a sigh of relief. I had at least a few days to process. I wished like hell I could talk to Cami about Sebastian and Death, but I knew I couldn't. Loneliness consumed me as the tears streamed down my face, and I allowed myself to crumble.

Chapter 47

Ella

I shuffled through the file at my desk, searching for the information my bosses needed for the newest case. It had been a week since I'd seen Sebastian, and my time was running out. Thank god, I had work to delve into and help me lose track of reality.

Blake, my boss, walked into my office. "Ella, Clayton and I are leaving and on our way to the courthouse before it closes. We won't see you until tomorrow, but it's good to have you back."

I smiled at him. "It's good to be back."

Blake gave me a little wave as he left my office. The bell on the front door jingled, signaling someone was coming in or out. I suspected Blake and Clayton were leaving, but I had to check. I poked my head out and scanned the waiting area, but no one was there. Checking my watch, I realized it was four-thirty. I could probably lock up, turn off the lights, and call it a day. Since the time had changed, it was getting dark earlier, and I considered parking on the street instead of walking to the parking lot behind the building.

Suddenly, my palms slicked, and perspiration dotted my forehead as the memory of Death chasing me through the parking lot and woods bombarded me. My core throbbed with the reminder of him catching me and pinning me down as he roughly fucked me, punishing me. Inhaling a deep, calming breath, I tried to suppress my building desire. The longing for his rough touch sent delicious waves through my body.

"Shit." I groaned. "I miss him. Both of them." I walked back to my office and sank into my chair, staring at the organized stacks of papers I had to read through. However, I wasn't sure I could focus. Not only was I missing Death, but I was also missing Sebastian. Even though we'd messaged a few times, he'd given me the space I needed. Little did he know that I wasn't actually sick.

It was time to decide once and for all to stay or walk away for good. Over the last several days, I'd realized it wasn't a matter of Death being who he was. I'd witnessed him firsthand. It was the fact that Sebastian, the loving, intelligent gentleman I'd fallen for, wasn't who I thought he was. At least not entirely. Maybe I had the best of both worlds and needed to embrace it. What if I could find peace in the arms of a man responsible for so much dark and twisted chaos?

The dread and fear of reconciling the two sides of Sebastian dissipated, and I knew in the depths of my being that I wanted to be with both of them.

Standing, I closed my laptop and stuffed it into my computer bag. I snatched my phone off the desk and located Sebastian's number. Adrenaline shot my heart into overdrive as I listened to the phone ring for the third time. Maybe he was asleep. As I prepared to leave a message, he answered.

"There's my girl," Sebastian said.

His husky voice and accent sent a tingling sensation through me and released warmth throughout my entire body.

"Hey." I smiled. "How are you?"

"Much better. Doc says I'm healing nicely. The stitches are out, and he said to take it easy but that I could work toward getting back to my life."

"That's wonderful. I'm so sorry I wasn't there to help, but the last thing you needed was to puke while you had stitches in your stomach."

"I missed you, but I was glad you stayed away. But ... are you better now?" I didn't miss the hope in his voice.

"I am. Can I see you soon?"

"Come on over, Ella."

"I need to lock up. I came back to work today, so give me a few. Depending on the traffic, I should be there in about an hour."

"I can't wait. Are you hungry? I can whip up something to eat. If you want a steak and baked potato, I have a great wine that pairs well with beef."

"Oh, that sounds amazing. I've not eaten since nine this morning."

"Excellent. Drive safely."

I closed my eyes, the gentleness in his tone sending delicious little shivers through me. "I will. See you soon."

He said goodbye, then we hung up. Ten minutes later, I was on the highway headed to his place.

My heels clicked against the hardwood floors in the hall of the penthouse floor. My heart thumped erratically, beating against my rib cage as though it might rip through my chest cavity. Sebastian might not understand that seeing him tonight was a monumental moment, but for me, I was all in with this man—*all* of him.

The door swung open, and the guy before me nearly stole my breath. His jeans were slung low on his hips, and my gaze took a slow hike up his shirtless, muscled body. Tension in my core tightened as his hungry stare raked over me.

"You look stunning."

"I forget you've not seen me in a suit or skirt before." I smiled, waiting for him to invite me in.

As if he had read my thoughts, he stepped back and waved me inside. My attention was glued to him as he pulled on a navy polo, his biceps and chest muscles flexing with each move.

"Let me take your briefcase and purse. I'll set them next to the couch."

I gave him my items but held onto my phone. Watching him walk away, I focused on the muscles flexing in his long legs and ass.

"You're getting around really well."

"Doc said I surprised him with how fast I'm healing." He strolled over to me again and wrapped me in his arms. "Now that your bags aren't in the way." His focus dropped to my mouth, then moved back up to my eyes before he pressed his lips to mine, and I melted into him.

Placing my palms against his chest, I relished the beat of his heart beneath my fingertips. I had almost lost him in the accident. It had been a wake-up call for how I truly felt about him.

His tongue slipped into my mouth, swirling and dancing with my own. Fire and electricity sparked between us, and it felt so right. Sebastian's hand traveled up my back, moved under my long, dark hair, and wrapped around my neck. His touch made my mind blink offline as my body took the driver's seat, responding to him on a level beyond my control.

I arched into him, pressing my hips against his thick erection, mentally begging him to be inside me. Even though I hadn't had sex with Sebastian, I had with Death. A little voice inside my gut reminded me that Sebastian wasn't aware that I'd slept with him already, so I had to play it cool and allow him to take the lead.

Sebastian broke our kiss and pressed his forehead against mine as he cupped the back of my head, cradling me in his palm.

"I've missed you so fucking bad. Stay with me tonight."

I laughed softly. "I would love to. I just need to leave early enough to change clothes before I have to be at work at nine."

"Done." He took my hand and led me to the kitchen. "I have to check on the food. I took the liberty of pouring you a glass of wine. It's best after it breathes for half an hour."

I smoothed my red silk blouse and sat at the small table in the nook. I sank my teeth into my lower lip as I watched him gracefully move about the kitchen.

"What?" he asked, grinning at me.

"You just seem very comfortable in here. I like it."

His brow rose. "Yeah? Guess I'll have to cook for you more often then."

"I can't support that until I taste your food. It might smell good but taste like crap." I laughed, enjoying the light conversation. The last week had been emotionally heavy, and I was ready to move forward.

My phone vibrated against the tabletop, and I snatched it up and answered.

"Hi, Mom. How are you?"

"Hi, honey. We're hanging in there. I wanted to see how you're doing and give you an update on your father."

My chest squeezed tight, wondering if it was good news. I shoved the hope back into a box and prepared for the worst. Over the last year, we'd thought each treatment would be different, but they all fell flat.

"I'm fine. Somehow, I'm managing to stay out of trouble." I said, keeping it lighthearted for a moment before she broke me with bad news. "But tell me about Dad."

"The doctor just gave us an update. He had some tests run the other day. I didn't want to tell you about them until we knew if the trial was working."

I stilled, holding my breath as I looked over at Sebastian, who had stopped banging pans when he realized Mom was on the phone.

"It's working, Ella. The tests show a big improvement already."

I slapped my hand over my mouth, tears spilling down my face. "Oh my god. Mom, they're sure? They're a hundred percent positive?" I asked around my muffled cries.

"Yeah. They're positive, sweetie. When we come home, he'll still have some appointments to monitor the progress and treatment. They'll keep him in the trial and track results over the next few years, but he's going to be okay."

"Mom." Emotions clogged my throat. "Tell Dad I love him, and I can't wait to see you both."

"Oh, honey, us too." She sniffled. "Tell me about work. How are the cases going?"

I grinned. Mom always changed the topic when she was super emotional. Apparently, I did the same, so I understood the need to redirect. "Good. I've just started a new case that's really interesting and keeps my attention. It's nice to be back."

"And your father mentioned you had met a guy. How is that going?"

A silly grin slipped into place as I met Sebastian's gaze. "His name is Sebastian, and things are going great. When you are home and settled, we can get together so you can meet him. You'll love him." *I do.*

"I'm so excited that you've met someone, Ella."

"Me too. He's an amazing guy." *Both sides of him.*

After chatting for a few more minutes, we hung up so Mom could get back to Dad. I set the phone on the table just in time for Sebastian to lift me off the chair and set me on my feet.

"Is it good news?" He peppered my cheeks with kisses, wiping the tears away.

"He's going to make it. The trial is working." I laughed. "You'll get to meet him soon if you want to. Just because I said that to Mom doesn't mean you have to commit to anything."

He smoothed my hair and pressed a gentle kiss to my mouth. "I want nothing more than to meet your parents. I look forward to it." He stepped away as the timer on the oven dinged. "After dinner, can we talk about what we look like moving forward? I want to make sure we're both on the same page."

If he hadn't just kissed me breathless, I would have panicked. My stomach clenched. It appeared that I was going to panic anyway. At least he tried to calm my anxiety before he asked to talk.

"That sounds good." I needed to speak to him as well.

Chapter 48

Sebastian

I caught the flicker of hesitation in Ella's expression as I mentioned talking after dinner. I hadn't meant to spook her, but I think I had. Call me stupid, but how I felt when Ella was around was mesmerizing. Everything about her sparked intense emotions inside me, and I had to know if she reciprocated those feelings. A quick conversation on the phone wasn't what I was looking for. I needed to see her face-to-face and read her body language.

Once I cleared the plates and refilled her wine, we headed to the living room. I set her drink down and turned on the gas fireplace. Ella sat at the end, curling her legs beneath her. From the rise and fall of her chest, she was nervous. She picked up her glass, and I caught a subtle tremble in her hand.

"I think I put you on edge when I asked if we could talk. That wasn't my intention."

Her lips pressed into a thin line, and she stared at the leather couch. "Usually when someone says something like that, they want to end things."

I closed the gap between us and took her hand. "I don't want to end our relationship, Ella. The opposite, actually." I cleared my throat, trying to control the spike in my heartrate. "Kip reminded me that I needed to talk to you before I just assumed anything."

She looked at me, attentive. "What is it?"

"Are you seeing anyone else, or is it just me?"

Her forehead creased. "No, I'm not dating anyone else right now."

I wanted to pull her into my lap and kiss her senseless, but I needed to continue. "Have there been other guys since we met?"

Her jaw briefly tightened. "There was someone at the beginning, but it was short-lived. You took up all my headspace." She smiled and ran the pad of her thumb across my knuckles.

"I want to take up more than headspace. I want you and only you, but I'm not sure if we're in the same place or not."

She took a deep breath, the rise and fall of her breasts begging for me to play with them, but I maintained eye contact.

"We are. I'm not interested in anyone else either, Sebastian." Her tongue darted over her lower lip, and I stifled my groan as I imagined it on my cock.

"Excellent." I leaned over, cupped her chin, and kissed her. "Be a good girl and tell me that you're mine."

Ella gripped the front of my polo shirt, her heavy-lidded gaze fixed on mine. "I'm yours, Sebastian."

My cock fought against the confines of my jeans, swelling to the point of pain. I trailed kisses along her neck, and she moaned softly, arching against me as she shifted to give me better access.

"Are you ready?" I nipped at her ear.

"Yes."

I pulled away and stood before my arm slipped under her knees and around her back, picking her up off the couch. She automatically wrapped her arms around my neck and placed her head against my chest as I carried her to my bedroom, where I set her down gently on my bed.

She slowly unbuttoned her shirt, her fingertips grazing her skin as she brushed the fabric to the side. I drank in every inch of her, and a wave of longing rushed through me.

I hungrily watched as she removed each item of clothing until she was standing there in only her thong. My eyes traveled up and down her gorgeous curves.

"Your body is a work of art, baby. You're beautiful inside and out."

Ella smiled. "Thank you."

"Lie down and get comfortable."

She settled in the middle of the mattress, and I kneeled, grabbed her hips, and pulled her to the edge of the bed. I lifted her legs and draped them over my shoulders. Gripping the back of her thighs, I gently pushed her knees to her chest, exposing her slick center. My body burned with desire as I worshipped every inch of her sweet pussy. She writhed beneath me, clawing at the bedspread as I thrust a finger inside her while feasting on her sensitive skin as if she were a delicacy. I licked down her wet core, and my tongue dove deeper, possessing every part of her.

Her hips lifted off the mattress. "Sebastian, oh god." She jerked before her legs trembled, and she screamed my name.

I stood and opened the drawer of my nightstand, rummaging through the contents until I located a condom. Within seconds, I tore the package open and rolled it on. I crawled up her body and pressed my lips to hers. Our tongues intertwined as I shared the taste of her. Ella grabbed my ass, pulling me closer as I kissed down to her neck and chest. Her breathing became labored as I cupped her breast and teased her nipple with my teeth. Ella shifted and ground her hips against my erection.

I propped myself up and lined my cock at her entrance. When I swiped the tip through her slick center, I moaned. I pressed against her opening, easing just the tip into her.

"I've waited until the time was right, Ella. You were worth it." I eased into her, savoring every moment of being with her. My fingers tangled in her hair, and I looked down at her through lowered lids.

Slowly, I pushed in and pulled out, her eyes locking on mine. Her walls clenched around my shaft, and I shuddered as pleasure rippled through me. But it was more than just sex. It was about her heart and mind. I wanted to take the time to cherish every amazing thing about this woman who had chosen to be with me.

Our bodies fit perfectly, and it was at that moment that I knew in my soul that she was made for me.

I moved in a gentle rhythm, filling her and reaching deep inside. Her breath hitched, and her mouth parted.

"That's a good girl. Cum for me, Ella."

She met me thrust for thrust as we consumed each other. Her whimpers filled the room and her core tightened around me. I drove into her, about to lose my damn mind. No matter how close I was to my orgasm, I needed Ella to come first.

Her fingernails scraped down my back as she bucked with her release. Her face scrunched with her pleasure and pushed me over the edge. My entire body seized as I came.

I looked at her, knowing that her flushed cheeks and glow were because of me. Lowering my head, I kissed her. My nose skimmed her jawline, and I pressed my lips to her ear.

I made my way to the bathroom, disposed of the condom, and ran the water until it was warm. After grabbing a washcloth, I returned and gently cleaned her. We stared at each other for what seemed like an eternity. "My sweet, Ella. You're my new addiction."

Chapter 49

Ella

Over the next month, Sebastian and I spent every free minute we had together. He had visited my place long enough to christen the couch, kitchen counter, and my bed before he packed my clothes and toiletries in a suitcase and put them away in the closet and dresser of his penthouse. He mentioned moving me in fully a few times, but I hadn't agreed yet. Once Sebastian changed and became Death, he would show up at my home, and I needed to be there for him.

Dope's car pulled up to mine in the Starbucks parking lot, and I exited my Toyota and locked it before I hopped into the backseat of his car.

"Hey," Kip said from the front. "I was going to give you this seat."

I waved him off, then fastened my seatbelt. "I'm good. It's a short ride."

Ten minutes later, we arrived at a small cabin nestled in the woods.

"Whose place?" I asked as we approached the beautiful red and blonde pine door adorned with a heavy, black knocker.

"My dad's," Dope said. "We meet here when we need to talk about Bass in private."

My boots scuffed the porch as we walked in. Dope flipped on the overhead lights and walked toward the kitchen. "Want a beer, Ella?"

"Sure." I sat on the brown leather recliner and waited for the guys to grab a drink. Curiosity reared its head with my burning question. I figured Kip and I knew each other well enough for me to finally ask it. "Hey, Kip? Why did you hire the attorneys I work for? I mean you don't have to tell me, but when I opened your file, it was full of blank papers. Honestly, I had no idea your legal name was Christopher Lytton. It wasn't until I saw a photo of you that was stuck to one of the sheets that I realized it was you along with your red jacket the lady brought into the bar that evening. The image must have just been missed because nothing else was in there."

Kip shot Dope a look, and he nodded. "I hired them on retainer in case Sebastian ever got caught."

I gawked at him. "My bosses know that Sebastian is a killer?"

"No. They know that Sebastian is a powerful man who helps relocate women and children, and when he keeps them safe, he's breaking laws. They're some of the best criminal attorneys around. Those are the men I want on his side. That file was blank because I asked them not to keep any record of what I'd shared. They probably slipped paper in it so it wouldn't arouse suspicion. Apparently, it didn't work."

The color drained from my cheeks, and I shot him a sheepish look. "Dope didn't tell you that I thought you were Death?" *And that I was freaking the fuck out when I thought I might be sleeping with Sebastian's best friend!*

"Must be all the mysterious disappearances that raised suspicions." Dope quirked his brow at Kip.

Kip glanced at the floor. "I'm not using drugs, if that's what you're thinking. Haven't touched the shit again. Between work and cleaning up Death's messes, it's a lot. Sometimes I just have to regroup and take some time to myself."

Tension filled the space as the guys stared each other down, the silence almost deafening. I didn't think Dope bought Kip's lame story any more than I did.

Kip finally looked away and returned his attention to me. "At least our efforts aren't in vain. I would much rather you suspected me than Sebastian until we knew you were going to stay by his side. Well, we hoped anyway. And, the wild ride is about to begin again. Death will be back soon."

"How do you know?" I took a drink of the pale ale.

"Has he been complaining about headaches to you?" Kip asked, hopping onto the barstool at the butcher block countertop.

"Yeah, but I just figured it was left over from the car accident."

"The headaches show up, his sleeping patterns change, and he gets agitated easily. Eventually you'll see that, but I think the two of you are too new and in the honeymoon phase. Kip and I usually meet here to make sure we're tracking him, cleaning up, and doing all of the other shit that comes with his killing sprees." Dope shoved a hand through his messy hair.

"This will be the first time I see Death and know the truth." My stomach clenched with the thought, but at least I knew they were the same man. Kind of.

"Maybe you can talk to him, tell him that you know who he is," Kip suggested.

My head whipped in his direction, horror twisting my expression. "I'm sorry, what? You're kidding, right?"

"No. Ella, he loves you even as Death. If you can get through to him, he might get help. We can't cover for him forever. We do our best, and now with you helping, it's easier ... but we know the cops are going to catch him sooner or later." Kip's shoulders tensed, his anxiety evident.

My gaze narrowed in on Dope. "I thought you said if he knew he had another personality it could drive him over the edge."

"Each person and how they react is different. It can cause severe anxiety, and when he stresses, he kills. It's a risk we are going to have to take, and we're running out of time," Dope said.

I tapped my foot against the floor, my nerves on edge with the idea. "He can't get caught. Besides, he's cleaning up the pond scum that are a waste of space. I hate to admit it, but I'm actually supportive of his rampages." I winced with my confession.

"Don't feel bad. We are too." Kip pursed his lips. "He's doing a lot of good. That's not the problem. It's that we need to move him, or he has to get treatment. He's been killing in the same area for too long."

A moment of clarity smacked me. "Because I'm here."

"Yup." Dope popped his 'p.'

I massaged my forehead. "I can't make the decision for him, to get help or to move, I mean." I chewed on the inside of my cheek. "What if he doesn't accept the truth? What then? We move?" I couldn't leave Portland.

Before either of the guys could respond, an idea barged into my thoughts. I added, "I will take him to other parts of the country. And I'll help you guide his kills." I threw my head back and barked out a laugh. I had lost my fucking mind.

The guys glanced at each other and nodded. "We've done what we can, but now we have someone with a stronger influence. You can keep him busy while we find more scum of the earth. We'll do whatever it takes to keep him out of prison or a psych ward. They'll throw away the fucking key if they catch him. I love my bro, and I have to do everything possible to keep that from happening."

"I love Death too." He's dark, powerful ... savage. My thighs clenched with the thought of him pinning me down and taking what was his. The sex with him was the extreme opposite of Sebastian. I craved both sides of Sebastian. Realizing that I was being selfish, I snapped out of my hormone-induced brain fog.

"We have a plan A and a plan B. I'll see what I can do when I see him again. He deserves the choice, and I'll do anything to protect him. My dad is still in the clinical trial, and I won't move away full time. I can't."

"We get that, Ella. We just needed to be on the same page for Sebastian's sake." Dope eyed his green beer bottle, then tilted it up and guzzled it, loudly burping when he was done.

I looked at Kip and shook my head. "How do you put up with him?"

Kip laughed. "He's a dude. Besides, when he burps and farts around you, then you know you're no longer a friend. You're family."

I laughed. "Lucky me."

Dope's phone chimed, and he removed it from his back pocket and tapped the screen. "Kip, can you cover the bar? I need to get to Sebastian and drop Ella off at her place. From the cameras, he's about to split and I'm guessing he's going straight to her place."

I swallowed the lump in my throat, dread sinking into my stomach like a stone in a lake. "I hope to hell this works."

THE SUN HAD SET AN HOUR AGO, AND I SAT ON MY COUCH, working and texting with Cami. Her day had been filled with multiple car accidents, and a few shooting victims. It had kept the ER running.

Listening for Death to creep into my house, I hoped he would show up. It had been a while since I'd seen him, but it was good that I was able to help Sebastian.

Spotting my empty glass, I snatched it up and walked to the kitchen, every nerve in my body buzzing with anxiety. The guys didn't have to tell me this might be dangerous, but I was already used to that part of Death.

A scream worked its way from my throat as I spotted the mostly hidden figure standing near the sink.

"Shit! You scared me. How long have you been there?"

He flexed his gloveless fingers. "Long enough. You didn't bother locking the door. How did you know I would be here tonight?"

I approached him slowly and set my glass on the granite counter. "Just a hunch." I reached up to touch his shoulder. His all-black attire blended in so well that it was challenging to glimpse his mask. But I wanted to see those grey eyes burn with fire for me. "Where have you been? I've missed you."

His hand shot out, and he grabbed the back of my neck, pulling me against him. His fingers wrapped around my throat as his mouth brushed my ear. "I know you've been with another man," he hissed.

Terror ripped through me as I clawed at his arm. Black dots floated in my vision as I struggled against him. In a last attempt to breathe through his jealous rage, I gripped his free arm as hard as possible. I stared at him, pleading for him to let me go.

Seconds before I lost consciousness, he released me. I collapsed in a coughing fit, struggling to pull air into my lungs.

He emerged from the darkness, his wicked laugh making the hair stand up on the back of my neck. Death gripped me by the waist and shoved me against the wall. "Did he fuck you?" He grabbed my crotch, and pain shot through my core.

"I've not been with anyone other than you." I reached up and played with strands of his hair in an attempt to break through his rage. "Only you."

His hold lessened, and he rubbed my pussy through my yoga pants. His grey eyes flashed with something I couldn't identify. I could almost see the wheels turning in his brain.

"Do you swear on your father's life that no one has touched what's mine?"

Without hesitation, I swore on my dad's life.

"If you're lying to me, I will find out, and I will. Finish. You." He fisted my hair and pulled my head back. "You will worship your god now, little lamb." Terrified that he would learn about Sebastian, I scrambled for an answer.

Death forced me to my knees, not letting go. With his free hand, he flipped open the button on his jeans and lowered his zipper.

My breath hitched in my throat. He hadn't understood what I'd tried to tell him, but at least he'd calmed down—for now.

His long, stiff cock bobbed free, and I wet my lips, ready to take him. I wrapped my fingers around his thick shaft and stroked. Kissing the tip, I tasted the drop of precum. I glanced up at him, ready to play his game.

"Show me how much you love your god, my cum whore."

I opened my mouth for him, waiting.

He slid his dick in, and I hollowed my cheeks as my tongue caressed the silky skin. I whimpered as I sucked and licked his cock, my pussy soaked and ready for him.

"Take it all, my dirty little slut."

Saliva coated his dick as I continued. His lips parted as he moaned. He was nearing his orgasm, and I needed mine too.

Death tightened his hold on me, forcing me to be still as he fucked my mouth. Prepared for his cum to hit the back of my throat without notice, I was surprised when he withdrew.

He sneered at me and forced his fingers into my mouth, prying it apart. Death spit and then clamped my jaw together so hard my teeth rattled. "Swallow." That gravelly, rich voice reverberated in my chest.

Obediently, I swallowed before he pulled me to a standing position. With a quick motion, he jerked my pants and thong down to my ankles. I stepped out of them as he tugged my sweatshirt over my head, exposing my breasts to the cold air. I shrieked as he swooped me into his arms and carried me to my bed. Placing me on the mattress, he backed away and, for the first time as Death, removed his clothes. He removed the sheath around his calf and pulled out his knife. The blade shimmered in the moonlight, and I sucked in air.

Death approached me again, his cock bobbing with each step. "Spread your legs."

I did as he asked as I propped up on my elbows.

"You're drenched, Little Lamb. Your juices are coating your

thighs. Do you like sucking my dick?" He stroked himself, pinning me with a heavy-lidded stare.

"Yeah."

He crawled onto the mattress and straddled me, pressing the blade against my throat. I tilted my head back, giving him access and showing him my surrender. I inhaled sharply between my teeth and forced myself not to move as Death dragged the tip between my breasts, and blood drops pooled on my skin. He leaned down, his tongue flicking over the wound he'd inflicted. With each cut, he licked it clean.

"More," I whispered.

"I'll give you more, little lamb. I'll give you so much you'll be begging me to stop as hot tears stream down your face. I will take everything from you tonight."

When my stomach was covered in cuts, he pulled back to admire his work. "Beautiful." He ran his finger through my blood and tasted it. "Tastes so good, and now I will sacrifice your body for my pleasure."

The corner of his mouth kicked up in a wicked smile that sent my heart into overdrive as he moved. He kneeled on the floor as he dragged the knife on the inside of my thigh, marking me the same way he had my stomach. My pussy throbbed, needing that skilled mouth on me.

He flattened his tongue and slowly licked my drenched slit.

"Please." At that point, I wasn't even ashamed that I was begging.

His eyes bored into mine as he flipped the knife around and pushed the handle against my entrance. "I have something special for my cock slut." He held up the weapon, and for the first time, I saw the silver nubs that started at the base and moved up on both sides. "It's ribbed for your pleasure." He pressed it into my entrance slowly, the notches sending shocks of ecstasy through me.

"What a dirty girl, getting fucked with the same weapon I take lives with."

"Yes." My back arched off the bed as I gave into his sickness, allowing it to consume me.

His mouth landed on my clit with a sharp bite. I cried out in pain as the pleasure followed on its heels. Death licked and sucked as my inner walls clenched the handle. I was powerless over my body as he bent me to his will.

"Oh, shit." As I seized, I clawed at the bedspread, bunching the soft fabric between my fingers.

Death removed the weapon before he flipped me over on all fours and rammed into me with his cock. I lurched forward as he thrust, claiming me all over again.

He spread my ass cheeks apart and spit on my skin, massaging it on my puckered hole. His finger toyed with my entrance before he pushed inside, and my tight walls gripped him.

"My little whore likes it in the ass." His hips picked up pace, the sound of our bodies slapping together.

"Your body belongs to me." He grunted.

My eyelids fluttered closed as I bucked and greedily moved against his hand.

"Do you like fucking a cold-blooded killer, Ella?" He drove deeper, stroking my slick walls just right. The familiar warmth pooled inside my belly, and my orgasm was a slow roll that swept through me.

Making a gruff sound, he pounded into me one last time before he shuddered with his release. My legs and arms trembled beneath me, and I struggled not to collapse on the mattress. I jerked from his bite near my spine. He planted a line of kisses across my back.

"You served me well, little lamb." He pulled out, and I melted onto the bed, catching a glimpse of his powerful legs striding to my en suite bathroom. The sound of water reached my ears, and I allowed myself to rest as he ran a bath for me.

Chapter 50

Death

"The silence of a lamb is not a sign of its ignorance." ∼ *Unknown*

After I'd stepped back into my jeans, I swirled my fingers in her bubble bath, testing the water. There was something different about my little lamb tonight. She was more willing and possibly less afraid of me. Eventually, she would become accustomed to my ways, but I would never allow her to not fear me.

When I'd arrived, my blood was boiling, and I had planned to seek revenge on the man who had touched my little lamb, but not until I'd punished her. But the look in her eyes when I was choking the life out of her nearly broke me. Since as far back as I could remember, I felt something other than darkness consuming me. Ella had just been a flicker of light in the past, but she'd infiltrated every part of me over time.

I returned to the bed and picked her up, cradling my little lamb in my arms as I carried her to the bath. Slowly, I lowered her into the water.

Ella turned to me and reached out, her fingertips tracing my arm.

I placed my palm over it, the warmth of her touch seeping into my cold, disturbed heart.

"Death?"

"Yes?"

A tired smile eased across her face. "I would burn down the world for you."

Ella's words struck me, sending me off balance. I gripped the bathtub, staring at her as if she'd spoken another language. She had.

"You don't know what you're saying, little lamb." I collected the cup she left at the side of the tub and gently tilted her head back. I scooped up the water and poured it down her dark locks.

"You would do the same for me," she said, allowing me to shampoo her hair.

"I have already, but I would do it again." She didn't know I had a surprise waiting for her, but she would soon. Ella groaned as I massaged her scalp, the stress physically leaving her body.

"I—I ..."

"We will talk later. Relax and let me take care of you."

She nodded and closed her mouth.

Once she was clean and I had made sure that the surface cuts hadn't been too deep, I dressed her in her favorite pajamas. I pulled her sheets and comforter down, and then she crawled into bed and burrowed beneath the blankets. Instead of leaving, I slipped in next to her. Whatever was different about her, I wasn't willing to leave her that night.

Ella snuggled against me, pressing her ass against my cock. I stroked her hair, the sweet smell of her vanilla and peach calming me.

"Death?" She shifted her head on the pillow and looked over her shoulder, our gazes locking.

"Yes?"

"I know who you are," she said in a whisper.

My hold tightened. I should have known, but I'd allowed this woman to break the fortress around my heart and let my guard down.

"And I love you," she added.

Her confession should have sent me scrambling out of the bed, but instead, I found myself rooted in place.

"Say something, Sebastian. Talk to me."

A jolt of pain surged through my mind as her words pierced through me. I grabbed my mask, ripped it off, and flung it across the room while I gritted my teeth. A shadow flickered through my mind's eye, something familiar but too far out of reach. Raw, pulsing fury throbbed through my veins as I glared at her.

"How dare you call me by another man's name?" I snarled.

She rolled over on her back, a show of submission. "I know you as two men. Death and Sebastian." Her fingertips grazed my jawline, and I stilled. Her touch was gentle and loving. The last woman who had touched me that way had laid in a pool of blood on my kitchen floor. Horrible flashes assaulted my memory, and I winced.

"It's okay. You're safe, baby. You're safe. What are you seeing?" Ella sat up and cupped my face. "I love you. I bleed for you. I cry for you. Everything I do is for you. Let me take your pain."

An anguished cry reverberated through my body as I held the sides of my head. Sharp, excruciating knives stabbed my skull. "Stop!" I tumbled out of the bed, my knees smacking the hardwood floor.

"Sebastian, listen to me. It's Ella. It's okay. Can you hear me?"

She climbed off the mattress and kissed me, briefly soothing my mental anguish. Ella wrapped her arms around me and held me tightly.

"What happened, Sebastian?"

"You don't want to know," I cried. Grief and horror ripped me in half and stomped on me until I was a bloody mess.

"Death. It was a horrible situation, but you made it through. You just had to cope the best way that you could." She rubbed my back, and the warmth of her hands on my bare skin pulled me to the present moment.

"What's happening to me, little lamb?"

Ella gripped my chin and forced me to look at her. "Do you

remember what happened that day after school when you went home?"

I nodded, unable to speak through the nausea rolling in my stomach.

"I'm so sorry. I can't imagine how horrible that was for you. You were young and innocent. It wasn't your fault."

"I was a sorry excuse for a son!" I roared. "I failed them both and hid like a coward as that motherfucker butchered her."

Ella stumbled backward and fell onto the edge of the mattress.

"No. It wasn't you that hurt your parents." She frowned, putting on a brave face even though I suspected she was terrified. "He forced you. He used and manipulated a scared little boy."

I stepped away until my legs hit the back of the chair. Sinking into it, I pulled my hair, the images flipping through my mind as I relived every moment I'd buried for years. Reminders of driving the knife into my father's body ricocheted violently through me. My head snapped up, a feral growl leaving me as an evil smile slipped into place. "My father was a sorry excuse of a man. He beat my mother, cheated on her, and started to touch me when I was nine. He was disgusting and filthy. Martin Fletcher deserved to die at my hand."

Ella stared at me, pale and trembling. "Your father molested you?" Tears streamed down her cheeks. "I'm so sorry, baby. I had no idea."

"That sick fuck snuck into my room when Mother was sleeping and forced me to do unspeakable things." I tore at my chest, my nails raking across my skin as the torment of those nights ignited a dark rage that took on a persona all its own. "Unspeakable. If you knew... if you..." My head dropped between my shoulders, hanging low with shame.

"Shh. Don't. Don't tell me. It's okay. I'm glad he's dead. I'm glad that he died at your hand, and you became Death."

Slowly, I looked at her.

My little lamb was on my side? "He did. And so did my mother. She never protected me from that monster."

Ella looked at me, dismayed. "She knew?"

I ground my teeth together, my breaths short. "She knew. She pretended that she didn't." Staring at the floor, I clenched my jaw as the anger returned, slamming into me with the full force of a tornado. "Mother caught him one night. When he had me bent over, fucking me with a glass bottle because I was dirty and shameful, she cracked open my bedroom door. I heard it creak and looked over my shoulder. Our eyes connected for just a moment before she backed away and disappeared, leaving me with him."

A pained look was etched into my little lamb's face, and I hated that I'd dulled her bright light with my darkness.

She stood and tipped her chin up as she walked toward me. "They deserved to die for what they did to you. If I had known, I would have helped."

Shock rippled through me as she stood in front of me. "You would have helped?" My skin crawled, itching with the need to destroy but not her. I would never destroy my queen.

"Yes. I love you, and I will always protect the people I love."

I rose, the sharp pains in my head subsiding to a dull throb.

"And I will always protect and love you, little lamb."

She slipped her arms around my neck. "I know."

Chapter 51

Ella

"I tried," I said to Dope and Kip, who were staring at me with eagerness in their gazes. When I'd called them, they'd dropped everything and showed up on my doorstep. They quickly made themselves at home on my couch as if they'd been here a million times. I stood in front of them, replaying the events of the previous evening in my mind.

"I tried to tell him that he was also Sebastian, but he got ..." I touched my neck, remembering the ghost of his rage. "He can't handle the truth, guys. We have to do something else." I wondered if they knew the horrible details about his parents. Dope had lived a block away but had seemed to adore his family. I seriously doubted that Sebastian ever confided in him about the brutality he lived through as a child. As promised, I would protect Death and Sebastian's secrets.

"Did he hurt you?" Dope protectively crossed his arms over his chest.

"Almost, but it was like a part of him snapped to his senses." I sighed with a heavy heart. "You and Kip were wrong, though. From what Death told me, he was around longer than when you and Kip met him. He gave me details of memories when he was nine."

The guys gawked at me, and a shocked silence hung in the air.

"What the fuck? I was at his house a million times when we were kids, and I never saw anything weird."

"You wouldn't know to even look for signs," I said softly, trying to console my friend.

"This is why you're so good for Death and Bass." Dope shoved a hand through his red hair, rattled.

"As horrible as that was to hear, it proves that you're good for Death. He would have never confided in us that way." Kip's forehead creased with worry. "Well, we either try to stop Death from coming out as much as possible, or we need to find people all over the country for him to take out."

"Since I learned the truth, I've been deep diving into research, and I don't think there is a way to suppress Death. We just have to look at it as if he's an assassin, ridding the world of evil. If we feed him his prey, then we can keep him moving." I folded my arms across my chest.

Dope released a low whistle. "Do you realize what you're saying? What you're committing to?"

I placed my hands on my hips. "I've had time to think about it, and I've made my decision. I'm all in. I love Sebastian, and I love Death. There's no turning back, and I understand that. I'm already in too deep. I can't walk away."

Dope and Kip gave me silly grins. "Welcome to the family for real, Ella. When Sebastian first laid eyes on you, he wouldn't shut the fuck up and drove me crazy with all things Ella. Now, I'm glad it was you and not anyone else. You're a badass, and I'm happy you've joined us on the crazy train."

Kip walked over and gave me a brotherly hug. "Whatever you need, I've got your back."

"Thanks." My chest warmed with his kind words.

"Yup. You managed to handle Death and break him as much as anyone could. You're a fucking badass in my book." Dope jumped up and hugged me before pretending he hadn't had a sentimental moment with me.

"Thanks, guys." I blew out a heavy breath. "Does this mean I can start assisting with relocating women and kids with you? I would leave my job if it meant I could help change lives." I beamed at them, loving the idea of the danger and adrenaline pumping through my veins.

Kip scoffed. "You'll be helping with that I'm sure, but it's up to Bass. Regardless, you're on the hunt for twisted fuckers with the rest of us."

I cocked a brow at him, questioning his choice of words.

"If we're providing the prey for Death, we have to hunt first," Dope explained.

"Understood." I eyed them and smiled. "Before we go, I need your help." Over the next several minutes, I shared my plan to protect Sebastian from Death trying to kill him again. If they weren't aware of each other, Sebastian was still in danger.

After the guys left my place, I headed to work for the day. The hours I was keeping were kicking my ass, but I wasn't sure how to manage my new roles. I knew that a super sexy bartender would be at Velvet Vortex that evening, and I needed time with my bestie.

I stared at the files still needing my attention, but my bosses had already left, and mentally, I was toast. I messaged Cami, asking her to meet me for a drink and dinner at the club. Her reply came in quickly with a *hell yeah*.

J.A. Owenby

Locking up all the sensitive information, I grabbed my belongings and left. Even though I was always on the lookout for Death, we'd reached a place where I wasn't as terrified of him. If he popped out from behind the building, I had a better idea of how to handle him— run—and let him chase me because the punishment would be absolutely delicious.

I laughed as I safely hopped in my car, started the engine, and drove out of the parking lot.

Butterflies ran amok in my belly at the thought of seeing and kissing Sebastian. It was crazy how much I missed him throughout the day. Even though I'd told Death I loved him, I had yet to speak those words to Sebastian.

My palms slicked with sweat, and I wiped them on my black pencil skirt. I hadn't brought a change of clothes for after work so Cami would get me in a full suit with a subtle blue blouse peeking out.

I pulled into the parking lot and parked near the entrance. "Fuck it." I laughed as I shucked out of my blazer and tossed it into the passenger seat. Pulling the hairpins from the tightly wound bun on the top of my head, I let it tumble over my shoulders.

Damn, that felt good. I ran my fingers through my strands before I collected my purse and exited the car.

As I neared the entrance, I heard a familiar voice.

"Bitch!" Cami yelled.

I turned around, grinning as she rushed at me wearing her green scrubs. She nearly knocked me over with her hug.

"How has it been two days without us talking?"

I hugged her, realizing how deeply I'd missed my bestie. "Because we're both busy getting laid when we're not working."

She broke our embrace, grinning. "Hell. Yes. And damn, is having sex on a regular basis the best."

I held my arm out, and she slipped hers through mine and flashed me a big smile. "It is the *fucking* best ... pun intended."

Laughing, we entered the club, "Love Like This" by Zayn

324

pumped through the rooms as we made our way to the bar and settled on some available barstools.

"There she is." Sebastian tossed a cocktail shaker into the air and caught it with the opposite hand. He tucked it away beneath the sink as he strolled over to me.

"Hi, beautiful." Sebastian cupped the back of my head and laid a searing kiss on me.

The small crowd around us responded with hoots and hollers. Embarrassed, I looked at Cami, who was laughing her ass off.

"What can I get you ladies?" Sebastian asked.

Sucking on my lower lip, I said, "I'm starving."

Sebastian's blue eyes flashed with desire. He leaned forward, and I did the same. "I have something to feed you." He kissed my cheek before he walked away.

Cami dramatically collapsed her upper body on the counter. "Fries ... and a burger ... and a fifth of Jack ... and an Uber home."

I whirled around, giving Cami a what the fuck look. "Cami, what's going on?"

She peeked at me from beneath her arm. "I think I'm in love, and I'm not ready for it to happen yet. Ryan was just supposed to be a fun fling."

I giggled and rubbed her back while I pushed down the niggle of worry about my best friend being in love with a damn police officer. "Welcome to the ride, babe."

Over the next few hours, we caught up on all things including, work, my dad, and our fears about the men we were in love with. Sebastian kept our drinks topped off until we were drunk.

"Fuck. I can't drive," Cami said, rubbing her face and peeking at me through her fingers.

I smacked my lips before I said, "Same. I'll have Sebastian call us an Uber."

Sebastian approached us, wearing a big grin. "No need. Kip will drive you to your place, Cami. Ella, he'll take you to the penthouse."

He kissed me goodbye as Kip rounded the bar and guided us out of the building.

Before we reached the door, I glanced over my shoulder. Sebastian winked, and I gave him a lopsided smile. It was crazy how far we'd come in a few months, but nothing else mattered when you knew you'd met the one.

Chapter 52

Ella

The room spun as I leaned on the toilet in my bathroom, my stomach heaving with each retch. My hands gripped the edges of the porcelain bowl, and my knuckles turned white from the pressure. The acrid taste lingered in my mouth, and I gagged even more. Tears pricked at the corners of my eyes as I struggled to catch my breath, waves of nausea washing over me in relentless succession.

I managed to pull myself away from the toilet, wiping my lips with the back of my hand. My heart pounded as I attempted to calm myself down. I groaned as I leaned against the wall and realized my period was about three weeks late. My cycle was like clockwork, no matter how much stress I had. Life with work, Sebastian, and Death had kept me so busy that I hadn't noticed I was late until now.

My mind traveled to when Death had taken my morning-after pill, but I'd quickly called the pharmacy and replaced the prescription. Regardless, Sebastian and I had fucked like bunnies every chance we'd had. Even though he used condoms ... Death never did.

"Shit!" I rubbed my forehead, my chest so tight it hurt. "How the hell am I going to explain this to Sebastian?"

Realizing I might be jumping to conclusions, I climbed off the floor and stumbled to my bathroom counter.

Taking a long breath, I closed my eyes and reached deep inside me for strength. With trembling hands, I grabbed the pregnancy test hidden in the back of the drawer. Slowly, I unwrapped it and followed the instructions, my pulse pounding wildly.

I paced the small room, glancing at my watch every few seconds. What if it was positive? How would I tell Sebastian? Would he be angry, disappointed, or worse, leave me? A thousand thoughts raced through my mind, each more terrifying than the last.

Two distinct lines appeared on the stick a few minutes later, one bold and unmistakable, the other faint but undeniably there.

I stared at the results as if it were a three-headed monster.

Shoving the used test back into the box, I walked into my bedroom and located my phone on the nightstand. I sank onto the edge of my mattress, numb with shock. I shouldn't be surprised. Condoms weren't foolproof, and from day one Death was determined to get me pregnant. It worked. He would be thrilled, but I wasn't sure about Sebastian.

I called my doctor's office and asked if they could squeeze me in this afternoon to confirm if I was pregnant. Home tests were known to be faulty at times, and a blood test would be more accurate. Once I scheduled an appointment for later that afternoon, I climbed back into bed and snuggled beneath the covers. My hand slid to my lower belly, and in my heart, I knew I was carrying Death and Sebastian's baby. Once the doctor confirmed it, I could talk to Sebastian later that evening when we all planned to meet at Velvet Vortex.

My eyelids grew heavy as I drifted off into a dreamless sleep.

Chapter 53

Sebastian

I shoved my hands in my jean pockets, my pulse pounding.

"Dude, don't give yourself a heart attack." Kip slapped me on my back as I paced my living room.

"Easy for you to say, mate. Even though things have been brilliant between Ella and me, you never know what will happen."

"Are you having second thoughts?" Kip arched a brow at me.

"Hell, no. There's no doubt that I want to spend the rest of my life with her. We've talked about marriage, kids, and what the future looked like together, but ..." I shoved my fingers through my hair. "I'm fully healed from the accident and ready to take the next step. But that shit fucked me up. Life is short, and the time with her over the last several months confirmed my feelings for her. I don't want anyone else."

Dope chuckled. "If you know it's the right time, then do it. We've been over this a million times, man. It's all good. Just don't forget to breathe. Apparently, oxygen to the brain is important."

I resisted smacking him upside the head. "Everything is riding on this ... what if?"

A knock at my front door stopped my full-blown panic. I hurried to answer it, peering through the peephole before I did.

"Thank fuck." I answered and pulled Cami into the penthouse. "I'm so happy you're here. You know Ella better than anyone, and I need to make sure this plays out well." My gaze landed on the men's pair of black shoes that stood behind her.

Goddammit. She brought Ryan. I was hoping she'd leave the cop at home.

"Hey, mate." I extended my hand. "I've heard a lot about you from Cami and Ella. It's nice to finally meet you." *Fuck!* I plastered a smile on my face, hoping like hell it was convincing because I didn't want a cop anywhere around. "Come on in." I moved back and waved them in.

Cami grinned, rubbing her hands together like a madman planning their final world takeover.

"Okay, this is how it's going down." She slid her purse strap off her shoulder and parked her handbag beside the entrance.

THE DANCE FLOOR WAS CLOSED TO THE PUBLIC FOR THE evening, but the restaurant was packed. I selected one of my favorite playlists. "Holy Water" by Freya Riddings played in the background.

Cami and Ella were all smiles at the bar. Ryan paid Cami enough attention that told me he was definitely into her for more than just a fuck. It seemed as though he was going to stick around, and since I loved Ella, I would have to figure it out. Every time her face lit up when she was with Cami, there was no question that they were inseparable and good for each other. I had to make it work with Ryan ... nothing made me happier than seeing my girl happy.

Kip tipped his chin at me. It was time.

"Unconditional" by Freya Riddings began to play, and the lights over the restaurant dimmed. I walked out from behind the bar, focusing on the only woman in the world. Her long black hair fell in loose curls down her back, and her black jeans hugged the curves of her hips and ass. Her eyes danced with excitement.

"Dance with me." I held out my hand.

Without a word, Ella slipped off her seat and joined me. Once we reached the dance floor, I pulled her close and pressed my forehead against hers as we swayed to the music.

"I came to an important conclusion today."

"What's that?" she asked, her smile infecting every part of my soul.

"That I love you, and I can't live without you. Ella, you made me breathe again ... believe again."

"Sebastian." Her palm moved over my cheek. "I love you too."

My pulse hammered against my wrist as I slowed our dance. "Ella McCloud, my heart only beats for you. I've rehearsed this moment, played it over in my dreams, but now all those scripts seem unworthy, and they pale in comparison to the reality of you," I admitted, the words tumbling out with an earnest chuckle. "You've made every day a new adventure, a story worth telling our grandchildren one day. You're my today, my tomorrows, my inescapable and wonderful always," I continued.

I dropped to one knee, everyone a silent witness as I removed the black velvet box from my jean's pocket and opened it to reveal a ring as radiant as the smile I hoped to see her wearing soon. "Ella, will you marry me?" I asked.

Her hands flew to her mouth, a mirror of the surprise I felt at the strength of my emotion. "Yes."

I reached for the two-carat princess-cut engagement ring and slipped it on her trembling finger. Standing, I pulled her in for a deep kiss.

She giggled against my lips and laced her arms around my neck. Laughing, I picked her up and spun her in a circle. Not once in my lifetime had I felt like this—happy and hopeful about a future with the one person I loved with my entire being.

I set her down on the floor, her gaze softening. She pushed up on her tiptoes, and I bowed my head to meet her lips.

"I have a surprise of my own." She grabbed my shoulders and pulled my ear to her mouth.

My eyes widened as the shock of her words torpedoed through me. I sank to my knees once again and placed my palm on her abdomen. Placing a kiss on her stomach, I swore to cherish and protect my child and future wife for the rest of my days.

She gently played with my hair as I kissed her belly again, then gave her a goofy grin. I stood and embraced her before I yelled at the top of my lungs.

"I'm going to be a father! Drinks are on the house!"

"And a non-alcoholic drink of your choice." I took her hand, eager to get her home and into my bed.

Chapter 54

Ella

Several weeks had passed without a single sign of Death's presence. With our diligence in minimizing Sebastian's triggers, the killings had decreased significantly. My heart swelled with joy as I saw him content and excited about our upcoming wedding and the news of our pregnancy. He had even stepped back from his duties in rescue missions and managing the bar, allowing us to spend more time together.

A gust of crisp air greeted me, and I turned around to find Death standing inside the kitchen door. My pulse raced with conflicting emotions—both happy and sad by his appearance.

"It's been a while since I've seen you." I pushed up on my tiptoes and kissed Death, grateful that I'd slipped my engagement ring into my jeans pocket while I was packing. The engagement on top of what I needed to tell him would be too much.

He released a sexy growl and pinned me against my kitchen counter, which was littered with dishes that I was packing.

His eyes narrowed. "Where are you going, little lamb?"

"I'm putting the house up for sale." I ran my fingertips over his cheek. "You'll have to figure out when to see me since I'll live in a penthouse." I wrapped my arms around his waist, his hard chest pressing against mine.

"No. This is *our* place. You're not selling." His tone was low and deadly.

My brow arched. "I have to pay for Dad's cancer trial. The medication is working. When I move, I won't have a mortgage payment anymore."

A hint of a smile graced his lips. "It's already paid for, little lamb. When I arranged for your father to have the treatment, I took care of it upfront. If there are additional costs, the doctor will contact me." He gripped my waist, digging his fingers into my skin. "I will always protect you, Ella."

I ran my palm over his muscled chest, his pecs tightening as I did. At times, I was well aware that Death didn't want me to touch him. He had to feel in control. I had to take it slow and make sure he felt safe.

"I need to move on, Death. Not from you. Not ever. Just a new location."

"Why are you pushing this? I said no."

"Because." I peered into his grey eyes, fascinated with how his looked different from Sebastian's, and with how Death had a Pacific Northwest accent. "I'm pregnant and need a bigger place for the baby."

The kitchen grew so quiet I could have heard a feather hit the floor.

"Pregnant?" His voice sounded full of wonder.

Delicious little goosebumps peppered my skin. "Yes. I'm a few months along."

He stepped away, staring at my still-flat belly. I suspected he was on an emotional overload. It was funny how, at one time, I refused to carry a serial killer's baby. I doubted I would say "never" about anything again. "I think it's a girl, but we will know for sure soon."

Death dropped to his knees and placed his cheek on my stomach. "I swear always to protect you. I will slowly dismember anyone who attempts to hurt you. I will be a better father than my sick and twisted one ever was." He lifted my shirt before he pressed a kiss to my abdomen as I stroked the back of his head.

"You'll be a wonderful father." Since I'd learned more about Sebastian's condition, I understood that Death knew the same father that Sebastian did, but their memories were separate. Death had taken on all the trauma, then his psyche couldn't handle anymore and split.

He stood slowly, his eyes blazing with sincerity.

"You are my queen, Ella. You and the baby will lack for nothing."

I threaded my fingers through his hair and cupped his neck. "See, already a good father." I smiled up at him, my heart full of what I felt for him and Sebastian.

"But we need to talk," I continued, "and I need you to hear me and not fly off the handle before I finish."

Death nodded, and his gaze narrowed on me. "Go on."

I released him and located my purse on the cluttered kitchen table. Rummaging through the contents, I found what I needed.

"After you see this, I want you to verify the information on your own. I'll give you what you'll need." I opened a kitchen drawer and removed what I needed.

I walked back over to him, my hands trembling as I unfolded two pieces of paper. Placing the proof on the counter, I set the baggie with strands of Sebastian's hair next to it.

"What is this?" He frowned.

"Two paternity tests. Don't freak out, you're the father ..." I tried to calm my racing heartbeat. If this didn't work, not only was I out of ideas, but I also wasn't sure the knowledge wouldn't push him over the edge and end very badly for the baby or me. I had no choice, though.

"Two? Why two if the baby is mine?"

He gripped my jaw so hard, pain bounced through my head.

"Please, please listen to me. If there is an ounce of trust toward me, I need you to listen."

He slowly released me.

"Do you remember the last time I saw you? I called you Sebastian."

He growled but remained quiet otherwise.

"The baby is yours ... and Sebastian's. I had a friend gather some of Sebastian's hair, and some of yours was in my bathroom sink. Look at the results. Please. You'll see they're the same DNA."

Death snatched up the papers, his eyes scanning both.

"This doesn't make sense. You had these made just to fuck with me!" He roared.

Shit! I shook my head and took a few steps back. "I would never do that to you. Never. All I ask is that you verify the tests, and when you realize it's true, promise me you won't try to hurt Sebastian anymore."

My knees wobbled, and I sank to the floor as a wave of nausea rolled through me. I glanced up in time to see him stomp out the door. For whatever reason, he didn't turn on me, and I suspected it was because I was pregnant.

Sobs shook my body as I allowed all the pent-up fear and anxiety to the surface. Only time would tell if Death would be back and what that would look like.

Chapter 55

Ella

Although I was excited to officially move in with Sebastian, it had been a long two weeks without Death. I was at my place as often as possible, hoping he would show up. Each time I slipped my engagement ring into my pocket. I hated lying to him, but until I knew the baby and I were safe, and he could at least promise to not hurt Sebastian, I couldn't risk it.

I glanced around my place with a combination of sadness and excitement. I had held off moving into Sebastian's penthouse with him, but I couldn't continue to put my life on hold. Tonight was my last night at my home.

Since there wasn't any furniture left, I sank to the floor and crossed my legs at the ankles as I leaned against the kitchen cabinet. My life had taken so many turns while living here. Dad nearly died, I had a stalker who ended up being Shadow Whisperer online, but Death when he wasn't behind a screen. I had fallen in love here, and it would always hold treasured memories. But it was time to give it to the next person.

I stood slowly and then the back door opened. Death's black

boots caught my eye. Wiping my suddenly sweaty palms on my jeans, I waited for him to speak.

"I don't understand, but the tests are accurate. I even had someone take Sebastian's DNA and had mine and his tested." He tossed the papers on the empty kitchen counter. "You weren't lying."

"I wouldn't lie to you, Death. The situation is confusing, but I only ran the paternity test so you wouldn't try to hurt him anymore. He's promised the same with you."

Death's confused gaze swung to me. "It doesn't make sense, and I've spent the last few weeks planning his slow, torturous death until my test results came back identical to yours." His hands fisted at his sides. "Someday ... someday I'll try to understand, but ... because we can't be the same person." He strolled over to me and gripped my chin, forcing me to look at him. "Not now. My instincts say it's a bad idea."

I traced his stubbled jawline. "Trust them. They won't steer you wrong." Deep inside, I understood that Death was cunning and manipulative. He wouldn't stop looking for answers. I only hoped that it would be a while before he continued to learn more.

His mouth crashed down on mine, and he dug his fingers into my side. When he finally released me, my lips were deliciously bruised.

I placed my palm on his chest. "I missed you. We will work out when we can see each other."

"I know." The turmoil in his eyes flipped to hatred with a dash of mischievousness. "I was going to wait, but I have a gift for you."

"Oh? I like presents ... but I'm not sure what to expect from you."

His sexy, wicked grin fell into place. "Always anticipate the unexpected." He leaned down and kissed me, roughly. His lips parted, and my pulse raced as his tongue teased and coaxed mine. Cupping my face, he tilted his head and kissed me deeper. His touch stole the air from my lungs, and my knees turned to Jell-O.

"Get your purse, we're going somewhere."

If anyone saw us together, they would see me with Sebastian. I just had to make sure no one engaged us in conversation. If we were in the car, hiding would be easy enough.

THREE HOURS LATER, THE SUN BEGAN TO SET, AND MOTHER Nature had painted the cloudless sky with streaks of pink and orange hues. Soon, I would be watching the sunsets while rocking my baby. The idea wasn't a reality yet, but everything would change when I started to show.

Death parked in the middle of the field near an abandoned warehouse that was barely holding up. Once he exited the car, he strolled to my side and opened my door for me. He protectively slid an arm around my waist, and I nuzzled against him, enjoying this rare side of him. When we reached the entrance with a padlock and bolt in place, he turned to me.

"You know who I am, little lamb. That will never change. I hunt. I torture. I kill."

A lump formed in my throat, and I swallowed it. "I know." A shudder worked its way through my body as I suspected he was holding someone inside.

"Is someone in there?" My voice cracked with emotion as I reminded myself that this would be my life with him. A part of me would have to fully embrace the darkness since I'd vowed to protect him, even when he had no idea that I was pulling strings in the background to keep him safe.

"Come." He took my hand and led me inside, the heavy door closing behind us and cutting off the stream of light. I stood in the pitch black, my heart stuttering in my ears.

The intense beam from his flashlight lit our path. He stopped me before I stepped over broken boards, grabbed my waist, and lifted me over them.

"They have nails."

He didn't have to explain. I understood what he'd meant. Stunned at his care of me and the baby, I stared at him in awe.

"Let's go, time is short, little lamb." Death took my hand, and we walked to the back of the warehouse. He opened another door and flipped on a light. A man in his boxers and a dirty, white tank huddled in the corner. He'd been badly beaten, and his knee and leg were bent at a strange angle. He would never walk again, but that was the least of his worries. A large empty cup and crumbs of leftover food on a paper plate were next to him. For whatever reason, Death had wanted to keep his prisoner alive.

We moved closer. His swollen bruises were the only thing I could see.

I was rooted in a haze of uncertainty, and I bit my lip, holding the swell of feelings inside.

"Ella."

My brain scrambled to understand who was in front of me.

Death walked over to the man in the corner and kicked his broken leg. "Talk like your life depends on it, motherfucker."

The man shrank in the corner, blubbering like an idiot.

"Look at her," Death growled. "Who do you see?"

The guy slowly rotated his head toward me, his piercing blue eyes like an icy dagger, making my heart gallop while cold shivers of terror raced through my veins. Dread danced around me like a black fog, threatening to engulf me.

"Ella?" The sound of his voice punched me in the gut and dropped me to my knees.

Death rushed over to me, grabbing my hair just in time for me to puke. The stench of the splatter hit my stomach harder, and I wretched again, chunks landing on the hand I was using to brace myself against the floor.

"Little lamb, look at me."

I spit the last bit of puke out of my mouth and wiped the dangling string of saliva from my lips. I turned my head, tears spilling down my cheeks.

"John Bordeaux will never hurt you again. He will never touch you or another child again. Do you understand what I'm saying?"

I nodded, and my emotions morphed into shock and then anger. My eyes were bleary with my body's sudden revolt at seeing that son of a bitch after all those years.

"I wanted to give you closure. Do you have anything to say to him before I finish what I started? If you want to strike first, he's all yours," Death whispered, brushing his lips across my temple. Deep concern embedded in his features.

I managed to stand on wobbly legs, and my chin shook. Slowly, I walked toward John. Adrenaline sizzled through me, and I clenched my jaw so hard that pain shot through the side of my head.

This had been the moment that I'd dreamed of since I was a child. Revenge on the man who molested me and sold pictures of me on the internet. The man who had befriended my parents. I cleared my throat and squared my shoulders. With tears in my eyes, I exhaled, searching for the right words that would wash me clean of the black stains he'd left on my soul. But there were none. Nothing I said would change the fact that this guy was a sick, fucked-up pedophile. Rage pounded through me, and my hands fisted.

A twisted laugh escaped me as I approached him and kicked him in the face with my booted foot as hard as I could. His scream echoed off the walls.

"Too bad you won't walk around blind for the rest of your life, John. You would never be able to take another picture or video again." I stomped on his left hand, which was on the floor beside him. His cries echoed throughout the room. "That's for every child you touched and scarred for life." I planted both feet on the ground, my breathing ragged and heavy with a rage I'd never allowed myself to experience before. Lifting my leg, I slammed my foot down on his dick and balls. His screams were deafening as I backed away, admiring my damage. Even if Death let John live, he wouldn't hurt anyone anymore.

I almost wished John would survive. The mental anguish of what he'd lived through would be a sweet revenge, but I knew that Death wouldn't let him go because, in the back of his mind, he would always be watching out for John to come after us. I doubted he would go to the cops since it would also lead to an investigation of him.

I backed away, my gaze still on John as my chest heaved with heavy breathing.

"Ella," Death said from behind me. "Look at me."

I turned slowly, my skin buzzing with anxiety. A storm of emotions pulsed through me as I focused on Death's extended hand.

"Take it." Death's knife lay flat in his large palm, beckoning me.

I reached out and touched the handle. The same one that had been inside me. The blade glimmered in the low light, and I wrapped my hand around the hilt, electricity sparking through my body.

"You can do this. Embrace what's inside you, little lamb. Embrace your darkness. As I've told you ... we are the same."

My attention drifted up to Death's. I nodded, then gripped the weapon in my hand. I walked over to John and kneeled beside him. Power coursed through me at the mere thought of controlling whether he lived or not.

John peered at me through red, swollen eyes, snot hanging off the tip of his nose. His lips parted but before he spoke, and before I talked myself out of it, I plunged the knife into his chest. The crack of his sternum echoed off the walls, and the room spun as images of John's abuse ricocheted through my mind. I pulled the knife from his body as blood spurted from the wound. Raising my arms up, I stabbed him in the stomach. His agonizing wails barely penetrated my hatred while I repeatedly buried the blade inside him. Finally, John's body went limp, his unseeing eyes staring at the ceiling.

My body shook violently as I stared at John's blood all over my hands and wrists. I'd killed him. I'd killed a man in a rage. The knife tumbled to the floor as I scrambled backward. My stomach rolled at the sight of John and all the blood, and I turned my head and vomited again.

Gruff hands held my hair back as my belly emptied its contents.

"You did well, little lamb."

He helped me to my feet and cupped my chin. "Don't ever apologize for saving the children who John would have taken and used."

I blinked rapidly as Death told me about the two little girls behind the wall that he'd saved. With the truth of what I'd done ... how I'd helped kids stay safe, I tucked away any guilt in a little box and buried it deep inside me.

"I'm ready to go," I said, tipping my chin up in victory. It was over. The man who had molested me died a painful death as I rid the world of him.

I allowed myself one more glance and let the sight of him, wrecked and broken, just like the children he'd hurt, give me a glimmer of peace. Raw, dangerous power flowed through me and for the first time, I understood Death's sick fascination. It was control at its strongest.

Without any effort, Death swept me up, his muscular arms slipping under my knees and around my back as he scooped me off the ground.

"Let's get you home, little lamb. I'll finish my work here later."

I gripped the back of his neck, marking him with John's blood as he carried me over broken boards and nails until we reached the exit. He set me down and opened the door. His grey eyes pierced my soul, and my body suddenly hummed with desire.

We reached the car, but instead of him opening the door and climbing into the driver's seat, he led me to the hood of the car and bent me over.

"You did well, Ella."

He slid his hand around my waist, undid my jeans and slowly lowered them over my hips and down my legs. Death helped me step out of them, then licked and nipped his way up my bare thigh.

"You'll be rewarded for your kill."

I shuddered as his breath grazed over my G-string, my pussy growing wetter by the second. Death hooked his fingers in the strings and dragged it down to my ankles. He spread my ass cheeks apart, exposing me to him.

On his knees, he hungrily devoured my core with his tongue, lapping at my slick folds and circling my pulsing clit with expert precision. Each lick sent shockwaves of pleasure coursing through me, and I moaned as he thrust his wicked tongue inside me. He savagely nipped at the sensitive skin around my entrance, igniting a fiery ache that only intensified my desire for him. His touch was fierce and insatiable, driving me to the brink of ecstasy with each tantalizing stroke of his talented tongue.

Death slid two fingers inside me, coating them with my juices before he trailed up to my asshole. As his lips latched onto my clit, he moved his hand to my tight asshole and pressed against it. With each thrust of his finger, I pushed back eagerly, taking in the full length until I was grinding against him like a wild animal. The combination of the kill's adrenaline rush, the blood staining my hands, and Death's skilled touch sent me into an uncontrollable frenzy. I screamed and thrashed as my orgasm exploded over his face, leaving us both panting and drenched in sweat and pleasure.

He stood and turned me over, his hands gripping my hip as he wiped my juices from his mouth and chin. With a primal growl, he freed his cock from his jeans and rubbed the engorged head against my slick slit. His eyes blazed with pride, wonder, and an intensity of love that I had never seen before.

As he slid into me, his gaze never left mine, locking us together in a fierce connection. He leaned down and traced his tongue along my collarbone, nipping at it with a mix of possessiveness and passion.

I wrapped my hands tightly around his neck, pulling him closer as he picked up the pace. Each deep thrust hit my clit just right, sending sparks of pleasure shooting through my body.

"You are my queen, Ella McCloud," he growled between breaths, his words fueling the fire inside me.

I circled my legs around his waist, meeting each of his thrusts with equal fervor. "Yes," I moaned in response. "And you are my king."

With every move, we were lost in a perfect rhythm, our bodies moving together in a passionate dance. "Cum for me, little lamb," he urged, his own pleasure evident in the huskiness of his voice.

My world exploded as my body seized with ecstasy. "Oh god," I cried out, clinging to him as wave after wave of pleasure washed over me.

"S-Sebastian," I stammered, barely able to form coherent thoughts as the intensity consumed me. And then in one final glorious moment, he roared as he released inside me. We collapsed together in a tangled mess of limbs and emotions, our bodies spent but our hearts united as one.

He looked up at me, and his knuckles grazed my cheek, then he kissed me on the forehead.

My stomach turned in anticipation of his anger at being called Sebastian, but it never came. He gently brushed strands of hair away from my face, his eyes full of awe and a hint of apprehension.

"Let's get you home."

A sense of peace washed over me as I realized that for a fleeting moment, Death had recognized Sebastian.

Chapter 56

Death

"Where predators roam free, the prey lives in chains." ∼ Unknown

A malicious grin slipped over my face as I stared at the mess my little lamb had made. I returned to the warehouse after I got her and my baby safely home. Pride had swelled in my chest as I watched Ella kill John. It wasn't right for me to have all the fun when she needed closure—especially now that she was pregnant. My little lamb had to understand that I would continue to rid the earth of foul monsters who preyed on innocent children.

I barked out a dark laugh, realizing I would soon be protecting a daughter. At least, Ella suspected it was a girl.

Blood moved across the floor, trickling into the drain. Once I disposed of John's body, I would clean up the remnants of my work.

I dragged his ass to the black tarp and dropped him so hard that the back of his head split open, exposing his brain. Whistling "Oranges and Lemons," I continued to prepare him for disposal and scrub the room. When I brought someone new here, I wanted it to be pristine before I started to torture them.

Footsteps slapped against the concrete floor, approaching

quickly. I glanced up, grinning at my longtime friend from college. One evening I'd slipped out of the dorm and stalked a campus rapist, and Ryan had learned my identity. I was young and dumb and hadn't checked my surroundings well. Once I tossed the guy in the trunk of my car, I drove a few hours away to take my time to kill the son of a bitch. When I reached the abandoned house where I would dissect him while he was awake, Ryan showed up. We fought, and I won. I tied him up and dragged him into the home where my victim was waiting for me. Ryan glowered at me, then asked who I'd kidnapped. I explained who he was and why I'd taken him—he'd raped eleven women on campus. It had to stop, and I could do exactly that. It took a while for us to trust each other after that night, but I'd quickly realized he was one of the good guys. He was on my side, and we'd become close friends. Once he joined the police force, I had someone to help cover my tracks so I could continue my work.

"Right on time."

"You know I wouldn't leave you hanging if I can possibly get here," Ryan said.

"Grab the fucker's feet."

Ryan strolled over, his expression grim as we picked up and hauled the body out of the building and tossed it into my trunk. I left the lid open, not wanting the stench of his sins to permeate my car.

I wiped the sweat from my brow. "Thanks for the help. It's always easier if I have a hand." I folded my arms across my chest, eyeing the cop.

"I'll keep them off your trail. I fed them a bullshit story the other day, so it should keep the team busy for a while. It's getting harder to get to the crime scenes and help clean up."

I rubbed my neck. "I know I need to lie low, but this one was personal."

Ryan chuckled. "'Lie low' is an understatement. They're sniffing you out. Shit, I'm helping clean up and throwing the cops off your trail as much as I can, but I can't be there for you all the time. Get your girlfriend and take a long ass vacation. You're going to be a father; you need to pick your kills a bit more carefully."

"I understand." My forehead pinched. "How did you know she was pregnant?"

"I'm dating her best friend, Cami."

"If you hurt her, you'll have Ella to deal with." I grinned. "That's not a place I'd want to be."

"It's always the best friend that you have to watch out for. I'll be good to her, but does Cami know about this?" He nodded at John's lifeless body.

"No. Ella would never give me up. She's in too deep."

"Aren't we all? When you gagged and tied me up in this warehouse, I changed my mind about you. As a cop, I have to be careful. I can't take sons of bitches out like you can, so I'll do the next best thing. Help you stay out of prison."

We went silent for several beats. "If anything happens to me ... promise me you'll take care of Ella and my baby."

Fuck! I can't go down like that. I have to slow down the kills.

Ryan took a deep breath, his chest rising and falling as he looked me dead in the eye. "You have my word." He extended his hand, and we shook. Unfortunately, there wouldn't be any way to tell if he honored his word, but I hoped I would never have to find out.

Chapter 57

Sebastian

"You're so beautiful you're glowing." I tipped Ella's chin up. "Are you ready?"

"Yes, I'm excited to learn what we're having." She smiled at me, love sparkling in her mesmerizing green eyes.

I picked up our luggage and took one last look around the penthouse before we walked into the hall, and I locked the door behind us.

"Hopefully traffic isn't too bad," she said, wheeling her carry-on bag next to her.

I pushed the button, and the elevator doors whooshed open. We piled in, laughing at the number of suitcases we'd packed, but we would be gone for a while. When the doctor had told Ella that she needed to lower her stress and relax, we'd decided to spend time at my house in the country. She'd never visited upstate New York, so it would be a perfect place to unwind and prepare for the baby.

After her dad and mom had returned from California, we took them to dinner and shared the news about the baby. I'd never seen parents so proud and excited. I believed it gave her dad something to continue to hold out for, even though he was in remission. Soon after, Ella gave notice at her job. I had expressed my concerns about her working around criminals while pregnant, but she grinned and told me she'd had plenty of practice and could hold her own. I didn't doubt it, but it was my responsibility to keep her safe. And, with the move, she agreed that it made sense to quit.

We were loaded into my car a few minutes later, and I pulled away from the curb. I turned on some music and smiled as Ella danced in her seat to "Silence" by Galli J. "I'll miss the club. Will you?"

"Sure. It kept me busy and probably out of trouble." I shot her a grin. "Until you walked in; then I knew I was in trouble."

Her giggle lit me up. A sudden wave of grief washed over me, and I took her hand. "I wish my parents could be with us today."

"Me too, baby." She squeezed my fingers.

Forty-five minutes later, we arrived at the doctor's office and were shown to a room. To my surprise, we didn't have to wait long for the doctor.

"Hi, I'm Dr. Glendon."

"This is my fiancé, Sebastian," Ella said, introducing us.

"It's nice to meet you." The doctor turned her attention to the love of my life. "Ella, how are you feeling?"

"Good. I'm a little tired, but the nausea has calmed down."

"Excellent. And as for your move to New York, I've already reached out to a wonderful doctor there. The front desk has her information for you when you leave. Call her and schedule your next appointment."

"Thank you so much for taking care of us." Ella placed her hand on the little baby bump.

"Are you ready?" Dr. Glendon asked.

"Yeah," we replied in unison.

The doctor patted the table, and Ella hopped up and laid down. The doctor raised Ella's shirt and squirted a gel on her stomach before she pressed the probe against her.

"Hmm," Dr. Glendon said, moving the wand around.

I froze. "Is everything okay?"

"Everything looks good. The babies look healthy."

Ella frowned before she bolted upright, knocking the doctor's arm away by accident. "Babies?" The color drained from her face as her gaze darted to mine.

I grabbed her hand, the news sinking in. "How many?" I managed to ask.

"Twins. Fraternal. One boy and one girl."

Ella fell back onto the bed. "Holy shit. Two?" she squeaked.

"One of each." I laughed. "That's amazing." I leaned over and kissed Ella, then whispered in her ear. "That's my good girl. You're going to look so beautiful with your belly swollen."

A cute blush graced her cheeks. "Wait until Cami finds out. She'll be planning to move into the guest bedroom."

"We'll need her." I winked at Ella.

AFTER THE APPOINTMENT, WE BOARDED MY PRIVATE PLANE. Ella had been quiet as she walked onto the aircraft for the first time. Initially, I thought she was recovering from the shock of learning she was carrying twins, but there was something else. It was almost as if she recognized the plane, but that would have been impossible. I hadn't even told her I owned one until after we were engaged.

Once we were in the air and settled, Ella reclined, and I covered her with a plush brown blanket. I sank into the seat next to her and watched my beautiful girl as she slept. I had a feeling I'd better do the same. We had a busy road ahead of us, but at least finances weren't a problem, and we could spend time with our babies.

SEVEN HOURS LATER, I DROVE UP THE LONG, GRAVEL DRIVEWAY that meandered through the property and led to my home. Both of us had napped on the flight over, and Ella was ready to stretch her legs. When I turned off the engine, she hopped out of the car and looked around. It had been a while since I'd been here, and I'd had to hire someone to clean and prepare it for us.

"Oh my god. It's gorgeous, Sebastian! You've been holding out on me."

The large country house nestled in the rolling hills was stunning. Its traditional two-story structure with a stone foundation and cedar shake siding was painted a warm, creamy white. Well-manicured lawns with maples and oaks surrounded the place with its wrap-around porch and swing overlooking the pond.

"If you can't find me, I'm curled up on that porch swing with a blanket and book," she added.

I walked up behind her and slipped my arm around her waist, careful of her slightly swollen belly.

"Can you see us building our future here?" I nuzzled her hair.

"Yeah. I really can. It's so peaceful." She faced me, her gaze finding mine. "I love you, Sebastian Fletcher. I can't wait to marry you and become your wife." Ella snorted. "After the babies of course. I want to look good in my wedding dress."

"Ella, you would look stunning with a round belly at the altar. Now be my good girl and get into that house. I've been waiting to make love to you all damn day."

I tickled her sides, her squeals and giggles music to my ears. She ran to the door and waited for me to unlock it. I swung it open, and she stepped inside, all smiles. I wondered if she realized that she owned every part of me. One thing I knew for sure: my search for love and a future had ended the moment Ella McCloud walked into Velvet Vortex and stole my heart.

DON'T MISS THE EPILOGUE! CLICK HERE TO READ MORE.

Illicit Obsession Sample

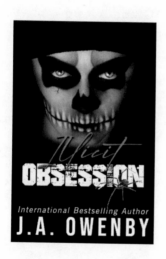

The day my stepsister died she took my heart with her.

Now, I'm a shell of a man, a cold-hearted monster.
Imagine my surprise when the love of my life shows
up at Whitmore University alive and well.

I'm ready to make her pay for destroying me.

This isn't a fairy tale, and I'm sure as hell no knight in shining armor.

I have no problem dragging her into my dark world along with me.

But when I dig for the truth about that fateful day, I can no longer deny my feelings about the only girl I've ever loved.

And just as I vowed to destroy her,
I vow to protect her even if it costs me my life.

Illicit Obsession is a **new dark, forbidden, sports, secret society standalone romance** featuring an **unhinged/ possessive hero and a strong, curvy heroine** who knows how to tame her **stepbrother**. In this second-chance romance, there's **no cheating, no cliffhanger**, **no third-act breakup**, and a **happily ever after** guaranteed!

This standalone is a **BRAND-NEW story with Jagger and Ariana from the Whitmore Elite Series. If you have read Forbidden Obsession, this book is **completely different** but with the same character names.

Each book in the Whitmore Elite series is a standalone and can be read in any order!

Download Illicit Obsession on Amazon or **FREE** in Kindle Unlimited! **Click Here!**

Turn the page for the Sample of Illicit Obsession.

Prologue
Jagger

"What the hell is this?" I blinked rapidly, trying to clear the haze from my eyes. "Where am I?" Despite the struggle against my restraints, it took me a few seconds to realize that I wasn't going anywhere due to the tightness of the ropes. I frantically searched around the room in an attempt to figure out where I was.

A dark chuckle bounced off the cement floor and walls. "Don't worry, Jagger Whitlock, it's all a part of the plan," the disguised voice said. He peered at me through the holes in the skull mask as he paced a circle around my chair. I recognized him from the society invitation video. *Fuck, what the hell did I do?*

"What do you want?" Despite the chilly air against my bare chest, beads of sweat formed on my forehead. The bastards knocked me out, drug me out of the field house, and tied me to a chair. Apparently, it would have been too much for them to grab some sweatpants for me. Instead, I shivered in nothing more than my boxer briefs. I had no idea who I'd pissed off, but I mentally skipped down that long list.

"You're one of the chosen. Try to relax and enjoy the ride." The fucker laughed even more.

My blood boiled in my veins. The familiar feeling of fury and hatred reawakened the beast inside me.

The masked and cloaked person didn't speak, but I felt the power bubbling beneath his skin. He might be crazier than I was. I wasn't sure if it was a good or a bad thing.

I attempted to control my breathing, but I had no fucking clue who was behind the mask and had taken me prisoner. If I bargained for my freedom, it would tickle his ego, and I would leave wherever I was in one piece.

"A brotherhood will fight for each other, but only if they have something on the line. Something to lose. In your case, you want a pro football career. I can make that dream come true, but why should I if you have no skin in the game?"

I blanched at him. "You can get me a pro ball contract?" A sense of foreboding enveloped me. This wasn't good. Whoever was talking to me was fucking with my head, and I strongly suspected I knew who it was. *Shit. This is bad. Real bad.* Until I found his weak spot, I had to play his sick game.

"If you can get me a deal with the Eagles, I'll give you my damn soul." Even though I realized it wouldn't serve me well, I gave him a disbelieving snort. "What are you, the devil's right hand?" What he didn't know was that I was the devil's left hand. Maybe we could work together and solve a big problem I had that refused to leave me alone.

The figure stopped in front of me and bent over, the nose of his skull mask a mere inch from mine. "I can make it happen, Jagger Whitlock, but what will you give me in exchange? I have no use for a wasted, dark soul like yours." He straightened, staring a hole right through me.

"Name your price. Hell, I've done a lot of dark shit in my life. I'm pretty sure I can offer you something you'll find valuable."

I shivered, sweat drying against my skin and making me even colder. Minutes ticked by without another word from him.

"What should I call you? Skull? I mean, you know *my* name. That doesn't seem fair, does it?"

He folded his arms in front of his chest. "You can call me Black Widow. I am the leader of a secret society, and if you pass the test, you'll join us."

I barked out a laugh. "Sorry, man. You should have led with that. You're wasting your time. I pledge to no one. This shit show wasn't what I signed up for." If he wasn't lying, it wasn't who I thought it was, which meant this situation wasn't as bleak as I first assumed.

A spotlight blasted through the darkness and I shrank away, trying to shield my eyes until my vision adjusted.

"It's easy, really. I'll make sure you have everything you want in exchange for your deepest, darkest secret."

My heart skidded to a stop, and I reminded myself to breathe. "No fucking way," I said quietly.

"Are you sure? You're ready to walk away from all of your dreams?"

"I don't know you, asshole. How am I supposed to blindly trust you?" I tugged on my wrist restraints again, as if they had magically loosened.

The light dimmed and moved, illuminating the rest of the small area. Several people stood on the other side of glass walls, all of them wearing the same skull mask and robe as the Black Widow, arms crossed over their chests in what could only be called a power stance. They looked immovable.

A voice began to filter into the room.

"Jagger," a female said.

My throat constricted as she continued to talk. "I love you, baby. Promise me we'll never be apart."

"I'll never let that happen," I replied on the recording.

"What the fuck? How did you get that?" I yelled over the recorded conversation. Her voice sliced through me like hot knives carving out my heart and tossing it on the cold ground.

"If our parents find out, they'll separate us," she said.

As hard as I fought against it, tears pricked my eyes. It had been years since I'd heard her speak.

"Tell us your secret, Jagger, then all of this will disappear. You can finally move forward. I'm doing you a huge favor."

My body trembled as the recording continued, with the sounds of us kissing and moaning as we made out. I remembered every sound, every breath. Even though I'd promised her, it had been our last night together.

Agony twisted my stomach into a million knots as I was overcome with grief—the soft lilt of her tone wreaked havoc on me.

"What happened, Jagger? What did you do?" the Black Widow asked.

I sucked in a huge breath, trying to clear my head.

"If you tell us, then you'll have everything you've dreamed of: a family, a career, and more women than you could imagine at your fingertips. Most of all, I can grant you hope. All I ask is for your darkest secret in return. Pledge your loyalty to each man here and they will do the same."

Frowning, I looked around the room at each person staring at me. I could have sworn a few of them nodded. Had they already talked about their pasts?

"Who are they?" I gestured to the strangers on the other side of the glass.

"Members. Each have shared their secret and now have successful lives and careers. They will forever be a part of the brotherhood. You can have the same thing. Once you tell us yours, they will share with you as well."

I swallowed hard, wishing I had some water. Closing my eyes, I listened to the recording continue to play. She had sent me the video later that evening. It was still on my phone, but I couldn't bear to watch it. Now, I was listening to it and so were the people in this room.

"You're a perfect fit for the society, Jagger. Name your price. We need someone like you."

"I want the pro deal. Nothing else matters. I have nothing left except football."

Moans of her pleasure filtered through the speaker, and it took everything inside me not to break down and sob.

"Then you'll have it. Don't misunderstand my intentions. I've hand-picked every member. You have skills and value. Let the society give you the world. All I need is something that proves to us that you're all in. Betrayal of the members is punishable by death, so are you willing to pay the price to make all your dreams come true?"

The recording finally stopped, and a heavy silence hung in the room as the others patiently stood and waited for my answer. I had nothing to lose. Whoever the Black Widow was, he realized what I would say, or he wouldn't have the recording. He was one clever son of a bitch. I had to give him that. If he could deliver on the pro deal in exchange for dirt that he already knew, what the hell was I really losing? The others had to share too. We would all be on an equal footing. I was familiar with the pledge process since my uncle was the president of an MC, the Dirty Bastards. I understood how that loyalty worked—a secret for a secret.

Taking a deep breath, I realized that if this asshole knew, anyone could find out, and that knowledge left me vulnerable. Hell, I would need some friends to help me bury it. All this time, I thought I was protected. As soon as I was finished here, I would need to find a way to erase my past once and for all. Maybe the Black Widow had done me a favor and saved my ass.

I squared my shoulders, ready. "I . . ." My voice cracked. "My biggest secret is—"

Need more? Download Illicit Obsession on Amazon or **FREE** in Kindle Unlimited! **Click Here!**

In the Shadows

J.A. OWENBY

Edited by: Emerald Edits and Lisa Carlisle

Cover Art by: Qamber Designs & Media

First Edition ISBN: 978-1-949414-78-3

Also by J.A. Owenby

The Whitmore Elite Series, Dark, Football

Forbidden, a prequel

Illicit Obsession, a standalone novel

Ruthless Obsession, a standalone novel

Sinful Obsession, a standalone novel

Toxic Obsession, a standalone novel

The Beautifully Damaged Series

Beautifully Damaged

Beautifully Broken

Beautifully Shattered

The Love & Ruin Series

Love & Ruin

Love & Deception

Love & Redemption

Love & Consequences, a standalone novel

Love & Corruption, a standalone novel

Love & Revelations, a novella

Love & Seduction, a standalone novel

<u>Love & Vengeance</u>

<u>Love & Retaliation</u>

<u>Love & Betrayal</u>

About the Author

International bestselling author J.A. Owenby grew up in a small backwoods town in Arkansas where she learned how to swear like a sailor and spot water moccasins skimming across the lake.

She finally ditched the south and headed to Oregon. The first winter there, she was literally blown away a few times by ninety mile an hour winds and storms that rolled in off the ocean.

Eventually, she longed for quiet and headed up to snowier pastures. She now resides in Washington state with her hot nerdy husband and three purebred Siberian cats who insist on using her computer as their napping spot. She spends her days coming up with ways to torture characters in a way that either makes you want to throw your book down a flight of stairs or sob hysterically into a pillow.

J.A. Owenby writes new adult and romantic thriller novels. Her books ooze with emotion, angst, and twists that will leamazon.-com/J.A.-Owenby/e/B00J77KCFKave you breathless. Having battled her own demons, she's not afraid to tackle the secrets women are forced to hide. After all, the road to love is paved in the dark.

Her friends describe her as delightfully twisted. She loves fan mail and wine. Please send her all the wine.

You can follow the progress of her upcoming novel on Facebook at Author J.A. Owenby and on Twitter @jaowenby.

Sign up for J.A. Owenby's Newsletter at www.authorjaowenby.com

Like J.A. Owenby's Facebook:
https://www.facebook.com/JAOwenby

*J.A. Owenby's One Page At A Time reader group:*https://www.face
book.com/groups/JAOwenby

Made in United States
North Haven, CT
30 July 2024

55601949R00226